THE DAEGMON WAR BOOK I

—THE—
GIFTED

MATTHEW DICKERSON

LIVING INK BOOKS

Writing Worth Reading™

The Gifted
Book 1 of The Daegmon War

Copyright © 2015 by Matthew Dickerson

Published by Living Ink Books, an imprint of AMG Publishers, Chattanooga, Tennessee (www.LivingInkBooks.com).

Print Edition   ISBN 13: 978-0-89957-796-8
ePUB Edition ISBN 13: 978-1-61715-440-9
Mobi Edition ISBN 13: 978-1-61715-441-6
ePDF Edition   ISBN 13: 978-1-61715-442-3

First printing—April 2015

Cover illustration by Kirk DouPonce, DogEared
   Design, Woodland Park, CO.
Map of Gondisle illustration created by Mark Dickerson.
Interior design by PerfecType, Nashville, TN.
Editing and proofreading by Susanne Lakin and Rick Steele.

Printed in Canada

15 16 17 18 19 - MAR - 7 6 5 4 3 2 1

For my good friends Louis and Susan, and for Jake, Olivia (#54), Jack, and Will, for being my test audience. Your friendship and support is a treasure.

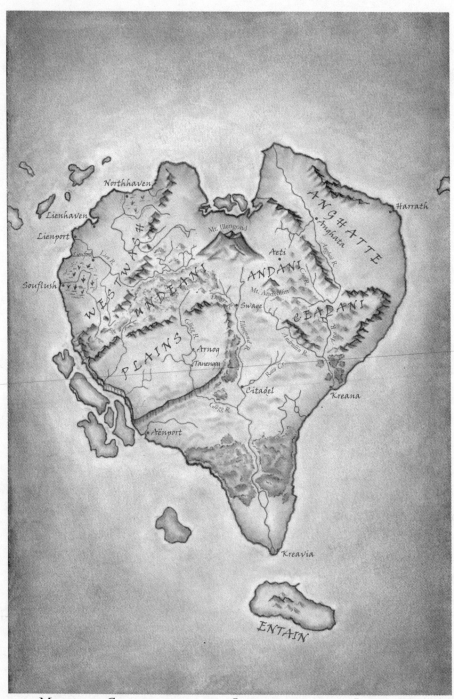

MAP OF GONDISLE AND SURROUNDING ISLANDS

CONTENTS

CONTENTS

1

ELYNNA

Even through the deep snowpack beneath her feet, Elynna could smell the heat rising toward her. It had become almost unbearable, and her strength was withering. Standing high up the slope on the thick icy crust of hard wind-packed snow, she gazed across the desolate valley, squinting against the glare of the afternoon sun. To her naked sight all looked barren and empty, but she knew it was out there. Wincing more from the mysterious pressure assaulting her than from the blinding whiteness of the snow, she lowered her head and squeezed shut her eyes.

Her companions watched her closely, waiting for her to speak. They could not feel the heat as she did. They followed her because they believed in her gift: a mysterious power none of them shared.

A power? Elynna wondered. No. Not a power. A weakness. It was as much vulnerability as ability. She was able to smell and feel their enemy the same way she could smell rotting fish or feel the bite of winter winds on her cheeks. If this was a gift, it was a gift she did not want. Yet, she could ignore it no more than she could have stood outside her home and escaped the smell of marsh air or the sound of the Lienwash River flowing past her village.

She tried to speak, but her words came out in a whisper barely audible over the soft moaning of the wind in the crags above them. "The Daegmon is near here." She stopped, leaving the rest of her thoughts unspoken. *The Daegmon is close. I can feel its presence growing stronger each moment.* She had made her claim too often over the past few days. How much longer would they continue to trust her?

She opened her eyes and brushed aside a few strands of black hair prematurely streaked with silver, revealing the high forehead and rounded cheeks characteristic of her people, the Fisherfolk of Westwash. She was tall though not broad. She stood shoulder to shoulder with most of the men in the company. Only the North-landers were taller. And though she lacked their strength and agility, her hands at least were strong and skilled from a decade spent mending fishing nets. How she wished she were standing by the sea now, wondering what time her father and brother would return in their boat for supper. Standing by the sea and smelling the salt air. Or perhaps the river air of her winter village. Smelling any scent that everybody else could smell too, and which did not make her skin burn. Yet her days on the Lienwash were a lifetime ago.

She shook her head. Strong fingers were of little use against this enemy.

She scanned the valley for some visible sign of the creature's presence—something her companions could see as well. But aside from the dull gray of granite cliffs, and a few green tufts where the tallest of the mountain spruce still thrust their peaks toward the sky, all she could see was ice and snow.

Into that emptiness Elynna now gazed. Her face, once smooth and lightly tanned, accustomed to warm salt air of the Westwash, was now cracked and burned from too many days in the bright skies and thin air of these high Ceadani Mountains. The past two years had aged her far beyond her twenty-five summers. Only the color of her eyes—"sea green" her mother had called them, though the green was more brown than blue—brought to mind the soft summer mists of a home untouched by this cold harsh climate. But they were pained eyes, and they too looked older than their years.

It was the lithe Plainswoman Tienna whose voice broke the silence. "I sense it too. There is a sickness in the earth. As if—" She paused. The others turned to listen. Tienna's opinions, on the rare occasions she shared them, were well heeded. She was, after all, a huntress from the Plains, elite among her people. She also possessed one of the rare gifts of power. She understood health. She could feel its presence the same way Elynna could sense the Daegmon.

"The buried trees. The dirt. Even the rocks," she whispered. Despite the heavy fur cloak on her shoulders, she was shivering. She was not meant for such a climate. Her sleek body had too little fat, and beneath her borrowed cloak she wore only a short sleeveless shift: the uniform of her rank. Only a thin layer of woven fabric covered the gap between her knee-high fur boots and the bottom of her cloak. "I know nothing of the feeling of which Elynna speaks, the scent of the Daegmon's presence, but there is a wrong here. I feel the ill in this snow and beneath it. It groans under some oppressive weight."

"She is right," Thimeon added. The sturdy Andan guide clenched his staff as he stared down into the valley through dark-brown eyes that matched his hair. Time and again over the past few weeks he had proven his skills at navigating and surviving these rugged mountains. Just keeping them all alive through blizzards and cold had been no easy task. But the burden was taking a toll on him too, and his voice now matched his furrowed brow. "It is still early autumn," he said. "Even in these high passes the deep snows should be many weeks away. I have never seen anything like this."

Thimeon lacked the strength of some in the company, and other than his proficiency with a hunting bow he claimed no skill at arms, but he was a natural leader. His broad shoulders and easy stance emanated security and rootedness. He had a strong face and a kind but penetrating glance. In the early days of their travels, when Thimeon's affection for Elynna had started to become obvious, the other women in the company had whispered to Elynna how lucky she was. Elynna, however, had adamantly refused to acknowledge any attraction for him. "Too plain. Like sand by the seashore. It all blends together. You may be glad it exists, but there's nothing special about one grain." When Siyen had pressed her about it, Elynna had made it clear she had no interest in Thimeon. She had told him as much too. More than once. Nonetheless, his leadership and skills she did not question, and she was aware as he spoke that the other Andani nodded their heads in agreement.

Elynna turned her gaze back on Tienna, who was several inches shorter and many pounds lighter than Elynna. The two were a study in contrasts. Tienna was the shortest and lightest member of the company, but her compact frame was far from frail. She possessed a fluid grace and agility Elynna had never before encountered. And a matching beauty too. Though Tienna didn't have what the fashion-conscious women in the capital city of Citadel would have called a full figure, her small waist accentuated her hips and curves—features the straight-bodied Elynna lacked. Tienna's long braided red-brown hair, dark green eyes, and high forehead wrapped her in a rare air of mystery that even the familiarity bred by their growing friendship had not eliminated.

"I have not often traveled beyond the Plains," Tienna said, turning toward Thimeon. "These high mountains are foreign to me, and if you told me there was snow here year-round, I would believe you. But whatever is here now is wrong. The trees and grasses are groaning beneath this. That I can feel. Something is sapping their health."

A shudder ran through Tienna as she finished, and Elynna also winced in shared pain. Yet she could do nothing to relieve Tienna's distress any more than she could relieve her own. Alas, none of the companions were immune to suffering. It had been some sixty days since they had left Citadel and come north into the highlands, pursuing a creature they should have been fleeing. None of them even knew what the Daegmon was. It was just a strange appellation from old legends, nearly forgotten even in story until it had sprung to life. Where it had come from, or why it was wreaking such destruction, or where it would attack next, or even how great its power was, Elynna had no more idea than anybody else. The old legends of village storytellers and the tales of a few traveling bards were her only sources of knowledge, if that could even be called *knowledge*. She had traveled all the way to Citadel looking for answers. To King Eughbran himself. And what had she found? Nothing. The king had not only refused her plea, he had denied there was even a problem. He had denied the very existence of the Daegmon. There was no aid to be found from Citadel—not a single ship, nor soldier, nor knight. Only more riddles. The journey to Citadel had accomplished nothing.

And it had cost her a brother.

But Elynna could not afford to dwell on her losses. Every member of the company had known loss. Villages ruined. Families destroyed. That was what had united them.

Alas. Even united their strength was so frail. Had not every one of them already faced the creature and failed? Elynna had run through the inventory a hundred times and come up wanting. Of twenty-two companions, only four numbered among the gifted. And of those four gifts, neither her own nor Tienna's were of any use in battle. A huntress Tienna was by vocation, skilled even by the high standards of her people, but she did not call herself a warrior, and her training was of no use against a Daegmon.

Their one hope lay in the brothers Cane and Cathros. Their gifts were the weapons of power. But what hope did those gifts offer? The brothers were only two, mortal and limited, whose gifts were neither tried nor understood. Though they would have been a formidable pair against mere human foes, they were now facing an enemy whose strength had not yet even been fathomed. Even if Cane could conjure the *sword flame* at will—a feat he had not learned—what would it matter? Nor could the *battle strength* that came upon Cathros be any match for the unnatural power of their enemy. They needed more of the gifts. But knowledge of the gifts, like knowledge of the Daegmon itself, lingered only in the old tales.

Then there were the ungifted. From scattered villages across northern Gondisle they had somehow found their way to Elynna. Unarmed. Untrained. *Ungifted.*

There were three others from the Westwash: Fisherfolk like Elynna—like nearly *everybody* in the Westwash. To *be* a Westwasher was to *be* one of the Fisherfolk. It also meant being ill prepared for war and even less ready for the brutal cold of these highlands. Until a few days earlier, none of them had ever even felt snow. Now Elynna had felt more of it than she wanted to feel in her lifetime. The young woman Siyen was little better off. Born of a Southland mother and Westwash father, and raised on one of the great farms near Citadel, she knew only a little about fishing, and more about harvesting fruits and grains. But knowing the seasons of blossoms and melons gave no more help against the Daegmon than knowing the seasons of the great runs of *grelsh* and *kellen* up the rivers of the Westwash, or knowing the techniques for catching them. Nor did the knowledge help them against this cold.

Only slightly better off were the Plainsfolk. They had some skills, to be sure. They were hunters and gatherers, experienced in the nomadic life, of night after night spent without permanent shelter. They knew the feel of biting winter winds that swept across the Plains. Yet none of them except the huntress Tienna had been trained for endurance and hardship. And none but Tienna were among the gifted. And the flurries that fell from time to time in the Plains were nothing compared to the blizzards, deep snows, and bitter cold of these Ceadani Highlands. Or so the Plainsfolk had said more than once.

Then there were the six Highlanders. All from the Andani tribe. None of them gifted. Born in the mountains and prepared for the cold? Yes. But soldiers or fighters they were not. The dark-haired Llian had apparently served as a soldier at Citadel some years earlier, but though the long scar across his cheek made him look fearsome, he had not fought in a single skirmish in all his years of service. He was quiet, and as far as Elynna could tell as gentle as a mother duck with ducklings. The sword he carried at his side might be rusted in its sheath by now. And though the somewhat younger Bandor had proven himself a gifted hunter and archer like Thimeon, he knew nothing of warfare.

At least the Anghare—the Northlanders as they were so often called, though Easterners would have been a more accurate name—were warriors. Anghatte was a hard land, and it bred a hard people: clans of warriors and miners often fighting among themselves. There were five of them in addition to Cane and Cathros. All five knew how to wield a sword, shoot a bow, and throw a spear. They were not cowards. But they, too, were among the ungifted. Thus it came back to the same thing. Among the Northlanders, only the brothers Cane and Cathros had gifts of power. Only in those two and their gifts did the company have hope to avail against their foe, the Daegmon.

Elynna scanned the company once more. Her eyes passed quickly over Thimeon, her Andan guide, but her thoughts did not leave him so quickly. In his heavy goat-skin and knee-high fur boots, he was at home on the barren snow-covered slopes. It was he and his cousin Theo who had managed to outfit the entire company in the Andani-made cloaks, hats, and mittens they now wore. Without these, they would have had to turn back days ago. Or they simply would have frozen to death.

Elynna glanced sidelong at Thimeon as a strange mix of emotions welled up within her. There he stood, unabashedly watching her through mud-brown eyes that spoke not only of trust but of longing. She turned away, but too late to avoid meeting his gaze. She grimaced, and for a brief moment her thoughts were diverted from the task at hand. Perhaps that was what bothered her most about him. He distracted her. It was not that she loved him. Indeed, knowing his feelings for her, she liked him all the less. Yet still, he distracted her. Something about him reminded her too much of her own inadequacy. No matter how much he cared for them all, he was destined to fail—not for lack of effort but because he was too weak. That was his greatest sin. He was the symbol of an effort well intentioned but vain. When it came to battle, he would prove impotent just like the rest of them.

"Perhaps," Thimeon suggested, "we should rest for a few days. Let us regain our strength. There is a large village not more than a day's journey from here, over that ridge—"

"Go if you want," Elynna interrupted in a harsh voice. "Lead the others with you. What good are so many out here in this barren wasteland?" Her words brought several heads snapping in her direction—the "others" of whom she had spoken: the ungifted. Surprise and hurt registered in their eyes, and she winced at her own thoughtlessness. She would give anything she had to save them. But she feared that what she had to give was not enough. And what did *they* have that might suffice where the gifts failed? They had even less. She did not retract her words. The fact that she would have perished three times over in these mountains without Thimeon's aid did not seem to matter now; all the efforts of the ungifted were futile against the Daegmon.

"I will go where you lead," Thimeon replied, lowering his head at the rebuke.

"And we will stay with Thimeon," came another Andani voice. It was the gray-haired Braddoc, a rough old shepherd old enough to be Elynna's grandfather. He could talk for hours about sheep and their ways. There was little else he knew. Still, he took a firm grip on the spear he had fashioned from his shepherd's staff, and glared at Elynna with a resolve that dared her to send him away. Others among the ungifted echoed the sentiment, vowing to stay with Thimeon to the end of the quest.

"And yet our pace might be faster if we were fewer," came a voice from among the Northlanders, thick with the throaty Anghare accent.

Elynna turned toward the voice and found herself looking straight at Cane. He returned her gaze without flinching. He was tall with a deep chest, muscular shoulders and forearms, and a stern jaw. Unable to match his will, she turned her eyes back to the distant hills. "What good are mere bows and staffs against the Daegmon? There are only a few powers that matter," Cane added. His proud and booming voice carried through the crisp air. Nobody missed what he said. The silence deepened as many of them turned defiant eyes upon him while he stood there, unmoved, staring at Elynna through small eyes as black as his braided hair.

Elynna groaned inwardly, suspecting that his impatience was directed at her. She guessed his thoughts. He despised her weakness as much as she admired his strength. She didn't blame him. She despised her own weakness. Did it not disqualify her from his love for which she longed? But she could not think of that either. She was no freer to pursue Cane's love than to flee from Thimeon's. "No," she began. "We will—"

"Listen," Tienna interrupted.

"—stay together as long—"

"Be quiet!" Tienna repeated. "Listen."

The urgency of the warning silenced the discussion. Elynna stood still, ears alert as she watched her friend trembling. At first she heard nothing. Several seconds passed. Then she noticed it. A steady rumbling, almost too low for her ears.

"Where is it coming from?" the old shepherd Braddoc asked, as he glanced around from slope to slope. In moments the sound had grown from a low murmur to a loud and steady rumble. "I have heard this before in the high mountains in spring. It is the sound of an avalanche. But I see nothing."

"Avalanche," Elynna muttered as her memory returned. "Let the sea rise over us. It is here."

Before she could say another word, it struck. A rush of terror, a physical reality of dread and horror as intense and agonizing as any pain she had ever felt. It swept through her body like a conflagration. She stumbled backward. Only Cane's quick hand on her arm kept her from collapsing. "Are you all right?" he asked calmly.

Elynna couldn't answer. At Cane's touch, a faint voice arose inside her. A thread of courage. A reminder. The danger had not grown or changed. She had known the risk, and had chosen to pursue the creature anyway. And Cane and Cathros had not been with her before, when the creature had attacked her village. They were with her now. It was not hopeless. She was *supposed* to be here.

But the voice faltered. And in an instant, all that remained of her reason fled—and with it, all the days and weeks of preparation for this moment. She stepped away from Cane. *Run.* She tried to shout. *The Daegmon is upon us.*

But nobody moved. No words had come from Elynna's dry mouth.

"There," Thimeon shouted over the noise. He pointed high up the slope to their left. The snow was convulsing. Ground heaved in giant spasms, shaking the valley and sending a half dozen of her companions tumbling backward. The rest of them braced themselves against one another to keep their balance. Still they watched. A huge bulge appeared in the hillside as snow tumbled down around it. The pitch of the rumble had risen to nearly a scream.

"The Daegmon," Tienna said in a horror-stricken voice. "I feel the ill. The earth groans in agony."

Elynna could only nod. The heat sense that smote her was like a blast of fire. Only once before she had felt the heat of the Daegmon's presence this intensely. She had forgotten what it did to her. Thoughts fled her mind, replaced by mere fear.

And it was not finished. With a burst of steam, smoke, and dirt, a dark rent opened up on the snowy slope. All eyes were fixed there now. And when the debris had cleared, they saw it. The Daegmon had begun to appear.

"Illengond protect us," Thimeon muttered as he stared at the grotesque scene. The foremost part of the Daegmon's body had already pushed forth from the ground—a cavernous mouth lunging toward the sky with gaping jaws of sword-sharp teeth. Though a mile or more away, Elynna and her companions drew back in fear and disgust.

In an instant, the creature was tossing its head from side to side, shaking its body free from the ground. Above steaming nostrils, large eyes glowed red with hate and power. As its neck shot up from the snow, it released another deafening roar. Then, with a powerful surge, two huge pinions broke free of the mountain, scattering snow and frozen dirt across the slope. The creature's wings, covered with black leathery scales and spanning forty feet, arched upward as it dragged itself free with its front talons.

The rest of the body emerged beneath the wings, and for a moment it stood looking downward. Then, in one fluid motion, it swept its wings backward and launched upward off massive rear legs. As its body took to the air, the rest of its long whiplike tail slid free of the ground, leaving a dark black wound in the mountainside.

While the companions watched, the Daegmon rose high into the air, its shadow blotting out a swath of hillside. It dwarfed them all. Once, twice, then a third time it circled, climbing higher with each loop. It was a display Elynna had seen before. They were all going to die. Unless . . .

In terror, her eyes swept the hillside and the valley below looking for an escape. But there was nothing to be seen. They had been led into a trap, and had followed like spawning fish into a net. The Daegmon flew one more circle. Then, with a final terrifying screech, it folded its wings and swooped downward.

The sound brought an end to Elynna's paralysis. "Run!" she screamed.

2

TERROR AND REASON

E lynna's companions were moving. Not the action they
had long practiced—the movements of a careful attack,
of pursuers cornering their prey. For the same irrational
fear that had overwhelmed Elynna had overwhelmed the others
also. She could see them around her, fleeing down the slope like
rabbits from a hawk, tumbling and sliding on the crust thickened
by sleet and rain.

Only Cane and Cathros remained rooted behind her. "No!"
Their simultaneous shouts reached her ear at the same time.

"Don't run," Cathros called out a moment later, and before the
echo of his voice could even return from the distant hillside, Cane
was giving his own order. "We must fight. We came to fight."

Nobody listened to either of them. Down the steep hill across
the wind-packed snow Elynna ran on the heels of her fleeing companions. Those in the lead were already fifty steps away before
the brothers' voices tumbled over them in the wind. Elynna, near

the back of the pack, could feel the Daegmon's eyes hailing down on her like a sheet of arrows. Off to her left somebody stumbled in the snow and fell. Then another went down.

She didn't slow. The Daegmon drew closer. She could feel it. Then her own foot found a softer patch of snow and broke through the crust, and she tumbled headlong into the snow to await her death.

Yet death did not come at once. The fall spun her around. When she stopped sliding, she was looking back up the hill. There was the Daegmon, jaws gaping wide, gliding down the slope in pursuit of its prey. Cane and Cathros stood their ground facing it, though neither of them had yet drawn a weapon. Tienna also had somehow managed to check her terror after a few steps. Or perhaps her pain was simply too great to allow her to flee. She stood a few yards down the slope from the two Northlanders, her arms clutched around her chest as she absorbed the wounds to the land around her.

"No!" Elynna screamed, as the creature's talons reached toward Cane to tear him from the ground. But at that instant, Cane swung his sword free of its scabbard. With a loud crack, a burst of blue flame engulfed his blade and shot upward toward the creature's belly. The Daegmon veered away, its talons missing its target by a several feet.

Cathros joined his brother's attack. With the battle strength upon him that had nothing to do with his innate human might, he had loosed from somewhere a massive chunk of ice that none of the other companions could even have lifted. He hurled it toward his enemy's exposed belly as though it weighed no more than a child's toy. But the ice that would have crushed another human shattered ineffectually off the creature's tough hide just as the burst of flames from Cane's sword sputtered. Unperturbed, the Daegmon continued over the trio and on down the hill toward less dangerous prey.

Elynna turned her head and followed the flight path of their enemy. There she saw her. One lone villager had straggled behind the others. It was the young Andan girl. She was limping. The Daegmon saw her too. Tilting its wings, it turned toward her. Elynna shouted, half in warning and half in fear. The girl heard the shout. Or perhaps she just felt the creature behind her. She turned and looked back up the hill just as it caught her. The terror registered on her face for an instant. Then her cry was cut short as powerful talons ripped into her spine and jerked her from the ground.

Elynna looked away. A moment later she felt a strong grip on her shoulder. It was Thimeon, kneeling beside her. "Come," he said. He tried to pull her to her feet.

She yanked free of his grasp and struggled to stand. Above her, the Daegmon circled higher, carrying the girl's body. Elynna was powerless to do anything. "Help *her*," she pleaded.

"It is too late," Thimeon replied tightly.

Just as he spoke, the Daegmon released its grip. From high in the sky, the small form dropped to the ground like a stone. Even in the snow, the thud of impact was audible. Elynna gaped in horror. The Daegmon's awful screech echoed across the valley, but for the moment her guilt and anger had overcome her terror. Why had she ever allowed the young girl to join them? Why had nobody protected her?

Thimeon put a hand on her shoulder again. "We must move quickly. Leave the hillside. We must find shelter somewhere."

Elynna was still staring at the broken body lying on the snow. "Why did you bring her?" she accused. "She had no chance."

It was unfair to accuse Thimeon, she knew. It was the shepherd Braddoc who had brought her. Thimeon had turned them both away at first, but they had followed the company for three days and refused to leave. And there was no place to have sent them anyway. But her own anger and guilt were too great to keep bottled.

Thimeon opened his mouth, but his words caught in his throat. He dropped his hand, and his shoulders sagged in defeat. Elynna scowled at him, then turned and looked up the slope. Cathros and Cane were now jogging down toward her, their dark braided hair flopping behind them as they ran. Tienna ran between them.

"Don't flee," they called as they came. "Stop running." Their eyes shone brightly, and there was no sign of panic in their faces. Cane held his sword high in the air like a standard. Blue fire flickered up and down the length of the blade and along his forearm. Even in the afternoon sun, the weapon shone brightly with its burning. And something in the flaming blade pushed back on Elynna's fear. A spark of courage returned.

When the brothers had come to a halt beside her and Thimeon, Cathros spoke. "We must not give in to fear. The Daegmon will destroy us if we do. Fear is its weapon." His voice was slow and measured. "It feeds on our fear."

Elynna knew intuitively—or through her gift—that Cathros spoke the truth. She could taste the creature's power growing with the terror of her companions. But what could she do? She couldn't stop being afraid. She looked down the slope. Except for the five of them standing there, and one who would not run again, the others were still fleeing. They were nearly a quarter mile away already, and spreading out as they went. The company was in ruins. Or soon would be. She turned her gaze back to the sky. The creature had already circled around and now dropped toward them for another attack. It opened its mouth in a great gaping grin.

Thimeon noticed what Elynna did not. "It ignores us and pursues the others."

"Thimeon is right," Cane said. "It avoided the flame of my blade, and will not come near me, I think. But the others are scattered. I cannot protect them. They run mad in all directions just as the Daegmon would have us do. It will destroy us one at a time. Our hope is to turn and face it together."

"There," Thimeon shouted. The Daegmon had bent its wings and now dove to the right where a distant figure struggled across an icy patch of hillside. It closed upon him quickly, its enormous talons stretched out to clutch its prey. From above, Elynna could only watch as the huge shadow engulfed the fleeing victim. Snow and ice exploded as claws and tail crashed into the hillside with enormous force. The watchers gasped and held their breath as the Daegmon rose up in the air.

"Look," Thimeon cried. "He's still alive!" Miraculously, the intended victim had risen to his feet just a few steps from the scar in the snow.

"It is Aram," Cathros said. "One of the Anghare. He is skilled."

"He is lucky," Cane replied. "We must make them stop running."

Thimeon was already yelling. "Turn around." His voice carried through the crisp dry air, echoing off distant slopes. "Stop."

Elynna added her voice to his. One figure stopped. Braddoc. But the others—too far away, or too overcome with fear to hear the call—continued to flee. Above, the Daegmon circled for a third assault. It had all the time in the world. The valley floor, even if they reached it, offered no more safety than the hillside.

"Come," Thimeon said. "We must help them." Without waiting for an answer, he started down the slope toward Braddoc. Cane gave his brother a grim look but went with Thimeon. Cathros, Tienna, and Elynna followed behind.

It didn't take long to reach the old shepherd. Like Elynna, he was strengthened by the presence of the blue flames that flickered up and down Cane's arm and blade. Only then, in the presence of that strength for the third time, did Elynna grasp something she had not before understood. Something she had not even thought about. The Daegmon was a powerful creature. She knew that. There was reason to be afraid. But this terror they felt now was beyond reason. Something crushed all hope. Some presence. Some power of the Daegmon. It could not be resisted by the will, unaided.

Yet Cane's gift, or whatever strength was in his blade, was more than just flame and power. She could feel that also. It warded off the Daegmon terror. In its presence she was still afraid, but with a rational fear; it did not paralyze her.

"We must regroup," Cane said. "If we can," he added, under his breath. The others nodded. Braddoc's face was white, but he understood. The six of them now continued down the slope. Cane and Cathros ran side by side at the lead with Cane's flaming blade held aloft. Tienna came a few paces behind the brothers. Though pain still showed in her face, with the discipline of a huntress she had put it aside. She now cast off her heavy cloak as well, and ran low to the ground like a tracker. Even in the snow, her stride was swift and effortless. Next came Elynna, her bow in one hand with an arrow ready in the other. Behind her came Thimeon and Braddoc, the ungifted, carrying their spears.

But the distance between the two groups was too great, and the Daegmon too fast. Before Cane and Cathros could close the gap, it was upon the others. And they still had not turned to face it.

"Falien," Thimeon cried out. "Turn."

His voice was drowned by a loud screech as the Daegmon extended its massive forelegs toward its next victim. Then the distant form did look, but there was little he could do. He ducked, avoiding the scooping talons that missed slicing him in half by mere inches. But his evasion was for naught. As the Daegmon sailed past, it lashed downward with its tail which fell from the sky like a great tree limb in a gale. The thunderous blow struck Falien in the back. He crumbled to the ground while the creature continued on over the heads of the others. Thirty yards ahead and to the right, Elynna watched another of the companions fall with a huge gash across his back and shoulder. It was Hruach. His sister Hrevia barely dodged a similar fate, then rushed back to his side.

Elynna looked around her. Her company was in complete disarray now. In their first real trial, she had utterly failed as a leader. Other than the few who stood with her next to Cane, only the Northlanders Aram, Kayle, and Annat had finally shown enough presence of mind to stop running. Or perhaps, even from a distance, they had felt the surge of Cane's power that was working in Elynna as well to keep the terror at bay. They stood together with weapons drawn. But they were only three, and they were among the ungifted. Above them the Daegmon circled for its next assault. Already the battle looked hopeless.

"Do something," Elynna shouted at Cane. "Do something now."

In response Cane swung his sword over his head and let loose a savage war cry. What followed surprised them all, perhaps even Cane. As he shouted, a burst of energy exploded with a boom from his raised blade. Flames engulfed his arm and shoulder, then shot thirty yards in the air like a fiery arrow straight toward their enemy. The force of the concussion hurled Cathros to the ground.

Out of the corner of her eye, Elynna saw Tienna dive to the side and roll to her feet many paces away. An instant later Elynna, who stood a few steps further back and whose reflexes were slower, simply fell and covered her face from the intensity of the power. Only Cane was unaffected, immune to his own power.

The involuntary display lasted only a second, then subsided. But the Daegmon had felt it. It veered sharply away from Cane, and Elynna sensed a faltering of its power. Seizing the opportunity, she yelled as loud as she could.

"Wait!" The crisp air felt good in her lungs as she inhaled and yelled again. "Stay together. We must not flee." Compared with the roar of the Daegmon, her voice sounded thin. Nonetheless, several more companions stopped. Turning toward the voice, they spotted Cane coming down the hill with his sword ablaze. Wonder and hope filled their eyes.

"It is not over," Thimeon warned. "The Daegmon is coming back."

Elynna looked up. Angered at the interference, the creature roared again more loudly. Its voice rose to a terrifying thunder that echoed off the valley walls. The mountainside trembled. Elynna threw her hands over her ears. She had seen grown warriors tremble at the sound. The companions who were still running fell to the ground and covered their ears. This time, however, the tactic backfired. For, when it was over, the companions rose again to their feet. Lo and behold, they were still alive. Pausing, they looked around. Others were calling out their names. Cane came toward them, his blade vibrant with power. For a moment their sanity was restored, and they heard Elynna's call.

But the Daegmon had destroyed whole villages. It was angered, not defeated. Eyes blazing, it began to swoop down again. This attack was no longer slow and lazy. Elynna would not reach the others in time. Further down the hill Jamesh stood alone, staring up at his approaching doom. His hands hung limp at his sides. He hadn't even drawn a weapon. She was about to scream at him, when she heard a sudden hopeful exclamation from Thimeon.

"It has turned back."

"What?" Elynna looked back to the sky. The Daegmon had inexplicably turned from its attack and was circling back toward where it had first emerged.

"It is fleeing," Braddoc said. His voice reflected the same mix of surprise and relief that Elynna herself felt.

"Now is our chance," Thimeon urged. "Hurry. Regroup before we are attacked again."

Two minutes later, the company had gathered around the brothers Cane and Cathros.

Cane's drawn and upraised blade drew them and held them together. Their panic had subsided. Cathros had scooped up Falien from where he lay crumpled in a heap on the snow, limp and lifeless. "His heart is still beating, but barely. His breath is shallow. He will need help soon, or else—" He didn't finish the sentence, but Elynna finished it in her mind. *Or else he will die.*

Hruach had fared better. With the aid of his sister he was back on his feet. His heavy cloak had been torn in half by the long raking blow of the Daegmon's razor-sharp talons. Miraculously, however, the wound to his flesh was not deep.

Then came Braddoc's voice. "Llana?" His eyes were scanning the hillside for her. He had not seen her fall and did not yet know, but there was desperation in his face as he turned back toward the companions. "Where is Llana?" he asked, his voice tight with pain.

Elynna glanced involuntarily back up the slope. She was surprised to see the distance they had come. "There," Cane said, pointing to a distant speck on the hard-packed snow.

"Llana!" The old shepherd said her name with a gasp. His grip on his spear tightened. "We must get her."

Cane shook his head. It would take them many minutes to climb back that high—far longer than it had taken to descend. They could not risk it. Not unless she was still alive. "No. We cannot."

Thimeon put his hand on Braddoc's shoulder. "I am sorry, friend. It is too late."

Braddoc shook his head. "I must. She is my brother's granddaughter. She is all that remains of our family."

"It is too late," Cathros said softly.

Ignoring Cathros, Braddoc started running back up the hill. Thimeon shouted his name. "Braddoc. No." Something in his voice—some hidden authority—made the old shepherd stop. "You can't," Thimeon went on more softly. "It's too late."

Braddoc's shoulders slumped, and he fell to his knees. Hands over his face, he began to weep. Thimeon stepped in front of him, pulled him to his feet, and wrapped his arms around him in sympathy.

"Come," Elynna said. "We must stay together." Without waiting to see who would follow, she turned her back and walked down to where her remaining companions were huddled together around Cane.

"We need a plan," Cane was saying. His blade still glowed dimly with the blue flame. "We need to be ready when it attacks again. There is no shelter and no place to run. We must fight. It is our only hope. It is what we came to do."

"Will it attack again?" Aram asked. He was another tall Northlander, with short-cropped hair the color of the bright-polished bronze head on his long spear.

"Yes," Elynna answered.

"And this time we will be ready," Cane went on.

It was clear from their faces that the companions did not share the Northlander's confidence. Nevertheless, Tienna spoke for them. "How? Tell us what to do."

A long silence followed. Cane gave no answer. Thimeon and Braddoc rejoined the others. Braddoc's face held a grim expression—a fierceness Elynna had never before seen in the old shepherd's eyes. She risked a glance at Thimeon. For once he was not looking back at her. His face was ashen as he stared blankly ahead.

"It is circling again," Cathros said.

"It will watch and choose its moment," Elynna said. She was surprised to hear her own voice. Her words did nothing to encourage the company.

Cane was silent a moment longer, lost in some internal debate or struggle. Then he snapped back to the present and began issuing commands in a clear and measured voice. "Form a tight circle. Thimeon, Bandor, Kayle, and Aram must guard the downhill side with your spears. Cathros will stay with me here on the uphill side. The rest of you fill in on the left and right and keep your backs to the middle. Those with swords, come closest to me."

"Shouldn't you and Cathros separate and defend opposite sides?" Aram asked nervously. "You are the only—"

"No," Cane replied, without waiting for Aram to finish. "It will attack downhill. It is too clumsy to fly up the slope. We will meet it above with our greatest strength. Cathros and I will bear the brunt of the attack."

"Do not fear," Cathros added more gently. "If it attacks from below, we will come to your aid."

Aram nodded. He was one of the Anghare too, and had a warrior's discipline. There was a determined silence as the company set about following Cane's orders. They formed a circle about thirty feet across with their backs to the middle. They had all taken off their heavy woolen mittens to better grip their weapons. Hruach, despite his wounds, drew his sword and stood at the side of his sister, who also held a straight double-edged Northland blade. With them on the left side along with Braddoc were the Plainsfolk Marti, Nahoon, and Beth. Llian moved to the right, along with Thimeon's young cousin Theo and the Westwashers Pietr, Jamesh, and Siyen. Thimeon and Bandor stood on the downhill side with spears in hand. With them Cane sent the ungifted Anghare Annat, Kayle, and Aram.

Elynna looked about her. Though because of her gift she was in some ways the leader of this company, she had always known that when it finally came to battle, Cane or Cathros would take charge. She was glad the burden did not fall on her. She nocked an arrow to her bow and stood half a step behind Cane and to his right.

Tienna, having stripped to her fighting shift, crouched down next to Elynna, ready to spring. She had drawn from her belt a hunting blade nearly as long as her forearm, and deadly sharp. Elynna looked at her again with renewed respect. If the huntress felt any of the terror that gripped Elynna, she did not show it.

From her first day in the company, Tienna had repeatedly and fervently denied being a warrior. She was a huntress, she said. She had a skill at both tracking and avoiding being tracked. She sought food for her people. And she found it. She had trained herself to be aware of her surroundings. Of every sound and smell and movement. Of the direction of the wind and the moisture in the air. Even of the silence. She had not told Elynna this in a boastful way. It was simply a matter of fact. And Elynna had seen enough not to doubt her. Tienna had already demonstrated the endurance born of discipline and hard training. But she was not trained for war, and had no desire to be. The folk of the Plains were peaceful and had not fought against each other for many years. And yet, for all her disavowals, Tienna had as well the grace and skill of a great warrior, though not the size or strength.

Cathros took his position last. He set Falien's unconscious body in the center of the circle and covered him with a blanket from his pack, then moved to his brother's side. Unlike Cane, he bore no weapon. Cane had told Elynna the reason when they first met. *Swords are useless for my brother. He had tried to wield a weapon against the Daegmon thrice before when the battle strength came upon him, but no weapon we have yet found can bear his might. Spears crumple in his hand like twigs, and strong swords shatter. It is a waste of steel.*

Thus they stood, poised and ready, as the Daegmon circled overhead. But the attack did not come. The creature continued its flight, circling higher with each pass. "What is it doing?" Elynna asked when she could no longer bear the waiting.

"It is afraid," Cane answered with a hint of disappointment in his voice.

"No," Tienna replied more softly. "It is not afraid. Listen." A rumble had started again, much like the sound they heard before the creature emerged. The Daegmon was circling high along the ridges now, its mouth open in a low-pitched continuous roar that grew louder as the creature rose higher. Again, the mountain trembled. Across the way, a huge section of snow over one of the cliffs broke free and crashed down. Still the roar grew in volume. The creature was exerting its power.

It was Thimeon who first understood. "It can't be! This is not the season or snow for it." His eyes were wide open. A moment later, he was running uphill toward Elynna and Cane. "Get us out of here now. It's trying to bring the snow down on us."

"What?" Cane asked. "I don't under—"

"Get us out. Don't you see? The Daegmon is starting an avalanche. It's going to bring this whole slope down on us." Even as he said this, the mountains began to echo the Daegmon's growl. The snowpack vibrated and trembled to the Daegmon's piercing call. In a few moments it would begin to slide down the mountain in a great crushing wave, and if they remained where they were, they didn't have a chance of surviving. Too late Elynna perceived that the Daegmon had been even craftier than she imagined. It had lured them to just this spot, toyed with them, and now would destroy them without a fight. She turned to Cane for help, but he was staring wide-eyed around him. His fearlessness in battle did him no good now. This was something he couldn't fight.

Boom. On the far side of the valley a huge block of snow crashed down over the ledge. The rest of the company was beginning to panic again. "Hurry," Thimeon shouted. "There's not much time. This snow will go any second."

"Where?" Elynna asked, looking back to Thimeon for directions and trying not to panic. "You are from the mountains. Tell us what to do?"

Thimeon didn't answer. He scanned the valley just as she had done a few moments before. The Daegmon had chosen its location well. There was no shelter to be seen that would withstand the force of an avalanche. "Pray to the All-Maker," he breathed.

The Daegmon still circled, its roar growing ever louder, more triumphant in anticipation. Passing the top of a ledge, it smashed its tail into the slope. The snow gave. A patch began to slide down the hill. As it slid, it grew, collecting in a wave, pulling the rest of the mountainside with it. A moment later, the entire rim of the valley above them to the south began to collapse. It spread in both directions along the ridge. Like the crest of a giant breaker, the valley was caving in.

"Down," Thimeon yelled, as some new hidden hope blazed in his eyes. "Down. Down. It's flat enough here. We can do it. Go down. Beneath the snowpack." Elynna stared at him with no comprehension, but he wasn't speaking to her. He was yelling at Cane. "Digging is too slow. The fire. Use the fire. Go down."

Cane understood almost at once. "Stand back," he ordered.

The ground rumbled as from an earthquake. A mile above them, a huge wall of snow was careening down the steep mountain.

Ignoring their impending doom, Cane drove his sword straight down into the snow at his feet. The blade burst into bright-blue flame, and the heat was so intense and immediate that everyone nearby leapt back and shielded their faces. In a small circle around him, the snow began to evaporate in a giant cloud.

In a second, Cane had dropped a foot down. But Thimeon yelled, "Faster!" He looked up. The crest of the avalanche was less than half a mile away. "Hotter! Use all the power you have." Without waiting to see if Cane could comply, he spun around and yelled to the others. "Come now. This is our only hope."

When they saw what was happening, the companions sprang toward the hole. The flame around Cane intensified as he responded with a surge of power, willing its force downward. It was like the blast of some giant furnace, or of a raging forest fire concentrated in one spot. An explosion of steam shot into the sky, and Cane dropped straight down into the snow, engulfed in flames and steam, while the others stepped back even further. In an instant he was gone completely, and the blue fire was just a glow coming through the steam from somewhere below.

Shielding his face against any heat, Thimeon leapt to the edge of the newly formed pit and looked down. Elynna stayed beside him, afraid to do nothing and equally afraid of what he would do. Steam smote them in the face, blinding them. She had no idea how deep Cane had gone, or whether it was safe to follow. She might as easily be burned by his flame or drowned in the melting snow. Yet there was no more time and no other choice. Down was unknown, but if she waited above, she knew what would happen.

They paused only a few horrible seconds hoping for the flame to cool or the steam to dissipate. Then Thimeon motioned for the others. He tried to urge Elynna into the hole first, but she stepped back. Was it a sense of duty, that she as leader of the company should be last to safety? Or was it fear of this blind leap? Or perhaps both. She could not have said. She knew only that Braddoc was first. He stepped over the edge and dropped out of sight into the steam. With Falien in his arms, Cathros followed. The crest of the avalanche was a hundred yards away now. The rest of the company poured in as Elynna stood aside and watched. Hruach and Hrevia, Aram, Kayle and Annat, Marti, Nahoon and Beth, Falien, Pietr, Jamesh and Siyen—in twos and threes they leapt through the small opening down into the hole. In seconds they had all disappeared into the steam. Only Elynna and Thimeon remained.

"Go!" Thimeon shouted at her.

Elynna stepped toward the hole just as the wave of snow crashed into her back. She stumbled forward. Then all went black.

3

THE BURNING
OF LIENFORD

S creams of terror shredded the dawn air. First one alone at a distant edge of the village, then another by the river, then a third closer still. Before long a cacophony of agonized cries were echoing off the stone buildings of Lienford. Elynna, in the throes of another vivid nightmare, awoke with a start. She was trembling and drenched in sweat. The shrieks rang in her ears, hollow and strangely distant, and she mistook them for the lingering grip of her dream. But this morning the screaming did not end when she awoke. Wakefulness no longer brought safety and release. These were real screams. The village of Lienford was awash in them, and it grew worse with each moment.

She sat bolt upright in her bed. As she did, the pain struck: a sharp searing burn like when she'd unwittingly brushed against one of the jellied balloon fish floating near the river mouth of her coast village. Only, now her whole body was aflame in agony, not just her foot or leg. She could barely move. Outside, the turmoil grew closer. Voices she recognized, rushing down the path in front of her house or darting past her window, were calling out in dismay or horror. What was it? She tried to shout, but no words came out, and she was afraid to know. She felt only the overpowering urge to leap out her window and flee with them.

Before she could move, her father rushed into her small room. He yanked her to her feet and almost threw her toward the door. "To the barn," he yelled, "There's no time to stop. Run!"

Still in shock, Elynna turned and stumbled through the eating room toward the front door. She stopped on the threshold. Despite her father's urgency, something prevented her from stepping outside. Her nerves were on fire, blotting out all of her senses. She did not smell the fragrance of water celery that always filled the air at this time of year, or feel the salty moisture from the early morning westerly breeze coming many miles upriver from the sea. She did not delight in the orange honeysuckle glowing in golden sunlight on the side of her neighbor's house, or the wood sorrel creeping across the ground nearer the river. She did not even see them. She smelled, or felt, or tasted only smoke and panic. And something very evil. She knew, without being told, that an unspeakable horror had come upon the village.

In the next room, her father was rousing her younger brother Lyn, urging him to get moving, not to ask questions. Elynna was only dimly aware as Lyn stumbled out into the kitchen smelling the air and looking about him in panic. "Father," she said dumbly, as though in a trance. He was digging through the tool cabinet frantically searching for something. "Father," she repeated. Something about the terror was familiar. She had felt it in her dreams all week. And she had the inexplicable and irrational fear that whatever had come to her village had come there after her. Finally the words came. "Father, please, don't leave—"

Another scream cut short her plea and propelled her father back into motion. His voice was frantic as he grabbed Lyn by the shoulders. "Go with Elynna. Get her to safety. Go to the stone foundation of the barn, by the corner of the salt shack where the structure is strongest. Lie there underneath, and don't leave until this is over—or until I come get you. Do you understand?"

Lyn nodded. He stepped to the doorway beside his sister. There he turned once more to ask what was happening. Father never answered. He pushed them both out, propelled them toward the small barn, then turned toward the growing melee in the center of the village and disappeared into the confusion.

"Come on," Lyn said. Trembling, he took Elynna's arm. "We'd better do as he says."

"No," she cried, staring toward the corner of the adjacent building where their father had disappeared. "We must stay with him."

It was too late. A wailing screech filled the misty air—a cry so harsh and terrible and full of power that could not have been mistaken for human. It rose above Elynna's thumping heartbeat, above the constant rumbling of the ice-choked river, above the screams that filled the village. Before the sound died away, she was bolting toward the barn. Barely slowing, she dove into the stone crawl space beneath the salt room. Lyn was close behind her, his face pale white. For a long moment they did not move. Neither of them could speak. By the time they turned around and looked back out of the opening, the panic had reached their edge of the village. Men and women were running wildly past their hiding space. They were men and women Elynna knew, but she had never seen them like this. Grown men who had a hundred times risked their lives against countless dangers on the open sea were now screaming in terror as if they had gone insane.

"Are we under attack?" Lyn asked. Though two years Elynna's junior, he was already as strong as an ox. Yet he was shaking like a fish in a net. It was the first time she had seen him afraid. "Is it Northlanders?" he asked. There hadn't been war anywhere in Gondisle in the memories of any in the village, and it had been many lifetimes since war had come to the Westwash. Yet all the old stories spoke of the Anghare as an aggressive and warlike people.

"I don't know," Elynna whispered. But it was not true. She knew even then it was not the Northlanders. It was worse than that. Far worse. It was more than the screams that terrified her. There was something deeper—a fear that froze her heart. She didn't know how to explain it. "That sound. I felt it coming in my dream, as if—"

She never finished. A shadow passed low over them, blotting out the gray sky like a huge cloud of black smoke, larger than a house. She saw it then for the first time—the Daegmon, its mouth open in a terrible gaping grin. It soared over the rooftops in pursuit of the fleeing villagers. Before she could breathe, its tail came down with a crash. Their house, where just a few minutes earlier she had lain asleep, collapsed in a heap of rubble.

"Father," she shouted, fearing that he had gone back inside. She cast her eyes for some sign of him in the ruins, but her sight was blocked as Lyn, overcome by terror, tried to back further down into the crawl space. "Father is out there," she said, almost weeping, "We have to—"

"Shut up!" he screamed in her face.

Something in his voice made Elynna cringe. She pushed his arm aside and peered out along the ground, struggling for some glimpse of their father. A pair of booted feet ran past. "Father," she yelled and stuck her head out.

A huge pair of jaws snapped shut not fifty feet from her hiding place. Where a man had just run past, the ground was empty. Overhead, a huge winged creature dropped the mangled body into the wreckage of a house. And the scream that Elynna heard now was her own. That the man wasn't her father didn't stop the terror.

The minutes that followed seemed like hours. Again and again the Daegmon swept through the village, ruthless in its destruction of everyone and everything in its path, raining death down upon all that moved. Each time its shadow passed over Elynna, her terror worsened. Soon flames were rising from burning homes. Broken bodies lay strewn about the ground. Still the screams continued, punctuated by the occasional crashing of another home. There was no escape from the creature. None but the icy-cold of the Lienwash River carrying the floods of melting snow high up in the mountains. In desperation, some took that route and were not seen again. Others fled to their boats, but few escaped the Daegmon that way.

Elynna wept, yet she could not look away. Outside she could see children. Their parents were lost, dead, or consumed by terror. She wanted to help them, but her own terror left her paralyzed. She could only watch as young children she knew lay huddled in the mud, whimpering. Now and then the Daegmon snatched up another, or crushed one with its tail. She could see their bodies now. Their innocent voices rang in her ears.

"No," she whimpered loudly. "Stop it."

Her face was pushed roughly into the ground. "Be quiet," Lyn rasped in her ears. "It's going to find us."

Blood was everywhere, splattered on rocks and doors, in puddles beside the fallen, seeping into the ground. The agonized moans of the dying droned in the background behind the harsh shriek of the Daegmon. Its cruel talons cut through the helpless fishermen as effortless as her father's best fillet knife took the flesh off fish. Gaping jaws snapped bodies in two.

"Father," Elynna called, frantic, hoping beyond hope that he still lived. All about her, crushing blows of a powerful tail were smashing even stone buildings from their foundations. The creature was everywhere at once. There was no end. The carnage kept growing. She saw them fall: cousins, aunts, friends, neighbors. Dying in agony with no hope. They had never faced anything like this. They were fishermen, not warriors. "Father, please," she pleaded, ignoring her brother's warnings.

Then he appeared out in the open toward the center of the village between a pair of burning houses. He was running toward them. She saw him the same instant he spotted her where she lay beneath the stone barn. Their eyes met, and the image froze in her memory—the momentary relief lighting across his face at his discovery that she was still alive. Then the cry of a child caught his attention. He turned away. He didn't see the Daegmon coming, but it wouldn't have mattered if he had. He stopped to help the fallen child.

"Hurry!" Elynna shouted between sobs as he scooped the child in his arms and ran toward the barn. That scene, too, was etched in her memory. From high above them, the Daegmon saw it all. It dropped down like a sea-eagle—only, a hundred times larger. He saw the shadow engulf him. Still trying to shield the child in his arms, he ducked and rolled as the creature swooped past. He was too slow. Talons raked across his back like four parallel sword strokes. He took two more stumbling steps, then toppled to the ground, the child still nestled safely in his arms.

"No," Elynna cried in horror. She started forward, only to be pulled back into hiding by her brother. She tried to break loose, but he was too strong. The Daegmon had circled for another pass through the village. It was flying slowly now, higher overhead, circling as if searching. She felt the heat once again—the burning that had plagued her dreams. And then the touch. The horror of its mind. She realized even then that Daegmon was searching for her. She was the intended victim.

4

TRAPPED

Elynna opened her eyes with a start, just as she had on that morning one and a half years earlier. And for an instant she thought she was back there again, reliving the nightmare. But all was dark. There was no screaming. Only dead silence. She blinked and rubbed her eyes wondering if she had gone blind. Or died. The throbbing in her head was the one indication she still lived.

"Tienna?" she asked, tentatively.

"I am here."

"I can't see anything. Is it dark here? Or have I—?"

"There is no light," Tienna answered. "Or if there is, I too have been blinded."

Elynna breathed a sigh of relief. The thought of being trapped in darkness was not as terrifying as the thought of losing her sight—of permanent darkness. She stopped rubbing her eyes and instead reached down and felt around with her hands. Her fingertips touched bits of rock and ice and something else just a little softer, perhaps frozen moss or grass. She listened more carefully

41

now, and began to hear the sounds of breathing all around her. She stuck her hands out to the sides. Her left brushed against another body. An elbow or knee. Her right hand felt nothing but air. Somehow they had made it down all the way to frozen ground in some sort of a cave. Cane had saved them all. She spoke his name aloud.

"He is spent," came Cathros's reply. His normally pleasant baritone sounded tired and ragged, and in the darkness gave no hint at the great physical strength behind it. "He lives, but his effort exhausted him."

"Let him rest. He saved us all."

"That is yet to be seen," Cane mumbled from somewhere nearby.

Elynna stared into the blackness. She had no idea where the voice had come from, but she knew he was right. Her head still pounded. "And you, Cathros?" she asked.

"I am . . ." There was a pause. "Alive."

The roll continued. "Thimeon?" No answer came. Thimeon had waited until very last to jump down. He had still been standing above when the front of the avalanche had swept her into the hole. Her heart pounded as she repeated his name louder, suddenly afraid she might have lost him. And she needed him too much.

This time there was an answering groan from not far away, followed by a weak voice. "I think I'm still alive."

Elynna breathed another sigh of relief. Slowly she spoke the names of all the companions—all except Llana and Falien. Though many sounded weak, all twenty answered.

Elynna felt beneath her once more. Her hands found frozen soil and rocks. "We came all the way down to the ground," she said. It was a statement, not a question. But Tienna answered her.

"Yes. The snow was deeper than we thought. We fell to the ground, and the avalanche sealed the entrance above. Fortunately Cane hollowed quite a cavern before he was spent. It was big enough for all of us. Nobody would have survived out in the open. It is miraculous we were not swept away or crushed even down here." *That avalanche was unnatural. I could feel it.*

Elynna nodded, though it was invisible in the darkness. "Was anyone hurt by the fall?" When there was no answer she asked, "How is Hruach?"

"I will heal," Hruach answered, "but Falien is badly injured."

Cathros confirmed the report. "He is unconscious now, but for a brief time he regained consciousness. He could not feel his legs. More than that I do not know. We need light."

"Light," said Thimeon, snapping his fingers. "Of course." There was a brief shuffling, and moments later the sound of flint striking stone. A torch appeared illuminating Thimeon's face and a large circle around him. He was sitting up, looking shaky but with no sign of injury. While Elynna watched, he removed a second torch from his pack. The light reflecting off the snow walls was enough to illuminate the cavern. It was roughly circular, about thirty feet in diameter and seven feet high, with walls and ceiling of crusted snow and a floor of dirt and ice. The ground sloped gently. At the far corner was a low gap where the melting water had rushed away. A pile of snow and debris marked where the avalanche had covered the entrance.

Elynna turned next to the dazed faces of her companions. They were arrayed about the rough floor, prone or propped against their packs. None of them looked well. Siyen was even paler than usual, and her long sandy hair hung wet and limp. Hruach and Hrevia sat side by side. Both had blood dripping from their long Anghare noses. Marti, Nahoon, and Beth, the dark-skinned Plainsfolk, were shivering from the cold and damp.

Tienna rose to her feet and stood for a moment with a nervous expression. "Something is wrong," she said, sniffing. She wheeled toward Thimeon and snatched a torch from his hand. She threw it to the ground, where it sputtered and went out. "The other one too," she commanded. "Put it out."

Though confusion registered on Thimeon's face, he obeyed. The torch dipped toward the ground. Then it was dark again. A few of the companions groaned.

"There is not enough air here," Tienna explained.

"But they were burn—" Siyen started to whine.

Tienna cut her off. "And we're breathing too. But we wouldn't be for long if we left the torches burning."

For all her usual gentleness and patience, the huntress was not overly fond of Siyen, nor sympathetic to her story, despite how many times it had been told to them all. Siyen's father had grown up in a Westwash fishing family, the youngest of several brothers. As a young man, he'd run off on a trade ship to Aënport, and married a young Southland girl from a family of migrant workers. Siyen was their only child. From the time she was old enough to pick fruit off the tree or vine, she'd worked with her parents as a hired hand on a large farm. But when her mother took ill and died, her father had returned to the Westwash and taken Siyen with him.

His family had welcomed him back warmly, and they were delighted to meet his daughter, the only female born into the family in two generations. They provided a boat and equipment for him and restored him to the fishing trade. The work was as hard as his farming life, but at least he'd become his own boss.

Siyen, however, while she inherited her father's love of the sea, never really liked fishing. Nor did the slow and simple life of the Westwash suit her. She'd been thinking of returning to Citadel. Then she'd fallen in love with a young Westwasher. They were all set to be married in the summer.

That was when the Daegmon had come, destroying the village and killing both her father and her fiancé. Siyen had gone to Citadel, with a group of refuges. She'd been hoping to find some of her mother's relatives but was instead drawn into Elynna's quest. That was her story. She referred to herself sometimes as a Westwasher and other times as a Southlander, depending on her audience. What she didn't say, but what Elynna had privately suggested to Tienna one day, was that Siyen had become enamored of Falien, another young Westwasher with dark hair and a friendly smile who'd made the voyage with Elynna. The one who now lay grievously injured, perhaps with his back broken. The one who might not live, and if he lived might never walk again.

"I don't think she would have come had it not been for Falien," Elynna had told Tienna just a few days earlier. "But I don't think Falien has any feelings for her, so I doubt she'll be with us long."

So far, though, Elynna had been proved wrong. Siyen had pressed on through weeks of travel and trials, often in the face of hardship and obvious danger. Nonetheless, for somebody who claimed to have labored hard all her life, Siyen never showed much willingness to work. This, Elynna had also mentioned to Tienna under her breath on more than one occasion. Tienna, who worked harder than anybody in the company and with never a word of complaint, had nodded her agreement. But Thimeon, overhearing Elynna's whispered complaints one day, shrugged.

"Maybe she works less hard than others. But we must be slow to judge. Who knows what role each of us will have, and what we'll be capable of doing when we're called to it."

Tienna had appeared chastised, and after that was kinder to Siyen. Even Elynna felt guilty. "I know Thimeon's right," she had acknowledged to Tienna. "I think I'm just jealous." For Siyen was, in her own way, quite beautiful. Marching around the wilderness with dirty hands and a pack too big did not suit any of the women well. But a young man who saw Siyen sitting on a stool in some inn or tavern in Citadel in a short dress with her long sandy hair pulled up, and earrings to match her blue eyes, certainly would have thought she was beautiful. And that was something Elynna could not say about herself. Indeed, she couldn't help but notice that some of the Northland men, including Cane, paid extra attention to Siyen in the evenings when they had time to sit around a fire. It was never difficult for her to find somebody to do her jobs for her.

That entire conversation flashed through Elynna's memory. Though she could see nothing, she imagined Siyen folding her arms in a pout as though Tienna had just scolded her. But nobody other than Elynna was paying any attention to Siyen. Several voices were speaking at once, asking questions of Thimeon. In answer he gave off a long, low whistle of realization. "Of course," he said. "I should have known better. I am a fool."

"What do you mean?" the voices asked, with obvious concern. "Are we running out of air?"

"I don't know," Tienna replied. "I can't explain. It is my *health sense*. I tasted grave danger from the torches—a sickness in the air creeping into our lungs. The fear ceased when the torches were extinguished."

"What do we do now without light or heat?"

"I do not know."

Elynna exhaled a long breath. "Tienna. Can you find your way over here? We need to talk."

"I will come," Tienna said. Silence followed. When she spoke a minute later, she was inches away.

"Tell me what you know," Elynna said. Her voice was barely above a whisper, but in that small snow cavern anybody who listened closely would have heard her words.

"They are not well," Tienna answered. "Falien's injuries are most serious. If we cannot help him soon, he will die."

"Can you feel the extent of his wounds?"

Her reply sounded tired. "It will take some probing. But yes, if given the chance, I can." She paused, then added, "He is not the only one in danger."

"What of the others? What is wrong with them? I only saw their faces briefly."

"Our escape was costly. The air down here was as damp as lake fog with all the evaporating snow. Most of us are wet through to the skin, especially the first few who followed Cane. They might as well have fallen into a river and stepped out into the icy air."

"What can we do?"

"Sitting still is the worst thing. If we do not get moving soon, I fear some will die from the chill."

Elynna shivered. Even in the dry mountain air the dampness lingered.

"And yet," Tienna continued, "in many ways we were fortunate. If we had been at the bottom of the valley, the water from the sudden melting snow would have filled this cavern instead of running out. And higher up where the slope is steeper, this whole cave might have been swept away by the force of the avalanche. Even where we are, it was miraculous we survived. Had the snow not been so deep or packed—"

"I understand," Elynna interrupted tersely. "Is Cane sore off?"

"He is uninjured," Tienna replied. "He is protected from his own flame—immune to its heat, though it drains his strength. He is the only one of us who is completely dry. But the others . . ." Her voice trailed off.

"What do you suggest?"

"I can tend to Falien. Perhaps by my gift I may bring him healing, though it will take all of my strength. For the others, we need to get them warm as soon as possible."

"Tienna," came Thimeon's voice from nearby. He had found his way across the small cave.

"I am here."

"I do not understand your health sense. I knew the avalanche was unnatural only because I know these mountains. But you *felt* the wrong. Can you"—he paused as if searching for the right word—"can you feel the land around us?"

"This is not the time," Elynna interrupted. "Leave us."

Thimeon ignored the interruption. "Are there living things nearby? Trees? Any of the mountain spruce?"

"How close do you mean?"

"Close enough to dig to through the snow."

Tienna was slow in answering. When she spoke, her voice came from near the ground. "Yes. I believe so. I feel the roots reaching out, drinking in the water beneath us. It is the only life I can sense other than us. And the only health."

"Where? How far?"

There was a shuffling as Tienna stood and found Thimeon's arm. "There. Only forty feet through the snow. But do not miss it. The trees are few in this notch."

"I understand."

"The tree is still alive," Tienna added. "That is why I can sense it. The wood will be green. Not good for burning."

"The mountain spruce is full of pitch. Even green, it will burn hot if we can get it started."

"Wait," Elynna commanded when she realized his intention. "Why do you want wood? You don't mean to start a fire after what Tienna told us. If there is not enough air for a torch, surely there isn't enough for a fire."

Thimeon was already gone. Elynna heard only her own heavy breathing and the squeak of his departing footsteps on the frozen ground. A short time later Braddoc's gruff voice drifted across the cave. "What does it matter?"

"It matters," Thimeon said in a gentle but insistent voice. "I need your ax."

A bout of coughing accentuated Braddoc's mumbled reply. Then there was more silence. Eventually Elynna heard the muffled sounds of digging: the soft thud of an ax in snow, the scraping of a blade gouging through crust, or hitting a piece of ice.

As Elynna stood staring into the blackness where Thimeon worked alone and invisible, her thoughts drifted back on the *coincidence* that had brought him and Tienna and several others into the company. It was late in the fifth month, halfway through the pale cycle of the last moon just before midyear's day, and more than a year following the destruction of her village. She had been traveling northward, fleeing Citadel after her disappointments there. They had set up their tents somewhere near the Dagger River on the wagon road to Aeti. With her were her newfound companions: Falien, Pietr, Jamesh, Cathros, Cane, and Siyen. They were a mix of refugees from the Westwash and a small delegation of Northlanders, all departing Citadel. All of them had gone to the capital city in search of aid against their foe. And they had failed to find it. Accident or fate, or a common need, or perhaps just common desperation had brought them together and given them their goal: pursue the enemy that had ravaged their people, and destroy it.

Still in desperate need of help, but no longer willing to wait, at the urging of Cane they'd finally left the city and begun a rash pursuit of their foe with their hopes of success resting in the gifts of Cane and Cathros. And in the gift of Elynna to lead them and help them find that foe.

That was the start of their quest, and there had been much to discuss and many decisions to make. They had wanted privacy, but coincidence had played it otherwise. Or Fate, as Thimeon had called it. "There are no coincidences," he had told her later. "Nothing that is not under the All-Maker's care."

"What about my village?" she had asked him, bitterly. "Was that under his care?" Thimeon hadn't answered. "Then I'd rather believe in accidents," she'd said.

Accident or otherwise, however, he had appeared that night at their roadside bivouac. Her fledgling small company had been engaged in an ongoing debate. Cane was arguing that they pursue the Daegmon immediately. Cathros had taken his brother's side, though not with as much fervor. Falien, however, supported by both Pietr and Jamesh, had wanted to find others to join them—to make the company bigger and more capable of facing their powerful foe. Elynna had not spoken. Her mind sided with Falien, but even then she had already come to desire Cane's approval, though she had known him only a few days.

The conversation grew heated, and in the cool evening air carried further than they intended. Without warning a stranger stepped out of the darkness into the light of their fire. Though he bore no weapon, something about him looked dangerous. Cane leapt to his feet sword in hand. Thinking Thimeon a robber, he threatened to run him through if he came any closer. He probably would have done so, too, if the stranger had moved an inch. Or maybe they all would have died. Cane did not know that the stranger had his own companions waiting in the woods with arrows on the string in case something went awry. But the man made no move. "I am Thimeon," he said. "An Andan hunter and ambassador of my people. I have heard your voices, and your words speak of your plight. I too came seeking aid against the Daegmon."

Before long they were exchanging stories. Thimeon, like many of the companions, had been chosen by his people to go to Citadel to tell the king of their distress. Two days earlier, at the village of Hilt, he had met and joined several other Andani and Plainsfolk traveling south on similar errands. His company had made camp on the road not far from Elynna's, and had overheard Cane's loud voice talking about pursuing the Daegmon. That had prompted the nighttime visit.

And so the conversation began. Thimeon and his group learned from Elynna of the gifts of power that she and the Northland brothers possessed. When she told him of the king's unwillingness to aid his people, he made the decision to abandon his own trip to Citadel and to join their fledgling quest. With Thimeon came Bandor, Llian, Theo, Marti, Nahoon, Beth, and Tienna.

The remainder of the company—Braddoc and Llana as well as a second Northland delegation of Hruach, Hrevia, Aram, and Kayle—had joined them later in Aeti.

Though it brought to their company another of the gifted in the person of Tienna, it was for Elynna a bitter meeting nonetheless. She had been full of anger at a brother who had so recently deserted her, bitterness toward a king who had refused to give aid to his people, and despair at her own failure to accomplish anything. And for some reason Thimeon, despite his kindness and apparent skill, more than anybody else reminded her of all her inadequacies. How then had he come to love her, who so little wanted his love?

Somebody coughed loudly, a harsh hacking cough. It could have been any of them. It was followed by a second, then a third. Within moments it had spread through the company. The whole cavern was full of rasping wheezes.

"Elynna?" Tienna said softly.

"I don't love him." Elynna mumbled aloud. Then, as though realizing she'd spoken aloud, she added quickly, but quietly so that only Tienna could hear, "And I owe him too much already. What will I do if he succeeds?"

"What will we do if he *fails*?" Tienna replied.

There was silence. Tienna was another to whom Elynna owed much, though she had known her only for the same number of days she had known Thimeon. It was a strange friendship, Elynna thought. They were about as different as she could imagine two women being, the young Plains huntress and the fisherman's daughter. Tienna was so self-sufficient, and strong, and graceful, and skilled at so many things. Compared to Elynna, who knew only the mending of nets, the tending of a garden, and the names of a few flowers and trees that grew along the river and salty marshes near her home, Tienna seemed to know everything. She was used to a life of danger, was comfortable being alone, and she flinched at nothing. Yet at the same time, she was more ready even than Elynna to rely on others. More than anything, it was Tienna's confidence that set them apart, at least in Elynna's eyes. Tienna was as secure and even hopeful as Elynna was full of doubts. Maybe it was these very differences that had led so quickly to such a close bond. Or maybe it was the one thing that they did have in common that gave them that close friendship: both of them had a gift they did not understand, that they could not ignore, and that caused them so much pain. Within a day of joining their companies, Tienna had become Elynna's closest friend and her tent mate as they bivouacked their way across the highlands of Gondisle.

"They will need heat soon," Tienna said, breaking into Elynna's thoughts. "Their condition will get worse."

"What am I supposed to do?"

Tienna did not speak again right away. "I will go and help him," she finally said.

Elynna's defensiveness was suddenly replaced by concern. "Are you well enough? You have so little . . . so little clothing."

"Work will keep me warmer," she replied. "In any case, I think he will not find what he seeks without my help."

Elynna did not object. She knew Tienna well enough now to guess that advice would be futile. She was a huntress. She would do what needed to be done. Besides, Tienna was probably right. "Can you help Falien?" Elynna asked instead.

"Not yet. I need time to prepare. And I, too, will require warmth."

"What about the air? How can we have a fire?"

"I do not know. Thimeon will have to find a way to make it safe, or we all shall die. Unless . . ." Tienna paused.

Elynna grasped for any hint of hope. "Unless what?"

Tienna's reply was a deep sigh. "We do not have enough strength for that."

Elynna did not ask for an explanation. It was not needed. She could still sense the Daegmon lurking out there somewhere, waiting for them. "No," she agreed. "We do not."

Tienna was silent as she departed, but when Elynna spoke her name a short time later there was no answer, only hoarse coughs.

Alone again, Elynna sat huddled on the frozen ground with her arms wrapped around her legs. All was still dark, and memories of her flight from Lienford moved through her thoughts. The days following that first Daegmon attack on her home were the darkest of her life. It was not the destruction of the village itself. She could have tolerated that. It was her father's death. For a few months, she and Lyn had tried to rekindle some spark of life amid the ruins. Though younger than she, he had already learned something of the fishing trade. And while much of the village was in ruins, fewer of the villagers had perished than she had imagined in the darkest moments of the raid. Many had found places to hide, or had fled into the woody marshes. Some of the men had already departed downriver in their boats for an early morning of fishing, and had returned later in the day after the attack to discover the devastation. Still, many others had perished, and most of their equipment had been destroyed along with their houses. Boats. Nets. Almost everything. Without their father, Elynna and

Lyn were lost. By autumn of that year, most of the survivors of Lienford—having already fled downriver to their summer coastal villages—had begun the much longer trek toward Citadel looking for work, food, help. Then, too, Elynna had begun to suspect the extent and nature of her gift. And Lyn had begun to resent it.

"We need to do something." Cane was speaking. He had found his way across the cave and now stood somewhere close by.

She bit back her caustic response and listened. Another seemingly disembodied voice spoke out of the darkness not far from Cane. "We need heat. Many are sick. Several of us lost our packs. There are not enough blankets."

Elynna recognized the voice. Cathros. "Thimeon has gone to look—" she started to answer.

"We know," Cane interrupted. "But it is unlikely he will succeed. Even if he does, we cannot wait."

"My brother must try to conjure the flame," Cathros explained. "For heat."

Elynna lifted her head. The pitch of her voice gave way her hope. "Can you?"

"I do not know. In the past it has come only in the presence of the Daegmon."

"He is still weak," Cathros added.

"I am strong enough," Cane said, but his next request belied his confidence. "Help Cathros support me."

"I will do what I can," Elynna replied. She rose to her feet and stepped toward the voices. She could picture the two brothers standing there. Cathros, the elder of the two, was leaner than Cane but stood even taller, and was every bit as strong or stronger even when the battle strength was not upon him. In their dark hair and darker deep-set eyes, sharp noses, and sculpted chins, they looked like brothers. If there was one difference in their faces, it was that Cathros's expression was softer, as though his age had given him a little more compassion. Or perhaps more sorrow. Cathros's voice, though still with the distinctive throaty Anghare accent, also was a kinder—a mellow baritone next to Cane's stern monotone bass.

A second later Cane's hand closed on her arm. Her heart raced at his touch. He pulled her a step closer and wrapped his arm around her shoulder. She felt his weight and began to tremble with an excitement that had little to do with the hope of heat.

"Are you ready?" Cathros asked.

"I am," Cane answered.

Elynna knew that any of her companions who were awake would have heard the conversation. Did they have any hope? Would it be another disappointment? The few quiet conversations going on around the snow cave came to an abrupt end, but the sounds of nervous breathing and scattered coughs seemed to amplify.

"Cathros, put your arm around me and hold me up. I need to draw my blade. It is the vehicle for the flame." He shifted, and Elynna heard a soft swish of a blade sliding freely from a leather scabbard. Her eyes were open wide as she stared into the blackness where she thought the sword might be. Cathros's breathing was audible beside her, deep and steady. Cane's breathing sounded more labored. Elynna could feel his pulse through his grip on her shoulder. She could smell his hair.

She strained her eyes for some sign of life in the blade he held in the blackness in front of her. Each passing second took forever. Did she see or only imagine she saw a tiny blue glow in front of her face? Another long moment passed. Nothing happened. Elynna stared more fervently into the darkness. Nobody spoke a word. She was holding her breath. Cane's breathing was slower now, less steady. The blade remained dark and cold. Finally came the release of breath as the Northlander gave up and collapsed.

Elynna almost fell under his weight. "I am sorry," she said, as though it were she who had failed.

"He is still too weak to call up the power," Cathros said, as he helped Cane ease back to the ground. "Or else it can only be called upon in battle. I do not know."

Elynna said nothing. She wanted to throw her arms around Cane. Even more, she wanted him to put his arms around her—to hold her with some sort of feeling and warmth. She wished she could see his face now. Instead, her own brother's face flickered momentarily across her memory, and she heard again his parting words. *"Go, if you want. You won't succeed. You destroy everything you touch."*

A short time later Cane and Cathros returned to their own spots, leaving Elynna alone again. She stared into the blackness thinking about Lyn while the time crept forward. Fatigue eventually overtook her, and she fell into a restless slumber, a semiconscious awareness of others coughing, full of dreams of the Daegmon. Still, it was sleep of a sort, and she needed it.

How much time passed while she remained in that state, Elynna did not know. An icy draft on her cheek aroused her. Suddenly alert, she sat up and peered into the darkness. There was nothing there. Nothing but the draft, and she did not yet understand what it meant.

Cursing the bitter air, she sat up. Her hunger told her it was morning. Unable to find any more comfort on the cold ground, she rose to her feet wondering how many meals were left in their packs. It was as she stood thinking about food that she heard, for the first time in several hours, muffled voices rising over the intermittent coughing. An instant later she noticed a faint light radiating throughout their snowy prison. She rubbed her eyes wondering if it was her imagination.

The light grew brighter. Around her she could again make out the crude shape of their cavern and the forms of her companions huddled under their blankets in little groups around the floor. Looking across a swath of supine bodies to the far wall, she saw a low tunnel from which the light was now coming. Beside it a huge mound of snow filled the corner of the cavern, attesting to the amount of work that had gone into digging it.

Even as she watched, Thimeon stepped out with his arms full of freshly cut wood. Following just two steps behind him came Tienna with the torch and another smaller bundle of wood. Snow crusted her hair, and her lips looked blue with cold, but there was an expression of triumph on her face.

At the appearance of the torch and the wood, her companions were soon on their feet. They crowded round the spot where Thimeon laid out the wood.

"Let's move the fire to the center of the cave," Cathros suggested.

"I do not dare," Thimeon answered. "There is little enough air as it is. A fire here will help draw fresh air down the tunnel."

"Does the tunnel reach the surface?"

Tienna answered for Thimeon while he concentrated on his work. "It does. We were fortunate indeed. It appears the main force of the avalanche swept around us or over us toward the bottom of the valley. Otherwise we would have been buried much deeper. Or swept away. Thimeon was able to work his way to the top of the tree and clear a path for air as he gathered wood. He has also made our exit ready for when the time comes."

Thimeon finished arranging the wood for a small fire. "We will need a vent," he said. "Even with the draft, the smoke will suffocate us if there is no hole in the roof."

"How—?" Elynna started, but Thimeon was already at work. He picked up a spear from against the wall of the cave and looked up toward the ceiling. Where he stood, the cave was about seven and a half feet high. The snow above was crusty from melting and refreezing. Stepping a few feet away from the wood, he poked the spear upward through the layer of crust. A shower of snow fell on his face. He shook it off and tried again. He stuck the spear up higher, working it around to make a hole.

"How far to the top?" Cathros asked.

"Near the tree it was about fifteen feet," Thimeon answered. He poked around with the spear. More snow came down. Soon he had opened up a funnel the length of the spear and about a foot in diameter. Still, it did not reach the surface. He gave the spear to Cathros. "How high can you throw this?"

Cathros shrugged and took the spear. Standing under the hole, he balanced the weapon in his hand, testing its weight and lining up the angle. Then he hurled the spear upward as hard as he could. It flew hard from his hand and disappeared in a puff of snow overhead. It hung there out of reach for a few seconds, then fell back down with another shower of snow. Cathros looked disappointed, but Thimeon picked up the spear and handed it back to him. He took a full dozen throws, each one penetrating higher into the ceiling. Three times the spear got stuck and had to be knocked out with another spear. On the thirteenth throw, the spear broke through the surface and then fell back. A speck of sky appeared above. Cathros threw three more times, opening the hole further with each throw, then lost the spear through the hole.

"It is enough," Thimeon announced. The others watched breathlessly as he pulled the torch from the snow and set it to the kindling. The torch sputtered in the wet wood and threatened to go out. Thimeon pulled it back until it burned brightly again. With the aid of Theo, who had come to his side, he rearranged the twigs and tried once more. Elynna's shoulders were knotted as she watched. A moment later she heard the crackling and popping of small twigs catching ablaze. There was a collective sigh of relief around their cave. Thimeon set the torch aside at once and dropped to his hands and knees. He blew on the flames and the fire began to grow. He fed it more twigs. They burned quickly, but the larger green wood showed no signs of catching.

"Here," he said, shoving the last of the twigs at Theo. He jumped up, grabbed the torch, and flew up the tunnel. Theo took over feeding the blaze. The companions squeezed closer, desperate for some heat. Just as the last twigs were consumed and the flames ready to die, Thimeon reemerged with another armload of the small sticks. The process was slow and frustrating, but eventually the larger pieces caught flame. It was not much longer before the fire was roaring and wind hissed down the tunnel to feed it. The room grew smoky, but heat radiated quickly and nobody complained.

Several minutes passed as the companions sat or stood staring at the fire and soaking up as much warmth as they could. It was the first sign of hope since the battle. But it was only a glimmer. Tienna had already turned her attention toward the unconscious Falien. Elynna moved to her side and watched her friend. Her eyes were closed and her hand rested on the wounded man's body. All of a sudden, she groaned and her body shuddered. She opened her eyes, and she jerked her hand away as if burned. "His back is broken here."

"Should we bring him closer to the fire?"

"No. Do not move him again. He must be healed soon."

"Can you do it?"

"I do not know. I am afraid. I do not comprehend my health gift. I have used it only a few times to bring healing. Never to so serious an injury. The effort is great. And this? This injury may be beyond the power of healing given to me."

"I understand," Elynna said, though in truth she did not. She looked down at Falien. His eyes fluttered as though he was regaining consciousness.

"He is a Westwasher, is he not?" Tienna asked. "Do you know him well?"

Elynna did not answer at once. Llana had died almost unknown to her, and though Falien had traveled with her for many weeks, he was still almost a stranger. "Pietr knows him," she finally said. Her voice sounded defensive. "They are not from my village, but from the coast somewhere to the north."

"When did you meet him?"

"He was among those who sailed from Westwash to Aënport after the Daegmon attacks. We met on the road to Citadel."

"Does he have any family? Any who survived?"

Elynna could only shrug in helpless ignorance. "You would need to ask Pietr."

Pietr, who stood a few steps behind the glow of the fire, heard them. "I do not know him well, but I have heard him speak of his parents and some brothers. I think they are all still alive. That was why he was chosen to go to Citadel. He came from one of the few families in his village who had a husband or son to spare after the Daegmon attack."

Tienna nodded and sighed. She took a deep breath, then leaned over the still form. Thimeon, who stood behind her, took off his heavy fur cloak. He had set it aside during the digging, but had come back from the task damp with sweat and had put it back on as soon as he got the fire going. Now he set it on Tienna's shoulders.

To Elynna's surprise, the usually self-sufficient Tienna accepted. She sat a moment longer, then bent over farther and placed her head on Falien's chest and listened. His breathing was shallow. There was no sign of his chest rising and falling. With one hand she probed his ribs while her other came to rest on his forehead. Then she lay still, bringing her breathing into rhythm with his.

Thimeon knelt beside her to offer help if she needed it, but she was silent now. Elynna sat across from them and watched. She had seen the healing once before. In one of the Andan villages, shortly after Tienna had joined them, they had come upon a badly burned child—a victim of a Daegmon raid. Moved by the little girl's suffering, Tienna had picked her up and rocked her in her lap. A short time later, she had turned pale and set the girl down. To their amazement, the child was healed.

There had been few witnesses then: Elynna, Beth, Thimeon, and the child's mother. Tienna had never since spoken of the event. Her power had frightened her. So had the cost. She had collapsed after healing the girl, and it had been several minutes before she regained the strength to walk. What the cost would be of such a healing as she now attempted, none knew. And none dared ask. They could only watch.

Several minutes passed. Tienna's eyelids slipped shut. Soon her body fell limp. A shudder passed through Falien and her. Then she began to hum. It was a soft melodic humming. She shuddered again but did not cease. Suddenly she clenched her hands into tight fists. The humming turned to low moans. Throughout the rest of the cave, all had fallen silent. Minutes passed. There was no sign of movement from Falien or Tienna.

Then all at once Tienna gave a shout. "No." Her eyes opened wide with the horror of some realization, and she jerked away from Falien as if to rise. Elynna rushed toward her friend to help her pull away.

Too late. A giant spasm shook Tienna's frame, and her body fell limp. Her hand slipped off of Falien's chest, and her eyes fell shut.

THE WEIGHT
OF SNOW

A low groan, almost a sigh, issued from Falien's lips. He opened his eyes and for a few seconds lay staring at the ceiling, flexing the fingers of his right hand. Then he lifted his head and looked around.

Elynna could hardly believe what she was seeing. "Falien! You're moving!"

There was a stir of excitement. Pietr came rushing over, followed by Jamesh and Cathros. Others crowded around too. Caught for the moment in the excitement of Falien's recovery, Elynna was not paying attention to Tienna. Not until Thimeon spoke the huntress's name aloud did she realize that Tienna was not moving. That her eyes were still closed, and her face was almost as pale as the walls of snow surrounded them. Thimeon was leaning over her listening. There was no sign of breath.

Elynna's felt her excitement drain, even as she saw the faces of those around her fall in fear. "What is it?" she asked. "Is she . . . ?" She couldn't finish. She felt her eyes welling with tears.

Thimeon put two fingers on Tienna throat and leaned close to her mouth. His face was expressionless, and to Elynna it seemed like forever before he sat up and spoke. "Her breath is barely perceptible, but there is still life within."

"Help her."

Thimeon nodded. Gently, he lifted her unconscious form and carried her closer to the fire. He laid her down next to the warm blaze and wrapped her in her blanket.

"What is it?" Elynna asked in a soft voice. "What is the matter?"

Thimeon shook his head "I don't understand. There is no sign of injury. And yet. It's as if . . ." His voice trailed off. He glanced up at Falien, who stood surrounded by disbelieving companions, flexing his limbs and assuring them that he was healed.

"As if what?" Elynna asked quietly.

"I don't know" Thimeon whispered. "I don't have her gift. But I wonder what price she paid."

The others quickly became aware of Tienna's condition, and the space became suddenly very quiet. It was Cane who said aloud what Elynna was thinking but was unwilling to voice. "We have lost one of the gifted. It was a costly trade."

An icy silence followed Cane's words. The companions cast uneasy glances at Tienna's wan form lying beside the fire as they resumed their silent waiting. Falien, aware of what she had done for him—and stung, perhaps, by Cane's words—took up sentry beside her. Elynna also stayed near her friend, taking a break from her watch only when they meted out food from their dwindling provisions. As morning progressed toward midday, sunlight began filtering down through the vent. With the wax-ing of day, the Daegmon retreated. Elynna's sense of its presence slowly diminished and then disappeared altogether. "It's gone," she finally said. Nobody asked her what she was speaking about. Either they understood the pronouncement, or they were too tired to care.

Sometime later in the morning, Thimeon broached the subject of their departure. "We cannot wait here forever." When Elynna stared at him blankly, he continued. "We don't know how long it will take for Tienna to recover. We must leave while we have a chance—while the Daegmon is far away. Though I am afraid to move her, our wood will not last more than a few more hours. And without her help I will not find more."

Elynna finally nodded. "We will leave at midday—if anybody can tell when that is."

Thimeon looked at her a moment longer as though about to say something more. Then he walked away. Soon afterward, the companions began preparing to depart. There were a few sidelong glances in Tienna's direction, but nobody spoke her name. Those with blankets rolled them and returned them to their packs. Oth-ers retrieved items of clothing they had attempted to dry by the fire. Siyen, Hruach, and Hrevia just lay were they were, coughing or trying to sleep.

An hour later they came together for a midday meal. Many were still sick and coughing, and Tienna's unchanging condition hung over them all like some massive precariously balanced rock. Elynna could not eat. She rose and paced the small cave. She stopped at the mouth of their escape tunnel and felt the contrast between the draft on her face and heat on the back of her legs.

Then came a yell from the cave behind her. "*Tienna!*"

Elynna turned and saw Falien kneeling by the side of the huntress. Tienna's eyes were open. Her cheeks were flushed.

Echoing Falien's cry, Elynna yelped with joy. "Tienna! You're awake. You're well." It was more of a question than a statement.

In answer Tienna tried to sit up, but fell over at once. "I am weak," she acknowledged. "But I will survive. Just give me food. And drink if we have any."

"There is plenty of water. The Northlanders have been melting snow over the fire. As to wine, there is not much left, but you may have what there is. They have warmed that as well."

The company waited only a short time as Tienna gathered her strength. When she walked over and dropped Thimeon's cloak on his lap with a word of thanks, they knew she was herself again. "Keep it," Thimeon offered.

As Elynna expected, Tienna shook her head. "I have spent many days tracking game across the snowdrifts on the windswept Plains in the winter. I can bear the cold."

Thimeon looked as though he was about to object, but then thought better of arguing with the strong-willed Plainswoman. Instead, he pulled from his pack a rabbit fur hat and a long-sleeved tunic woven with multihued threads. He handed them to her instead. She hesitated. "This is not yours," she said, for she could see that the tunic was too small for the sturdy Andan guide.

"The tunic is not," Thimeon acknowledged. "But please take them both. As you can see, the tunic would not fit me. And the hat is a spare."

To Elynna's surprise, Tienna accepted. She turned the tunic over in her hands and admired it. It was intricately woven, and she took a moment to admire the workmanship and the pattern made of natural red, tan, and white threads with hints of blue. "It is beautiful. Where did you get it?"

"My mother wove the fabric on our loom from the wool of our *gyurts*. My sister Siarah has not yet learned the art of weaving, but with our mother's help she sewed the tunic."

"She should have kept it for herself. It is beautiful, as is your sister. She would have been lovely in it."

Thimeon did not answer right away. When he did, his voice was low. "She sewed two tunics from the same long piece of cloth. This was the first, made with much direction and help from our mother. The second one she finished the week before our mother was killed. She kept that one for herself."

Tienna bowed her head for a moment, then lifted her eyes and looked at the tunic again. "The dye is beautiful, as is the weaving of your mother. Our people spin and weave and dye also. We know the secret of red, but not of this blue."

"There is no dye," Thimeon answered. "These are some of the natural colors of the gyurt."

"I have not seen this animal. A 'gyurt' you call it? What does it look like?"

"Bigger than a sheep, and with long necks and tall pointed ears. They are more the size of the Anghare goats, but woolier and not so ornery. They are not common among the Andani, who prefer sheep. But the Ceadani folk live in a wilder and steeper land, as you can see around you, and with more predators. The gyurt thrive here and need less care."

"Do you trade with the Ceadani for the wool?"

Thimeon shook his head. "My father traveled widely around Gondisle, before he met and wed our mother. After he returned to start our farm, and my sister and I were born, he did not travel much. But he did journey long enough to buy two breeding pairs of gyurts, and two pairs of Anghare goats as well. Now we have a small herd of both along with our sheep." He paused. "My sister has them at my uncle's house now. If you had stayed a day or two longer when you came through Aeti, you would have seen them. Come visit again when all this is over, and I will show them to you. They are beautiful animals. Or perhaps we shall see some if we go down into the Ceadani villages. In the summers the *gyurtherds* are up in these hills with their flocks. But with this early and bitter onslaught of winter, I'm sure they have returned to the lowlands."

"I would like that," Tienna said. "To visit the farm your father built, and to talk more with your sister. I could see she was special to you, and it was difficult for you to leave her." A shadow passed across Thimeon's face. Tienna went on quickly. "It is a precious gift, and I am honored to wear it and think of your sister. And your mother."

Now Thimeon smiled. "Siarah would be honored to know you wore it. Though she met you only once, I know she admired you. Maybe she had you in mind all long, for she insisted I take it with me, saying that *somebody* was bound to need it. So I've been carrying it since we left Aeti." He smiled wryly and added, "Instead of extra food."

Tienna returned the smile. "Your sister was right. And I will wear it with honor." Binding her long hair in a knot upon her head, she slid into the pullover tunic and pulled on the rabbit fur hat. The tunic was only slightly too big, reaching down to the tops of her thighs. The hat was huge. Even with all her braided hair tucked underneath, she was still able to pull it down low over her ears.

"You *might* be mistaken for an Andan weaver woman or shepherdess," Thimeon said with approval. "Though perhaps a weaver who didn't know how to measure."

Tienna laughed. It was the first laugh any of them had heard in several days. "How about an Andan hunter? For it is true I would not know how to measure a garment any more than I would know how to weave."

"Our women rarely hunt," Thimeon replied. "But they are skilled in many other ways, most especially with the weaving of fine cloth. But also at knitting."

"How come your women do not hunt? I thought the Andani were good hunters."

Thimeon shrugged. "When I was young I thought it was because our men were stronger—more capable of drawing a heavy bow, carrying an animal after the kill, and other tasks needed for hunting. But now I think it is simply because our women are more skilled than our men at so many other tasks and cannot be spared from those duties." Then he laughed. "My mother would send our father hunting sometimes just to get him out of the house. That, maybe, is the *real* answer."

Tienna looked as though she was about to respond. But then she pinched her lips shut and said no more. She pulled a rope from around her waist and retied it around the tunic to gird herself once more. Then she announced her readiness. The companions began to move. Those who had not lost their packs hoisted them on. Others grabbed the few remaining pieces of wood. One at a time they stooped over and headed down the low tunnel.

It was about forty feet to where Thimeon had found the tree. The last companions were still in the cave when the front of the line reached the exit. Where the tree had been, the tunnel turned abruptly upward. Sunlight streamed down from above. With the tree gone, the climb proved difficult.

Theo, who was light and used to climbing in the snow, was sent up first with a rope. Though his cheeks were red from a mild steam burn, he had recovered quickly from the chill. He worked his way up, digging into the hard snow with his fingers and the toes of his boots. With several impatient companions waiting, he disappeared out the top of the shaft. A short time later one end of his rope dropped back into the hole. "It's secure," he called down.

Braddoc, his face now grim with determination, climbed out next. Elynna stepped forward to follow him, but Thimeon insisted she wait until he could survey the scene to make sure it was safe. He climbed third, and Elynna followed after him.

As soon as she emerged into the open, the cold wind slapped her in the face. The brightness of the sun was deceptive; the day was colder than the last. Still, it was good to see the sun again. It was early afternoon, the day after the attack. Though it felt like an eternity, they had spent only one night and the following morning beneath the snow.

While the others climbed up behind her, Elynna scanned the slopes for a sign of the Daegmon. The force of the avalanche had ravaged the whole side of valley. The only sign of life was the thin line of smoke filtering out of a hole in the snow a dozen steps east of where she stood. There was no sign of the creature that had caused the destruction.

She turned to Thimeon. "Where can we go for help?"

"What do you mean, 'where can we go?'" asked Cane, coming up behind her. "We go after the Daegmon. The battle is not finished. We have come too far to turn back. It took many weeks just to find this beast. We cannot give up."

"We have given battle and lost," she replied bitterly.

Before Cane could object, Thimeon interrupted with his own proposal. "Let us follow the course of the avalanche to the bottom of the valley and out to the east. If we then turn back northwestward around the jut of the hillside, we will be headed toward Gale Enebe, a large Ceadani village. Chal-char is the chieftain. He is counted among the wisest of the Ceadani. He and his people will give us whatever aid they can. Whatever we ask."

"How far is it to this village?" Elynna asked.

Thimeon looked around, but they had descended too far into the valley to get bearings. Even the high triune peak of Illengond was invisible behind the nearer ridgeline. "I cannot say. I have been Gale Enebe only thrice. I do not often travel this far south."

"Guess," she demanded.

Thimeon shrugged. "One day of hard travel might bring us there in good weather. In this snow it will be longer."

"We will lose the Daegmon's scent," Cane grumbled. "If we turn away now, then everything we have endured will be for nothing. Is this what you desire? With one defeat, have you lost heart and given up the quest?" He looked first at Elynna, who turned her eyes downward, then at Thimeon.

"No," Thimeon replied. "You are right. We must not concede. If we sit and do nothing, it will destroy every village in Gondisle. Better to bring the battle to our enemy than to wait for our dooms."

"Then why do we run away?" Cane pressed.

"We are tired and our supplies are low. We must regain strength."

"And learn how to fight it," Elynna added, attempting to salvage some honor in Cane's sight.

"How can we learn to battle such a creature?" interjected Cathros, who had quietly come up behind his brother.

To this there was no reply. Not even from Cane. By then the remaining companions had emerged. Despite their bruises and fatigue, all were eager to move away from that place. The decision to go to Gale Enebe was nearly unanimous. After a rest in the village, they would decide whether to renew their quest. Even Cathros agreed it was a good plan. Only Cane dissented.

The going was slow at first. It took more than an hour to travel just half a mile. The avalanche had followed several courses down from the rim of mountain and wreaked havoc on the valley floor. A hundred yards to left of where they stood, the slope had been stripped bare. At the bottom, huge piles of snow and ice were everywhere, along with several giant boulders. They had to pick a careful trail over the uneven ground, and now and then were forced to plow through or scramble atop deep and heavily packed snow. The stronger members of the company had to help those who were the most tired or sick.

For a while, Thimeon led the way. Where the snow had been swept away, or where it was packed solid, Bandor walked at his side. In places where they needed to wade, they marched in single file and took turns breaking the trail. Elynna followed behind, her gaze alternating between Thimeon's back and Bandor's. She did not want to look at Thimeon. Not even at his back. But Bandor was worse.

Since meeting the Northlanders Cane and Cathros, he had also begun braiding his bright red hair in a tail in the Anghare fashion. The braid reached a third of the way down his back and swung from side to side where it stuck out from his woolen hood. No matter how much she tried to think of something else, it reminded Elynna of the red braided mooring rope that always dangled from the bow of her father's *lall*—his shallow riverboat their family kept in their winter village of Lienford. And that made her think of her father. If he were with her now, would he be ashamed of her, running from their enemy?

She wished somebody would come talk with her. Distract her. Tienna. Or Cathros. Or even Siyen.

Or Cane. Or perhaps not Cane. She could not bear the look of judgment on his face.

What she wished for did not matter, however. Nobody came to speak with her. Nobody spoke at all. Not until they paused midafternoon to share some of their little remaining food. Even as they ate, few spoke, though many were coughing.

Once beyond the reach of the avalanche, travel grew easier. Onward they trudged, silent save for the jingling of packs and the squeaking of boots in the snow. They were following a valley that ran almost due east. Two more hours of hiking took them to a long, narrow ravine and a steep descent. There they encountered several deep drifts that went from wall to wall. There was no way around, and each such wall took many minutes to break through. It was late afternoon before they had completely escaped the high alpine bowl where they had spent the previous three days and had their disastrous encounter with the Daegmon.

When they finally emerged from the ravine as evening began to fall, the snow was barely above their ankles. Here Thimeon turned them northward, and they continued their journey following the ridgeline of peaks they had just departed. They going became easier, and had they not already expended so much energy, they might have continued on for another hour or more; though the sun had disappeared behind the tall peaks, there was still plenty of daylight. But they were exhausted.

Spotting a sheltered hollow, Bandor suggested they stop for the night. At the mere mention of rest, the companions collapsed. It was Thimeon, not Elynna, who urged them to set up their camp, and several minutes passed before any of them had the energy to respond. Eventually the discomfort of the cold ground prompted Elynna to action. When she stood and began to follow Thimeon's instructions the others joined. It was the grumbled curses of a few of the Anghare that alerted her to their predicament: with their lost packs they now had only two tents among them.

She turned to Thimeon. "What do we do?"

For once Thimeon was at a loss. "This is not a night to sleep in the open," he told Elynna in a quiet voice. "Too many are already sick and weak."

Elynna, who was used to relying on Thimeon, had no answers. Thimeon turned to his fellow Andani. Bandor had no ideas either.

"*Quinzhees*," Theo said.

Elynna stared at him. Theo had not spoken for two days. Not since before the battle. In the aftermath of the attack, even after Thimeon had gotten the fire going and some warmth had begun to seep into the air, Theo seemed to remain in shock. It was the news of the loss of Llana that had started it. He had been especially close to her. The two of them had been the youngest members of the company. Practically children. Well shy of twenty summers. Elynna was sure Theo had allowed to join the company only because he was Thimeon's cousin.

He had not yet shown any particular skill except for starting a fire and keeping warm.

And what was he talking about now?

"Quinzhees," Theo repeated, looking right at Thimeon.

Thimeon gave a gesture with his right hand as though he should have thought of that answer himself. "Of course. That's the answer. This is perfect for it, but we'll have to get started right away or the snow won't settle properly."

Elynna stared at them with no idea what they were talking about. From the expressions of those around her, she was not the only one. Theo had to explain to everybody but Braddoc and Thimeon the concept of a Quinzhee: basically just a large mound of snow with a cave hollowed out of the middle, though there were a few important tricks to making them to ensure they didn't cave in. Several of the others—especially the Northlanders—were skeptical that they could pile up snow and dig a cave big enough and strong enough to sleep in, or that such a cave would keep them warm. A few of them said so. Thimeon looked as though he was about to reply, but then he then just turned and walked off.

While Tienna and Aram prepared a thin stew of roots and squirrel from their depleted supplies, the Andani ended up doing most of the work of piling up and digging in the snow, and the shelters were smaller than they might have been. Yet, when they did drop off to sleep not long after their meal, the Andani and Plainsfolk sleeping in their dugout snow caves were the warmest, and the Westwashers and Northlanders crammed in the two remaining tents who complained most of being uncomfortable through the night. They would have been even colder had not Thimeon, against their wishes, insisted on piling snow up against the sides of the tents for extra insulation.

Elynna woke first in the morning. It was not physical discomfort that woke her but her awareness of the Daegmon's return—an awareness that penetrated her thoughts even during sleep. She did not have the sense of impending doom she'd felt before earlier attacks, but she knew instinctively that the creature followed them somewhere in the distance. Fighting the panic rising within her, she woke the others, urging them into motion as best she could without burdening them with her own fear and knowledge.

The Northlanders, normally the most disciplined members of the group, with the exception perhaps of Tienna and Thimeon, were slow to start moving. She wanted to yell at them. While she pulled the laces tight on her fur boots, she could hear one of them—she thought it was Aram—grumbling at Thimeon in the thick Anghare accent. "You Highlanders live a hard life in a hard country. Sleeping under the snow is a strange way to make it less hard, and an even stranger way to keep warm."

She could hear in Thimeon's voice that he was as annoyed as she was. "I don't know what you call 'Highlands'—applying one name to such a vast land. I suppose you mean the mountains of both the Andani and Ceadani, and perhaps the Undeani as well? To me, they are all different, and all require different skills. Perhaps these Ceadani *highlands* may build even more hardihood in its people than the more gentle Andan farmlands, and there is more I wish I knew about them. Any region is less harsh if you know how to live in it. Your hot, dry Anghare desert seems harsher to me than our snows and colds."

Be quiet, she wanted to say. *The Daegmon is near. I can sense it.* But instead, without even turning to look, she simply said, "This isn't the time to fight. We need to move quickly."

But Thimeon, uncharacteristically, kept going. "You can always put on more clothing when cold, and snow can always be turned to water, but what can you do when the air itself is boiling? Melt sand and drink it? Who knows? Maybe you know how to find water. You have learned to survive there for generations. So if I were in Anghatte suffering from heat, I would take what remedy you gave me. My cousin now gave you a remedy for the cold. You should have accepted it."

"Sorry, friend," Cathros said. Elynna turned to see him place a friendly hand on Thimeon's shoulder."

Despite further impatient urging from Elynna, several more minutes still passed before everybody was moving and preparing to depart. There was no food left now except dried fruit and a few nuts the Andani had brought. They drank from their water, which they had learned to keep beneath their sleeping skins at night to prevent it from freezing. Then finally they had the two remaining tents in their packs, and they were ready to go. Throughout the morning they pressed northward along the same general line they had been following at the end of the previous day. To their left a range of mountains rose up steeply, though its highest peaks were hidden behind the nearer ridgelines. To the right, in the direction of the rising sun, the range of hills was lower and more rounded for many miles until they collided with the north-south ridge of mountains that separated the Highlands from Anghatte, which most folk called the Northland.

Thimeon once more took the lead, but now Cane had joined him. Occasionally, one or two of the Andani—Bandor, Theo, Braddoc, or Llian—would scout ahead. They had been traveling a few hours, and the sun was halfway up the sky when they came through a cut at the far end of another long valley and found themselves looking down a long slope toward the northernmost expanse of the Ceadani highlands that eventually gave way to the Raws. For the first time in days, they could see many miles to the north and west. Only a single large mountain that Thimeon named Ceathu dotted the landscape to the north.

"How much longer to this Ceadani village you spoke of?" Elynna asked. She had walked up beside Thimeon as they prepared to descend the long slope. She tried to mask the fear in her voice, but she had just felt another twinge of that heat—the sense of doom that preceded an attack.

"Farther than I thought. Those three rounded peaks to the west are—" He paused as if searching for a word in another language. "They are known as the Maker's Knuckles. From those mountains the village takes its name, though in a different tongue: Gale Enebe. We must head in that direction."

"How far?" Elynna repeated impatiently.

"The village is by the base of the last two knuckles. Most of the homes are set in the cliff side and are difficult to see. In the winter the village can be spotted from a distance by the steam rising from the hot springs. At this pace, we will be lucky to make it by nightfall tonight."

Cane and Cathros were walking nearby. Elynna chose the time to confide in them. "We are being pursued."

"What?" Cane asked in a voice that turned a few heads.

"The Daegmon," Elynna said as softly as she could.

"It is near?"

"I feel it. It is pursuing us."

Cane looked around. In a voice devoid of expression he commented, "There is no place to flee if it attacks us here," he said, with no more expression than if he were telling them what he had eaten for breakfast. "We will have to fight it."

Elynna followed his gaze. "We must hope to make it to the village."

Then Cane's voice grew sharp with sarcasm. "I'm sure the Ceadani will be thrilled when we lead the Daegmon to their home."

Elynna did not answer. Cane's words stung, not only because of the tone but because she knew his critique was well founded. What could she say? What other choice did she have? After a moment, she turned to warn the rest of the company. As word spread of their enemy's return, their pace quickened. Fortunately, there were no mishaps on the steep slope. At the bottom, the terrain grew friendlier. Thimeon was now able to change their course more to the west. They were in the wide Ceadani plain. It stretched north many miles, dotted by a few stray peaks and ranges of hills. A light dusting of snow had fallen during the night, and northward the sky was blanketed in dark-gray clouds, but overhead it was almost clear with only the faintest wisps of high clouds contrasting with the blue. The sun would follow a clear path that day. And as it continued its climb, the air warmed several degrees.

The sense of the Daegmon's presence dissipated at noon, and the company risked a brief rest. Despite their fatigue, they had made good speed, and the peaks of the Maker's Knuckles were noticeably closer. Thimeon announced that if they pressed on through the afternoon, they would make Gale Enebe at nightfall.

In the afternoon, however, a bitter breeze came up from the east. Though it came at their backs and seemed to push them onward, it did nothing to make the sick and tired company more comfortable. Several of them began to grumble, and only

Elynna's awareness of her role as leader kept her from adding to the complaints. It was Thimeon, and not she, who urged them to pull their cloaks tightly about their necks and continue on. Travel was generally easier on this more level terrain, but though the snow was much less deep, it had been windswept into high dunes and drifts, causing occasional delays and detours.

About two hours past midday, Elynna became aware of the Daegmon's return. She cringed with the first touch of its heat and tried to harden herself against the pain, but as the afternoon progressed, the burning in her nostrils increased. Against her will, her memory kept drifting back to a conversation with her brother Lyn shortly before their relationship had gone sour. She'd confided in him a fear that the Daegmon had been after her in particular when it had attacked their village—that somehow she was responsible for the destruction of Lienford. He'd been incredulous at first and called her ridiculous. Only later did he come to believe her. And to blame her. "For the destruction of Lienford" is what they said aloud, but they both knew what the blame was really about: the death of their father.

And now she was leading that creature to another village? Cane was right to blame her. She couldn't do it.

6

PREY

By the time the sun had dropped half way toward the horizon, fatigue had overtaken them. Despite the desire for haste, several of the companions were lagging behind. Cane and Thimeon were forced to slow the pace. As the sun dropped farther, the Daegmon's presence grew stronger. Twice Elynna thought she caught sight of its massive wings high in the sky behind them. Once she stopped and was almost knocked over by a wave of heat, as if it had somehow assaulted her from a distance.

"What is the matter?" Tienna asked, concerned.

"Didn't you feel that?"

"I felt only your own weakness, as though something was assaulting your health and sapping your strength."

"Not the Daegmon's presence? The evil?"

"No. I do not have that sense. Is it near?"

"I felt it—" Elynna paused and bit her lip. "There is plant that grows along the river near my village. Nettle, we call it. All children learn to recognize it when we are young. If you brush it with bare skin, even lightly, it burns and raises bumps."

83

"We have a plant like that as well. We call it *ga-am*. It grows along gullies."

"That's what it feels like," Elynna explained. "What it has always felt like. Except the pain is inside me. In my head especially. Like it's brushing all my bones. But now it is more than that. I felt it attack me. The creature is *aware* of me."

Tienna looked toward the sky. "Do you mean it can *see* us?"

Before Elynna could respond, she felt it again: a burning touch, inside her skull. It lasted only a second, but she winced at the pain, and Tienna reached out to grab her. "Are you okay?"

"No," Elynna gasped, as for the first time she finally understood—she wasn't just sensing the Daegmon's presence; she was feeling its *thoughts*. It was aware of her, just as she was aware of it. It was probing her mind, tasting her intentions as much as her location. And it was that touch of its mind in hers that caused the most pain.

"Tienna," she said with horror. "It is searching me out. It knows me. It knows . . ." She struggled for the right words. "It doesn't just know I'm here. Somehow, it can feel my mind."

Tienna took her by the shoulders. "Elynna. What are you talking about? Are you well?"

"This is what I did not understand before. It is hunting *me*. It can feel my presence. It knows my thoughts. Or something of them, anyway."

"Are you sure?"

Elynna looked Tienna back in the eye. She could handle distrust from almost anybody in the company, but not from Tienna. The opinion of her friend meant too much. And the opinion of Cane also. "You do not believe me?" she asked softly.

The rest of the company had passed them and were waiting a

short distance ahead. Thimeon started back, but Tienna motioned for him to stop. She turned back to Elynna. "I believe you. We must tell the others."

A short time later Tienna had explained their situation to the companions. "The Daegmon can feel Elynna's presence even as she can sense it. She has felt its touch on her mind."

Others had the same question as Tienna. *Was Elynna sure of this?*

"It pursues me," Elynna blurted out in fear and frustration. "It knows of my gift, and it wants to devour me." Several of them took an involuntary step away from her, as though she had some disease they might catch. Then they turned their eyes from her toward the skies.

But Cane remained where he was. "Then we must protect you," he said calmly.

Elynna shivered. "We are all in danger, but my presence increases that danger. Maybe I should turn aside and not go into the village. I cannot let another village be destroyed because of me."

"We will not abandon you any more than you would abandon one of us," Thimeon replied. "Let us make haste. I have been to Gale Enebe. There are few places in Gondisle where we could be safer."

"They are tired," Tienna interjected. She looked around at the companions. "They are fishermen and farmers, not warriors."

"Perhaps," Thimeon answered, meeting Tienna's gaze. "But they are hardy. Do not judge the strength of a shepherd because he is not a warrior. Or," he added more softly, "the skill of a weaver."

She met his eyes and nodded. "I do not judge. If they can endure, let us move faster."

"Come," Thimeon said aloud. "The Daegmon is at our heels. Let your hearts provide what strength they may."

At once he set off at a trot. Drawing either from their fear or perhaps from some hidden reservoirs of energy, the companions responded with a surge of speed. As the sun continued its decline, they marched across the wide valley. The mountain peaks were a mile or more on either side now, and the way before them was open. Thimeon pointed out some distance ahead the steep slope and cliff face where they were headed—where the Ceadani village had been built many generations earlier. Despite their fatigue, the companions began to feel some hope that they might make it. The anticipation of rest and warmth and food. Still, Elynna's uneasiness grew as the late afternoon wore on. More than once she turned toward the sky and ducked. But she did not see the Daegmon, unless only a glimpse of it wheeling high in the sky far off.

Though weeks earlier near the start of their trip Thimeon had said more than once how beautiful the Ceadani lands were, what Elynna saw around her was far from cheery. The early winter had turned the scene bleak. Green leaves were frozen to the trees. Somewhere far off to her right, across the northern Ceadani Plains and the Raws, the lofty peak of Illengond towered even above the clouds that continued to stack up in the north. There were some in the company—and many more throughout Gondisle—who looked to the mountain for hope and comfort. She knew it was there somewhere, lost above the bleak gray blanket, with its familiar circular crown and three spires pointing skyward. But she could not see it. And Elynna was not one to find hope there anyway.

As the sun dipped toward the horizon, level with the tops of the tallest peaks to the northwest, snow clouds swept in from the north. Thimeon announced that they were nearing the village. A stream came down from the hills ahead, steaming in the cold air. They turned to follow its course and found a worn trail. By this time, Elynna was in pain almost constantly.

Thimeon put his hand on her shoulder. She pulled away from his touch but listened to his words. "The trail leads between these low hills and up a steep slope," Thimeon explained. "The village is against the bluffs. The homes have been built into the cliffs. You will be safe there."

"It follows me," she said. "I do not understand why, but it seeks me. I can feel it getting closer. Its power grows as night comes."

Now it was Cane who put a hand on her. "Are you sure of this?"

She did not pull away from his grip. "Yes. I feel its presence. I do not know how to explain." She squeezed her eyes shut and tried to fight the panic, to talk coherently. "Part of it is like a terrible stench. Or a burn. But there is a presence behind it, as though the stench were attacking me." She opened her eyes again, and for a moment she met Cane's gaze. "It is like knowing something and feeling something at the same time. And . . . And . . ." She stopped.

"Tell us," Thimeon said. "What do we need to know?"

Elynna took a deep breath. "It is that terrible sense of doom—of something about to happen. I feel it nearly as strongly as I did before the attack two days ago. By it is more than that. The creature probes my own knowledge. It is aware of me. I'm sure of it. Perhaps it is aware of all of us—of all of our gifts: of Cane, and Cathros and Tienna also. That's what I was trying to say. The stench enters me. It's like it is smelling *me*."

"Then there is no doubt that we are being pursued," Cane stated.

Elynna bit her lip and shook her head. "No. There is not," she whispered.

"Then I fear to lead the creature into the village no matter how strong and secure the village is," Cane went on. "Perhaps it is time we turn and fight." He looked at Elynna as he said this, waiting for her to respond. Elynna thought of Lienford in ruins. She knew Cane was right. But her words stuck in her throat.

It was Thimeon who spoke in response. "How?"

Elynna was relieved when Cane turned his eyes away from her and toward Thimeon. "We are not without weapons. Do not forget that the Daegmon avoided my blade at our last encounter. It has fled from us for many weeks, or so it seemed, until it ambushed us in the mountains. If it did not have *something* to fear, it would not have delayed attacking us for so long. Perhaps it knows I can inflict harm upon it."

"Perhaps," Thimeon agreed. "But then why wouldn't it avoid you once again and attack the rest of us?"

Cane did not answer at once. "Does the trail enter narrow ravine or gorge in the hills ahead?" he asked instead.

"As I said before, I have been here rarely and not in recent years."

"You have not yet failed as our guide. Tell me as best as you remember."

Thimeon closed his eyes and sighed. Then opened them again. "As I remember from my past visits, at its narrowest, where the stream cuts through a shallow defile, a strong deer could almost leap across the top from one ledge to the other. The walls are steep, but it is not deep. In some places it is as tall as the mountain spruce, but in other places a man could jump down from above and avoid injury. The defile runs half a mile or more before it levels out at the top of the slope. Unless I have confused this place with some other in my memory. There are countless rivers and ravines in these mountains."

"Could we walk along the top of the ledges on one side or the other?"

"In daylight it could be done with little difficulty. At night it might be more dangerous. What do you propose?"

Tienna and Cathros were now listening, as were some of the others. "I hesitate to speak my mind because of the danger involved to Elynna."

Elynna started to tremble. "Say it," she said. Her voice cracked as she spoke. She was not sure if anybody even heard her.

But whether he heard her or not, Cane went on. Once more, he looked directly at her as he spoke. "If the Daegmon senses your presence more than the rest of us, then it may be that we could use you as bait in a trap."

"*No!*" Thimeon and Tienna spoke at once.

Elynna's trembling grew more pronounced. "How?"

"Just a simple ambush," Cane explained. "If some of us can get higher than the Daegmon and attack it from above—keep it from flying away—we may be able to strike a fatal blow," He was looking at Elynna as he spoke, as though gauging her strength of will. She looked back at him. Mingled with her fear was another feeling, almost as strong. She longed desperately for him to find her worthy. Did he realize this? He put a hand on each of her arms. "If you wait at the end of the defile, it may fly down low enough seeking *you* that the rest can surprise it from above. We repay its ambush with out of our own."

"But what do I do when it reaches me?"

"I will stand beside you," he said, still holding her by the arms.

Elynna made her decision at once, while memory of a ravaged Lienford was in her mind, before fear could turn her away. "I will do it, but we must make haste. It approaches even now."

Tienna protested the plan at once, but Elynna reminded her that if she were called on to fill the same role, she would not refuse. This was something Tienna understood, and she did not object again. At once Cane began explaining his plan and shouting instructions as they began a quick dash up the hill. He explained his plan and the timing of the ambush as they ran. Thimeon and Cathros were already dividing the company into two groups, preparing the ambush. Yet to Elynna it seemed they were more like rabbits fleeing to a hole than soldiers readying for battle. As the walls of the defile started to rise on either side, they split up. Cathros and Tienna led one party up the left side, while Thimeon took the others up the right. Elynna stayed on the trail at the bottom with Cane beside her. Her companions' silhouettes were visible above her, but all was silent except for their scrambling feet.

Then a screech filled the sky. A shadow passed forty feet overhead. Elynna ducked. "It will see them," she cried. Her voice had a desperate edge. "It knows. The trap won't work."

"It may guess our plan," Cane replied, "but if it feels your presence as you say, perhaps it will come after you anyway and ignore the others." With a hint of disgust in his voice he added, "So far we have given it little reason to fear us."

A moment later they found the sort of spot they were hoping for. A large boulder, about shoulder high, stood in the middle of the ravine. The path went around one side, and the stream flowed around the other. "We will stand here," Cane said tersely. He swung himself to the top and pulled Elynna up after him. "When it attacks, jump backward to the ground behind the boulder, and crowd as close to it as you can. Do not go out into the open."

Elynna nodded. She had lost her voice. Another screech filled the air, and her terror grew. The Daegmon was returning. It swooped over them again, lower this time. She would have had an easy shot with her bow, but she knew now that arrows were useless against its tough hide.

At the bottom end of the defile, against the pale sky, it turned back. She looked at Cane. His hand rested on his sword hilt, and faint flickers of blue light rolled up and down the sheath and along his fingertips, though he had not yet drawn the blade. A dozen feet above on both sides the companions had now found their places and were looking down at the scene. If their faces held the same terror as Elynna's, it was too dark to tell. The Daegmon approached the final time. It beat its wings slowly as it flew up the defile, eyes blazing red and talons extended.

It was coming straight toward them, right up the defile, just as Cane had hoped. And as Elynna had feared. She could see it clearly now. It was bigger even than she remembered. Its wingspan was so broad that its wings kept brushing the walls on either side, sending showers of rocks and debris into the air and down onto the trail. A hundred and fifty yards away, it opened its cavernous jaws and let out a third roar that shook that walls, almost knocking Elynna from her feet. The distance between them closed with remarkable speed. Only at the last instant did Cane's blade flash free of its sheath, bursting into a blaze of vivid blue flame that danced up his arm like lightning.

"Jump away," he shouted.

It was too late. Despite the Daegmon's great size, its onrush was swift. Elynna was paralyzed. She could only watch.

"Leap!" Cane shouted again, but he was no longer looking at her. Radiating a power of its own, his blade flashed brightly in his hand. Flames engulfed his arms. Unafraid, he stood facing the enemy.

Then the Daegmon—its talons already reaching out to seize its prey—perceived Cane's power, and for an instant it faltered. Elynna felt an unmistakable diversion of its deadly might—an uncertainty about this new power that was opposing it.

In that split second of time the Daegmon pulled back. Its head shot upward away from the blade, and its strong legs pulled in as if it hoped to soar over its foe. But it was already too close. There was no place to turn. Cane saw his chance. Uttering his Anghare battle cry, he lunged upward toward its exposed neck with a mighty stroke of his blade.

The Daegmon was not so easily trapped. With agility that belied its size, it threw its head backward, simultaneously snapping its tail forward underneath it. Cane's lunge fell short of its target as the creature executed a giant mid-flight flip. Its tail slammed full force into the boulder just below where Elynna stood beside Cane.

Boom. The concussion shook the boulder and jarred Cane off his feet. Already off balance from his sword stroke, he started to fall straight toward the Daegmon. Reaching toward him—perhaps to help, perhaps to save herself—Elynna lost her own balance and stumbled forward. Her arms flailing to find Cane, she screamed as she toppled over the edge.

The descent was short, but her knees slammed hard on the frozen ground. The impact sent a jolt of pain up both legs as she fell forward onto her hands. Yet her fear overrode the pain, and spinning around she hurled herself rolling toward the boulder, away from the Daegmon.

A few feet away, Cane somehow managed to land on his feet with his flaming blade still in hand. He had no time to collect himself. The Daegmon's somersault had sent its tail too far forward for flight. With a thud that shook the ravine floor, it crashed to the ground on its back just beyond reach. Cane rushed forward, blade poised to deal a stroke to its exposed belly.

Yet again they learned that this enemy was too crafty. Even as it struggled to its feet, it thrashed blindly with its tail and rear talons. Cane was hard-pressed for his own life.

Boom. The tail slammed against the wall like a battering ram, missing his head by inches and showering shards of smashed stones and ice down on Elynna. *Boom.* Another blow exploded at his feet, sending him stumbling backward almost onto Elynna's lap. The tail slammed into the stream. A wave of cold water drenched them both.

And before they knew what had happened, the Daegmon had rolled to its feet and spun around. Its head, ten feet above the ground, towered over theirs while its eyes blazed down with contempt upon its puny adversaries. Elynna wilted beneath its evil stare and squeezed further back against the rock. Sensing the distress of its prey, it Daegmon opened its mouth wider. With a long hissing laugh, it rose higher still, towering twenty feet tall on its rear legs like a grotesque imitation of a rearing horse.

Cane stood undaunted. His blade was subdued but still glowed blue. The creature watched him for an instant, evaluating his power. Then it attacked.

Talons extended, it lunged downward, sweeping its claws in a fierce blow aimed at his foe. Cowering in a crevice below the boulder, Elynna saw four razor-sharp blades rip out a hunk of rock inches above Cane's head. Yet somehow he rolled free of the blow, and with a warrior's agility he slashed upward with his own blade even as he spun around.

This time the stroke connected, exploding in blue flames. The Daegmon roared in pain. But before Cane could take advantage, the beast recoiled and nearly ripped the blade from his hand. He stumbled forward, struggling to hold on to his weapon while the flames flickered and threatened to be extinguished.

The creature was back at him in an instant. A snap of its jaw missed his head by a breath. It snapped again, and Cane was forced to roll to his side. His blade once again flamed blue with a surge of power, but the creature gave him no other chance to strike a blow with it. The jaws lunged toward him again, and again he rolled away, missing death by a few inches. He slashed blindly with his blade, carving a bright blue arc in the air, but to no avail. The Daegmon reared again to full height, spreading its wings to the side.

Then Elynna saw what Cane did not see. She saw, and she understood, for she could feel the very thoughts of the Daegmon. It was as though she were in its mind for that instant, aware of the bunching of muscles, the intake of air, the power in its claws. While the Northland warrior struggled to retain his balance in the face of slashing claws and teeth, the creature had moved backward toward the north wall of the ravine. As it did so, it bent back its mighty tail preparing to deliver the death blow. The Daegmon had the opportunity it needed. The only opponent in a hundred years that had given it cause to fear would come to an end. It opened its mouth to finish him with a single snap.

"Look out," Elynna shouted. But her warning cry distracted Cane, who turned to look behind him.

Yet the Daegmon, too, had made a mistake. It had seen the companions lining the ravine walls above, but thought them too puny and insignificant to worry about. Elynna could sense that knowledge, also, and the disdain that came with it. And so it had ignored them and gone after the one enemy who might do it harm. Now, at a signal from Thimeon, the companions sprang their ambush at last. Down leapt Cathros squarely upon the creature's back. With him from the same side of the ravine came three of the fiercest Northland warriors: Aram, Kayle, and Annat. And into the fray jumped also Llian, with the Westwashers Pietr and Jamesh.

The battle had now begun in full. Sensing the supernatural power of one of the humans on its back, the Daegmon reared in surprise. Cathros, with all his might, drove down into the creature's hide a huge hunk of rock that would have crushed a mortal.

The Daegmon roared in pain and fury, shaking the ravine from end to end. Then, writhing like a snake, it toppled on its side, sending its two riders tumbling off. Cathros landed on his feet, but Annat was not so lucky. He fell forward beneath the Daegmon's flailing talons and was not quick enough to escape a savage blow that tore open his belly.

An instant later the Daegmon was back on its feet showing no sign of injury. Eyes glowing more angrily than before, it looked over the ten foes now facing it. All except Cane and Cathros backed away in fear before the deadly glance.

Then another figure leapt down from above, unseen and somehow unfelt by the Daegmon. But Elynna saw, now, with her own eyes. It was Tienna. As the creature stepped toward Cane, she held tightly to its neck. Aram charged in with a spear. The Daegmon snapped its huge jaws on the shaft and threw him aside like a cat tosses a mouse, then dropped the spear in splinters as Aram struggled to rise.

From the other side of the ravine Bandor and Theo jumped down from above, and sprang to Aram's aid to pull him to safety. Nobody else yet dared make a move. Feigning with its talons, the Daegmon drove Kayle, Pietr, and Jamesh back. Then it spun again toward Cane and Cathros. The brothers held their ground as it stepped toward them. With the boulder behind them, they could not have retreated if they wanted to. And Elynna, looking out between Cathros's legs, knew they were all that stood between her and death.

Cane held his blade aloft. Flames danced in the sky. The Daegmon howled at the sight of the talisman. Its own power flared in response, and Elynna felt the searing heat of its hatred. With no warning, the huge tail came whipping around toward its target with the power of an avalanche. Rocks and sand flew in all directions. A short but horrible scream split the air as Jamesh, standing too close, was caught unaware. The tail slammed him in the ribs, throwing him twenty-five feet through the air. As the tail continued toward its target, he hit the rock wall with a horrific crack. Elynna heard a scream and realized it was her own.

Yet Cathros was not so easily moved. The battle strength was upon him. He had now become like part of the rock itself. The tail caught him in his midsection with a loud thud. He stumbled backward with the blow, and yet did not fall. In his powerful arms, he took hold of the Daegmon's tail before it could withdraw. Elynna could sense a momentary surprise in her enemy. She had heard of

Cathros's gift, but would not have believed this was possible had she not seen it for herself. He was holding on to a creature a hundred times his size, and for an instant it could not escape.

That was the instant Cane needed. Elynna watched as his blade flashed down like lightning, driving deep into the Daegmon's tail. The creature's roar was no longer one to terrify its enemy but a cry of pain. It tried to pull free. Cathros held tightly just long enough for Cane to land one more blow. The blade came down again in an explosion of blue flame. Shards of flaming metal flew through the air.

Cane fell. His blade had shattered in a concussion of power too great for it. Cathros also stumbled backward, holding in his arms a severed tail.

The Daegmon lurched, withdrawing the stub of its once powerful weapon. Everybody froze, watching and wondering what would come next. Elynna felt her thin hope start to grow.

But it did not last long. Madder than ever, the enemy rose high on its rear legs and spread its wings. It was as though it had been merely toying with them up until now. It could destroy them any time, raged its thoughts. Once more, Elynna believed those thoughts. She looked around. Cane held the shards of his blade in his hand—all that remained of his weapon. There was nothing now to contain his flame, without which he was defenseless. He and Cathros stepped backward. They pressed their backs to the wall as the Daegmon came toward them, jaws gaping.

Then, the lithe figure of Tienna, still clinging tenaciously to the Daegmon's neck, rose upward. The movement caught Elynna's eyes. Balancing on her legs with the extraordinary skill of a Plains huntress, Tienna let go her hold of its neck for just an instant and drew her long knife. With both hands, she plunged the blade downward with all her might into its head. It was a fierce blow, and the enemy stumbled forward, stricken.

Still it did not fall. Its skull was thicker than its skin, and though Tienna was a deadly hunter, she was not exceptionally strong even by mortal standards. The blade sank halfway to its hilt and there it stopped. Aware now of its rider, the Daegmon twisted its head around until one eye was just a few feet from her head.

"Jump," Cathros shouted as it snapped at her knee. Tienna didn't move. The Daegmon ground its teeth bare inches from her body, but she was well positioned. Despite all its furious twisting, it couldn't reach her. Fearlessly, she held her place and grabbed the blade to wrench it free for another blow. The creature didn't give her a chance. Unable to reach her with its jaws, it lifted its head once and jerked it down. The sudden motion sent Tienna flying forward through the air, thirty feet over the boulder against which Elynna crouched. All at once she was gone, and the creature roared with a sound Elynna knew was laughter.

The battle continued. Emboldened by Tienna's maneuver, the final members of the company came leaping down from both sides of the ravine: Marti, Nahoon, Beth, Siyen, Falien, Hruach, and Hrevia. All who had held back.

Last came Braddoc. The old shepherd had been biding his time along the north wall, waiting for the right moment to strike his blow and avenge the death of his brother's granddaughter. Now his moment had come. His hands held tight to the spear that had once been his shepherd's staff. Even in the failing light, the grim determination on his face was visible. With a shout that echoed off the stone, he landed squarely on two feet directly between the Daegmon's wings. Then, as quick as lightning, before he could be thrown aside, he drove the spear down with both arms.

It was a blow like Tienna's, only Braddoc was half again as strong and heavy, and his spear much longer. The hard iron head sank deep into his enemy's back. Again the Daegmon howled out in anger and pain.

With a toss of its wings, it hurled Braddoc hard against the wall, where he fell lifeless to the floor. Nobody could come to his aid now. The Daegmon had gone wild. No more methodical advancing or retreating.

Before Bandor and Llian could dive out of the way, a flick of the long stub that remained of its tail sent them flying. Bandor crashed into the wall. Llian was not as lucky. He landed just a few paces away and was eviscerated by a swipe of talons. It turned next upon Pietr, who was still trying to help the wounded Jamesh stagger away. There was nothing he could do for his friend now.

Elynna screamed as Jamesh disappeared behind a snapping jaw. Pietr rolled free, just escaping the creature's range. On it came, snapping at the others as they sought to scramble to safety. The Daegmon was on a rampage. Nobody could touch it now. Yet miraculously the spear remained where Braddoc had impaled it, protruding from deep in its back like a giant thorn between its wings.

Cane gave a great shout. The stub of his broken blade flashed with blue flames. The Daegmon turned toward him. It was no longer afraid. Three steps carried it across the short distance separating them. Its eyes darted between the brothers, as though sensing their gifts and assessing their power.

Then it saw Elynna, crouching behind them. Their minds met. She felt its searing hatred even as it sensed her terror. It struck, lunging toward the brothers headfirst as if to devour them both with one swallow.

Instinctively, Cane and Cathros dove in opposite directions. Elynna, behind them, was unable to move as the huge jaws came toward her. With a crash, the top of the Daegmon's head slammed hard into the boulder a few feet above her. For just a moment, as she waited for the jaws to snap shut and crush her, she found herself looking down its horrible bottomless throat and tasted the smell of its rancid breath, sharing with it the certainty that it had destroyed her.

However, Tienna's blade was still imbedded in the creature's skull. Whether because some other force was at work, or the blade was well-forged by some ancient forgotten craft, it did not break. Thus the force of the Daegmon's own blow against the boulder did what the young huntress had not had the strength to do. The creature drove the blade deep into its own skull, right between the eyes.

The ensuing roar was deafening, louder than any it had yet released, and the moments that followed were the most terrifying Elynna had ever known. Wildly, it thrashed around the ravine floor, throwing itself against boulders and splashing through the stream in a vain attempt to ease the pain in its skull. The companions ceased trying to fight, but scattered, seeking safe refuge from the death throes of their enemy. Those who did not flee quickly suffered hard for it.

And then, as suddenly as it had begun, all was quiet. Beneath the fading red of a cloudy sunset, Elynna looked out and saw the Daegmon lying dead, its body choking the ravine.

7

AFTERMATH

The Daegmon was not moving.

Elynna stared ahead. Her ears still rang from the roaring, her eyes and nostrils and mouth stung from the creature's acidic breath, and every limb and muscle and nerve in her body quivered. She struggled to use the one other sense that remained to her, the one sense she had never wanted but could not ignore—her so-called *gift*. But though the Daegmon's body lay in front of her—grotesque with power even in death—the awful sense of its presence was gone. She could feel nothing. No heat. No touch of its mind.

She looked around in surprise. All was still. No sound reached her ears except the gentle rumble of the brook and the stirring of the wind along the ledges. Somewhere behind her the sun had just set. The sky was pale gray. She leaned her head back against the rock, and gazing down the ravine she let her eyes drift upward toward the eastern sky. Caradon, the fisherman's star, had already appeared. Though it was long since she had taken the time to gaze at it, she knew it well. It was the first star every child in the Westwash learned by name—the first to rise at night, shining in the east to guide tired fishermen home from the sea.

The distant flickering held Elynna's gaze until a movement nearer at hand caught her attention. Cane was rising to his feet. He glanced in her direction but didn't speak. His clothing was torn, and his face covered with sweat and dirt. The flames on his sword arm were gone, and he looked smaller. A dark red-brown stain drenched his left shoulder. He tossed away the shards of his broken weapon and took a few slow steps, letting his injured arm dangle at his side. Cathros rose also and made his way to his brother's side. He reached out once to touch Cane's wounded arm. Then together they approached the twisted neck of their fallen enemy. It stared at them through red glazed eyes, but it did not move.

Cane drew nearer. He placed his foot on its neck. "It is dead," he proclaimed.

Only then did Elynna rise from beneath the boulder. She was still trembling. Her legs were barely able to hold her. Around her, the dim forms of her companions struggled to their feet.

"It is dead," Cane repeated. "We have won."

Swallowing, Elynna took a step forward. She realized then how cold and sore she was. She was soaked with sweat, and both ankles were in pain. Still she moved forward. The Daegmon's body filled the center of the ravine like a giant scar. Water rushed over one of its wings that had fallen into the stream. Elynna stood a moment longer as Thimeon approached from somewhere off to the side and joined her, looking at their defeated enemy.

The Andani guide had already retrieved his pack from the ravine floor. He pulled out two torches and lit them. Their dim light reflected faintly off the walls as he placed them in nooks in the rock. A few of the other companions were stirring also, moving out from wherever they had gone for shelter. Cane and Cathros moved around the body to examine it. Already a vile odor of unnatural rot was rising from the corpse. Elynna stepped up to the head. One huge eye still stared at her. She tried to push it shut with her boot, but the creature had no eyelids. Then a heavy odor of decay wafted up from its open jaws. She turned away, her stomach threatening upheaval.

For a time, as the companions moved about the bottom of the ravine and surveyed the scene, nobody spoke. They had not yet fathomed the reality of their enemy's death. Or perhaps the carnage was too great and the victory less sweet than they had hoped. Elynna did not know. She did not know even how she felt herself. She was still too numb. In the torchlight, she looked around for the bodies of the fallen. To her left, Bandor and Theo had found Llian. Their somber movements made it clear that he was already dead. She turned away. It took her longer to find the other victims. Jamesh had not survived the crushing blow. Annat, too, was dead; Aram and Kayle were pulling his broken body away from the Daegmon.

"Elynna," Thimeon called with some urgency. Following his voice, Elynna spotted him kneeling beside the stream, tending to someone.

"Who—?" she started as she approached, but she recognized the prone body before Thimeon could answer. On the ground lay Braddoc, bleeding and covered with snow knocked loose from the bushes along the ravine walls. Thimeon had found him half in the water, too weak to crawl out by himself. His eyes were open, but he wasn't moving.

"Elynna?" Braddoc groaned, making a futile effort to sit up. He could barely turn his head. "Is she here?"

"Lie still," Thimeon said, holding him down. "She has come."

Elynna bit her lip to hold back her tears, and knelt at the wounded man's side. "What is it, Braddoc?"

"Where is it?" he asked. Blood spilled from a pair of deep gashes in his belly where the Daegmon, in its final assault, had caught him with its talons. "Did we win?"

"It is dead," Thimeon answered as he struggled to stop the bleeding with a piece of his shirt.

"We have defeated it?"

"We have," Elynna answered. To her dismay, Thimeon's efforts to staunch the flow of blood were unsuccessful. The old shepherd's midsection was one giant wound. "You dealt the death blow, Braddoc. It could not dislodge your spear."

"Then I have avenged Llana."

"You have."

Thimeon suddenly turned to Elynna, a flicker of hope in his eyes. "Tienna. Her healing power. Where is she?"

A flicker of hope flashed across Elynna's thoughts as she remembered Falien and his miraculous recovery. Ignoring her fatigue and the sharp pain in her ankles, she rose to her feet and looked about, desperate to keep Braddoc from becoming one more victim. The companions were gathered in small clumps around the fallen forms. She scanned their faces, looking for the Plains woman. The healer. There was no sign of her friend. Then it came back to her: the scene she had forgotten in the depths of her own terror, and then again in the momentary relief of victory. Tienna had been flung over the boulder, thrown by the might of the Daegmon. Thrown impossibly high and hard. Hard enough to have killed her.

Panicked, Elynna called her friend's name. Her shout echoed

down the gorge. There was no answer. As quickly as she could on her twisted ankles, she hobbled up the trail toward the boulder over which the Daegmon had so easily tossed the small huntress. To the left, the stream flowed deep between the boulder and cliff. On the right, a tall mound of fallen snow and debris clogged the trail. Trusting her momentum to carry her over the top, Elynna lunged up the mound. When her momentum failed, she fell forward and scrambled with her hands until she rolled over the top and down the far side. There she struggled to her feet. Crying as much at the fear of yet another loss as from the new cuts and bruises that racked her body, she started up the trail, frantically calling for her friend.

In the near darkness, it took a moment to spot her. Tienna lay on the far side of the stream in a small heap against the bottom of the rock wall. Her body, unmoving, looked twisted and broken.

"No!" Elynna wept. She lurched forward, tears streaming down her face, and plunged heedlessly into the icy stream, stumbling in the knee-deep water.

Was it a trick of the light? Elynna slowed as she stepped out of the numbing water. Tienna was sitting upright against the wall. She had opened her eyes, and was now following Elynna's approach.

"Oh Tienna," Elynna cried, falling to her knees and throwing her arms around her friend.

"I thought you were dead," Tienna said when they released each other.

"And I thought you were dead as well. But the Daegmon is defeated. Defeated," she replied. "Finally. We have won."

"I am glad. I feared the worst for all of you."

"*You* feared? I wasn't the one who went flying thirty feet through the air. But come. We have no time to waste. The Daegmon is destroyed, but three of the company lay dead, and Braddoc is sorely hurt. He will not live without your help. Do you have the strength?"

"I am ready, but you will have to carry me."

"What?" Elynna looked at her friend more closely. "What is the matter?"

"My left leg snapped when I landed." Her voice was dispassionate, as if she were describing another's injuries, but tracks in the snow showed where she had dragged herself across the ground. "My other ankle is badly twisted, though it is not broken."

Elynna shook her head, marveling at her friend's determination. But injury or not, she didn't dare delay any longer. Wrapping her arms around Tienna's legs and waist, she struggled to pick her up. The attempt failed. She slipped and fell, and Tienna cried out in pain.

"I'm sorry," Elynna sobbed.

"Do not worry for me. Get me to Braddoc. Though I cannot help myself, perhaps I can help him."

Elynna nodded and tried again. This time she succeeded in standing, with Tienna wrapped in her arms. After a pause to adjust her balance, she staggered toward the stream. She rested a moment at the edge, then stepped in. The current pulled at her legs, and she struggled on the smooth rocks to keep her burden above the water. Thrice she slipped and almost fell. By the time she got across, she was exhausted. She managed three more steps before she had to set Tienna down. The icy water numbed the pain in her ankles, but made it difficult to feel her footing.

Feeling nearly hopeless, she cried out for help, but her voice was lost in the steady rumble of the stream and the whistling of the wind down the ravine. She shouted louder. Still there was no answer. She struggled again to her feet and lifted Tienna once more. This time she made it eight steps. But she could go no further. In her condition, the mound of snow and dirt was an insurmountable barrier.

She was at the edge of despair when Cathros appeared, torch in hand, half climbing and half plowing his way over the top of the mound. "Is it Tienna?" he asked, seeing Elynna with her burden. "Does she live?"

"Her leg is broken, but she is not bleeding. Braddoc is much worse off. We must get her to him so she can help."

Cathros shook his head.

"He bleeds badly," Elynna protested. "We must get—"

She didn't finish her sentence. The look in Cathros's eyes told her enough. She was too late. Braddoc had already died. She sank to her knees and set Tienna down on the snow. Then the dam of her emotions broke, and she began to weep.

Drained by her ordeal, Elynna did not return to the scene of battle. She remained instead with Tienna while the others tended wounds, gathered their belongings, and took care of the fallen. The sky was black by the time they gathered again around Elynna. The torches had burned out, so they stumbled the last hundred yards up the defile in the darkness. There they collapsed.

They were on level ground in a small circle surrounded by boulders and low shrubs. A light wind whistled around their heads, but they were too exhausted to build a fire or look for shelter. Thimeon and his young cousin Theo, who normally would have taken the initiative, sat mourning beside the broken bodies of Braddoc and Llian, the fallen Andani. Bandor, despite a broken hand and a badly bruised shoulder, had made an initial effort to gather some wood, but then he too had collapsed against a tree, the pile of dead branches lying at his feet unlit. Cane leaned against a boulder and held a bandage to his bloody shoulder. The other Anghare sat in their little circle a short distance from where Annat's body had been lain. Hrevia was tending to her brother Hruach, who moaned in obvious pain. Pietr and Falien had covered Jamesh, the fallen Westwasher, and were now tending as best they could to each other's wounds. Siyen huddled against a tree shivering and whimpering.

The Plainsfolk were the only people among the company who had not suffered any casualties in the battle, but they had not escaped unscathed. Tienna did not complain, but her face was drawn and pale. Nahoon and Marti had both lost considerable blood from multiple cuts and gashes, and Beth had been knocked unconscious and now sat moaning and holding her head. Only Cathros made any effort to move about, and even he soon gave up and sat down.

After a while, Elynna drifted into numb sleep. How much time passed in this state, she did not know. She awoke to see flickers of light high up on the hillside. Was it a dream? All was silent save the sough of wind through the branches overhead. She watched the lights for a while, transfixed. Were her companions leaving her? She felt too tired to care. She could only gaze at the lights through half-closed eyes. It took two or three minutes before she realized the lights were coming down the trail toward her and not departing.

Somebody was coming. She began to wake more fully. "Thimeon," she called into the darkness. Why had she called *his* name? she wondered. Why not Cane? Or Cathros? Or anybody else?

"I have seen," Thimeon replied from somewhere not far away. "Six torches. Maybe seven."

"Who are they? Have they come to help? Or are they—"

Thimeon cut her off abruptly. "We have no enemies in these mountains save the one we just defeated. We are still deep in Ceadani land, and they are a peaceful folk. Those torches must come from Gale Enebe. They are Chal-char's people. If they are not . . ." His voice trailed off, as though he could not finish that thought.

"You know their language. Speak with them. Ask them . . . Accept whatever aid they offer."

"I will do what I can."

Steadily the torches approached, disappearing now and again behind slopes or trees and then reappearing a little closer each time, until six distinct flames were visible. About five minutes after first appearing, the approaching party disappeared a final time around a bend in the trail and then reemerged just a short distance away. They almost stumbled over the feet of Hruach and Hrevia as they entered the glen. They were lightly armed with spears and bows.

For a few seconds they stood staring at the circle of companions who lay on the ground staring back. Finally, the torchbearers separated and made a path between them. As they did so, there came into the small clearing an older man with deep wise eyes and a gentle smile. He was white-haired and white-bearded, with many years of wrinkles upon his face. A circlet of silver adorned with a single blue stone hung about his neck. He was taller than Elynna, though shorter than Cane or Cathros. Despite his obvious age, his back was straight and his gait steady.

As he stood there, the object of Elynna's scrutiny but also

clearly the object his own people's honor, his eyes searched the circle, moving from face to face in the torchlight. At first Elynna saw in his expression—the widening of his eyes and the lowering of his jaw—something like either surprise or amazement. But as he took in the sight of the covered bodies, and state of those who had survived the battle, the look turned to one of compassion and sorrow. And for the first time in many days, Elynna started to feel at ease as a burden she had been carrying lifted, for a time, off her shoulders.

A few moments passed before the stranger began to address them in the common trade language, in a voice low and cracked with age but not weak. "We greet you in the name of the All-Maker." He did not wait for a reply. "I see that you are tired and sore. We saw the Daegmon and were preparing the village defenses, when we saw and heard the signs of your great battle from a mile away. Many have fought the Daegmon, and all have lost."

"We have defeated it," Cane said flatly.

"I see that," the stranger said with a smile. "For it is evident that you still live—unless we are seeing ghosts—and that fact alone can have only one meaning."

Cane shook his head, his tired mind unable to follow the old man's speech. A brief silence followed. Then Thimeon rose to his feet. He took a deep breath and bowed, then replied in a language Elynna did not understand. The villagers, pleased to hear their own tongue spoken, murmured their approval as Thimeon and their leader conversed for several minutes.

The old man spoke again in the common trade language of Gondisle. "You honor us by speaking the tongue of the Ceadani. I rejoice also that your people have not forgotten us."

"The mountains bind us together," Thimeon answered, "and Illengond towers over us all, reminding us that the Maker is the All-Maker. The Andani do not forget."

"You are welcome among us, fellow Highlanders," the man replied. Then he turned to Elynna. "I am told you are the leader of this brave company. I am Chal-char, Elder of Gale Enebe. You and your people are welcome in our village and among the Ceadani. You have won a great victory, and for that we honor you."

Elynna sat in silence. She wanted to answer, but no words came to her lips. She was too spent, physically and emotionally, to answer. When she did not reply, Chal-char motioned with his hand, and as he spoke, a number of his people stepped forward from the shadows. "I know your people are tired, but you will be safer and warmer if you return with us this night to Gale Enebe. There we can offer you beds, and feed you if you are hungry. The way is not far. Let us first tend to your wounds and provide sustenance to strengthen you for the short walk. Then we may depart."

Though Elynna did not try to count them, her impression was that the Ceadani numbered about twenty. As they began moving around her and her prone companions, she noticed that only four of them bore well-forged weapons. The rest were armed with hunting bows, makeshift spears, mining axes, and other crudely fashioned implements that might serve as weapons under desperate circumstances. Though all were dressed in similar garb—high warm boots, thick woven trousers, heavy cloaks, and fur-lined hats—they were in many ways a varied group. They ranged in age, from a lad who looked a year or two younger than Theo up to Chal-char, who might have been old enough to be a great-grandfather. There were six or seven women among them, though in their heavy cloaks it took Elynna a moment to realize this. All were ready to help. Some carried litters, others pouches of herbs and ointments for healing, and others flasks of drink.

Aware suddenly of her hunger and thirst, Elynna waited eagerly as they passed one of the flasks first to the wounded Tienna, then to Nahoon, then to herself. It was a warm beverage that reminded her a little of an herbal brew the folk of Westwash drank during the rainy season, though the Ceadani drink was stronger and sweeter, and had an unusual fragrance that made her think of the mountains. It was at once soothing and refreshing, and she could feel vitality seeping back into her bones.

She could tell from their expressions that her companions felt the same thing. As they warmed to the drink and felt some of their strength return, others of the Ceadani examined the injuries. With efficiency that even Cathros later said was astonishing, they stitched together the wound on Cane's shoulder with a fine thread—a process none but the Northlanders had ever seen performed—and then redressed it with fresh cloth. They also attended to several other cuts and wounds suffered during battle. To the bruises and sprains they applied a soothing ointment with a fragrance similar to the hot beverage in the flasks. To the open wounds they applied a different ointment that stung for an instant but numbed the pain. They did not try to remove Tienna's splint, for they said both that it had been well done and that its removal would be painful. Instead they bound her to one of several litters they had brought with them.

They had also brought a small supply of dry clothing of good Ceadani workmanship and style: cloaks, boots, gloves—all made for cold weather. To those who had lost their packs, or had fallen in the water, or were simply not equipped for the cold of the Highlands, these gifts proved the greatest boon of all. Elynna accepted a dry pair of fur-lined boots from a young woman her age. The boots she had been wearing were not only torn and frayed from wear and battle, but they had gotten soaked when she crossed the stream to find Tienna. The Ceadani had blankets too, to put over the litters of those who were too wounded or weak to walk on their own: Nahoon and Beth, who had been wounded in the Daegmon's final rampage, and Hruach, who had twisted his knee badly landing when he had jumped down from the ravine to join the fray.

Finally came the unpleasant task of caring for the slain companions. The bodies of the four who had given their lives in the battle were placed with great honor on litters and covered with blankets to be carried back to the village. When all was done, they were ready. Between the slain and the wounded, there were eight litters in all, and most of the Ceadani were occupied carrying them.

The companions still capable of walking, refreshed somewhat by the drink and eager to find food and shelter, had risen to their feet. A few had even begun to talk, introducing themselves by name to their new hosts. Though not many among the Ceadani spoke the trade language, they could understand at least the exchange of names. It was good to hear voices, Elynna thought. Less than an hour had passed before all were following Chal-char toward Gale Enebe.

A few stars were visible overhead. The air was cold, but the strong beverage had a double effect on Elynna of both warming her inside and making her a little dreamy, like when waking from a long afternoon nap in the sunshine. Or perhaps the second effect was due to her fatigue, or the mystical quality of torchlight on snow, or the stark foreign terrain. Whatever the cause, she found the journey mysterious, and was later unable to remember how long it took.

Chal-char led them steadily uphill along a narrow winding trail that no longer followed the path of the river. Despite his age, his pace was brisk, and Elynna had to work to keep up. Twice she stumbled when her sore ankles gave out. Both times a figure emerged from the shadows to catch her. She had a vague sense that the trail, after cutting back and forth through tight turns, leveled and took a big wide bend to the left, and then straightened out. She found herself looking up at the star Caradon and realized she was now facing east. But then clouds thickened and even the brightest stars disappeared. She lost all sense of direction. Her eyes wandered as she walked, but the torches revealed only scattered trees to their left and a steep mountainside to their right. The snow was not deep, and felt soft beneath their feet. Soon she saw the dark shape of a mountain looming higher on their right. Its silhouette was clear against the stars high above her.

Shortly after that, the trail disappeared into a dark tunnel of rock. There followed a long climb up a torch-lit stone staircase surrounded by rock. Just as she was wondering how long she would have to continue, she heard hushed voices around her coming through holes in the rock and echoing along the staircase. Now and then she felt a draft as they passed gaps or doors or vents in the surrounding stone. After a few minutes of climbing, lights became visible beneath doorways on either side. At first there were only a few spread far apart, but these grew in number as they ascended. The air also became warmer—much warmer than outside—and strangely moist like the air of her mother's kitchen on days when fish stew simmered all day over the stove.

Even as she was noticing all this, the torches leading the way began to separate. Before she realized it, all but one torch disappeared. Elynna was alone with Thimeon, Chal-char, and two other of the Ceadani guides.

She did not want to be alone with Thimeon now. "Where are the others?" she demanded in a voice sharp, suspecting some plot on his part.

"We are being taken to separate dwellings," Thimeon explained. "You will stay here in Chal-char's home. In the morning, we will meet again." In a whisper he added, "You are being given a great honor."

Before she could reply, Thimeon headed off down a walkway with two of their guides, and Elynna was ushered through a heavy wooden doorway on her left. As one of the torchbearers lit a lantern on each wall, she got her first look at a Ceadani home. It was a huge square cave carved in the mountainside, about twenty feet wide and thirty feet deep, divided by a long woven blanket. The word *cave*, however, did it injustice, for though it was carved in rock, it looked just as warm and inviting as her own home had years earlier when her mother was still alive. There was beautiful wooden furniture: chairs, stools, tables, and shelves stacked with all sorts of useful pottery. Numerous hangings of woven tapestries and other artwork decorated the walls, and there were enough torches that nobody who wanted light would lack for it. And everything, however beautiful, looked meant for use.

"In the name of the Maker, welcome," Chal-char said in the common tongue, and he bowed.

His skin was tougher and more wrinkled than Elynna had first realized, and his white hair thinner. This made the brightness of his green eyes more compelling. There was something about him that she could not quite identify. It made her both feel safer than she had felt in many weeks and at the same time uneasy or unsettled. She must have stared at him for longer than she realized, for he bowed again and repeated his welcome. Elynna awkwardly returned the bow, but found she didn't know what to say. She was self-conscious—both of her lack of knowledge of the Ceadani culture and of how dirty and worn she must look. When she didn't speak, he motioned toward a table in the corner of the room where a small meal had already been prepared. He offered her a seat and said no more until she had been given ample opportunity to eat.

The meal was what Westwash Fisherfolk might have called light fare: warm bread, more hot drink, and a few thin strips of dried meats. In her present state, however, it was to Elynna a feast. She had no trouble consuming everything on the tray. All the while as she ate, Chal-char remained silent. Only when she had finished did he speak, and then only to offer more food. Now that she had something in her stomach, however, her fatigue returned. With words of thanks—almost the only words she had spoken in his presence—she declined the offer.

"Then," Chal-char began, as though reading her mind, "it is time for rest. I have many questions to ask you, for I desire to know about you and your company and how you came to fight the Daegmon. I can see from your skin and hear in your voice— few words though you have spoken—that you are from far away. You are not an Andan, as are some of your companions. Nor are you one of the Anghare. Perhaps you are from the lowlands?" He didn't wait for an answer. "Tomorrow will give us a time for questions. Now you shall sleep." He led her to a corner of the cave, where he parted a hanging woven fabric she had earlier taken only as a wall decoration. The opening revealed a small sleeping alcove off the main room. A small torch burned dimly in the far corner, giving off just enough light to move about the room. "Is there more I can offer you this night, other than sleep?"

Again Elynna declined. Her tongue had grown strangely heavy as if the mere mention of sleep had cast a spell upon her. Her eyelids began to close. Chal-char bowed once more, then turned and left. She stayed awake long enough to peel off her outer layer of clothing, now crusted with dirt and sweat. Then she lay down on the low mat of hay and fell asleep at once.

8

CATHWAIN

When Elynna awoke late the next morning, it was to the smell of something baking. Aroused by the delicious aroma, she rose from her bed and stretched, then looked around. The tapestry had been drawn back, and soft light streamed into her little sleeping alcove. Her few belongings still lay beside her mat where she had left them. However, next to her pack sat a bowl of fragrant water, still steaming, along with a pair of cloth towels. She splashed her face several times before drying off. Then she peered around the corner into the main room expecting to see Chal-char waiting for her, but she was alone. Only the fragrance of yeast and the bowl of water gave evidence that anybody had been there.

She looked back at the warm water. How long since she had last bathed? She couldn't even remember. It must have been in the rusted tub in her dingy quarters in Citadel. Such an opportunity was too good to pass up. She pulled the tapestry back over the door, peeled off the rest of her clothing, and for the first time in

119

many weeks washed her entire body. By the time she was done the water was brown with dirt. She shook her head in dismay.

If mother were still alive, she thought. Then she looked at her clothing. It was even dirtier and more worn than she remembered. All that remained clean in her entire pack was a single set of undergarments she had saved. She put them on, and then sat for a while longer staring at her pile of dirty raiment. Only when she heard voices returning to the house did she pull from her pack a lighter woolen tunic and trousers, slid them on quickly, and walked out into the main room.

Chal-char had returned. With him was a young woman of about fifteen summers. She had thick dark hair bound in braids halfway down her back and wore a long dress of some soft thick fabric. Silver chains that formed an intricate leaf pattern decorated each shoulder of her dress. It was belted at the waist with a wide black sash set with translucent green stones. The young woman, though slightly plumper in the middle than a young woman in the capital city would have wanted to be, was attractive. Her nose was small and straight, her ears delicate, and her figure full. She looked out from dark-green eyes that reminded Elynna of her own mother.

"This is my youngest granddaughter," Chal-char said. "Her name is Cathwain. She has come to offer you what service she can."

Elynna flushed with embarrassment at her own state. Somewhat self-consciously, she stood as straight as she could and tried to brush the wrinkles from her plain attire. Growing up in the Westwash, she had never thought of herself as plump or unattractive. But her time in Citadel had made her think differently—more self-consciously. And while the arduous journey had dried and toughened her skin, it had done little to help her figure. Whatever weight she had lost from the scarcer rations seemed to have come off in all the wrong places. Her hair, which she had not cut or tended in many weeks, hung snarled and limp down her back. Not that it had ever been beautiful, she thought. But at home in the Westwash, at least she had kept it washed and brushed, and trimmed to a manageable length, and even braided at times with fine braids pulled back over her ears. It would take a brush with bristles as thick as fishing spears to go through her hair now. And she was sure her face looked ten years older than it had before the attack. She wondered how Cane saw her. She was neither particularly attractive nor was she a skilled huntress like Tienna or a swordswoman like Hrevia. Whatever men of the Northland desired in a woman, she didn't imagine that she had any of it.

"I am pleased to meet you," she said awkwardly, and a little jealously.

Cathwain bowed her head politely as Chal-char spoke for her. "She is young, and has not yet come of age. But she speaks your tongue—better than she will admit," he added with a sideways glance, "and she was persistent in her offer. I thought you might be better tended by a woman your age than by an old man." Again there was a slight smile as he said this. "Besides, I am sure she will do better at fitting you." He paused as if searching for the right words. "When you have been fed, my granddaughter will bring you to the Gathering Place to join the others. We have proclaimed today a holiday and gathering. All of Gale Enebe will join together to celebrate your victory. We will talk more then." He turned and disappeared out the door, leaving Cathwain and Elynna staring at each other.

There was a long awkward moment before Cathwain said, "I will wash you?"

"I have already washed," Elynna answered.

"Your hair?" Cathwain asked.

Instinctively Elynna put her fingers to her hair, though already knew what state it was in. "My mother would have said a winter storm hit it, I think," she finally said. And to her own surprise, she laughed. "I think it's worse than that, though."

"I'm sorry! I did not mean to offend you."

"Don't worry," Elynna replied, still smiling. A lightness of mood was descending upon her. She had experienced nothing like it since her mother had died. "You are right. My hair does need washing. It is as stiff as spruce needles. I'm afraid there isn't much warm water left, though, and I couldn't ask you to wash it."

"Other things Gale Enebe may be lacking," Cathwain replied, "but hot water we have in plenty." She picked up the tub, which looked as though it weighed at least a quarter of her weight, and lugged it to a sink in the far corner of the room, where she refilled it from a continuously flowing tap in the wall. Before returning, she took a few yellow leaves from a pouch on the shelf and broke them into the water, releasing the now familiar fragrance into the room. "I will wash your hair now," she said.

Elynna objected, but the young Ceadani woman persisted. A short time later Elynna was leaning over backward with her head in warm water, enjoying a luxury she had not experienced in a long time.

"The clothes I brought you did not fit? Or perhaps you did not like them?" Cathwain asked when she was finished. There was a hint of disappointment in her voice.

"What clothes?"

Cathwain disappeared into the other room and returned with a pile of clothing made of colorful woven fabrics. She measured Elynna with her eyes, then pulled from the stack several items including tunics, trousers, and dresses. "I think these will fit you," she asserted, handing Elynna a dress much like her own, but without the patches on the shoulder.

Elynna hesitated an instant, then took the dress. The cloth was wonderfully soft to touch, more like the fur of a young otter than like anything woven. It made her own Westwash fabric feel coarse in comparison. She stood and held the dress up, wondering as she did what Cane would think of her in it. Then she looked back at the beautiful young woman in front of her. She put the dress down. "Perhaps the tunic and trousers," she said. "I am not pretty enough for this dress."

Cathwain frowned, but obeyed. Elynna, feeling suddenly ashamed of her body, took the clothes into the other room. They fit well and were as soft as they looked. Without ceremony, she threw her old clothes in a heap beside her pack. When she came back out, the washtub had been removed, and the small table was set for eating. She was treated to a meal similar to that of the previous night except the bread was heavier and served with slices of strong gyurt cheese.

As Elynna ate, Cathwain began querying her about her life. Where was she from, what sorts of foods did she eat, how old was she, and what was her family like? As Chal-char had suggested, his granddaughter's knowledge of the common tongue was quite sufficient, though her grammar was awkward at times. Her natural friendliness soon put Elynna at ease. Elynna found herself speaking comfortably of the rivers of the Westwash, and the great runs of silvery *kellen* and *grelsh* that moved up from the ocean to spawn. She named and described the different types of boats—the river floating *lalls* and the larger *shultees* used on the sea or in deeper rivers near the coast.

"I cannot imagine a body of water so big you cannot see across it," Cathwain exclaimed, her voice soft with awe. "Do you have a . . ." she stopped, as though searching for a word. "A husband? Or a man friend? Are you married? Or betrothed?"

"No," Elynna answered, partly ashamed that she had no betrothed, and partly ashamed that she would feel ashamed. She wondered if Cane would return to the Northland now that their quest was over. "No. I have no beloved."

Cathwain looked disappointed and fell silent. Elynna finished her meal, and Cathwain offered a glass of a hot gyurt's milk. Elynna accepted and sipped it slowly while Cathwain took the pottery dishes to rinse in a stone sink fed by the hot-water tap in the wall. "It is time to leave," the young Ceadani woman announced when she had finished cleaning up after the meal.

Elynna's face fell in disappointment. "Must we leave the village already?"

"No," Cathwain said with a smile. "Today is the Day of Celebration. As the Elder told you, we go atop the bluff to the Gathering Place. We will return here after dark."

Elynna breathed a soft sigh and nodded. She grabbed her heavy cloak from atop her pack and followed her young guide out the door. Exiting Chal-char's home, she took in her first daylight view of Gale Enebe. Expecting an underground maze of stone caves and tunnels, she was surprised by a broad swath of open sky directly in front of her. They were at least three hundred feet up the face of a bluff looking northeast. She was afraid to peer down over the edge. Nevertheless, the altitude put her at a great vantage point to view the surrounding land.

She had a magnificent view of the Ceadani highlands through which the company had spent several days trekking. Seeing it from a distance and knowing that the Daegmon was dead, it looked much less foreboding. Soon, however, her eyes were drawn further away and higher up the horizon. The sky above was clear and blue, and Illengond was visible far to the north. Even from this distance, its height was impressive. Snow covered its slopes from as low down as she could see almost to the summit. But its three stone peaks of solid rock were too sheer to hold snow. With a cloud nestled in the bowl between the peaks, it really did look like the crown of some ancient king. In the evening light, or beneath the light of a bright moon, the different veins of red, black, and blue-gray rock that twisted round each other appeared as jewels.

Some tales about the mountain had reached even down to the Westwash. But the Andani, who lived in the shadows of Illengond, were full of stories and beliefs about the great mountain. In her short time in the town of Aeti, and the somewhat longer time spent traveling with Thimeon, Theo, and the others of their people, she had heard many of them. Nobody had ever climbed high enough to look within that bowl between the three spires. Of if any had, they had never returned from the trip with the tale of that adventure. Some believed the mountain rose above even the thinnest of air. The top of Mountain Androllin, at only half the height of Illengond, was so high that those few who had approached its summit said it was hard to breathe.

But there was more to Illengond than its height. It had always been said to be the home of the All-Maker. It was considered a holy place by all of Gondisle.

Or it had been at one time. Fewer people believed in the All-Maker now, and she couldn't remember the last time any from the Westwash had taken a pilgrimage to the mountain. It was a long voyage.

Only when Cathwain spoke her name did Elynna lower her eyes from the distant mountain and turn toward the village itself. As Thimeon had told her, Gale Enebe was built into the cliff. The dwellings were carved out of the rock of the mountain. A stone walkway, wide enough for three people to walk abreast, wound along the cliff face in both directions, with several doors like Chal-char's opening into the rock. To the left, the cliff curved outward with several more doors and many levels of walkways above and below the one she was on. There were numerous window openings too, out of which some of the villagers were now looking.

"It is beautiful, is it not?" Cathwain asked.

"It is unlike anything I have ever seen," Elynna admitted. "Are there other Ceadani villages like this?"

"No other like this," Cathwain replied. Her face beamed with obvious pride. "These last many weeks, it has been good Gale Enebe so large and strong. Many fled here when homes destroyed by Daegmon."

"Is your family from here?"

Cathwain's face darkened. "My grandfather is my family now." An awkward moment of silence followed. But then her face brightened again. "Come. It is time we leave for Gathering."

She turned and began walking briskly in the opposite direction from which they had come the night before. Aware of the long drop off the edge of the stone walkway, Elynna followed keeping a step closer to the wall. They had gone a hundred feet, when Cathwain stopped and pointed to the rock. Inches from her fingertips, a line of steaming water trickled down the face. "This one is too small for use, but there are many more, some large and some small."

Elynna looked around. And for the first time she noticed dark smudges running down the wall every forty or fifty feet along the bluff where another spring came seeping through the stone, giving off a thin line of steam in the cold dry air. She turned back to her guide to ask a question, but Cathwain had already started off.

The walkway followed a gradual ascent along the face of the village. There were homes all around now. Some had wooden doors like Chal-char's, but most were hung with heavy skins or woven fabrics. A web of stone stairs led in and among them, connecting the levels. Some walks switched back and forth along the face of the cliff, while others disappeared into tunnels. There were also a myriad of balconies, windows, and terraces of one form or another. Most were carved into the rock, but a few, here and there, had been made of wood, cantilevered out from the rock face. What railings they had were mostly made of wood, but in many places there were no railings—just a sheer edge and a long drop. Elynna shuddered at the memory of her dark torch-lit ascent the evening before.

After a few minutes of walking, they turned left through an open archway into a darker tunnel that led to the bottom of an enclosed spiraling stairway carved into the rock. The stair was steep, and too narrow to walk side by side.

"We must climb for many minutes," Cathwain explained. "Are you ready?"

Elynna looked up the steep winding climb, unsure of the answer. But she did not want to admit that she was already feeling tired, so she bit her lip and nodded. At once her guide turned and started the climb. Elynna paused a moment longer and looked upward once again. Raised on the flatlands of West-wash, she was accustomed neither to strenuous climbing nor to being enclosed. However, anything was better than the dizzying heights of the open ledge along which they had just come.

Taking a deep breath, she plunged ahead. To her surprise, the air was warm and pleasantly moist, much more comfortable than the outside mountain air that had left her skin dry and cracked. And so, for a time, she enjoyed the climb. There were several doorways around the sides, and though she didn't see anybody, she thought she heard echoes of other footsteps. For much of the way the stair spiraled upward, but now and then it broke off at an angle or climbed straight for a long stretch before spiraling again. Elynna quickly lost her sense of direction, and after a time the doorways ceased. It grew even warmer then. She removed her outer cloak and climbed in her light Ceadani tunic.

In a few places the stairs widened, and then Cathwain would walk at Elynna's side. During those periods Cathwain spoke more about the village and its people. Since long before anybody could remember, Gale Enebe had been a gyurt-herding community, though they also had some sheep and hunted game in the fall— wild goats in the mountains, small deer, and an occasional bear. They grew only a few vegetables because of the poor mountain soil and short growing season. They were not a wealthy people so they did little trading, but they did barter with other Ceadani villages that had smaller herds but better soil for planting.

The conversation stopped and started several times. Cath-wain did most of the talking, but even she had to save her breath at the steepest portions of the climb, or cease talking when the passage grew too narrow. When they could walk side by side, and where the ascent was less strenuous, Cathwain would pick up right where she had left off, pausing only when she needed to search for a word, or ask Elynna whether her use of the trade language was wrong. Elynna corrected her now and then, but was too breathless to do much more than just listen.

Whenever they slowed or stopped to rest—which was always because of Elynna—they were passed by other villagers, usually traveling in groups of two or three or four. Some looked old enough to be her parents or grandparents, yet moved with the youthfulness of Cathwain. *"Thiuwa,"* they said as they passed, greeting Cathwain and Elynnna in the Ceadani tongue. Or sometimes *"Thiuwa Wa."*

"Thiuwa," Cathwain replied, to the younger ones. And at other times she replied, *"A ha le, Thiuwa."*

After a time—and with some coaching from her young guide—Elynna tried offering the same greeting, and those she greeted smiled broadly to hear their own tongue spoken, and went on to say more as though Elynna would understand. But equally often those passing by glanced in awe or curiosity at the stranger in their village, as though she was some sort of hero. Or perhaps even with some fear. Elynna did not feel like a hero. She had done very little in the battle, except to serve as bait. And others had died to protect her.

After some time, they passed the highest level of the village and there were no more places to rest. The constancy of the surrounding stone might have felt more oppressive had it not been for a series of stone paintings, mosaics, and engravings adorning the way. They were part of a continuing history of the village, Cathwain explained. There were a variety of styles among different artists working in different eras and in several mediums, and yet it still possessed a certain continuity.

"I have not yet learned all this history," Cathwain confessed. "But my grandfather comes here to study and meditate. I like to come with him and listen and look and talk. I don't think even he, though he is wisest of our elders in many generations, understands all of this story. He will ask me questions about what I think, or more often simply about how the art makes me feel." She stopped and paused before a striking mosaic of small brightly colored pebbles. It depicted a gyurtherd standing by a river. "My grandfather's questions, I think, are intended to teach me. But I believe he himself continues to learn, and he listens carefully to my answers."

Elynna, glad for a moment to rest her legs, nodded as she stood next to Cathwain and admired the mosaic. She had been too occupied by the climb to pay much attention to the murals or attempt to follow the thread of story they told. But when Cathwain started forward again a moment later, Elynna made the effort to pay more attention to the art. Now and then a particularly fascinating scene captured her attention, or else Cathwain would pause and explain some important character. In one large mural a huge winged creature flew high in the distant background. There were dark clouds around it, and in the foreground angry Ceadani warriors shaking spears. Elynna stopped and looked twice. She shivered, and wondered aloud if she was looking at a depiction of the Daegmon.

"I cannot answer," Cathwain admitted. "This one is very old, and I know little about it. Perhaps my grandfather can tell you."

Several works—elaborated painted murals, tapestries, simply drawing of shapes, and mosaics alike—had some depiction of Mount Illengond with its distinctive circular crown of three peaks. Some showed it from far away, its great mass towering over the landscape. Others depicted only the crown rising above the snow and clouds. In many of the later images, the peaks surrounded a hollow bowl. Elynna wondered how the artists knew to draw the mountain that way if nobody had ever actually looked in. Perhaps the bowl was just in the imagination of viewers, though the clouds that nearly always settled within the three peaks did seem to be held in some sort of hollow.

But Elynna could not linger too long to look, for Cathwain kept urging her on. "We've been climbing all morning," she grumbled, but Cathwain said they had been walking for less than the time it took to bake a loaf of bread, and that they would arrive soon. Elynna didn't complain again, but before they reached their destination, her legs were exhausted, her bruised ankles throbbed, and she felt ready to faint. Only her stubborn unwillingness to admit her fatigue in front of the young Ceadani woman kept her moving.

Eventually the stair came to a low arched doorway carved in the rock. On the other side of the door the way began to widen and abruptly ceased spiraling. They were now climbing along a natural chasm. Sunlight streamed down from above, and the blue sky became visible. Elynna drew on her last reserve of energy and finished the climb.

9

SANCTUARY

W e are here," Cathwain said in a soft voice full of awe. A strange light had come into her eyes as she spoke. Elynna looked around. They were on a small circular plateau about a hundred and fifty yards across. Steep rock walls with sheer cliffs rose hundreds of feet on three sides, cutting it off from the outside world. Only to the east did a narrow gap open in the walls. On that side, a thick cluster of evergreens guarded the small vale. It would have been impossible to find had she not been led there through the village, and the effect was one of solitude and protection.

Though she didn't know what it was or how to identify it, something about the place felt sacred. It was both beautiful and also strangely peaceful and solemn. She half expected to see eagles above her circling around aeries high on the stone. Only much later did she wonder why there was no snow and instead a thick spongy mosslike grass, blue-green in color.

"What is this place?" she asked after a moment's silence.

"The Sanctuary, it might be called in your tongue. Galena Ceati it is also called in ours." She paused. "I know not how to say it. It means 'gift of the Maker', but also the 'gathering place of the Maker.' But that sounds wrong in your language. It is the Maker's belonging, but it his people who gather there." She stopped and shook her head. "I think *Sanctuary* is better word. It is a holy place."

When Elynna did not respond, Cathwain continued. "All who are not too ill to come will be here. Chal-char has called us. Though tonight is a night of the new moon, and we are still twelve days from our festival of harvest moon, our elder has declared a victory feast of celebration. We will celebrate as though it were the yellow moon of harvest."

Elynna was about to ask more questions, when her eyes were drawn to the group of about sixty Ceadani on the far side of the bluff. Standing among them were Canc and Cathros. Cane's arm was splinted and bandaged, but otherwise he appeared to be in good health. Cathros looked even better, with no sign that he had even been in a battle the day before. Elynna walked over to join the two Northlanders, and Cathwain followed.

Cane greeted Elynna in his usual unemotional manner. She returned his greeting as warmly as she dared, and also introduced her guide, who blushed and bowed low. She turned to Cathros. His welcome was cheerier. He told her of his morning with his host, a young Ceadani shepherd, and how they had arisen early and traveled all around the village. "It is much larger than I would have guessed. The tunnels extend far back into the mountains."

"Do people dwell down deep?" Elynna asked. The thought of living far underground made her shiver.

"No. The dwellings are together near the front face. Most of the villagers' time is not spent under the rock at all but outside, where the gyurt and sheep are tended. There are various leas above as well as below the village, with a number of tunnels leading there. I think the tunnels may have been mines long ago, though I saw no sign of any remaining ore. My guide also said that in a long siege they would have plenty of cool storage for food, and no shortage of water. He also hinted that some of the tunnels lead to secret escape routes."

Cane, who was listening to his brother, shrugged. "The village is impressive, but as for the tunnels themselves, they are nothing in comparison to Anghatte mines where our father works. And he hasn't even begun to tap the deepest lodes."

Elynna continued to talk with Cathros and Cane about Gale Enebe and its inhabitants, and what life must be like here, and about how well they had been treated, while Cathwain listened. Tienna, hobbling on one foot with the help of a crutch, soon joined them, along with Thimeon, upon whom she occasionally leaned to rest her ankle. Others of the company followed in ones and twos, ascending from dwellings below and emerging on the plateau through one of two different stairways—the one Elynna had ascended and one other that came up against the cliff face and the eastern side. Soon, all the surviving companions were there, along with several hundred villagers.

The last to arrive was Chal-char. Only after all the others were gathered near the center of the plateau did he come up the eastern stair and onto the grassy lawn. When he entered their midst, the folk of Gale Enebe bowed their heads and ceased talking. Elynna followed their example. Meanwhile, Cathwain stepped up silently beside her and in whispers began to explain what was happening.

"He is our chieftain. The Elder, we call him, though the village has several elders, and all help to govern us. Still, he is the eldest of the elders, and counted the wisest. Few ignore his council. You were shown great honor to be his invited guest."

"Please tell him I *am* honored," Elynna responded absently.

"Few women have stayed in his house since the death of his daughter. He worried that you would not feel welcome."

"Where do you live?"

"I live with my father's sister and her husband. They have two daughters near my own age. I wanted to live with grandfather, but he thought it better I live with them."

Elynna stared at Cathwain for a moment as her words sank in. Then it dawned on her. "Chal-char's daughter? That was your mother?"

Cathwain nodded.

Elynna closed her eyes and swallowed. Had this young girl experienced the same tragedy? It took her a moment before she could bring herself to ask, "And your father too?"

Cathwain did not answer. Chal-char had come to the middle of the gathering and all was silent. He turned, and one at a time faced the four corners of the compass to bow to his people. They returned his bow, then sat, leaving the Elder standing in the center. All eyes were upon him now, yet for a time he said nothing. His face was still and serene, like the rock surrounding him.

As she looked at him, something stirred in Elynna. When he finally began, it was not so much a speech as a song or chant. He lifted his hands to the heavens, and in the language of the Ceadani intoned a long sort of invocation. Others of the Ceadani also lifted their hands, and some were moving their lips. It was obvious the words were known to them. Elynna, though she did not understand the words, had the impression of something sacred.

"It is a prayer to the Maker," Cathwain whispered. "Words of thanksgiving and praise." Beyond that, however, she never translated this part of the celebration. The young girl's eyes were closed and her hands were uplifted. When the Elder was done, he lowered his hands. He paused while the folk of the village opened their eyes and raised their heads. Then, in a voice seasoned with age but still loud, he began to speak again still in the language of the Ceadani.

"What is he saying?" Elynna asked, when she could wait no longer.

"He is speaking to our people now," Cathwain whispered. "He tells them of your victory over the Daegmon, and how you have freed us. He speaks also of the loss of your companions. There is more he says, but I know not how to put all in words. Perhaps he will say the same to you."

Elynna nodded and waited. Several minutes passed before Chal-char finished. By this time, several of the Ceadani villagers were murmuring. Finally Chal-char turned and faced Elynna. Their eyes met and he bowed again.

"We greet you," he began in the trade tongue. Others of his folk echoed the greeting, and several reached out to welcome the companions nearest them. "You have come to us as foreigners—a strange company of many different peoples from across Gondisle." He spoke with a slow rhythmic intonation that added weight to his words. "As strangers you have come among the Ceadani and brought our deliverance. We thank you and

welcome you. Be strangers no longer." There was another murmur of approval from the gathered villagers. He quieted them
with his hands and went on. "For many weeks we have suffered
oppression. Torment and hardship the Daegmon brought upon
us, as it did of old in the days long before even our grandfathers'
grandfathers when Gale Enebe was first built."

A chill ran down Elynna's spine. More folktales of the Daegmon from the Gondisle of days long past? Entranced, she closed
her eyes and felt the power of Chal-char's voice. "In those days
there were mighty warriors who arose from our midst, and lasting alliances were forged among the peoples. The Ceadani and
Andani were brothers, along with the Fisherfolk of Westwash and
all the peoples of the Plains. Even the Undeani joined their fellow
Highlanders in this fellowship. At our head came the warriors of
the Northland, who had raised up a king to lead the peoples of
Gondisle. Thus we prepared even as our enemy gathered itself to
destroy us all. Up from the south, from the stronghold of Entain,
came the Daegmon and with it a vast host ready to cast down
the mountains themselves. Great was the army of Gondisle and
powerful were those who led it, but greater still was our enemy,
until the Maker Himself came upon mighty Illengond and drove
the enemy away."

The histories flowed across Elynna's vision until she heard
words no longer but saw instead images of faces and changing landscapes, and Gale Enebe grew old and her origins were
forgotten, and Citadel was raised and the king grew strong.
Centuries flowed past, and for a time the Daegmon was forgotten. But then, just a few fortnights ago, it had appeared again at
the gates of Gale Enebe, attacking and killing a small band of
shepherds as they returned home for the evening. Then came a

second attack more savage than the first. While the wise of the village sought the old histories for a name of this new tormentor, three of the mightiest warriors of Gale Enebe were sent out to defeat it. None returned. Other Ceadani villages also encountered the same enemy and were destroyed. No help was to be found. Countless warriors from scattered Ceadani villages had fought vainly against the beast, leaving mothers widowed and children orphaned. At last Chal-char had forbidden the people from trying to fight while he continued to search the lore for tales of their enemy. For long days they had been forced to live in terror and in hiding. More refugees had fled to Gale Enebe, the only safe haven. Yet even there, beneath the stone, they dwelt in fear. Harvests were destroyed. Gardens and crops razed. The early winter had come upon them. Until the All-Maker had heard their cries of distress and sent Elynna and her company of great warriors to rescue them.

Of the battle itself, Chal-char said little. He had heard accounts of it that morning, perhaps from Cane or Cathros, but he did not dwell on the details. He spoke instead of the bravery of Braddoc and the others who died, as Elynna struggled to hold back tears. Then he spoke of the final joy of deliverance, and of the goodness and protection of the one whom his people called the Maker, but whom others knew as the All-Maker, who dwelt in Mount Illengond.

All the while Elynna listened as if it were somebody else's story, barely noticing when the speech came to an end. When she realized that all had become silent, she lifted her eyes and saw that several other elders had risen to join Chal-char in the middle of the clearing. They gathered together in a circle facing inward with hands clasped. The rest of the folk of Gale Enebe also rose to their feet. The elders then spoke in softer voices, one at a time, and at the end all raised their voices together in a common chant. When they were done, there was a moment of silence.

Then the celebration erupted. There was no announcement. No invitation or formality. The food simply appeared as if it had sprung from the ground or fallen from the skies. Baskets of bread in small dark nutty loaves. Jugs of wine. Blocks of cheese. Pastries of meats and dried fruits and pies of nuts. Elynna stood staring in astonishment, wondering where it had come from, until she saw Cathwain looking at her and giggling.

"Eat. It is time," the beautiful young Ceadani woman said.

"Where on earth—?"

"It is part of tradition—the mystery of the feast," she said with a laugh. Then her voice grew more serious. "It is a feast that is to remind us of the mystery of how the Maker provides."

Elynna nodded. Then she realized Cathwain hadn't answered the question. "But who . . . ? How . . . ?" She never finished. Her question was lost in the noise. All around her, the folk of Gale Enebe were now moving about—laughing, talking, and singing. She spotted Cane and Cathros engaged with some villagers who spoke the trade tongue. She watched Cane for a moment, aching to talk with him. Then she turned away.

With Cathwain at her side, she found Falien, Pietr and Siyen—her fellow Westwash Fisherfolk—if Siyen could really be counted as such. They greeted her and exchanged comments about the celebration. All of them were smiling. At Cathwain's urging, the five of them sat down to sample the fare. It was as varied as it was abundant. Although she was not overly fond of the strong flavor of their meats—lamb and goat and gyurt and wild game—or of the spices they used to preserve them, the rich pastries and varieties of cheeses were extravagant. And then she discovered the dark-brown bittersweet morsels the likes of which she had never before tasted. The treats seemed made to go with the hot drink she had tasted the night before, which also flowed in abundance. For the first meal in many weeks she was not longing for some good Westwash fish.

Meanwhile a group of musicians had risen and scattered to various corners of the gathering, where they began performing. Elynna counted twelve of them. Four played flutes, two of them carried small Ceadani harps, and the other six performed on an instrument Cathwain named a *cindel*—a lute similar to those played in the taverns of Citadel but wider, deeper, and with seven strings instead of five. There were both men and women musicians, and all wore the same uniform of bright red with blue sleeves and a heavy fur headband. They were scattered around the bluff, each playing for a different group, but from time to time they moved from one place to another so that before the afternoon was over, everybody had the chance to hear them all.

The beauty of the strings particularly overwhelmed Elynna, who had grown up where the only common instruments were twelve-note reed flutes. Each musician was playing a different tune, but whenever she was in a place to hear more than one, she noticed that they were in harmony and rhythm with one another and that the same melodic themes were weaving in and out of all the songs, though with different variations. After a time she suspected they were all playing different parts of the same song rather than different songs. Yet, for her lack of training— or maybe because of the subtlety of the musicians' skills—she couldn't quite put the pieces together. Only much later in the day, when all the musicians found their way together, did she discover that they were indeed playing a single grand symphony, harmonizing with one another with intricate overlapping themes. How they had managed to keep in time while scattered over the bluff, she never did discover.

By the time the musicians had gathered back together into a small group, most of the folk of Gale Enebe had also come together in one large ring filling the center of the Sanctuary. It was early afternoon. The sky was clear and the air warm. Elynna had long since abandoned her cloak. The icicles on the ledges were melting as though spring had returned, and with it hope. There was still food left and plenty of drink, but not many were still eating. All were content to listen to the music. And for just that short while, such was the power of the music and the serenity of the place and the hospitality of the Ceadani that hardship and loss were forgotten.

Then came an end to the music but not to the celebration. Before Elynna even had time to sigh, the musicians disappeared and the storytellers emerged. Again there were twelve of them. They were dressed in brightly colored cloaks, each different from the rest, but all with a dark blue sash around their middle. Like the musicians, they moved to different spots around the ring and commenced with their stories. The folk of Gale Enebe had been waiting for this part of the celebration, and silence fell over the group. Only the voices of the storytellers could be heard above the sough of breeze through the cliffs above.

Most of these storytellers were speaking in their own Ceadani tongue, but for the sake of the visitors to the village, there was almost always at least one within Elynna's hearing speaking the trade language. The stories were about heroes of Ceadani folklore. Some were short tales or poems, while others lasted several minutes. What made it confusing was that all the while they were speaking, they were continually weaving around the ring so that all twelve passed in front of Elynna several times. If they had moved at the beginning and end of the stories it would have been fine, but the movement, though slow, was continuous.

Only when she paid careful attention did she begin to see that this too had a pattern. All the stories were somehow interconnected—as if each teller knew what the other had told and where to take up with a new tale, or how the two tales were woven together—so that the story also had the effect of one large symphonic history that spanned the whole of Gondisle, with mention of the Maker or All-Maker and of Illengond his holy mountain woven through it all. And though she sensed that much or all of it was true history, not a moment of it was boring. Her only regret was that she did not understand the Ceadani tongue, and so much of what was told she missed.

This part of the feast lasted close to two hours, but there was still food and plenty of hot drink. At the end of that time all the storytellers also came together in the middle, and their voices grew in volume. By then there was no surprise that they were all telling the same story. Or rather, fragments of the same interconnected story, which was the history of the Ceadani, and Gondisle, and the Maker, and Mount Illengond, and several other interwoven themes. Not that they were using the same words, or even the same names or language, but like the songs sung by the earlier musicians, it all somehow fit together in a strangely fascinating way Elynna later found difficult to describe. Whatever it was, it was an amazing thing to watch, and she could have listened all day and into the night.

When Cathwain apologized that they were not as good as usual because of their struggle to use the trade language, Elynna could only laugh. "I can't imagine how it could be any better than this. I have never heard anything like it."

Finally the storytelling came to an end. The sun had dipped halfway to the horizon. There was a short time of quiet conversation and contemplation, and then Chal-char arose again to speak. He stood in the center of the gathering facing directly toward Elynna. All fell quiet. When he spoke it was in the Ceadani tongue. Cathwain translated for Elynna and the few of her companions who sat nearby.

"The feast must soon draw to an end, but the most important part still remains. The setting of the sun is but two hours away. Then we will celebrate the *Valqui*."

It took a few seconds for Elynna to realize they were awaiting her reply. "What is the . . . the Valqui? I do not know that word."

At a nod from her grandfather, Cathwain explained. "When the last hunt of the season has ended and the harvest is complete, we carry through the village the best of the produce and game. It is part of the celebration. We remember how we have been—" She paused, searching for a word. She turned toward Thimeon, who stood a few paces away, and said something to him in her own tongue.

"They acknowledge how they have been blessed," Thimeon said in a soft voice.

Cathwain repeated the word. "*Blessed*. Yes. We give thanks to the Maker for his provision." She paused again. "Do you have nothing like this among your people?"

Elynna thought for a moment. "Well, in the evenings during fishing season, when all the boats have returned safely from the sea, each family gives thanks for the bounty of fish and for the deliverance from harm. Sometimes we gather together as a village and do this together."

Cathwain smiled. "Then you understand well what I will say next, for you have spoken not only of provision but also of deliverance from your enemies. Though I have not seen it in my time—it has been more than a generation since any foe has attacked us—we have the same tradition during times of war and pestilence. When deliverance comes, we bear in parade the weapons of our defeated foes so that we may celebrate the gift of freedom. So you see . . ." She hesitated and searched Elynna's face. "The elders thought you would cut the head or claws off the Daegmon, or retrieve some other token of its death, and bring it through the village after the setting of the sun. In seeing our vanquished foe, we could again thank the Maker for deliverance."

As Cathwain spoke, Elynna's heart sank. She did not reply for several long moments, but stood in awkward silence. The deep peace that had enfolded her all day began slipping away. She turned to look for help and found Thimeon standing beside her. She was part annoyed and part relieved. "Did you understand what he said?" she asked him.

He met her pleading gaze and said softly, "I did. It is an important tradition, as Cathwain has told you."

She cursed him under her breath. "Four of my companions died in that battle. I have no desire to return to the scene."

"Nor do I, but I will go."

"I can't," she said firmly. "I will not look upon it again, dead or alive. You go if you want."

Before Thimeon could reply, Chal-char spoke again. He was still using the Ceadani tongue, and Cathwain had to translate again.

"The Elder says you are under no—" She paused again searching for a word. This time, however, she did not need Thimeon's help. "No duty. It is a rite to our people only. Yet such traditions are not taken lightly. We must remember." Then she added more softly and personally, "Elynna, it is an honor that you are asked. As the leader of your people, you were the means of a great deliverance not just for the Ceadani but for all the people of Gondisle. This is not a time that should ever be forgotten."

"I can't—" Elynna started to say.

At that moment Cane stepped forward. "I will go."

The voice and the offer startled Elynna. Such was the confidence and strength Cane radiated that Elynna half expected him to toss his splint and bandage aside and flex a fully healed arm.

"Why?" she asked. The moment the word was out of her mouth, she wished she had not spoken it.

"Let us show them that they have nothing more to fear."

Elynna stared at him a moment. She turned toward Tienna hoping to find some sympathy. But the huntress, who lay on a stretcher with her leg in a splint, looked as though she wanted nothing more than to jump up and join Cane. Indeed, her expression suggested she was seriously considering a way she could do it.

"You need not go," Cane said to Elynna.

Elynna thought there was a hint of disdain in his voice.

Thimeon repeated Cane's words but with greater gentleness. "You need not go. Your ankle is still weak, and even if the descent is not difficult, you will still have to climb back up all the stairs."

Elynna nodded. But the truth was, although the climb that morning had been tiring and caused a dull ache, her ankles had not bothered her since arriving at the Gathering Place. However she had reinjured herself in battle when she fell from the boulder, something about the salve they had applied that night before, and even more about the very air of this place, had a healing effect. She closed her eyes. What would the people of the village think of her if she refused? What would Cane think?

She looked at him, eager to depart on this trip. "I will go too," she said.

A short time later, she, Cane, and Thimeon departed with Cathwain as their guide. Though the sun would disappear soon behind the high cliff walls that enclosed them to the west, it would still be three hours and a little more before it set somewhere far off in the west. They would be able to make the descent in daylight, and if they did not delay long, Cathwain thought they would have time to reach the canyon and be back not long after dusk. Cane's sword had been broken in the battle, but Thimeon—perhaps knowing something of the Ceadani traditions—had brought his long hunting knife with him and left it near one of the stairs. He picked it up now, and then turned to follow Cathwain.

Rather than descending the stair, Cathwain led them toward the one gap in the surrounding rock walls where a hidden trail disappeared through a low hedge in the midst of a thick stand of trees. There they followed a steep trail down the eastern face of a bluff through a hidden defile. The way was difficult, but in places where the going might have been dangerous, a stair had been cut in the stone. And though Elynna's ankles began again to ache dully, the Ceadani boots she now wore supported them well, and she did not suffer a fall. After a lengthy descent, they arrived at the bottom and stepped out through another dense thicket. They were back on the trail they had hiked the night before, a good bit of the way in the direction of the ravine. Looking back up the steep slope of the defile, Elynna saw no sign of a trail.

"It is well hidden," Cathwain said. "Come. We still have some distance to go, and we should return not too long after sunset when the great fire is being lit."

Elynna nodded and turned to follow. It was a solemn walk. Thimeon had become strangely quiet. Cane was his usual grave self. Even Cathwain, who had been talkative through the day, had fallen silent. Elynna said nothing. She kept to herself as she trudged along a few steps behind the others. When they came to the head of the ravine, she had to stop. Even in the remaining daylight something was frightening. She had almost screwed up her courage to continue, when she felt an uncomfortable tingling of her added sense. It was light and disappeared almost at once, but Thimeon must have seen her expression. "What is it?" he asked.

"I don't know."

"I've seen that look before."

"No," she told him. "It isn't *that*." But she was not so sure herself. Maybe it *was* the Daegmon she was sensing. Was that possible? Wasn't it dead?

"Are you sure?"

"Yes," Elynna said, more to assure herself than the others. "I thought I felt something. But not like before. It's just that I wish— I wish we didn't have to do this."

"I think we should. This is not just for Chal-char. He would understand if we didn't. But something about the old tales we heard today and the paintings in the village make me nervous."

"I do not understand," Cathwain interrupted.

"It's okay," Elynna said. "We will go on."

Thimeon took the lead, and they started down the trail. It dropped steeply beside a small waterfall. Before they had even reached the bottom of the first slope, a harsh odor assailed their nostrils. It was the whiff of decay Elynna had smelled immediately after the battle; only, it was much stronger now. "What is *that*?" Cathwain asked, wrinkling her noise.

If the others guessed, they did not say. A few dozen yards down, the ravine snaked to the right. The smell was growing stronger. They came around the bend past another series of smaller cascades. Then the path flattened out. They could see ahead of them the back of the large boulder where Elynna and Cane had stood awaiting the Daegmon. The stream forked to the right, while the trail veered left over a mountain of debris. The ground was covered with their own footprints. The four of them paused. Both Cane and Thimeon had stern expressions. Nobody spoke. Thimeon strode a few paces ahead. He was the first past the boulder. "May Illengond rise up and shield us!" he cried.

Cane rushed to his side, and Elynna and Cathwain joined them a second later. All they could do was stand there. Confused, Cathwain asked, "Is this not where the battle was? The Elder said it was beyond this boulder."

Elynna thoughts went blank. There was no explanation for what she now saw. Or for what she didn't see. She was not sure whether she should be relieved or terrified. Instead she just felt numb, and she could only force herself to say, "It was."

"Then where is the creature's body?"

That was the question. And Elynna had no answers or insights. "I don't know."

She had not wanted to see the Daegmon again. Not even its corpse. But to find it gone? What could that mean?

The signs of the battle were still clear: broken spears, shards of a shattered blade, hundreds of footprints, and debris everywhere. Except, in the place where the Daegmon's body had fallen, there was now only a large black patch of charred dirt. In every direction the oily ash covered the ravine. From it all there arose a vile stench. Even the stream looked dark and cloudy. But there was no sign of the Daegmon's body.

10

THE ENEMY

Thimeon was the first to venture past the boulder. Cane followed a step behind. Elynna did not move. She looked down at the smeared prints left by their boots in the soot-stained soil. "Don't go down there!" she wanted to tell her young host, but Cathwain was already moving to join the others.

Ahead Thimeon stooped to examine the ground. He dislodged something with his boot, looked it over without touching it, then continued on searching for more clues.

"Come back," Elynna pleaded. A terrible premonition of danger had come over her. But her soft voice was lost beneath the steady rumble of the stream and the whine of wind in the rocks above. If the others heard her, they did not heed.

Cane had already passed Thimeon and was walking down the ravine. Thimeon was moving more slowly, studying the ground. Cathwain was close behind him now. When he bent over to examine something else, she asked a question. Elynna heard only Thimeon's reply. "I do not know. It may be. It is what I fear."

He straightened and looked around. Then he turned to his right and strode to the stream.

Elynna took a few stumbling steps forward. Her legs had no strength, and she felt like vomiting. But she did not want to be left behind. And she needed to know what the others were saying. As she passed the spot where Thimeon had first stopped, she saw what he had dislodged with his boot. It was a broken spear shaft half hidden in the soot. Braddoc's. The one that had impaled the Daegmon. She recognized it. The head had snapped off, leaving it more like the shepherd's staff it once had been. It was where the Daegmon had been, but where was it now? She moved more quickly and caught up to Cathwain and Thimeon beside the stream.

"Why is it so murky?" the young Ceadani woman was asking. "We've had no flooding upstream." She reached down to touch the water.

Thimeon caught her by the wrist before she could. "Don't," he said in a gentle but firm voice.

Cathwain withdrew her hand quickly. "What's wrong?"

"I don't know, but this is not silt. The water *is* clear upstream. Something here is fouling it. I have no doubt that it is the source of this stench. Don't touch it." He moved downstream to where Cane stood staring up at the ledges above.

"I do not like this place," Cane said, when Thimeon approached. "The smell has grown worse."

Thimeon nodded but said nothing. After a moment he shook his head in disgust, then turned and started back toward Elynna and Cathwain. Cane followed him.

"Let us depart from here," Elynna pleaded again.

Cane started to reply, but the words died on his lips when he saw her looking toward the sky. Thimeon had turned pale. An instant later, the four of them were walking briskly up the steep trail.

It was a long, painful walk back. Not until they were nearly back to the village did Cathwain venture to speak. "You do not understand what this means, but you are afraid?"

"I am afraid," Elynna admitted.

"This creature—the Daegmon. Yesterday was not the first time you fought it?"

"It was not."

"Why—"

"It destroyed my village."

Cathwain's voice grew soft. "Did you have any family?"

"I had a brother. And a father. It killed my father."

"And your mother?"

"She died when I was young."

Cathwain nodded. "The Daegmon has attacked other Ceadani villages, but we have been safe at Gale Enebe." She was quiet again for a minute. They passed the hidden entrance to the ravine trail, but she did not turn aside. "We will go back through the village. This path is difficult to ascend, and the ravine will grow very dark. There are torches on the stairs in the village. The stairs will be easier."

Elynna looked up. The first stars had already appeared in the east, and the moon was just rising. She was startled to see it dark blue. She had lost track of the long days of the pale moon. Then she remembered what Cathwain said earlier. It was the first night of the moon's forty-day cycle—the start of the eighth month.

It would be blue for three nights: dark blue tonight, then tomorrow night a brighter blue, like the Lienwash when it was running clear on a summer day or like the petals of the wild river roses, and finally on the third night a pale blue like the morning sky. Then on the fourth night of the cycle it would enter its longer green phase. Eight days it would be green before finally returning to its most familiar pale yellow. Where would she be when next she saw it pale?

She thought back on the last time the blue moon had risen and the cycle had started anew. Forty days ago. They had been in Aeti then, staying with Theo's family on their big farm. It was the last time the company had all slept beneath solid roofs: some in the farmhouse and some in the barn, but all warm and secure and well fed. The following morning they departed on their quest to find and destroy the Daegmon. They had been resupplied with food and warmer clothing. Thimeon's pretty little sister Siarah had helped her aunt, Theo's mother, make a big breakfast for the whole company. And then Siarah had spent the entire meal sitting next to her brother pleading with him to take her with him. He had resolutely denied her request. He would have denied Theo, also, if he had been allowed. But Theo's own father had spoken to Thimeon. "I know he is young, but his heart will not be denied. And though he is no warrior, he has some skill that may be of service."

"I cannot guarantee he will return," Thimeon had replied. "It may well be that none of us will return."

Thimeon's aunt and uncle both had tears in their eyes. "We understand. And if he does not come back, we will miss him greatly. But the All-Maker would not have us hold back even our own son. And we both have a sense he will be wanted on the quest."

Thimeon had relented, though it made it even more difficult for him to say no to Siarah.

Then two days after that, the last two members had joined the company: Braddoc and Llana. Llana, who was not much older than Siarah, and who before coming on this quest had never strayed more than a few miles from her small mountain village. If her parents had not died in a Daegmon attack two moons earlier, she would still be at home carrying cooking water from a creek and tending goats. Llana and Braddoc, who would never return to their homes.

And now they could not find the body of their foe. The thought crept into Elynna's mind. *Had their deaths been in vain?*

"We will have to tell the others." Cane's voice, quiet but clear, carried up from behind.

The pit in Elynna's stomach grew larger. Thimeon stepped up beside her and put his hand on her shoulder. She pulled away and gave him a reproachful glance. "Please," she said, as if that word explained everything.

He pulled his hand back. "I only wanted to offer to tell the others so that you would not have to. Cane is right that we must tell them. Yet it will be difficult. We just don't know . . ." His voice faded.

Elynna closed her eyes for a moment, trusting her feet to carry her. "I was the leader. I will tell them."

"Even an ox yoke is made for two. Will you not share this burden?"

"Not with you," she replied crisply. Before he could speak again, she accelerated past his reach and caught up with Cathwain.

Sometime later, the four of them had entered the base of the village and begun the long ascent up the stairway through the network of paths and tunnels in the elaborate rock dwellings of Gale Enebe. They passed behind the village and for a time saw the many doors on one side or another. Then the side doors came to an end and the artwork began. Thimeon, who had earlier ascended by the other stair, stopped in amazement at the image of the great flying creature. But Elynna did not want to look at it again and pressed on with the others, and he soon joined them.

By the time they reached the top, tired and out of breath, the sky had grown dark. It would be many hours before the dark blue of the new moon had risen high enough to peek down over the high rock walls of the place. Dozens of torches, some set on poles and some in holders in the rock walls, lit the enclosed lea. The air had cooled, but the hollow was sheltered from the wind. In the center of the clearing a large fire burned, adding to the light of the torches. Around it sat most of the companions listening to the musicians and storytellers. A few other smaller fires glowed around the perimeter. Cane went at once to his brother's side and whispered something in his ear. Cathros's expression gave no hint as to what had been said. Cathwain also disappeared. Elynna stood for a moment listening to the melodic language of the Ceadani carrying across the grass over the crackling of flames. Thimeon stepped beside her again. "Let me tell—" he tried.

"No," Elynna replied, yanking her arm free of his grip. Her voice was bitter. "I don't need your help. Just leave me alone."

She turned and stepped toward the crowd of villagers. One of the women storytellers, accompanied by a musician strumming a cindel, was singing a story. Chal-char sat beside her translating the tale for the visitors. When he saw Elynna approach, he motioned for the song to end. All eyes turned expectantly toward Elynna, waiting for her to produce some visible sign of their victory. Instead, she just shook her head. It was all she could do to keep from shouting at them.

It took a moment for the gathered crowd to understand what she was telling them—to read it in her numbed expression, or surmise it from the fact that she had nothing to show. Whether she actually said anything at all, she didn't remember. Her mind went blank. It was as if she were a distant observer watching herself speak, and not quite hearing all that was said. There were a few seconds of surprised silence during which her other companions as well as the villagers stood in confusion, not sure what to make of everything. Then the questions began.

"What happened?"

"Why have you returned?"

"What does it mean?"

"How can this be?"

It took many minutes to convince the companions that the Daegmon's body had disappeared. Even when Cane and Thimeon verified her words, many were incredulous. Everybody wanted an explanation, but nobody had one to offer. They began to crowd around. Elynna grew dizzy. *No*, she agreed, *there had not been enough time for all traces of the body to have been devoured by wild animals. What wild animals would eat such a carcass? Nor could such a large creature have been dragged away or washed away. Something different had happened.* But what? She was on the edge of falling now. Her thoughts were drifting.

Chal-char's voice was the last she heard. "In days of old," he said sadly in his slow, heavy speech, "the wise of our village knew the meaning of these things. I grieve the loss of many of my people's tales."

The next thing Elynna knew, she was lying on her back close to one of the fires. Somebody had covered her with a blanket, and Cathwain sat by her side. She tried to rise, but the pain in her head prevented it. "Lie still a while longer," the girl said. "You have fainted from exhaustion. When you are ready, I will give you something to drink."

Elynna nodded. She closed her eyes and put her head back down and listened to the voices. Cane's was loudest. "Let us search for the carcass farther downstream, beyond the scene of the battle."

"No," Chal-char answered. "You will not find it, I think."

"How can you know without looking?" Cane asked. "If you knew, why did you send us the first time?"

The Elder did not answer. Others spoke. Some agreed with Cane and some were not sure, but none had any desire to return to the defile. "Then I will return alone," Cane said in a taut voice.

"I will go with you, Brother," Cathros added. His was one of the few calm voices in the group. "Yet I believe in my heart what Chal-char has said. We will find no body. The beast is gone."

"Is there nothing to be done?" Hrevia asked, her voice tinged with despair.

A long silence followed. Elynna finally sat up and looked around. She did not know how long she had been lying down. Or, if she had fainted, how long she had remained unconscious. The fires were burning much lower now. Only Chal-char, Cathwain, and a few older Ceadani villagers remained with the companions. Others were milling about in groups here and there. Most had gone back to their homes. It was Hruach who answered his sister.

"Why must we do anything? We have defeated the creature. We saw its lifeblood spilled onto the ground. We saw with our own eyes the fall of the Daegmon. Did we, or did we not? Surely we have not suffered in vain."

Hrevia continued where her brother had left off. "No. It was not in vain. Do not question what our companions have given their lives for. We saw the victory with our own eyes." What the Anghare woman said next made Elynna choke back a sob. "Do not say that Llana, Braddoc, Llian, Annat, and Jamesh all died without cause." How much Elynna wanted to believe that! And how afraid she was that the words were *not* true.

"You speak the truth," Cane agreed. His voice was fierce as he reversed his previous decision to return to the site of the battle. "It was not in vain. We won the battle. We need not return."

But Thimeon and Chal-char were shaking their heads. A short time later the Gathering ended with the burials of four slain companions in a Ceadani tomb atop the high plateau. They also honored Llana; though they had no body to bury, her name was carved in the face of the rock. Then they dispersed. Elynna returned alone to Chal-char's home, where she lay awake long into the night.

The company stayed two more days at Gale Enebe, recovering from the wounds of battle, the grief of loss, and fatigue from many days of hard travel. Elynna spent most of that time in Chal-char's home with Cathwain. When she ventured out into open spaces, she caught glimpses of her companions standing on the balconies in twos or threes, or gathered in larger groups on the terraces and common spaces. But she did not often join them, for—though she would not admit it to the others—she was not comfortable on the high exposed walkways of the village. When she did join them, she stayed as far from the cliff face as possible and kept her back pressed against a wall. And she added little to their conversations, which were mostly about their various plans for going home. Elynna had no plans. She was not ready to make any.

Her discussions with Cathwain were mostly about the village. Many refugees began departing the village the day after the Gathering, making their way home now that the Daegmon had been defeated. Others chose to stay at Gale Enebe, for they had no homes to return to. Chal-char's people, meanwhile, simply returned to their daily lives: gyurt herding, gathering a few root crops still in the ground, preparing for winter, raising children, caring for the sick and wounded, telling stories, making art, cooking and eating food. The Ceadani, as Elynna learned, loved cooking and art, especially song and story. "I have heard strangers visiting our villages say that our lives are hard," Cathwain said. Just in the course of two days, her comfort with the trade tongue had grown considerably. "That it is a demanding and unforgiving land we dwell in. And yet despite that—or perhaps because of it—my people devote much time to the making of art."

Elynna thought about that for a time. The Fisherfolk of Westwash also worked hard. The land—and the sea even more than the land—demanded it. During the long, late summer days when the grelsh were running, they worked from the first hint of morning light until the stars were out, slept but a few hours, and started again. But her people were not artists. They sang simple songs in the evenings, but paintings and tapestries such as the Ceadani had were not found in the Westwash. But then she thought about it more, and an image came to her mind, and with it an answer. "My people do craft fine boats," she said. "They are works of art, with thought given to beauty as well as to strength and function."

Cathwain nodded, and the conversation turned to other things.

Though she was staying in his home, Elynna did not see much of Chal-char during the daylight hours. Since the Gathering, he had become preoccupied with old village scrolls and tapestries. Or so Cathwain had said. On the first day he did not appear in his home until late in the afternoon after the sun had disappeared behind the mountains to the west. His granddaughter seemed to be expecting him, though, for she had set three places at the table for supper. He arrived as she was finishing preparations for their evening meal: a rich stew of sausage, herbs, and roots served with hearty bread and gyurt cheese.

After the meal they sat for a few minute and drank the hot Ceadani tea, and he asked Elynna a few questions about the West-wash. Though he had heard about the sea—Gondisle's Womb, as the Ceadani referred to it in story—he had not seen it except once from afar, standing in some gap in the southern mountains looking down the Ana River Valley at a distant blue expanse. The sea was not even depicted in the art of the Ceadani. He listened as Elynna spoke of boats and fishing nets and tides and weather, and was surprised to hear that snow rarely fell on the ground in the Westwash except in parts far inland and upriver. "I always think of snow as forgiveness."

Cathwain and Elynna both looked at him curiously. "Why, Grandfather?" the younger one asked.

"It is a beautiful thing," he explained, "though sometimes difficult to accept. And it covers many wounds and scars."

Chal-char departed soon after, and did not return again that evening. Nor was he there the following morning when Elynna awoke and broke her fast with a bowl of hot grains in gyurt milk. She did not know if he had slept that night in his home or somewhere else. Or perhaps not at all.

The second day he returned again just as Cathwain—this time with help from Elynna—was finishing preparation of the evening meal. His granddaughter had a friendly scold in her voice. "What have you been doing all day?"

"Still puzzling over a riddle," he answered.

Elynna had a guess what the riddle was, but she did not wish to talk about it. He kissed his granddaughter on the forehead, gave a blessing to both her and his guest, and sat down for a meal as Cathwain laid it out on the table. It was Elynna's last night with them, and she could tell it was a special meal. Cathwain set out a sauce made of wild fruits harvested in the mountain. It had been preserved for the winter, but she opened one of the jars and served it with the bread. She'd also made a meat pie with rich buttery flaky crust, and dried fruits mixed with the root vegetables. After the pie, she served bowls of streaming broth, not as thick as the previous night's stew but dashed with interesting spices and every bit as flavorful.

After the meal, Chal-char said he would stay with them for the evening. Again he asked Elynna about her land and this time pressed more to hear how her life was different from those of the Highland peoples. When Elynna mentioned how many of her folk had left the Westwash and headed south to Citadel after the Daegmon attacks, Chal-char's attention grew more focused.

He asked how the creature had behaved, where it had come from, and especially how she could sense its presence. The conversation made Elynna uncomfortable and dredged up painful memories she had hoped to keep buried. That Chal-char kept speaking of the Daegmon in the present tense did not help. Was it only due to his lack of knowledge of verb tenses in the common tongue? When he gave her a chance to turn the conversation toward her family, she took it.

She told him about her father and mother, and how her mother had died of illness a few years ago, and about how she and her brother—like almost all Westwashers—had joined in the fishing trade. How she learned the crafts of net making and net repair, and sometimes fished in the rivers during the inland season, but had rarely gone to sea with her father. She did not mention her father's death, or how she and her brother had become estranged while in Citadel. And Chal-char not ask her about either beyond what she told him. After she spoke of their exodus to Citadel, Chal-char did tell her one thing she found interesting—the Ceadani folk did not have much written lore. Not compared with the great archives in Citadel. Nevertheless, for years beyond count, Gale Enebe had been the center of Ceadan culture, and what little that had been written by their people could be found here. And Chal-char had studied that lore carefully, especially as of late.

What Gale Enebe did have in abundance, along with springs of hot water, was visual art: paintings, mosaics, carvings, and especially tapestries. The Ceadani honored it more than written words. And so, seeking some knowledge of the Daegmon, Chal-char had been working with the other elders piecing together the old written lore with a more careful study of the murals and tapestries of the village. That was where he had spent the past two days. In doing so he had uncovered a clearer story of the languages of Gondisle.

"Our tales tell that long ago a great evil filled the southern half of Gondisle," he explained to Elynna, in his slow sonorous speech. "In the north, we Highland tribes—along with the Anghare to the east, the Plainsfolk, and the Fisherfolk of Westwash—dwelt in the shadow of Illengond under the protection of the All-Maker. The further we went from the great Mountain, the more dangerous life was. But when the peoples of the north had grown in numbers and were ready, the All-Maker drove that evil out of the south and gave that rich land as a gift to those who had dwelt around his mountain. The Fisherfolk of the Westwash, with their many boats and nowhere else to go, were the first to receive the All-Maker's promise and sail south. They landed first along the west coast of Gondisle and settled there first, where they could remain near the ocean. Gradually, however, they migrated inward and took up agricultural in the fertile soil. Two or three generations later the Andani also turned their thoughts southward, moving down into the center of Gondisle along the Illengond River, settling the upper valley, and moving south from there. As the Andani went south, they found already established settlements of emigrants from the Westwash."

This tale fascinated Elynna. Though her folk at times had been known as shipbuilders and explorers as well as fishers, she had never thought of them as important among the peoples of Gondisle. Was it possible they had once played a role in history?

"The Andani and the Westwashers got along well, for both were a peaceful folk," Chal-char continued. "And over time their languages, which were not altogether different to begin with, blended and became the common tongue of this new Southland. As both peoples continued to travel back to their homelands, the new language traveled with them even as it grew and changed. Eventually this new common tongue became the languages of both the Andani and the Westwash peoples even though some differences in dialect remained."

"But what of the Anghare?" Elynna asked. "The Northlanders? I thought they were the first rulers."

"The first *rulers*, yes," Chal-char answered. "There was no king in the south. No great city. And the people there—the descendants of the Andani and Westwashers who had first settled—wanted no king except the All-Maker. But in time the more warlike Anghare came south also. And they established the throne, and built the fortified palace of Citadel in imitation of their own fortresses. *Castles*, the Anghare call them. But when folk began to settle outside the walls of the castle, and a small trade town grew up, they gave it the name Citadel, which in their tongue means 'little city.'"

"It does not seem too little to me," Elynna interjected.

"I have not been there, so I do not know," Chal-char replied. "A few of our folk have traveled there and described it to me, but it is difficult to picture in my mind: manmade buildings the size of mountains, with more people than live in all the Ceadani villages together. No wonder they are so proud."

Not as large as your mountains, Elynna thought. But she said nothing aloud.

"But the city was not so large in those days," Chal-char went on. "It was dwarfed by the great city of Anghata, or even by their coastal port at Harrath. But still there was an Anghare castle there. A place of strength made for war. And slowly it grew. Until in time the Anghare built the new city walls in magnified imitation of the fortified stone towns that dot their own land far to the north. And they became kings."

He paused. "I do not know how many years or generations passed. I have heard some say that for a time after the Anghare came down from their Northland, there was still no king. For the people would not have one. Some say that the Anghare conquered the Southland, and by force made themselves rulers over the blended descendants of the Westwashers and Andani who had settled there. Others say that there was no king until another evil arose again, and that all the peoples of Gondisle united to oppose it, and willingly took the Anghare king in order to lead their armies against the evil. I do not know which story is true. Perhaps there is truth to both. But in either case, while the Anghare became the first kings of Gondisle, they did not willingly teach their own tongue to others. Instead they took as a second language the new common tongue already spoken there, for they were always fast learners of language. Slowly, as trade grew across Gondisle, and the roads and seaways grew safer, that common tongue of the Andani and Westwash spread. Now even some of my own people learn it."

Chal-char told her a little more about that time, but before long conversation turned to the ways of the Ceadani. Elynna, drinking more of the warm drink, found herself growing tried. She remembered little of the conversation that took place after that.

11

WHAT HOMES
REMAIN

On the third morning after the Gathering, about an hour after the late autumn sun had risen over the mountains to the east, the company met at the base of the village. After the Gathering, they had come to a consensus that they would travel together for as long as possible. Though some were still sick or wounded, none wanted to delay departure any longer. They had been treated well and shown honor in Gale Enebe, but they were strangers and didn't fit into the routine of the village. Elynna knew also that they were a burden to feed for a people whose resources had already been stretched by the flood of refugees. In any case, most of the companions were eager to return to their own homes, and to whatever family they still had. Even Tienna, though the healers of Gale Enebe had confirmed that she would not walk again for many weeks or months, expressed an eagerness to depart. "I feel trapped," she confided to Elynna. "I do not want to be a burden on the journey, yet neither do I want to be a cause for delay."

Elynna understood Tienna's feelings. She shared some of them herself. But there was one difference between them. Elynna had no home to return to. And no family. Leaving Gale Enebe meant the breaking up of her present relationships, but without any promise of more to replace them.

Thimeon arrived last. Elynna had not seen him at all during those two days. She heard from the other Andani that he was out in the leas above the village helping in the herding work of the family with whom he was staying, and trying to learn more of their secrets for raising gyurt.

As they loaded and double-checked their packs, they once again discussed their plans for travel. The Andani were traveling north, returning to their own homes and villages: Thimeon and Theo to their farms near Aeti, and Bandor to a smaller village in the northeast. They had the shortest distances to go. For the Northlanders also, the best route home was also north into Andani land, aiming to intersect the highland trade road somewhere east of Aeti. From there the trade route ran east past the southern shore of Tungmare Lake and the easternmost of the Andani villages before beginning its descent alongside the Tungmare River and down into Anghatte and the Anghare desert. Eventually it led to Anghata, the main city of Anghatte and the only large inland settlement in the Northland. Anghata had been built on bottomlands fertilized by the silt of annual floodwaters at the confluence of the Tungmare and Anghatte Rivers, which began in the Ceadani highlands as the Cea River. Passing through Aeti would take the Northlanders perhaps half a day out of their way further west than they wanted to go, but they had agreed to the plan.

"We should float home on the Cea River," Hruach had suggested, when he learned that it was one and the same river as the

Anghatte, and that it passed through the hills less than a day's journey away. Though his knee had recovered somewhat from the battle, he was still moving about with a limp and was not eager for long days of hiking. "Save us all the walking through this blasted wilderness. The river would bring us almost to our doorstep."

Chal-char had laughed as though Hruach were joking. When he realized the Anghare warrior had been serious, he explained why it was not a good idea. "That way cannot be traversed. The Cea Falls is but one of a dozen waterfalls in the canyon that would crush you, and even if we could build you enough boats here, there would be no way to portage them around the falls."

Hruach sulked, but consented to the long walk home and did not wish to wait until his knee fully healed.

For Tienna and the Plainsfolk, the fastest and safest route home started off northwest toward Aeti. From there, however, they would turn southwest, in the opposite direction from the Anghare, following the highland trade road around the northern slope of Mount Androllin and in the southern shadow of the great Mount Illengond. The road would take them as far as the trade town of Swage. From there they would turn back northwest along the Undeani road toward the village of Hilt and then due west through a wide valley into the Plains. There was no real road westward out of Hilt, but travel was not difficult.

"It seems like a long way," Nahoon had remarked. Among all the Plainsfolk, he was most eager to get home. He had left behind a young woman he had been courting for more than two years. Their families had finally agreed to marriage arrangements, and they would have been wed that fall had Nahoon not been chosen by his people for this quest. Two cycles of the moon—a full eighty days—had passed since his departure from her, and his beloved had heard no word from him since. Though he was more fit for travel than Hruach, he was just as eager to save walking. "It seems a waste to travel north, and then south, and then north again. There must be a shorter route."

Thimeon, whose head was full of maps and directions, replied. "Certainly there is. If you could fly. Follow the setting sun, and it will bring you somewhere near the northeast corner of your land in little over one-third the distance you will travel if you go all the way north to Aeti and back down. It will save you from circling Mount Androllin, the largest mountain in Gondisle, save Illengond itself."

"And?" asked Tienna, who noticed the little smile Thimeon could not conceal.

"It will bring you across the Androllin glaciers and snow-fields. So large you can spend all day walking and not touch anything but ice. Steep in places too, and full of hidden crevices. They are quite beautiful. Very much worth seeing. And probably the last things you will set your eyes on if you try to cross them."

Nahoon snorted. "I've had enough snow to last a lifetime. I'll go through Aeti."

Thimeon nodded. "I think that is wise, if you wish to see your beloved again."

For the Fisherfolk of the Westwash there was simply no easy return home. Their land lay far to the west and north. As Thimeon told them, a straight path following the flight of geese would bring them first directly over Androllin, and then through Undeani land, which most other folk avoided. The Undeani were not known to be hospitable. And while various descents from the Undeani high-lands to the Westwash were said to be passable in places where small rivers spilled down toward the ocean, once at the bottom there were few good routes across the marshy lowlands without a boat. Those among the Fisherfolk who wanted to return home would need to travel southwest through Citadel and to the coastal city of Aënport. From there they might eventually find passage, but probably not until spring after the stormy season.

Some of the Westwashers, including Siyen, didn't know if they would ever return. Their homes had been destroyed. They considered staying in the capital. But in either case, Citadel was their first destination. Thimeon explained, however, that a straight line to Citadel ran southwest over the southern spur of the Androllin range, the most rugged mountains of Gondisle. Though further south than the glaciers of which he had earlier spoken, these mountains were nearly impassable, with jagged crags, hidden defiles, and almost constant snowfall in the higher elevations. The quickest passable route to Citadel was to head east and south and then back west in a wide loop around the Ceadani peaks, and then southward through the Ana Notch and down to the coastal city of Kreana. From there they could follow a main trade route west to Citadel. But that would mean they would have to part ways almost as soon as they left Gale Enebe. Instead, they could also travel with the entire company as far as Aeti, and then continue on with the Plainsfolk as far as Swage, though it would lengthen their route to Citadel by two or three days.

There was little debate, for while all were eager to return to their homes, all also expressed the desire that they not disband the company any earlier than needed. For that, at least, Elynna was grateful. The entire company would thus remain together for several days, as far as Aeti. Thimeon had not sought to sway the decision, but once it was agreed upon, he showed obvious delight and offered his hospitality to any who wished to stay at his home.

That got the companions talking about Aeti. "I have traveled through the town more than once, on trade caravans bound from Anghata to Citadel," Hrevia had said.

"And what did you think of it?" Cane asked.

"Truth be told, it is a small and dirty town. Nothing like our Anghare cities. But the beer is good. And the people friendly. And the surrounding hills are beautiful."

"I cannot disagree," Thimeon acknowledged. "On any of those descriptions. I do not live in the town. My sister and I live on a farm our father built northeast of Aeti. We are far enough away that wild animals roam through our pasture and many of the townsfolk have never seen our home, but near enough that if I start walking toward town at the first hint of light, I will reach the farms on the outskirts before the sun is shining on my back. We are a half-day's walk west of where you stayed with Cousin Theo and his family. It is a similar landscape, though our farm is much smaller. Still I'm sure we can show hospitality to you all, before you continue your journeys."

Theo laughed. "Though I have no doubt my parents have taken good care of her, I think Siarah will be happy to see you again and to return to her own home. But perhaps less happy if you bring so many strangers with you, and she thinks it is her duty to feed us all."

"Your parents will have taken good care of her indeed, as they did once before," Thimeon replied. "Of that I have no doubt. It has not been easy on her since our parents died."

Conversation turned then to Llana and Braddoc, who were from the village of Aeti. Before the company disbanded, they hoped to find some distant family with whom they might share memories and tokens of their lost companions. Then they would sunder and go their separate ways. Elynna and the other West-washers would turn south along the trade road to Citadel. And where then? Elynna did not know.

"How long will it take us to reach Aeti?" Elynna asked, as they stood together at the edge of the village. From their vantage point, they could see out over the high mountain plains to the distant triune peak of Illengond that stood silhouetted against a dark-blue sky. Except for the three bare rocky spires on its crown, it was covered in snow as far down as they could see. A small cloud filled the bowl, but there were no other clouds in sight.

"Five days, I fear," Thimeon replied. He had not spoken to her since their return to the Gathering the previous evening, and even now he avoided her eyes. "More, if the weather is bad. As a goose migrates, it may be only sixty-five miles. But the road winds along rivers, and between hills, and we will want to skirt the Raws. By foot it is a journey of a hundred miles."

Elynna nodded. She knew already that the Ceadani had given them supplies to last two days. It was a generous gift, but they would still have to hunt or forage along the way, or buy food from whatever villages or settlements they passed.

"Tienna will have to be carried," he added a moment later. He had lowered his voice, and finally looked at Elynna. "She will not have the use of her ankle for many weeks. It was badly broken and may never heal correctly. Her best hope is to keep off of it for a long time. And others are also ill. It will be slow travel. If may be more than five days if we are forced to hunt long."

"Then let us depart as soon as we may," Elynna said. She turned and walked away.

With a last glance at the face of the village in the cliffs above, the company departed. Those not injured took turns carrying

Tienna's litter, with Falien insisting on the first shift along with Cathros. The others carried their own packs. Their path took them northward out of the village, down from the hills by a different route than they had taken in. They did not have to pass through the scene of the battle, and for that Elynna was happy. They traveled the remainder of the morning at a slow, steady pace gradually veering northeastward. The path took them along a wide tumbling brook and down again into a broad valley. The land was much higher in altitude than anything in the Westwash, and the surrounding peaks were higher still. They hiked about four hours along the brook as it grew to a stream and then a small river. In the middle of the afternoon they reached another river flowing down from the north as it took a wide bend eastward. This river was wider than the one they were on, but only a little deeper. On the other side a well-traveled road ran north.

Thimeon, walking alongside Tienna's litter, was talking to her about the land. "We are near one of the two main headwaters of the River Cea. This is the West Branch. It descends out of the glacier and snowpack of the Androllin Range and flows almost due east across the Ceadani highlands picking up small streams as it goes before it reaches its other major tributary—the North Branch of the Cea. Here we will turn northwestward. For the next day we skirt the foothills of Ceathu Mountain and follow the river upstream. Then we turn back due north and then northeast to skirt the eastern edge of the Raws."

He paused for a moment, as if lost in thought or memory. His voice was softer when he continued, so that only Tienna and Elynna could hear him. "I traveled here some years ago, first with my father and then alone. The Andani are not known as travelers, but my father journeyed much before he married and settled down to his farm. When I came of age to travel, he took one more trip with me, so that he could share with me his favorite memories of Gondisle. Then I continued alone for a time, trying to learning something of the peoples and landscapes of the realm. I had hoped to travel more, but then rumors of the Daegmon drew me home."

Tienna's voice sounded wistful as she replied. "Until this summer, when my people sent me in search of help, I had never before left the Plains. I had felt neither desire nor need to do so. But though I miss the Plains and am eager to be home, I am now glad to have seen something of the broader realm of Gondisle and to have stood closer to the shadow of Illengond. I can see also how it is you have gained so much knowledge—how it is you know of the passes and routes down from the Highlands. It is from your own travels."

"That, and maps," Thimeon replied. "My father made and collected maps, and we loved to look at them together. Maps from all over. I don't think you could find a bigger collection of them without going to Citadel or perhaps the library of some merchant mariner in one of the coastal cities like Aënport of Kreana. All in a little farmhouse in Andan hills." He laughed, and his voice grew a little louder again. "If we turned east from here, and followed the river downstream, we would find the road wandering through a few Ceadani villages ending at the edge of wilderness. The River Cea, however, continues to grow as you follow it downstream past the end of the road and into the wild. A half-day's journey beyond its confluence with the North Branch and past the last Ceadani village, it turns southeastward and plunges hundreds of feet through a beautiful and treacherous gorge. It is a spectacular sight. I would love to see it again someday." He closed his eyes and took a long deep breath. "After the gorge, it turns north and drops over thundering falls into the Northland—"

"And there," interrupted Cane, "it becomes the Anghaë—the lifeblood of the Anghare. Some call it the Anghatte, but that is more accurately the name only of the desert through which it cuts its course. Many long miles it flows on its journey to the sea— nearly two hundred from the Cea Falls to the end of its course, I have been told. It is beautiful to my people, this river is. There is little water in Anghatte—what you call 'the Northland'—save for what flows between the banks of the Anghaë and its one main tributary, the Tungmare."

"I have traveled little in Anghatte," Thimeon admitted, "save for one brief visit to Anghata and a few days of travel along the coast by ship."

"Is your land as barren as stories tell?" asked Tienna.

"It is not green like this," Cane answered. "Yet it is beautiful. I would not call it 'barren.' And the jewels we mine there are as alive as these trees, though they grow underground."

The companions were at the water's edge now. They paused to drink from the deep pool at the confluence of the two streams. Then they forded at a shallow gravel bar downstream. Tienna, who had repeatedly complained about riding in the litter, refused to be carried across the ford. Grumbling that she was a huntress and not a sack of grain, she limped through the icy water with Thimeon and Nahoon supporting her. On the far side they took a short rest, sharing an afternoon meal as they warmed their wet feet beside a hastily built fire. Long before their boots were dry, however, they resumed travel. They were on a road now, heading west-northwest, having left behind the mountains of Gale Enebe. Higher and wilder peaks were visible several miles to the east, and due north was the peak of Ceathu, but the land around the river was tame. Wide flatlands spread out ahead of them, marked only by a few giant pines and an occasional cluster of dwellings on some distant hill. Though the early winter could still be felt in the cold air, travel was easy compared to the previous weeks.

As they walked, Elynna's thoughts wandered again back to the days after the destruction of her home in Lienford. As she considered where to go now, she began to retrace in her mind her departure from home. Bereft of parents, she and her brother Lyn had eventually made up their mind to go to Citadel. Travel by foot across the marshes of the Westwash was dangerous and excruciatingly slow. Countless detours around bogs and wetlands were enough to discourage the most dauntless traveler. Indeed, other than short hunting trips usually taken in the winter, when ground was drier and in places frozen, beyond the confines of their villages the Westwash Fisherfolk traveled almost exclusively by boat. So they had joined seven other families in a flotilla of five boats and headed down the Lien River together, following it as it flowed northwest to the large coastal fishing town of Lienport.

It was a voyage she'd made many times in her life, though always in the past she had done so with her father. Like many Westwashers who lived inland, her family spent almost three months every year in a village on the seacoast. This was in late spring when the rivers were high and turbulent from melting snow but the seas unusually calm. These were the times they fished the open waters from their shultees, either going deep with lines for the variety of bottom-dwelling fish common among the coastal isles or chasing grelsh near the surface with nets. Their own coastal dwelling was in a seasonal village south of Lienport toward the harbor town of Souflush. But there were numerous fishing villages—a few occupied year-round but most of them seasonal—spread all along the coast from Souflush up past Lien-haven and eastward even beyond Northaven.

Of course the rest of the year, in late summer when grelsh were running upriver to spawn, and through the fall and winter when kellen were running, they were back home in Lienford fishing the rivers from their smaller lalls, which were better adapted to river travel. From Lienford, they could usually reach the sea in two days, and they could reach tidal water in little over a day. As long as they departed before the snowmelt was in full force, it was not a difficult voyage, though the trip back upriver in early summer was somewhat more tedious.

This time, however, even the downriver voyage had not been easy. The boats had been crowded and the water unusually high for autumn. This forced them to portage around rapids several times on the first day, and they covered only half the distance they usually did. On the second day they had arrived exhausted at a small village at the upriver boundary of tidewater, only to discover it had just been attacked by the Daegmon.

On the third night, camping at the edge of an island village only a few miles from Lienport in the broad mouth of the Lien River, Elynna had woken from a nightmare with knowledge that the creature was approaching. She had warned the village whose inhabitants escaped to a nearby cave just in time. Angry at its loss of prey, the Daegmon had wreaked havoc all morning.

At Lienport things had gotten a little better. The Daegmon did not appear again after they reached the sea, and within a few days Lyn had found them passage on a trade vessel bound for Aënport and the Southland. For a time, then, the two of them had traveled together in peace, brought closer together by their common suffering.

Elynna's mind was traveling southward along the coast of the Westwash, a melancholy memory of wind-tangled hair and salt spray on her cheeks, when the excitement in Bandor's voice jarred her back to the present.

"These are fresh," Bandor announced. The company had come to a halt, and several of them stood looking down at a tremendous number of large animal of tracks in the snow. Small marsh deer lived throughout the inland portions of the West-wash, but Elynna had never seen tracks of an animal this large.

Cathros concurred. "I do not know the ways of these mountain elk, but there are many of them, and they cannot be far from here."

"They're looking for food," Thimeon explained. "The early cold has caught them unaware."

"We, too, are looking for food," Cathros reminded him. "Or we will be soon. And if these are the same creatures we saw from afar many days ago, one of them would provide several good meals for us all."

Thimeon hesitated a moment, but finally agreed. "Yes. We must hunt. Yet we should kill no more than one. The early winter will take a heavy toll on the herd, I fear."

Tienna's voice rose from the litter. Along with Thimeon, she showed more concern than excitement at their discovery. "Something is ill. I sense it even from a distance."

"So their tracks indicate," Thimeon answered as he scanned the valley on both sides of them, following with his eyes first the approaching and then the departing tracks. "This herd is already distressed. They rush almost in a gallop. Then they turn sharply to the side. Then they go in all directions. Something is upsetting them. Nonetheless, Cathros is right. We will need food soon, and one of these elk will feed us all for many days. Unless they run themselves to death, we should be able to catch them."

A short time later, Thimeon, Bandor, Theo, and Cathros disappeared over the hill following the trail. It was two hours past midday, and they hoped to return before the sun had set. The rest of the company started another small fire and gathered around to wait.

Elynna sat beside a silent Tienna. "Tell me about the Plainsfolk," she said after a time, both to encourage her friend and also to learn more about her, for Elynna was continually appalled at her own lack of knowledge, even about those most dear to her.

A few minutes passed with no answer. When Tienna replied, her voice was unusually distant, almost like a reprimand. "You speak of the Plainsfolk as though we were one people. That would be like lumping together as Highlanders *all* of the folk who live in these mountains: the Ceadani, the Andani, and the Undeani. Though they have some customs in common, they are also different in many ways."

Elynna mumbled an apology and then waited for Tienna to continue. The silence lasted so long she was afraid the huntress would say no more. But Tienna was only gathering her thoughts, and after a time she began to speak. "There are many tribes scattered across the Plains. How many depends on whom you ask. Probably you would count five major tribes, but then there are several smaller tribes who share languages but in other ways keep themselves distinct. There are the fishing tribes of the Great Lake Umgog. Beth and Marti are numbered among them. Then there are the Uëtha, the wheat-gathering tribes to the east. Nahoon is an Uët."

"And you?" Elynna asked.

"I am from the Arnei. We are a hunting people. Like the Uët, and some of the smaller shepherding tribes, we are what you would call nomadic. We move from place to place as seasons change."

"Do you all speak the same language?"

"No. Each tribe has its own dialect, though the languages of the various fisher tribes are no longer different."

"What of the trade tongue? Is it spoken in your larger villages, or by your traders?"

"We have few villages in the Plains. Only two tribes have permanent settlements around the great Lake Umgog. There is also one other large village to the far west, but some say those folk are not kin to the Plains tribes. Even the village to the north of the lake is empty in the fall." Her voice slowly warmed as she spoke, and it was pleasant for Elynna after all the hardships of the past few weeks and the uncertainty of her own future to just sit and listen. "The language of the lake tribes is the accepted Plainstongue. Most of the Plainsfolk even from other tribes speak that language as well as their own. Some also speak the trade language of Gondisle, the Southland tongue that is spoken also by the Andani and among you Westwashers. But few traders come to our land from the outside. It possesses little that other folk would call riches. Jewels such as are found in Anghatte are not common even in our mountains."

"Tell me more about the land."

Tienna exhaled a longing sigh. "The Highlanders might call it flat, covered with tall rich prairie grasses and the mysterious wild wheat that appears in different places each summer. There are a few small forests and woods, and a range of low hills several days northwest of the lake. One large river crosses the land, with many smaller tributaries, all flowing from north to south down out of the Undeani mountains and plunging over the cliffs and into the south.

Around Umgog there are also wide spring-fed marshlands that drain into the lake and provide home for waterfowl and many other birds. Another river cuts off the northwest corner. In the spring there are other rivers that spring up out of the Plains with the seasonal rains, but they are small and most do not last until autumn."

Tienna paused and closed her eyes, as though perusing some map visible only inside her mind. "There is one other west-flowing river that rises in southwest, and even in the summer it remains deep enough to float a small boat and hold fish. So I am told. I have not been there, except to its very headwaters in the wooded hills of our southwest."

"Do the tribes ever war among each other?"

"There were such wars long ago—one tribe fighting against another—but none in my lifetime. There is land and food for all." She smiled. "One only needs know how to find it. As for weapons, you would find that the Plainsfolk do not gather such weapons of war as other people do, though we do have hunting implements and some few weapons for our defense."

"My great grandfather spoke of these wars," interrupted Nahoon, who had walked up beside them. "They occurred when even he was young. There was great loss. When they were over, the folk of the Plains vowed never again to fight one another. Now even Tienna's tribe, who of all the Plainsfolk were most known as warriors—and even now they are considered the most skilled hunters—are peaceful folk and slow to hostility. They scorn all but the simplest of arms—the knife and longbow. These they use with grace and precision."

By this time many of the others had ceased their own conversations and were also listening. "Are all your people hunters?" asked Falien, who had missed the start of the conversation.

Tienna, who had remained lying on her back where they had set her litter down, now sat up and turned to see who had spoken before she answered. "All of the Arnei can shoot an arrow, and at times of need will pick up the bow. Only a few are chosen to be trained as hunters and huntresses. It is a long and arduous training."

At Beth's prompting, Tienna went on to tell how as a young girl she had been selected, and of the rigorous discipline she had undergone. She spoke of the long-distance runs that lasted all day as they pursued herds across the Plains. She told how they selected the weak of the herds to kill, so that the strong would live to reproduce. Then, almost wistfully, she described how they competed for food with the tigers that came down out of the hills in the evenings.

"Aren't you afraid?" Siyen asked.

"Yes," Tienna said. "One who did not fear those beasts would be a fool. Yet we are taught how to fight one if we are ever attacked."

"Have *you* ever fought one?" Beth pressed.

"My grandfather was one of the greatest hunters our tribe has ever known," Tienna replied. "He became a legend for wrestling a tiger with no weapon save his waist rope. As for me, I have yet to face one. There are no living huntresses who have faced one. If I do this—and if I survive—I would receive the highest rank of my people."

"I hope you're not going out looking for one," Falien said with a laugh.

Tienna didn't answer. When she continued speaking a minute later, there with a tone of awe in her voice. "For all the skill of the Arnei hunters or huntresses, greater than any of them are the Amanti. They are hunters and warriors without equal in

Gondisle." At this Cane smirked, but Tienna didn't see him. She continued. "Fifteen is their number. Their vows are strict and their training is known to none save themselves. It is said that they can run five days without sleep, that they ride tigers and swim waterfalls, and that they speak with each other on the wind."

"The tales are true," Nahoon said. "I have seen them. That is to say, I saw one of them when I was a child. It is rare that any will see more than two or three together. One is enough, I guess. Even with my father, three older brothers, and both of my uncles beside me, I was afraid. But of course the Amanti are from my tribe, the Uëtha, so I had nothing to fear."

"Are they?" Beth asked. "I had heard that their numbers were chosen from the best of all the Plainsfolk."

"They speak the Uët dialect," Marti interjected. "That much I know."

"They're sworn to speak no other," Nahoon confirmed.

Cane was still shaking his head in incredulity. "How is it that they are never together? And what kind of warriors can they be if they have no army?"

"Nobody said they are *never* together," Nahoon replied. "I only said they are never *seen* with more than three together. I have heard some say that when a new Amanti is chosen and trained, that they all gather for the testing. Though others say the trainee is taken out by one of the old Amanti and trained alone. I have heard both of these stories told, but nobody knows except the Amanti themselves. And they do not say. I've also heard that the Amanti know when they are going to die, and that each trains his own successor. Other stories I've heard about them, too. I don't doubt them. They're legends, the Amanti are, but true legends. Living legends."

12

THE SMELL OF SMOKE

It was shortly before sundown when the four hunters returned from wooded hills to the east. Tienna heard their voices carrying along the wind and alerted the others. Elynna grabbed Nahoon and Martin and then walked out a short distance to welcome them. She ended up helping carry the load back to the camp, for the hunters had returned with several slabs of freshly butchered meat—at least a hundred and forty pounds—and they were tired. As they warmed their hands by the fire, Theo told how they had tracked the herd over the hill and through a dense stand of spruce before coming upon the stragglers. Elynna, despite all she knew of the fishing trade, knew very little about hunting and listened eagerly to Theo's tale. The hunters had chosen one animal from the herd to shoot. Then each of the archers had marked their arrow and shot all at once. Three of the four arrows struck their target, but Bandor had won the prize for coming closest to the heart. The animal had fallen at once, and the rest of the herd, barely aware of what had happened, wandered away. The rest of the time had been spent butchering the animal and preparing the meat, which could last many days in the cold weather.

By then it was nearly dark. As the company was in no particular hurry, Elynna suggested they bivouac where they were even though it had been a short day of travel. There was a loud agreement, especially from the four who had gone hunting. While some of them set to work putting up their shelters, Thimeon supervised the cooking of two huge slabs of loin. All were in high spirits as they sat around the fire and partook of a good meal of fresh meat and shared from the skins of Ceadani wine from Gale Enebe. As they were finishing the meal, the moon peeked its head over the hills to the east. It was the first night of the green phase. It would last for eight days, followed by a single night of bright yellow—Elynna's favorite night of each month—and then twenty-eight long days in its pale phase before the blue moon appeared again and it all started over.

Not long after the moon rose, its pale-green tint casting a ghastly glow on the snow-covered mountains, Elynna crawled into one of the tents with Tienna. She fell asleep almost at once and dozed deeply beneath her warm fur blanket.

They awoke the next morning before the sun had crested over the eastern peaks. The day looked to be clear, and warmer than it had been for more than a week. Elynna felt in good spirits, and the moods of those around her seemed to echo that. Cane even removed his splint saying that the break in his arm had been only a small fracture, and that in the days since the battle all the pain had disappeared. Tienna, probing with her health sense, concurred. "It is not yet fully healed. It needs a few more days. But unless you enter into another battle it should be fine."

Cane flexed his fingers, and wrist, and elbow, and nodded. "It feels good," he said.

As they broke camp, Thimeon described the plan for the forthcoming day of travel to anybody who wanted to listen. Elynna, though she kept her back to him as he spoke, paid careful attention. "We follow the river upstream for a dozen miles or so. If we make good time, then in the late morning we should reach the Ceadani village of Gale Ceathu. On the other side of the village, the river valley turns westward."

"And we continue north?" Tienna asked.

"Yes. This western branch of the Cea tumbles down out of the Androllin Range to our west. Once out of the high peaks, it crosses many miles of shifting wetlands and forests upriver to the west of us before it reaches Gale Ceathu and more settled territory. I have journeyed that land twice before. If you stay too close to the river channel, tempting though it is, you end up wandering endlessly around ponds and marshes where springs and tributaries flow in from both sides. The river flows like the braids of a woman's hair. You need to stay on higher ground a mile or two off the river if you wish for less difficult travel. But there are no roads there, and it does not follow the direction we want. Shortly after the village our road leaves the river and continues north for another day and a half, following the edge of the Raws of Androllin, and then veers northwest."

"The Raws of Androllin?" Cathros asked. "You spoke of it before on our journey south many days ago, and again yesterday. It is an ominous name. What is it?"

Thimeon smiled. "The land is as bleak as it sounds. It's an uninhabited and inhospitable territory, stretching west almost to the slopes of Mount Androllin. Most of the moisture moving eastward across Gondisle divides around the high mountains of the Androllin Range to the west, or the clouds simply empty themselves as snow onto the great glaciers. Little rain falls on the Raws, and there are few natural springs."

"Lack of rain is something the Anghare understand," Cane interjected. "Even less water makes it over the next range of mountains and down to the land we call home. And we have a name for the result. We call it a *desert*. It may not sound as ominous as your 'Raws,' but I assure you it is every bit as inhospitable."

Thimeon did not reply right away. When he did, his voice was quiet, without the haughtiness of Cane's. "The Raws are a desert, I suppose," he finally said. "They are dry, but not hot. It is a cold desert. And not as large as the great desert of the Northland. Still, it is enough to dissuade the ill-prepared traveler. The Raws divide the lands of the Ceadani and Andani and maybe explain how the two peoples became sundered many generations ago. We avoided the Raws on the way south because we were higher in the eastern hills."

He paused again, lost in thought for a moment. "As I said, water is scarce in the Raws, though not completely absent. Equally difficult for us, the afternoon winds are notoriously high. We can skirt the region again and travel through the eastern hills, but that will cost us a few days since our destination lies farther west. At this time of year, I recommend we stay on the road and angle across the northeast corner." He looked around to see if there was any dissent, but none of the companions raised a complaint. "If we are going to cross even the edge of the Raws, it would be good to start the journey early in the day so that we travel in the morning when the winds are low. For this same reason, Chal-char recommended we spend the night at Gale Ceathu.

He is well known to the folk there, and said we would be welcomed in his name. Had we not stopped to hunt, we would have reached the village last night. It will make today yet another short day of travel, but . . ." He shrugged and left his sentence unfinished.

"Let us wait and see," Cane suggested.

After a short breakfast of cheese and cold meat, they departed. Their journey continued in a direction more west than north, following the Cea River upstream. With Hruach hampered by his knee, Siyen and Beth coughing almost continually and grumbling of fatigue, and Tienna still in her litter, their pace remained slow. Yet not even those most eager to get home complained of the delays. It was a pleasant morning, and the companions talked cheerfully. Even Tienna was in a sunny mood, though she still grumbled at having to be carried.

"We're the ones who ought to be complaining," replied Thimeon with a good-natured smile. He, along with Aram, were currently taking a shift carrying her. "You are none too light. I'm only glad it isn't Cathros with the wounded leg."

It was Nahoon, as midday approached, who first observed the smell, saying it reminded him of the peculiar scent on the Plains when there was a distant brushfire. Once he commented on it, others noticed as well. Then Elynna began to grow nervous. Two or three times she thought she felt the faint twinge of the Daegmon's presence. It was almost undetectable. Perhaps her imagination. She didn't tell anyone. The breeze shifted back toward the west and the odor dissipated. Ahead, the river came out of a narrow ravine. The road veered to the right and followed an easier path over a hill. As they trudged up the slope, the murmur of the river faded. Elynna was near the tail of the pack, her eyes fixed absently on a long tress of Tienna's hair that hung off one side of the litter. When the litter and hair stopped moving, she lifted her head. They had come to the top of the hill, and the leaders were looking down the other side. Cathros let loose a long low whistle. Tienna rose to a sitting position to see what was the matter.

"May the mountain protect us," Thimeon moaned. He started forward, but Cathros grabbed him.

"Wait! We do not know what caused this."

Elynna ran ahead to see what the others were looking at. What she saw made her fall to her knees and bury her head in her hands in despair. The little Ceadani village lay in ruins, with smoke still rising from the burned buildings. A few houses still stood, but many lay in piles of rubble or smoldering in ashes. It was a horrible sight, though one that had over the past year become familiar to nearly everybody in the company.

"Elynna," Cane said, turning toward her. "Do you sense—?"

"No," she answered before he could finish. "Not now." But at the same moment, another thought came to her mind: a response to Cathros's words from the moment she saw the state of this village. *Yes. We do. We do know what caused this.*

"Then let us go down without delay," Thimeon enjoined. "There may be survivors."

"Wait," Cathros warned again. He glanced at Tienna lying helpless on her litter, and Elynna understood the gesture. "We don't know how old this is," Cathros continued. "There might still be danger. Let a few go ahead and scout."

Thimeon nodded. "I will go with you." He looked around. "Elynna, Cane, Falien, and Nahoon will also join us. The rest wait here. If we do not return—" He paused. "If there is danger, flee southward. Return to Gale Enebe. Bandor will guide you."

The others nodded grimly and moved back down the road out of sight while Cathros and Thimeon led the smaller group into the village. All but Elynna had drawn their weapons and were approaching cautiously, looking around as they walked.

They were halfway down the slope when three figures emerged from a building carrying a large load between them. "Looters?" Cane asked.

"No," Thimeon answered, with a sad shake of his head. "They are not looters."

An instant later, what Thimeon understood became clear to Elynna and the other companions as well. The three men were walking in solemn procession. The burden they carried was a lifeless body. Thimeon lowered his spear and began to move faster. The others followed a few steps behind. When the rest of the scene came into view, however, Elynna stopped again. A row of bodies lined the ground in front of the building. She turned away.

Thimeon stopped too. He turned and looked at the others, and then at Elynna. "Go back," he told her softly. "You have seen enough."

Elynna shook her head, denying Thimeon by habit, but it was a few seconds before she could move. By the time she was able to walk, the men in the village had seen the strangers approaching. They moved a few yards away from the bodies and waited, their eyes cold and full of grief. Thimeon bowed low to them and spoke in the trade tongue.

"We have come at a time of grief. Words of greeting would be hollow."

The men looked back through eyes too pained to be suspicious. "Turn and go back where you came," one said. "This land is not safe."

"No land is safe anymore," Thimeon replied. "That is why we are here. Let us help you. We have been through this." Then he said something in the Ceadani tongue, making mention of Chal-char.

The man who had spoken looked Thimeon over again. "We are destroyed. How can you have been through this?"

"We all come from villages that have been ravished."

"By the creature?"

Thimeon nodded. "The Daegmon it is named in tales of old. We have fought it." He paused. "And lost."

Several voices broke out at once, but Elynna barely heard them. *Lost.* The word rang in her ears. *Lost?*

When her attention returned to the present, one of the men of the village was speaking. "We heard rumor of this creature. We had been warned, but we did not understand." He had been gazing at the ground as he said this, shaking his head slowly. Now he turned and looked at Thimeon. "You speak our tongue. Yet you are not Ceadani?"

"I am not," Thimeon replied. "I am Andani, and those with me are from all across Gondisle."

"Then this—this evil creature attacks everywhere? The stories are true."

Thimeon's voice was soft and full of compassion. "It does, but we will not speak of it now. Let us help you with this task."

But before the man could reply, Elynna stepped forward. "Are there other survivors?"

"A few. They wait on the far side of the village. We will

depart as soon as we are finished—" His voice caught. Suddenly his words found passion. "We tried to fight, but it was too strong. No weapons sufficed against it—"

Thimeon reached out and placed a hand on the man's shoulder. "Enough. Do not relive it."

"My wife and child," the man said. "We should have gone—I should have taken them to Gale Enebe when we were warned. But I didn't understand . . ." He fell silent.

"Go and rest," Thimeon offered. "We will do your work, and we will not fail to give honor to the fallen." Then he spoke something else in the Ceadani tongue. The man nodded and turned with his two companions to depart.

Thimeon turned to Nahoon. "Tell the others what has happened. Have a few go with Tienna around to the far side of the village to wait. Any who wish to help can join me here. We will bury and honor the dead."

The men from the village had gone several paces, when Cathros suddenly called out to them. "Wait." One of the men turned and looked back, his eyes aching with pain. Thimeon winced and put his hand on Cathros as though to silence him. But Cathros turned to the companions, and said in a quieter voice. "We *must* know."

"Know what?" Elynna asked.

Cathros ignored her. His tone was urgent as he posed his question to the men. "When did this happen?"

"Yesterday evening," the man replied. "As the sun was setting."

A long silence followed as the men walked through the village and disappeared. Elynna understood all too clearly the implications of their words. Still, it was painful for her to hear Cathros speak it aloud. "Yesterday evening. After our battle. And so the Daegmon still lives. We have failed."

"Perhaps we failed to kill it," Cane acquiesced. "Or there were more than one."

Or both, Elynna thought. The idea struck her for the first time. Maybe this creature was not alone; maybe there *were* more than one. And maybe they could not be killed.

"I will have to find a new blade." Cane stated in his usual even tone.

Thimeon was still lost in his own thoughts. "This is what Chal-char feared or foresaw four evenings ago when the Daegmon's body disappeared," he murmured, almost to himself. Then he said more loudly, looking around at the others. "This is why he felt so strongly that we must go back and check the ravine. This evil we now face is shrouded in some mystery I fear we will not quickly unravel." He looked up the slope where the other companions waited, then back at the line of slain bodies. "What we do next, I do not know. The need is urgent and yet—" He paused. "Our decision must wait until the evening. For the sake of those who have suffered, let us first do what we can do here. There will be enough time to talk afterward."

Cane looked as if he was about to object, but Cathros spoke before his brother had a chance. "Well spoken, friend. Do we not all know what it means to have our lives shattered by this evil? We have accomplished little enough in our many weeks of pursuing the Daegmon. An afternoon spent here will not hurt us overmuch."

Cane yield to his brother, and Thimeon and Cathros started walking toward the building. Elynna, feeling the need to make some decision—to take some action—turned to Nahoon and repeated what Thimeon had told him a moment earlier. "Go tell the others. Bring here any who are willing to help."

A short time later, several of the companions trudged down to join in the task while the remaining few escorted Tienna around the village to the northern end. Under Thimeon's direction they searched the village for bodies of the slain. It was an unpleasant task. Elynna saw bodies full of wounds from talon and tail and claw as well as fire. Some had been killed in the open by the Daegmon, in the act of fleeing or fighting. Like her father. Many more had been crushed or burned in their homes while trying to hide. There was little talk as the companions worked, and they did not stop for food. For Elynna as for many of her companions, memories of burying their own families were too fresh. They laid the bodies side by side in a long shallow ditch scraped out near the center of the village. When they were done, they filled the grave with a shallow layer of dirt, and then covered them with a pile of stones to mark their collective grave.

A few of the survivors from the attack came back to help with that final duty, placing stone monuments and laying freshly picked flowers on the graves. Then together they held a silent vigil over the fallen. After several minutes of silence, Thimeon recited aloud an old Andan blessing, spoken commonly when the dead were buried. He spoke first in the Ceadani tongue and then in the common trade language. "All-Maker, grant that those who have fallen may find rest in your mountain, and give comfort to those who remain." Then, after a moment's pause, he added, "And give us wisdom that we can see your deliverance from this enemy."

By the time the burial was complete, the afternoon had passed and evening was upon them. The companions joined the folk of Gale Ceathu at the northern end of the village for a small and somber meal. Both parties shared what food they had, but most of them ate in silence. Only Thimeon was moving about, with Theo at his side, speaking in a soft voice words of encouragement among members of both parties.

But though she was dimly aware of his words and efforts, Elynna did not know how he, or anyone, could find anything good to be said. Counting children, there were about fifty Ceadani who survived the attack. The companions had laid to rest at least sixty bodies. There might be even more they had not found, buried under rubble or taken by the creature. It was worse even than Lienford. How could they go on? Elynna wondered. She could not bring herself to look in the faces of those around her.

As darkness fell, Elynna sat by herself and stared out at the evening sky. The village was in the foothills on the western slope of Ceathu Mountain. Behind her, to the east, the land rose steeply in a wooded hillside that blocked the view of the mountain. To the south, from whence she had arrived a few hours ago, there was a natural break in hills—a steep cut through which the road ran, starting up a small slope and then quickly disappearing around a sharp bend to the left. Northeast, the road continued on around another bend and again disappeared from view. But in broad sweep from north to west, where her gaze now fell, the land was open, descending in a long gradual slope down to the wooded valley of the Cea River. The sky had cleared except for a faint row of thin clouds in the west, and the sun was disappearing in a blood-red curtain over the distant Androllin Range now covered in snow. Northward, across the Raws, the brightest stars of the Great North Tree were just popping into view. A cold dry wind blew across the Raws. She pulled her cloak more tightly about her.

When all were finished eating, and darkness had fallen, the Ceadani began to move away to a small encampment they had made at the northern edge of their ruined village. One of the companions lit a fire behind her. Elynna did not see or hear who it was. Soon the others had all gathered around it. Even Siyen, who had not helped with the burial but had instead wandered off by herself for a time, joined them. Elynna had only to turn her body around and she was in the circle of companions, facing the fire.

Thimeon spoke first, saying what they all now knew. The Daegmon still lived, and their task was not yet finished. There was murmur of voices. Some in agreement, some in dismay. Some looked at Elynna, but she remained silent. Thimeon let the voices go on for a few moments, then he spoke again, suggesting they had been through too much that day to make any decisions. Several nodded their heads. Even Cane and Cathros agreed that it could wait for the morning. "Then let us rest," Thimeon said. "The All-Maker knows that we need it, and may He grant it this night."

One by one the companions found places to sleep in their various tents or on the ground near the fire beneath the stars. The last ones awake were the folk of the village, who sat by their own fire a stone's throw away staring into the flames.

Elynna's sleep was restless, but despite her fatigue when she awoke in the morning, she was eager to rise and start moving. Tienna was already awake, lying in her litter and staring at the top of their shared tent. "Many of the folk here are badly wounded," the young Plainswoman said. "I could see it, and I can feel it."

"What can we do?" Elynna asked.

"I don't know. I thought about it much last night. I could not help with the burial, but I could try—"

"No," Elynna interrupted. "Not you. There are too many injuries, and you are already weak. Where would you stop?"

"If not me, then who?" Tienna asked. "Who will help them?"

Elynna did not answer. She pulled her boots on and left the small tent in search of one of the village leaders whom she had met the day before. She found him standing atop a slope on the western edge of the village looking out across a wide expanse of highlands. Gale Ceathu was one of the northernmost Ceadani settlements. Behind them, the Cea River gradually grew as it wandered eastward toward the edge of the highlands and then plunged down into the Northland desert. To the west, upstream, the river disappeared off into the distant mountains from which it flowed, pulling its water from the melting packs of snow and ice. To the northeast of the village, out of sight on the other side of the hill, the well-worn trade road ran off northward toward Aeti. That was the path they had planned to take.

Elynna's eyes were drawn to the north and west, however, following the gaze of the Ceadani village elder who stood silently beside her. They were looking toward the Raws. Even from here, she could see it was a hard land. There were few trees, and north of the Cea no sign of water. No lakes or rivers or even any wetlands such as were common through most of the highlands. How did folk survive here even apart from attacks by the Daegmon?

She turned to the man beside her. She realized she didn't even know his name. Nor did she know if he even spoke the trade tongue. "I am Elynna," she said awkwardly, when he made no effort to acknowledge her presence.

The man hesitated before answering. "I am called Noab," he answered, also in the common tongue.

"Is there anything more we can do for you?" she asked.

"Can you restore the dead?"

Elynna winced. "I am sorry."

"And I too," the man said, ambiguously. Then his voice softened. "Forgive me. My demand was unfair. You are not responsible for what happened, and your compassion speaks for you that you, too, have suffered this fate."

Elynna closed her eyes and nodded. She tried to reply, but no words came to her mind. The memory was still fresh. When she opened her eyes, Thimeon was standing at her side supporting Tienna, who stood on one leg and leaned against him. She had not heard them coming. Noab looked at them, nodded, and then continued. "Already you have done much to help. For that we give thinks. As for us, I do not know what we will do. We had thought perhaps we would travel to Citadel . . ." His voice trailed off.

Elynna clenched her fists. "They won't help. The king doesn't even care."

"What?" Noab asked, eyeing her sharply.

"Never mind," Elynna replied. She poured all the bitterness and cynicism she was feeling into her words. "Go to Citadel. Let all of Gondisle go to Citadel."

Noab looked away and sighed. "Alas, not even the king can restore what we have lost."

"Some of us may be traveling together as far as Aeti," Thimeon offered. "That was our plan, though it may have changed now. The trade road runs west and south from Aeti toward the capital. There is no other faster way. You are welcome to join us—"

"Elynna," Cane interrupted. He and his brother had followed Thimeon and Tienna up the slope. "Do you still intend to go to Aeti with Thimeon? The Daegmon still lives. We know that now. Our quest is not over."

"Cane is right," added Cathros. "We have work yet to do. Whatever the others decide, the gifted at least should confer about our course."

Even as the brothers spoke, more of the companions were emerging from their tents. They saw the gathering and began to approach in ones and twos. Elynna watched them a moment. How many of them had the will to continue? Or the strength? Some, at least, needed rest and healing. Tienna. Hruach. Even if they were willing—and Tienna certainly would not want to give up—she could not lead them back into such danger and hardship without some hope of victory. And yet where could she go? For her, at least, there was no longer any safe place. Wherever she went, it seemed, the Daegmon would be after her. If she did not pursue it, then it would pursue her. She would not be responsible for bringing its fury against another defenseless village. She would have to pursue it. Even without hope. Even if it meant her certain death.

She turned to Cane. "Yes," she sighed. "You are right. At least for me. I must go on. And others, I think, will choose to come with us. I do not have the courage to send any away. We must gather the company and bring the question before them all. Let all each for themselves."

Elynna was about to start back down the slope toward the tents, when somebody called out something in the Ceadani tongue. Elynna and the others turned in the direction of the voice and saw, coming toward them, one of the three villagers they had first seen when entering the village the day before. By his looks, he was close kin of Noab—a little taller and not as rugged, but with the same brown curly hair and pale deep-set eyes. He continued to speak loudly as he approached up the hill. Elynna heard Noab's name, but she understood nothing else in his speech. To her left, however, she saw Thimeon turn and gaze in the direction of the road where it entered the village from the north, trying to peer over the low ridge that obscured the view in that direction.

When the man arrived, he pointed where Thimeon was looking and said something else in the Ceadani tongue. Then he looked at Elynna and said in the familiar trade language, "Come. Look."

"What is it, Noaem?" Noab asked.

"More visitors. Riders. Many of them. I hear their horses."

"Riders in the mountains?" Noab's surprise was evident in his rising inflection.

"I am sure of it," the one named Noaem replied. "They are . . . They are . . ." He paused, searching for words. He gave up and spoke in his own language.

Noab turned and translated to Elynna. "Riders are approaching from the north, down the trade road. They will be here soon. My brother says that the horses are hard-pushed and complain of ill treatment. They are many." He turned toward his brother, and the two strode forward over a low outcropping to get a better view up the road. A few long strides took them the thirty or so yards to the wide, flat rock that marked the top of the low ridge that jutted northwestward out of the village.

The companions followed more slowly, with Thimeon coming last, supporting the hobbling Tienna. They joined Noab and Noaem atop the flat rock, where they could look off toward the north and east and see the road as it approached the village.

"I hear nothing," said Cathros, who had the best hearing of any, except perhaps Tienna.

"Nor I," Noab stated. "But when it comes to animals, my brother is rarely wrong."

"Who is approaching? I wonder," Thimeon said, more to himself than to anybody else. "Large parties on horseback are uncommon here."

"I do not know," Noab answered. "We did not expect you when you arrived at our village yesterday. We do not expect them." He paused. "And we did not expect the Daegmon."

As the small group stood looking off to the north, the rest of the companions—curious, perhaps, about what was drawing everyone's attention—made their way up from the edge of the village where they had spent the night. Within a few minutes they were all gathered together atop the small rise with Noab and Noaem. Even from this vantage, however, they could hear and see nothing in the distance. When Thimeon explained what Noaem had said, a few of them looked skeptical.

"They come," Noaem said again a minute or two later. "Many horses."

"I don't see anything," Bandor said. But the words were barely out of his mouth when the first riders crested the top of the slope a mile north of the village. More followed behind, spread out across the road, streaming over the hill. Within seconds, more than fifty of them were riding down the trail toward the village.

"Who are they?" Cathros wondered again. "Has Citadel come to our aid at least?"

"It is a large war band," Cane answered, and his hand went to his sword. "If it is a band of raiders, we will be hard-pressed to defend ourselves. It might be wise to—"

"No," Thimeon interrupted, shaking his head. "There are few robbers in these mountains. This is not like in the Anghare Northlands, where raiders and war bands from rival tribes are common, and where tribal mines must be guarded by castles. Life here is too hard. And," he added a moment later, "there is too little of value to steal."

"And yet," Cathros observed, "this is no mere embassy. These men are ready for battle."

"That, too, I'm afraid is true," Thimeon said. "The crown sends none to these remote parts for the same reasons there are no raiders here: there isn't enough wealth here for Citadel to care about us. What have they to do with trees and sheep and gyurt?"

"But these riders are certainly from Citadel," Cathros said when the approaching war band drew closer. "Look. They wear the blue of the king's own troops."

"Have they finally heard our cries?" Elynna wondered aloud. As though drawn by that possibility, the pressed forward several more steps, down off the wide rock and out onto the frozen turf. Cane and Cathros flanked Elynna on either side, with Noab and Noaem to the left of them and Tienna hobbling up on the right, leaning on Thimeon.

Before any of them could say anything else, the mounted soldiers had arrived at the edge of the village at a canter. At the sight of the group awaiting them, they slowed their pace to a trot and then to a walk, and then spread out. They came to a halt just a dozen steps away, five rows deep of soldiers and fifteen horses wide. Most were dressed in plain blue uniforms with pants and matching coats that looked too thin for the cold air of the mountains. A few had blue woolen hats. Five, however, were decorated as officers, with medallions and marks of honor on their chests and sashes around their waists. The officers also wore expensive and much warmer fur caps. Their horses were mostly brown or black, of the larger breeds common in the Southlands, not the smaller white or mottled Highland mounts occasionally seen among the Andani or even less frequently among the Ceadani.

"Welcome," Elynna called out excitedly. At the sound of her voice, one of the men dressed as an officer moved his mount forward two steps and looked at her. He scanned the remainder of the company, then brought his eyes back to rest on her. "We have been hoping—" Elynna started again.

"Silence!" the officer warned sternly.

Elynna's eyes opened in stunned surprise, but her lips snapped shut.

"What is this?" Cane asked, stepping forward. "Why do you speak thus—" His foot had barely touched the ground in front of him before three riders had drawn their bows and were aiming at his heart. He froze, words dying on his lips.

"This is the one?" the officer asked, still looking at Elynna.

"Yes sir," came the answering voice. It was a voice Elynna recognized all too well even before she saw the face that went with it. And not even the sudden appearance of the Daegmon would have disturbed her more, left her more off-guard, or caught her more by surprise than this voice. From behind the first row of soldiers came a young man, unarmed but dressed in the same uniform as the others. He was tall and sturdy, with brown hair and dark-brown eyes that reminded Elynna of her father. It was a painful reminder, for other than his eyes, her brother had few of their father's traits.

"She is the one," he said.

"Lyn," Elynna muttered. Then more loudly, "What are you doing here? What have you—?"

"Silence," the officer commanded again. He turned to Lyn. "What of the others? Do you know them?"

Lyn looked around. He pointed at Falien and Pietr. "Those two came with her from Westwash. The others I do not know."

The officer nodded, then turned back to Elynna. His next words were loud enough for all to hear. "You are under arrest for the wielding of unlawful powers, for the destruction of villages under the protection of Citadel, and for the deaths of countless citizens of Gondisle. By order and authority of the king of Gondisle, I take you as prisoner." He turned to two soldiers. "Bind her up."

It took a moment for Elynna to realize what Golach had said. *Unlawful powers?* Did he mean the very gifts they had used against the Daegmon? How had he known about them? And why was it a crime to use them? Still, she had felt dismay at the realization that Lyn was somehow involved in her arrest. However estranged they had become during their voyage to Citadel and their time there, she would not have imagined him capable of so totally turning against her. But upon hearing Golach's words, that dismay began to turn to anger.

She was not the only one who was incensed. "What are you—?" Cane started to yell, stepping forward with clenched fists. Only Cathros's strong hand on his shoulder held him. The soldiers with bows had nocked arrows and drawn them taut once more.

"Perhaps we should bring them all," suggested one of the other officers. "The king will be pleased if there are fewer—" He paused a moment, searching for a word, then continued, "*witnesses* roaming free."

The first one—the one in charge—nodded. "Yes. Take the others too. There may be more that possess unlawful powers. We will bring them all to Citadel to await judgment."

"Wait," Thimeon cried out. "You are mistaken." He pointed over at Noab. "Speak with him. Ride twenty yards over this mound and look at his village. It was destroyed two nights ago, before we even arrived. We came to help. The power that did this is gone. Give us your aid and we will pursue it. If you are unwilling to help, at the least do not hinder us."

There was a moment of silence as the officer stared down at Thimeon. Then a fierce smile spread over his blank face. "Bind them tightly, and gag them since they are unable to obey the command of silence."

"Captain Golach," came the voice of a third rider who also bore the blue velvet of an officer. At Thimeon's words, he had glanced past the companions to the much-larger group of survivors from Gale Ceathu who were huddled on the north side of the village watching the scene unfold from a safer distance. "It will be difficult to bring them all to Citadel, especially in secret."

"If your company cannot take captive a band of unarmed civilians that numbers fewer than you, perhaps it needs another commander," the one named Golach replied in a sharp voice.

Before the other officer could reply, Noab stepped forward. One of the archers turned his bow at him, but the Ceadani leader held his hands up in peace. "Wait. Please." He continued forward slowly until he stood in front of Golach. "Do not take us. We do not know these people. They are strangers."

Elynna gasped. Another betrayal from the very ones she had just aided? Cane and Cathros also turned fierce eyes in Noab's direction. Only Thimeon and Tienna remained expressionless.

"Who are you?" Golach demanded. "And who are they?"

"I am from this village." Noab said, pointing toward where the village lay in ruins behind him. "Gale Ceathu it was called, before it was destroyed. It happened the evening before yesterday. We were still taking care of our dead when these strangers came by. They offered to help us and we accepted. We did not know *they* were responsible."

Elynna could not longer restrain her anger. "Responsible?" she screamed. "We helped you! How can you—?" She never completed her question. At a gesture from the captain, one of the soldiers who had dismounted silenced Elynna with a sharp hand to her mouth. She stumbled backward in pain.

"Which are your people?" Golach asked Noab.

"My brother Noaem here, and those over there," he answered, avoiding the companions' gazes as he pointed to the makeshift shelters where his people were.

"All of those are from your village? You have not seen these strangers before?"

"It is as you say," Noab replied. "We had never seen them before yesterday." He lowered his head. "And now, if it pleases you. We have lost everything. Let us go in peace."

Golach nodded. "Take your people and depart at once. You are to say nothing about what you have seen."

Noab nodded. Avoiding the furious gazes of several companions, he and his brother turned quickly and walked away. Elynna stared after them cursing under her breath until the captain spoke again.

"Disarm them and tie their hands. Take what weapons are of value and destroy the rest. Leave their legs free to march, and let them gather their own packs after you have searched them. Leave them food and cloaks. We don't want to feed and clothe them all the way to Citadel. Take everything else. And on second thought, don't waste time gagging them. If they try to speak, find some other way to silence them."

Elynna could only stand and watch in horror as the soldiers obeyed with surprising efficiency. Within a few minutes, companions had been herded into a small circle. Their hands were bound as their packs were stripped of any weapons. Bandor and Nahoon argued briefly against the injustice, but they were soon silenced with a few hard blows to the face and ribs. Siyen began to weep. Cane and Cathros each cursed under their breath, but knew better than to fight. Only Thimeon risked a brief argument on Tienna's behalf.

"Be careful," he protested. "She is injured and cannot walk. We need to carry—"

A gloved hand struck him hard across his face. He stumbled backward, releasing Tienna, who fell to the ground with a sharp cry of pain. There was flurry of activity among the soldiers as they bound the rest of the companions.

Elynna felt her anger mounting. Anger at the soldiers for their cruel treatment of Tienna. At the villagers from Gale Ceathu for not coming to her defense. At her brother. Especially at her brother. She was barely aware of the ropes taut around her wrists. Her eyes were fixed on Lyn, who sat astride his horse near the back of the company watching her from between the archers, gloating as if he had just won a battle. But somehow she bit back the angry words that came to her lips when she realized the futility of speaking them—and the satisfaction it would give him if she did.

Still, though she held her tongue, she was glaring harpoons at Lyn when Captain Golach rode up beside her and shouted instructions at the other officer and the soldiers around her. "This one is dangerous. Give her an extra guard, and keep her apart from the others." Then he turned to Lyn. "And you. Keep your distance from her, or you may suffer the same fate. Now that we have her, you are expendable."

Lyn's eyes opened in momentary surprise, but he obeyed and backed away after giving Elynna one final smirk. Then Golach gave the order to march. "And keep them silent," he added. "If any try to speak, do what it takes to stop them. They are worth nothing to us and may be disposed of if they cause trouble All except this one," he said, indicating Elynna.

13

THE POWERS THAT BE

The sun had been up for little more than an hour when a bound Elynna began her forced march westward out of the rubble of Gale Ceathu. After the initial shock of seeing her brother—and the dismay of realizing he was somehow involved in her arrest—she had regained enough of her wits to make some assessment of their captors. There were about fifty mounted soldiers, and another eight laden packhorses tied together on two long leads. The one named Golach was clearly in charge. The Citadel officers seemed almost afraid of him. They argued only briefly about their path. Elynna, who was kept closer to Golach and away from her companions, overheard enough to get the gist of it. Two of the officers spoke in favor of traveling north along the road, claiming it would be faster and easier, and that they would need to pass through Aeti to get more food. At the mere mention of Aeti, however, Golach, rejected the plan. He did not want to travel along a road, and above all did not wish to pass anywhere near any settlement in the highlands. He got his way.

He pointed at the pack animals. "Make our supplies last," he ordered, and they were off.

With the officers from Citadel barking stern orders to the troops and threats at the captives, they set a brisk westward pace away from the village on a trackless path heading into Ceadani wilderness. Forced to walk on foot beside mounted soldiers, Elynna looked wistfully at the packhorses. But the prisoners were left to travel on foot. Suddenly she felt very alone. All she could see between the legs of horses were booted feet. Then the crack of rope across her back spurred her forward. Cursing her brother, she forced her legs into motion and began the march.

They descended a long slope and crossed a narrow thinly wooded valley. To their left, they could see the land fall away further toward the river and the trees grow denser. But Golach and his scouts kept them on higher and easier ground for the first short stretch.

Soon, however, their path began a steady climb uphill. Elynna and her fellow prisoners found themselves in a rocky land of short scrubby spruce and fir trees, and wild thornberry bushes. They were on the southern edge of the Raws approaching the foothills east of the great Androllin glaciers and snow fields. A thin layer of snow had fallen on the ground, but wind had blown it clear in some places and into drifts in others. At the pace Golach set over the difficult terrain, however, Elynna didn't have much time to look around. Her body, already sore from the previous day's labor in Gale Ceathu, began to ache almost at once. The smell of horse sweat filled her nostrils and added to the misery. But her soft groans of despair, like the sound of her feet, were lost beneath the squeak of harnesses and the clatter of hooves.

For a time their path paralleled the Cea River on its northern side as they followed it upstream, but while the river meandered through a cut to their left, Golach led them on a straight path. They were rarely close enough to see the river or to hear the rush of water over gravel. One of the soldiers, apparently an Andan, mentioned to another that they were passing near the Ceathu Cascades and that they were beautiful in the spring and summer. But Elynna was offered no glimpse of them, and the only rumor of waterfalls was in the steepness of the incline and distant low rumble. Somewhere upstream of the falls, however, when the terrain had again leveled, their path finally took them to the side of the river. For a time they followed its course.

Another hour and a half of hard travel took them to the confluence of two branches of the river. The larger branch flowed in from the southwest. The smaller branch continued due west. Just as they reached this point, one of the advance scouts returned with a report for Golach. The officers halted their troops and gathered a short distance away from Elynna to confer. She could hear most of their voices and gathered something of their whereabouts from their discussion. The band *might*, she gathered, be able to continue some distance following the western branch upstream toward the mountains. However the land was growing steadily steeper, higher, and wilder. The Cea River was a regular series of cascades and rapids now. Due north, by contrast, a gentler descent led them down to the edge of Raws.

"Are there any settlements nearby?" Golach asked one of the men in his patrol.

"We are eight miles or more from the road," a man answered. It was the voice of the Andan who had earlier spoken about the Ceathu Cascades. "An occasional Ceadani hunting party may come into these hills, but they are otherwise uninhabited. None of the Andani live this far south."

"Then we will turn north here," Golach said. "Head across the Raws northwest, and make to skirt the northern slope of Mount Androllin."

Without waiting for debate, the captain spun his mount to the north and spurred it to a quick trot down the hill. For a short time then, thanks to the change of direction and pace, the soldiers fanned out and left more space between them. Ahead, Elynna caught a glimpse of the Raws. Thimeon's description had been accurate. It was a desolate land of sand, rock, and red clay, with little vegetation except an occasional scraggly pine and sedge grasses that grew in thick but sparse clumps. Already the wind was picking up from the southeast.

Before she could see any more, however, a horse came up behind her and a booted foot on her back propelled her forward. She was again surrounded by horses, and her companions were out of sight. The day was not yet half over and already her muscles were complaining bitterly. Only the threat of the hard yank of the rope or a boot on her back kept her moving.

Of the agony of her journey across the Raws, Elynna later remembered few details, only general impressions: the biting wind on the back of her neck, the cutting of the rope on her wrists, her fatigue, the spear butts propelling them forward, the condescending glare of Lyn looking down on her whenever the path of his horse brought him near. And step after step across the cold sand. From the position of the sun, Elynna could tell they were heading more or less northwestward. It was only later she learned from Thimeon that they were cutting across just the southwestern corner of the Raws and had not ventured through the heart of it. Ahead, if she could have seen it, was the peak of Mount Androllin of which Golach had spoken. It was the northernmost and tallest peak in the range with which it shared a name. But the range was actually much wilder and more dangerous to the south; the lower slopes of Androllin on the northeast side were gentle, though only sparsely inhabited and traveled.

The sun was well past its apex when the company came to a spring trickling off a low hillside. It flowed only a short distance from its source before ending in a small frozen oasis. On the west side of the pool, on the bottom of a steep rounded hill, lay a narrow wood of a few dozen tall gray pines. They were the first trees they had seen for several miles. Here Golach ordered a short rest. The prisoners were allowed a drink alongside the horses.

The halt was just long enough for Elynna to realize how much pain her legs were in. When they continued, however, the pace was a little slower. Their path crossed the spring and wound around the wood. From there, the land grew friendlier. They were back in the foothills of the Androllin range, on the west side of the Raws, but north of the glacier out of which the Cea River flowed. They were entering the southern reaches of what was marked on maps as Andani land, though in fact it was still uninhabited and mostly desolate. The sand gave way again to some hardy grasses along with a few scattered shrubs. Two hours more of marching beyond the oasis brought them to the far edge of the scrub lands. A small north-flowing stream delineated the western boundary of the Raws. Had they turned back east or northeast, they would have had many more miles to cross—at least a full day of travel before they were off the Raws, and another half day to get back on the trade road. Golach was not bringing them that way, however. They were taking a more direct route, cutting as close to Mount Androllin and as far from Aeti as possible.

Beyond the stream, against the hillsides, the surrounding countryside looked greener with bushes and trees and tall mountain grasses. In the open meadows, hardy wildflowers and wild winter grains rose up above the thin powdery snow. On the trip south many days earlier, Thimeon had told Elynna the names of many of these flowers, but she did not remember them now and had little attention to give them despite their beauty. Over the next few miles the evergreens gave way to alpine hardwoods. As sunset approached, they caught a glimpse far to the north of the first cultivated farms and homesteads.

It was not the change of scenery but a familiar voice that brought Elynna's thoughts whirling back into focus. "How many of your people died?"

She turned her head upward to see Lyn riding beside her. "How many villages?" he asked, in a voice meant only for her to hear.

A sharp retort died on Elynna's lips as a memory rose unbidden in her mind of the body of young Llana lying broken and crushed in the snow. Lyn disappeared back into the ranks of soldiers.

Sometime later, when the sun had set and the cloudy sky had grown too dark for travel, the captain ordered a halt. By this time, Elynna was numb of body as well as mind. The instant they stopped moving, she dropped to her knees. Only the thin layer of snow deterred her from laying her head down and falling asleep. She watched through half-closed eyes as lanterns were lit and soldiers set up their own tents with practiced proficiency. She was dimly aware that somewhere nearby Siyen was being forced to set up one of the companions' tents they had been made to carry. Then guards came, pulled her to her feet, dragged her a short distance, and threw her through a dark opening to lay a heap until another soldier stepped in with a lantern. The light caused her to blink. Having been kept separated from her companions throughout the day, she was surprised to find herself in a tent with Tienna and Siyen. She was more surprised when the soldier freed their hands long enough for them to drink some water and get blankets from their packs. She tried to rub life back into her numb fingers, but the freedom did not last long. They were bound again, hand and foot. The tent flaps were shut and all was black.

Several seconds passed before Elynna noticed the soft sobs coming from the far side of the tent. "Siyen? Are you okay?" she asked.

Siyen did not reply. Elynna turned toward and spoke toward where she imagined Tienna sitting in the shadows. "Tienna?"

"I am here," her friend answered out of the darkness.

"Are you okay? Did they make you walk?"

"No," Tienna replied bitterly. "Thimeon paid dearly for the privilege of dragging my litter."

Elynna shuddered. She was silent for a moment before asking, "What is happening? Why are they doing this?"

"I was hoping you would explain."

Elynna almost laughed, but it came out a sob. "What is happening? In one day our victory over the Daegmon had been proven in vain and our lingering hope that the king would send help has been dashed. There is nobody left to fight the Daegmon. It will be a long march to Citadel."

"They were looking for *you*," Tienna replied in a flat tone. "Why?"

"Didn't you hear them? They are blaming us for the destruction of the villages."

"I heard. They charged you with the use of 'unlawful powers' and the destruction of Gale Ceathu. Did you notice how concerned that captain was with identifying those of us with *gifts*? At first he just wanted you, but then he arrested us all."

"To keep the others silent?" Elynna guessed.

"Why?"

Elynna's voice was laden with the despair and cynicism she felt as she answered. "Maybe so the whole of Gondisle doesn't discover how evil our king is."

She had not meant her words as a serious answer. But Tienna's response showed she took the words seriously. "Yes. That might be. There is something going on as evil as the Daegmon's attacks. I would wager my bow that this captain *knows* we're not to blame for the destruction of the village. In any case, if the king truly cared what had happened, he would have done something long ago. So why did he arrest us if he doesn't believe we are responsible? What is he trying to find?"

"Or trying to hide?" Elynna asked.

"He is hiding something. That much is clear. There is too much that does not make sense. How was it they knew another village had been destroyed? Our captors showed up at Gale Ceathu just a day and a half after its destruction. Word can't have reached Citadel in that time."

Elynna pondered the question a moment. "They must have been already in the mountains looking for us. The only way they could have known about the village was if the king himself—" she stopped short as a horrible thought crossed her mind.

"If the king what?" Tienna asked.

"If the king himself ordered it. But no. That can't be. We know already that it was the work of the Daegmon and not of soldiers."

"Okay," Tienna agreed. "That brings us back to your other guess: that they were already nearby searching for us. So how did they know where we'd be? Or even who we were?"

"Lyn," Elynna replied, grinding out the name through gritted teeth. But she didn't explain her answer. Instead, she changed the subject. "How is your foot?"

"The pain is great."

Elynna closed her eyes against the darkness. She knew Tienna would never admit pain unless it was unbearably bad. "Will it heal?"

"I do not know. The bones are no longer in line. The splint was jarred when soldiers pulled me away from Thimeon." She paused, and then for a moment her voice trembled. "I need to do something soon or it will come together improperly. And I will be crippled." Despite tears at the corner of her eyes, Tienna's voice was steady—like a village healer discussing the wounds of somebody else, or a commander speaking about a military situation.

"Can't you use your gift of healing?" Elynna pleaded.

"I think not. Not on myself. I can feel my injury. Not just the way one feels pain—though I do feel the pain—but I can feel it with my gift. I can see with this inner eye where the bones are improperly set. I could even direct somebody else in setting them right. But I have not been able to use my healing power on myself."

"You tried?"

Tienna nodded. "I attempted the healing twice. Once during the battle when it was first broken, so that I could return and help my companions. Then again today. Nothing happened. I don't understand this—" she paused, searching for the right words. "This power. But one thing has become evident. I need the health of one body to bring healing to another."

"Then what can we do?" Elynna asked, her voice carrying the sense of desperation that Tienna's voice lacked. "Shall I speak with the soldiers and ask to reset the splint on your leg?"

"Thimeon has already tried. Several times. Captain Golach did not appreciate his persistence. Thimeon will sleep with welts on his shoulders for his efforts on my behalf."

"He is courageous," Elynna admitted for the first time. "I pity him, and I am shamed. I don't think I would have done the same for him."

"He would have for you," Tienna said.

Elynna felt herself blush and was glad the tent was dark. "What of Cane? How did he fare? I could see his anger simmering. Was he able to hold his tongue?"

"He is a warrior, and he is no coward. I fear what would have happened if he still had his sword. But he understands when words are of no avail and when it is best to hold his tongue."

Elynna pondered Tienna's comment a moment. She thought of the harsh words Cane had spoken to the companions at times. They were often words that needed to be spoken. Thoughts she'd had herself. But she'd wished he had spoken them more gently.

"What shall we do?" she said at last. "We must try *something* for you."

"I fear for my leg if we do not, but I am at a loss."

The two fell silent. Elynna's fatigue came seeping back over her. Despairing of the possibility of finding any help, she gave in to her weariness. Laying her head down on a lump of ground, she closed her eyes, and despite the discomfort of her bonds, she drifted off to sleep listening to Siyen's soft whimpering.

At the first gray of dawn, the three women were woken by one of the officers nudging them in the sides with a booted foot. Elynna rolled over painfully and sat up. She had a dozen different aches she would have rubbed if her hands not been tied. But her captor gave her no time. He drove her out with threats of kicks. Siyen squawked when he went after her, and she came shuffling out quickly. Tienna had to drag herself out. When they were out, he untied their hands.

"Pack your tent," he said. "If you work quickly enough, you can eat." Then he turned and strode off, leaving the three women under the watchful eyes of other guards.

"Wait," Elynna called out when she realized what he had told her. "The others have the food." She was thinking of the portions of elk from the hunting expedition, and of the dried fruits and nuts. But she was too late. The officer had already disappeared.

She turned to the soldiers guarding her and pleaded with them, but instead of offering help, they warned her that she was wasting the little time she had—and that if the tent wasn't rolled when the officer came back, he would make them regret their laziness.

Elynna cursed under her breath, but set to work with Siyen loading the parts of their tent back into their own packs, which they would be forced to carry. As she did so, she found in her pack a last bit of bread left from Gale Enebe she had put there after the meal the previous evening. Surprised and thankful, she shared it with Tienna and Siyen. They had barely finished their meager helping, when the officer returned and ordered them bound again.

It was only then that Elynna took the time to look around her. The sun had still not peeked above the eastern mountains, but it was light enough to see more than the dim outlines of trees. They had bivouacked in a wide meadow about a hundred yards up an east-facing slope looking out over the Raws. To the northwest, the familiar tower of Illengond was obscured by the eastern slopes of the nearer peak of Mount Androllin, whose own summit was engulfed in dark clouds.

She tried to place where they were in the dim map in her mind. Androllin, though it rose only half the height of Illengond, was still a towering mountain and could be seen from all around the central Highlands with its distinctive triangular peak like a crow's beak pecking at the sky. Weeks earlier, when the growing company had traveled through this region, it had been visible for days. She remembered seeing it from Aeti on a clear day, and again from the hill near Theo's home. She gazed in that direction, hoping against hope that the Andani people might come to their aid. Yet Aeti was a journey of at least two days to the northeast from where they were now. Perhaps more, if this wilderness was as trackless as it appeared. And who would come to their aid?

She looked back to the north and west, as though her eyes could see through mountains or pierce the clouds engulfing the peak. The trade road from Citadel to Aeti wound around the west and north sides of the mountain. She had heard Golach tell his men to avoid being seen. Yet she guessed he was heading for that road eventually. A more direct route to the road and Citadel, such as an eagle might fly, would have brought them around the southern slope of Androllin. But as Thimeon had explained, the terrain there, though free of the great glaciers, was laced with hazards: dangerous precipices, steep bluffs, narrow chasms, and deep winding gorges. Like the rest of the Androllin Range, it was virtually impassable. They would have to skirt around the northern slope and meet the road on the western side. About three days of travel would bring them to the trade road, she guessed, and then five or six days more and they would be at Citadel.

Captain Golach, perhaps counting those days himself and eager to be back in the fortress, began shouting orders at his soldiers urging them to haste. The last of the tents were down, and the prisoners were bound and ready to march. Soon the soldiers were mounting their horses. Nahoon and Bandor were sent over to pick up Tienna's litter. Then once again Elynna was cut off from her companions. With the threat of a whip or spear butt to prod her, she forced her sore legs into motion.

Fortunately the horses did not enclose her as tightly as on the previous day, and Elynna could see some of her surroundings as their forced march ate up the morning. Their way climbed up and down over swells of rolling hills and wooded valleys, with the latter growing deeper, wider, and greener as they wound their way northward. The air was mild. Although they were traveling north, it had grown warmer. The had left behind the snow of the preternatural winter, and also descended in elevation from the peaks south of Gale Enebe where they had first battled the Daegmon. Though the air was still colder even than a typical winter day in the Westwash, it felt to Elynna more like a late autumn day in the highlands. Indeed it was a pleasant land, despite their proximity to the Raws. Or it would have been pleasant under other circumstance. But she was a prisoner, and Golach drove the company at a pace that might have been easy on the mounted riders but was grueling for those on foot.

The fatigue of the forced march combined with harsh treatment from the soldiers and the lack of fellowship with her companions made the journey miserable for Elynna. Had even one of her fellows been at her side, it would have been more bearable. Instead, she kept raising her eyes to see her brother riding a few paces beside her, waiting for her to look up at him so he could return her gaze with a gloating smile before disappearing back into the ranks of soldiers leaving her wondering how he had become so cold and callous in so short a time. Their parents were nothing like this. Even when Lyn had grown angry with her after the death of their father, he'd at least shown passion and concern. This was far worse. And far more painful for her to bear.

Yet there was nothing she could do. She had no chance to talk with him. And what would she say even if she could? She did not know. It was almost a relief that she did not have to try. That the grueling labor of the forced march spared her the pain of experiencing more of the hurt she was sure he wanted to inflict on her.

On through the morning, the large band traveled. Despite fatigue and a rash of blisters growing on her feet, Elynna kept moving. With the sun behind a veil of high thin clouds, she had little sense of time. She was glad when they finally took a brief rest to drink from a stream. By that time, Lyn had ceased making visits to torment her. Her refusal to respond must have bereft him of the pleasure.

Unfortunately, something else began to annoy her: another premonition that she was slow to understand. Midday came and passed. Golach ordered a halt. The soldiers dismounted and ate while their horses rested. A soldier gave Elynna water, but they kept her away from the others. When she had taken her drink, she collapsed to the ground exhausted. Her head had barely touched the grass when Golach was once more shouting orders and the soldiers were mounting their horses. She lay still, unable to go further.

Through her closed eyelids she felt a shadow cross her face and heard a voice yelling. She didn't respond. There was some cursing, and a moment later heavy boots landed on the ground beside her. She had barely opened her eyes before she was yanked to her feet by the rope around her wrist. The soldier who did it was smirking as he bound her hands to his saddle with a short rope, then remounted and dug his heels into his horse's flanks.

Tears came rushing to Elynna's eyes as she stumbled onward at the end of the leash. And at the moment of her despair, it struck. The suddenness of the burning sensation made her stumble, and she cried out in pain and surprise. It was unmistakable this time. Turning her eyes skyward, she ducked her head expecting the worst.

Yet there was nothing to be seen. The sky was empty. As quickly as it had come, the burning touch disappeared, leaving Elynna alone again. She lowered her eyes. At the sound of her panicked outcry, the soldiers around her had stopped and were looking at her. She gazed back at them wide-eyed, then stood up straight and tried to regain her composure. Her guard urged his horse onward, and she stumbled forward once more.

"Cane?" she called hesitantly, illogically hoping he might hear her but that the soldiers wouldn't. There was no such miracle. A spear butt in her back warned her not to try again. She considered shouting one brief warning and taking the consequences, but then the truth struck. What good would it do even if she warned them? Her companions were bound and unarmed just as she was. They could do nothing.

An hour went by. There was no sign of Lyn. Aram and Kayle appeared in front of her briefly, but a horse stepped in between her and them. Her fatigue and hunger had once more taken pre-eminence in her mind, driving out the thought of the Daegmon. They were following a long gradual ascent when she felt the burning again. It was not as sharp or sudden, but it was just as unmistakable. Crawling up her backbone like a flame came the gnawing touch of the Daegmon's presence—the burning smell she had come to know. Within minutes it had sapped her strength. And without the nearby support of Cane and his gift, she had no defense against its terror.

"Cane," she called out in desperation. "It is nearby."

The flat of a sword caught her hard in the back, leaving a sharp sting despite her heavy cloak. She cried out and stumbled forward, but she understood the warning and fell silent. Once again that afternoon she felt a faint touch of the creature some-where in the distance, soaring high overhead or hidden on a hillside.

As evening came and Elynna's fatigue crept beyond extreme to uttermost exhaustion, the war band came for the first time into more settled territory. Here and there could be seen flocks of sheep grazing along green slopes and a few small houses nestled beside streams. They came upon a small road that might have served the cart of some local farmer, and or perhaps the wagons of loggers who worked the northern slopes of Androllin. It was even smaller than the wilderness road running from Gale Ceathu up to Aeti and not nearly as wide or as well-traveled as the trade route that ran from Citadel through Aeti to Anghata. But it was going roughly in the direction that Golach wanted to go. Without stopping to consider their plan, the soldiers moved down onto this road.

Shepherds on distant hillsides turned and gazed at the strange sight of a company of mounted soldiers riding along a little-used road. Golach ordered the guards to tighten their ranks. After passing a larger farmhouse across the valley and then coming unexpectedly upon a small trade caravan of Northlanders carrying pelts, he ordered the patrol to leave the road once more. It was about an hour short of sundown. Elynna heard him explaining to his officers.

"Even this rutted excuse for a road is too well traveled. And if we continue to follow it, it will undoubtedly lead us northward toward the trade road, where we do not want to go just yet. Not while still among the Highlanders, so far from Citadel. We will veer directly westward across wooded country and cut off the wide loop of road that passes through Aeti. It will save us a day and a half of travel and avoid several villages."

There was some grumbling among the soldiers, but not in Golach's hearing. A short time later they plunged into the trees. Away from the road, travel grew more difficult. Elynna's strength and concentration had long since disappeared. She was unable to avoid several bruising tumbles. Yet Golach continued to push his captives much harder than they had pressed themselves during the quest. The threat of blows gave Elynna the endurance to go on. Not until the last sunlight disappeared over the northern slope of Mount Androllin did they halt.

By this time, Elynna was far too tired even to think about her hunger. She was thrown together with Hrevia and Beth, whose hands had been temporarily unbound so that they could set up a tent. When the job was done, the two were tied again and together with Elynna were sent through the flaps with warnings not to leave the tent. When Hrevia managed with tied hands to open her last small package of meat to share, Elynna summoned enough strength to swallow. After that, not even the thought of the Daegmon's return could keep her awake.

The following morning, however, she awoke early to a plethora of sore limbs and muscles. She tried to roll over, but the sharp pain in her wrists reminded her of the bonds. Even her legs were tied. Between the ropes, the cramped quarters, and her aches, the attempt to find a more comfortable position failed. After a few minutes of squirming, she gave up and lay on her back staring at the roof of the tent. How long she lay listening to the heavy breathing of her companions, she was not sure. Outside it grew lighter. About the time she realized that the roof of the tent was visible above her head, she heard the first voices. A minute or so passed, and then a soldier ducked in through the low tent flap. Before Elynna could move, he was rudely shaking her feet and growling.

"Get moving. If I have to come in and get you, I'll drag you out by your hair."

Even if she had dared to ignore the threats, Elynna was too uncomfortable to stay on the ground any longer. She rolled to a sitting position and sat rubbing her hands for a moment. After exchanging whispered greetings with Beth and Hrevia, she exited. She hoped her wrists might be untied long enough to get circulation flowing in her hands again. Maybe even long enough for a bite to eat and a few words with the others. Golach showed no such grace. When Thimeon petitioned him for food, he replied with a sneer, "Give the prisoners water."

Elynna's heart sank, but there was nothing she could do. Pleading with Golach had proved useless. With their hands still bound, she and her fellow prisoners were sent to the spring in twos and threes for the quick drink that was to be their sustenance for the day. At least two of the others must have been unbound temporarily, for their tents were taken down and again spread among their packs, but Elynna did not notice who did it. Her stomach already growling for something more substantial, she waited her turn for water under the scrutinizing gaze of two surly soldiers who looked no happier than the prisoners.

As she was dipping her face in the spring, she remembered the unmistakable presence the previous afternoon. "The Daegmon," she whispered to Beth and Hrevia, who knelt at the spring beside her. "It's back. I felt it yesterday afternoon. I think it is following—"

That was all she had time for. Whether the guards heard her or not, the next moment they were pushing her away from the water and hurrying her off into isolation. She glanced around. The soldiers were mounting. Through a gap between horses she could see her companions lined up several yards away. Guards were double-checking their ropes, making sure they were tight and secure.

As usual, she turned her eyes toward Cane, drawn to his strength and resolve as she had been since the day they had met. But she was just as far away from him as ever. For a moment she tried to look at him as merely another of the companions, without the desire she felt for him. There was a firm set to his jaw, and the gaze he gave the soldiers was stony and defiant. Something simmered dangerously just beneath the surface. She could see it. Indeed, all the Northlanders looked that way: Cathros, Aram, Kayle. Even Hruach and Hrevia. They had not given up. Though for a time they were wise enough to hold their tongues in check, their fierceness was aroused. Their race bred this resistance in them. She wondered if the guards saw it too.

Without meaning to, Elynna looked at Thimeon next. He had several welts and bruises on his face and neck, yet fire burned in his eyes too. However most of the others—the Westwashers, the Plainsfolk, and the rest of the Andani—were more subdued. Tienna, lying on her litter, was in obvious pain. And Siyen, though uninjured, was staring blankly with glazed eyes. That was all the time Elynna had to look around.

Then began their third day of forced march. And the third day proved the worst yet. Elynna had not taken more than a dozen steps before all her pains shot back into her body. The night on hard ground had done nothing to ease them. And the situation grew worse. Before an hour had passed, loose leather on her boot had worn her right heel raw. Unfortunately, even had her guards been inclined toward compassion, they were not willing to risk Golach's wrath by stopping to allow her to lace them more tightly. She had no choice but to persevere.

As the morning progressed, they moved gradually deeper into the southern Andani wilderness crowded by trees and steep hillsides. During the morning they skirted the most densely forested areas, but avoiding trees and undergrowth eventually was impossible. It was midmorning when they entered the first thickly wooded area. It was a dark forest of mixed evergreen spreading out of sight in both directions. Golach ordered a halt at the edge. Elynna collapsed to the ground, too fatigued even to feel relief. When she saw the reason for the stop, any remaining shred of hope of some possible escape disappeared altogether. The guards were binding the prisoners together in long columns to prevent any one of them slipping off into the trees. Each column was tied front and back to the saddles of one of the soldiers. Elynna was the last to be tied. It was all she could do not to weep. Even being tied to one of the horses might have been an improvement had she been linked to the chain with her other companions. But she was left alone.

The trip through the forest took the rest of the morning and into the afternoon. It was difficult going. They had come into the steeper hills along the northern and northeastern ridge of Mount Androllin. The trees were straight and tall—thick and green at the top but limbless near the bottom. Many were old and rotted, and the ground was littered with their fallen trunks. Golach's company was constantly veering around them, or going under or over.

A multitude of streams and small rivers crossed their paths also, making travel even trickier. In spots springs made the ground soft and wet, while in other places it was frozen hard and uneven. And if the trees and bad footing weren't enough, the ground alternately rose steeply and fell away just as steeply as they made their way over numerous spurs and ridges emanating out from the central slope of Mount Androllin. Elynna stumbled several times, and without the use of her hands to check her fall, many of the falls resulted in new scratches and bruises. Worst were the tumbles into wet ground that left her cold, muddy, and miserable. Even Golach questioned the route, and Elynna could hear him scolding his advance scouts. But rather than slowing the pace, he ordered it faster. When one of his officers suggested they turn back toward the road, Golach threatened to run him through with a spear or anybody else who made any unwanted suggestions.

Onward they pressed. At one point Elynna became so miserable she lost even her fear of punishment and complained bitterly to her guards. They were unmoved. Her choices were to hobble forward on her sore feet or be dragged by the horses. The only redeeming feature of her physical misery was that it had grown to the point where she forgot about her brother and even about the Daegmon. Not until much later did she realize with relief that the day had passed without either of them making an appearance.

Only once, after they had come out the far end of the forest and found themselves at the base of a long steep scree with open ground all around, did Golach allow a short rest. It was early in the afternoon. They were close enough to Mount Androllin that its peak, now almost due south, was occluded from view by the steep slopes of the nearer foothills. The soldiers dismounted, and after seeing to their horses and making sure the prisoners were secure, they took a small meal. Elynna managed only a swig of water offered by one of the guards. Then, despite the rocky ground and all the noise, she fell asleep. A soft poke in the ribs awakened her. She groaned and rolled over without opening her eyes, but the booted foot jabbed her a second time less patiently. She looked up to see a young soldier staring down at her. "Come on," he said, with surprising gentleness.

Elynna looked around. The others were preparing to depart. Golach was already astride his horse. The terrain to the west promised more difficult travel. She forced herself to sit up. With the soldier still watching her, she somehow managed, despite her tied hands, to tighten the bindings of her boots. It was too late to help much. Her feet were already raw and bleeding. She rose only to collapse again from pain. This time, the soldier reached and firmly pulled her to her feet. He held her arm while she found her balance again.

"Here," he said, handing her a small piece of dried cheese. "Golach ordered these rations. You were asleep so I saved it for you."

Elynna asked no questions, accepting the offer gratefully for fear it might be rescinded any moment. As she ate, she stared at the soldier's young face more closely. He had the high cheekbones of the Andani, and kind, sad dark-brown eyes like Llana's and Theo's. As she looked at him wondering what his name was, he took his own water bottle from his pack and placed it to her lips.

"Hey," came a growl. One of the officers was staring down at them from astride his horse. "Get moving. You want Golach on your case?"

The soldier needed no further warning. He disappeared before Elynna could utter a word of thanks.

"And you," the man snarled at Elynna, but whatever he was going to say never came out for he was suddenly distracted and rode off.

Then they were moving again. The companions were no longer roped together, but travel was not much easier. The ground was loose and uneven, and they were constantly climbing or descending hillsides or traversing the sides of slopes. It was steep enough that several times the soldiers were forced to dismount.

It was about an hour after their stop that Elynna took an especially bad fall. They were on a steep descent. One of the horses next to her, stepping on a loose rock, lost its footing. When it lurched toward her, she stepped out of the way. Her foot caught, and the next instant her balance shifted precariously forward. Trying to avoid diving facefirst down the slope, she brought her right foot around as fast as she could and planted it firmly into the ground. It came down on a small ledge and twisted inward beneath her. The next moment she was lying on the ground writhing in pain.

"Get up," yelled one of the soldiers—the one who had almost gone down beneath his own horse. Elynna just sat there, gritting her teeth and clutching at her ankle. "Get up, I said," he yelled again and leapt down, then yanked her to her feet. When she collapsed again, he hauled her up with a viselike grip on her upper arms. Weeping from the pain, she collapsed a third time. The soldier was about to grab her again, when somebody came flying down the hill toward them.

"Stop it. Can't you see—"

Even as Elynna recognized Thimeon's voice, there was a loud thump and a pained grunt. She opened tear-blurred eyes to see him doubled over on the ground next to her and the soldier standing over him with clenched fists. Before he could rise, a foot caught him in the shoulder, knocking him backward several feet down the slope. The soldier stood over him for a minute, then straightened and walked back to his horse. Without looking back, he swung astride and started down the hill, leaving Thimeon unmoving on the ground.

Half a minute passed before two other guards rode up beside them. "Can you stand or do you need to be dragged?" one asked.

In reply, Thimeon rose slowly to his feet. He walked over to where Elynna lay. "Is it broken? Your leg?"

"I don't think so," she replied, wiping the tears from her face.

He knelt beside her and felt the ankle. She winced as he gently bent her foot around. "Twisted. We'll see what we can do later."

"Enough talk." The order was punctuated by a prod with a spear butt. Thimeon rose and helped Elynna to her feet as well as he could with bound hands. She stood for a moment testing her strength. The pain eclipsed even the burning of the raw skin, but her foot held her weight. She nodded at Thimeon. He stepped alongside her and hooked his elbow and forearm beneath her upper arm as securely as their tied hands allowed. Together they continued down the slope without interference from the guards.

For once Elynna did not despise Thimeon's company. He was not sent away until Golach came back an hour later and had angry words with the guards. By then Elynna was past caring. When the sun approached setting, she was barely stumbling along the rough ground. One ankle throbbed from the bad sprain and threatened to give out on her, while the other stung with the ache of raw flesh. Every muscle in her body screamed with fatigue. Five or six times late in the day she had to be hauled to her feet by one of the soldiers.

Finally Golach ordered a halt in a small hollow with steep slopes on three sides. Elynna would have dropped to sleep instantly had it not been for the pain. Instead, she fought with her laces and tried to loosen her boots as others of the companions, under guard, unpacked and set up tents. She succeeded with her bound hands at untying one of her boots, but not the other. Then one of the guards—the young one with the kind face—came and led her to the tent. Trying to keep her weight off the injured ankle, she hobbled after him and crawled through the flap.

"Are you all right?" came an unexpected voice.

14

OF THIMEON
AND TIENNA

E lynna was surprised to see Thimeon kneeling at the other end of the tent with Tienna on her litter beside him. "How—?" Elynna started. Before she could finish, the young soldier slipped through the flap behind her. Without a word he untied Thimeon's hands. Then he turned, glanced nervously out through the tent opening, waited a moment, then disappeared.

"Now," Thimeon said, "First things first." After untying the two women, he pulled from his pack a full water skin. He offered it first to Elynna, who grabbed it eagerly and had to restrain herself to keep from finishing it. When Tienna had also drunk her share, Thimeon took a large drink for himself, then capped it. Next he produced a handful of edible roots and a roll of spicy smoked lamb. He didn't explain how he had gotten the food or water, and Elynna was too busy eating to ask. A long silence followed as they consumed their small meal. Outside they could hear loud talking and laughing.

"We're far from any dwellings," Thimeon explained when they were done eating. "I heard Golach give permission for the men to drink and light fires. I think there will be revelry among the soldiers tonight. We might not get another chance like this."

"To escape?" Tienna asked.

Thimeon did not reply. Blazes were already springing up in the clearings around the tents, casting flickering glows on the outside of their tent. Elynna had seen that sky was clear, and the moon, though still in its green phase, shone brightly. Added to the glow of the fires, there was enough light inside the tent for the companions to see each other. Tienna's face was pale and drawn from pain. The swelling in her leg was visible through her leggings. Thimeon was little better. A huge lump on the side of his head marked the blow he had received for coming to Elynna's rescue, and crusty blood matted his hair. He looked at her through bloodshot eyes as he spoke. "Let me check your injuries."

Had Elynna not been so tired and in such pain, she might have resisted. She did not want to owe him more than she already owed him. But he was already loosening her boots. She cursed aloud his lack of gentleness, but it felt good to have the boots off. Blood from the chafing and ruptured blisters covered her left foot. Her right foot was swollen and dark blue.

"First, the open wounds," Thimeon said. He removed salve from his pack and applied it to the raw skin on her feet. The soothing effect was almost immediate. "In the morning I will give you more and a bandage to help protect it as you walk. For tonight it would be better to let these wounds have some air. Now let me look more closely at your ankle." He had her roll onto her stomach, then took her right ankle in his hand and gently bent it back and forth. A sharp pain shot up her leg, and she scolded him again.

"You have some tearing in your muscle here," Thimeon said, touching the top outside of her ankle. His voice was angry as he spoke, though the anger was not directed at her. "There is little I can do. You should be made to stay off this foot for at least seven days. If Golach had any compassion—" He shook his head. "I will apply numbing balm. It will help you feel better and maybe help you sleep, but healing will take time. In the morning make sure your boots are well laced. The more support your ankle has, the better."

He applied the balm, which took longer to penetrate and relieve the pain than the other salve, but when it took effect the result was better than Elynna could have hoped. The pain was reduced to a dull ache. In the meantime he had moved up her back. "There is blood soaking through your shirt. What have you done?"

Elynna was surprised. Her ankle hurt so much that she had barely felt her back. However, now that the salves were having their soothing effects on her feet, she noticed the other pains more acutely. "Maybe when I fell—"

"Take off your shirt," Thimeon ordered.

Elynna turned red with anger and self-consciousness, but before she could answer she caught Tienna's gaze. The huntress was watching calmly, showing no sign of surprise at the request. To her, Thimeon was just a healer. She would think no more of letting him bind her naked wounds as a healer than she would of fighting him if he were an enemy. It dawned on Elynna then. It was not modesty she felt; it was shame to expose the inadequacies of her own body—the fat where she didn't want it and that wasn't where she did, the boniness of her shoulders, the skin wrinkled from too much sun. Even before Thimeon—for whom she had no affection—she was ashamed of her lack of beauty. Aware of her own ridiculousness, she sat up quickly and before she could change her mind began pulling off her tunic. The action made her more aware of the state of her back. She gave a small cry of pain when the fabric ripped off a scab from her shoulder. Then she felt the cool autumn air on her bare skin. At once she pressed the front of her body back down on the mat. "Well?" she said caustically. "Are you just going to stare?"

"She's done now," Tienna said more gently.

Elynna looked over her shoulder and saw that Thimeon had politely turned his face to the door while she undressed. And for the first time in several days, there was a grin on Tienna's face. "What are you laughing at—?" Elynna started to say, but the sudden shock of Thimeon's cold hand on her back caused her to take a sharp breath.

"You didn't do this in a fall," he said. "This is from your pack strap. You have a large welt and several blisters. Your skin is almost as raw here as on your feet." He applied more salve, rubbing it firmly into her back, shoulders, and neck. When he was done, he put a large bandage over that area and then turned around while she sat up to dress.

"And now you," Thimeon said in a more sober voice as he turned to Tienna.

"I am ready."

"I have no salve that will stop such pain as this will cause you."

Tienna's voice was stoic. "It must be reset. It is better to feel hurt now than never to heal."

Thimeon nodded. "This is true, but the knowledge will not lessen the pain."

Tienna's voice was even softer when she replied. "I trust you. With my gift, I was able to see the wound in Elynna's ankle—the swelling and the tearing. I was going to tell you about it so you could treat her, but then just from feeling it you described it exactly as it is."

"Let us hope I can do something for you," Thimeon replied. Carefully he pulled back Tienna's blanket. Her broken leg looked horrible. From below the knee all the way to the ankle was dark blue. The ankle was as swollen as the day she had injured it. Even Elynna could see that the bones were not straight, and for a moment she felt guilty about her self-pity. Tienna's wound was much worse than her own.

Thimeon shook his head, and his voice dropped to a bare whisper. "The journey has not been good for you."

"Do what you need to do," Tienna replied. "I will guide you. Though I cannot heal myself, I can sense as clear as day where the injuries are."

"Here," Thimeon said, pulling another pouch from his pack. He unrolled a small wrapping that contained a half-dozen red leaves. "Chew on one of these. You will find it bitter, but it will help with the pain. If only I could make some tea with it." His voice trailed off.

While Tienna chewed on the leaf, Thimeon felt her leg and applied balm to the swelling. Now and then she groaned and there were tears in her eyes, but she did not complain. After a few minutes, he spoke. "Now is the time. Any relief the herb will give has taken effect, and I don't know how long before I'm taken away."

"I am ready."

They locked eyes for several moments, as though drawing strength from each other. Something in the way Tienna was looking at Thimeon caused Elynna to look at him again also. Did Tienna see strength in his gentleness and compassion, whereas Elynna saw only failure? Thimeon put his hand on the top of Tienna's head, gently curling his fingers through her thick hair. She lowered her head and closed her eyes.

"May the Maker bring you strength," Thimeon said. Tienna lifted her head and opened her eyes. Reaching up, she took his hand in both of her, and kissed his palm.

Thimeon slowly withdrew his hand. He turned to Elynna, instructing her to hold Tienna down and immobilize her upper leg. Elynna nodded, but even as she did, she doubted she had the courage to help. What if something went wrong? How could her friend endure so much pain?

Thimeon gave her no choice. As soon as Elynna was in position, he grabbed Tienna's lower leg with one hand on each side of the break in her bone. "You had better squeeze this hard and try not to yell," he said, giving her his cloak to hold. She nodded, and he went on. "I'll set it as best I can. If your health sense guides you more clearly than my hands, tell me what to do."

He took a deep breath, then gave a sharp jerk. Tienna's face contorted in agony. Elynna looked away, starting to feel faint, wanting it to stop. Thimeon did not let up. He continued pulling the leg straight, while feeling the bone. Elynna forced herself to turn back and watch. Even in the dim light, she could see the sweat gleaming on Tienna's forehead and the tears streaming down her stretched and clenched jaw, but somehow she kept her groans muted.

Those few seconds seemed like forever. Then Thimeon stopped. "I am sorry," he said, placing a hand on hers. He was crying as he wiped her sweaty brow with his shirt.

A minute or more passed before Tienna could bring her breathing under control. "You have done well," she replied through tightly clenched teeth. "It is straight."

"Alas, I wish I could splint it better. I fear the jarring of the road will knock it out of line again."

"If only you could use your healing gift on yourself," Elynna suggested feebly.

"Perhaps I can."

Elynna started in surprise. Had she heard correctly? There was something in Tienna's voice—was it a note of hope?—that made Elynna think she had heard correctly. "But you said—I thought—"

"I have tried twice and failed. But I was trying it alone. If I had a *vehicle*—a healthy body."

"I don't understand," Thimeon interjected before Elynna could voice the same thing.

"Neither do I," Tienna answered. "It is a power. Something incomprehensible. But one thing I do know. The few times I have used my gift to heal somebody else, my own body was somehow part of the healing. I don't know how to explain it other than this. It is as though I take the other's wound temporarily on myself, and through me it passes out of both of us. That is why it is so tiring. And so frightening. I have not spoken this before, but when I healed Falien I was sure that for a split second I could feel my own back breaking. The pain was incredible, and then for an instant I could feel nothing at all—as though I, too, had become paralyzed. I was afraid and I tried to stop, but it was too late. Then I fainted."

"Wait," Elynna exclaimed. "Are you saying it might be possible for you to use somebody else's health? That another person might become the vehicle for your healing of yourself?"

"I do not know. I have not tried. For even if my gift could work this way, I would not want to ask anybody to take that burden."

Thimeon's eyes lit up at once. "We must try. If it will help you, I will gladly be the one—the vehicle, as you say, for the healing."

"Now?" Tienna protested. "I don't think I even have the strength. And you—"

"Now," Thimeon replied before she could finish. "Every day will get worse for you. And if what you say is true, then maybe it is my strength that you need and not your own."

"Maybe," Tienna agreed. "But I cannot ask you to take that burden."

"I am willing. You would do the same for me, as you have already done for Falien. Just tell me what to do."

Tienna looked at Thimeon closely, and something unspoken passed between them. "Thank you," she said, and lay her head back down. "Lie down beside me as I am lying, and stretch out your legs."

Thimeon obeyed. He rested his head beside hers and took her hand in his. Tienna closed her eyes. She reached out with her other hand and put it on his elbow. There was another long silence, during which Elynna held her breath and watched. Nothing happened. Tienna opened her eyes. "It is no good. We need to be closer."

Thimeon slid over so that their shoulders were touching.

"No," Tienna ordered. "Turn around. Put your feet by my head so that I can feel your leg."

Again he obeyed. When he had spun around, she reached out and grabbed his leg in the same place that her own was broken, feeling the health and strength in his ankle. The look of concentration on her face was deeper and more solemn. Sweat beaded up on her forehead once again, and she shuddered and almost pulled her hand away.

Elynna knelt beside them and put her hand on top of Tienna's where it rested on Thimeon's leg. To her surprise, the power surging through Tienna's hand was palpable. Instinctively she pulled back, but only for a moment. Then she set her hand down once again. For an instant she felt what Tienna had spoken of: the sense of health and strength and soundness in Thimeon's bones, as real as the taste of food or the smell of flowers. Then it was gone. The flow of power changed.

Elynna could feel pain now. Or, more accurately, she could sense that pain was felt, for the pain did not touch her but rather passed beneath her through Tienna's hands. Appalled at the sense of brokenness, she opened her eyes. She heard Thimeon groan. There was a loud crack, or snap. Elynna jumped backward and pulled her hand free. To her horror, she saw that Thimeon's leg had bent in an unnatural fashion. She knew at once that it was broken. She looked back at Tienna's leg, expecting to see it healed. But it too was still broken. Something was horribly wrong.

"Your strength," Tienna said weakly. "Come back, Elynna. Now."

Elynna hesitated. She couldn't. What if this happened to her also?

"Now," Tienna croaked. Elynna looked down. Thimeon's face was buckled in agony. His whole body squirmed. Yet by strength of will he held on. "Now!" Tienna commanded.

Elynna knelt. She put her hand back upon Tienna's. Thimeon was in great pain now, but somehow the pain didn't touch her. She closed her eyes and gave up a little more. Now just a hint of the pain tingled in her fingertips. She tried to absorb it. More power flowed through Tienna's hands. She felt her friend straining, exhausted but somehow gaining strength rather than weakening. There was a moment of intense pressure. Then suddenly it let up. Tienna's grip relaxed and her hand fell away.

Elynna moved backward, afraid to look. Thimeon's face was ashen white. Beads of sweat rolled off his forehead. His breathing was heavy. He barely managed to open his eyes. Tienna was already sitting up. She reached down and felt her leg. Though there was still a trace of bruising, the swelling was gone. It looked straight. The women both turned toward Thimeon then. His eyes were closed. His lips were parted as if he meant to speak, but all that came out was a whisper. Elynna leaned forward to hear.

"Tienna," he whispered again. "Is she well?"

"She is healed. And you?"

"Tired," he said. "Very tired."

Tienna was sitting. Despite the circles beneath her eyes, she looked better than she had in many days. The agony was gone from her face, replaced by a look of amazement as she stared at her leg. She reached forward and felt it with her hands. Then she rose tentatively on one knee and tested her weight. "So that's what it's like on the other end," she said softly. Then she turned toward Thimeon. He was still prostrate. His eyes were shut and his breathing was slow and laborious. His face and hands were bruised and cut, and his cheeks gaunt. "You look awful," she said, as if noticing for the first time.

"Thanks," Thimeon whispered. His eyes were still closed, but a hint of smile curled his lips.

Elynna looked at him more closely. "Are you okay? You look like—" She stopped short, not wanting to tell him just how bad he looked, and also feeling ashamed that she hadn't noticed before.

"Like what?"

He had done so much for her wounds. And even more for Tienna's. And she hadn't even noticed his condition. "Like something the Westwash surf has pounded around for a few hours then tossed up on the beach."

"I know what tent to come to for encouragement," Thimeon replied weakly. Again he attempted a smile. "Believe me, you're not the first women who have said such things about my looks."

Elynna would have laughed if anybody else had said that. Did he have some strength even beyond that of Cane? Something she had not before fathomed?

Thimeon opened his eyes halfway, and his expression grew more serious. "I'll be fine in a minute," he said. He struggled to sit up, but fell back down again with a groan. Fresh blood trickled down from a cut above his left eye.

For the first time, Elynna found herself wanting to lean forward and comfort him. Help him. Offer support. Care for him. But Tienna acted first. "Thimeon," the huntress cried in dismay as she knelt and peered at his face more closely. "These cuts and bruises aren't from your part in my healing. You're pale. What have they done to you? Where did you get these wounds?" She didn't wait for an answer. "Where are your ointments?"

"I don't need—" he started. "I have little to spare. We need to save it."

Tienna was already sifting through his pack. "Why has nobody done anything for you?" she mumbled as she removed some salves. "These wounds are bad. I don't even need my health sense to see that." She touched a deep cut on the side of his head. He winced at her touch. "Perhaps I can—"

"No," Thimeon interrupted firmly. "Nothing is broken and you're tired already. The ointments will be enough. There are powerful herbs in them." He paused, then added in a whisper, "And don't use too much. Others might have a greater need later."

Elynna could only watch as Tienna nodded and began to apply salve to Thimeon's wounds, chastising him as she did. "Why did you not take care of these wounds yourself? You should know better than to let this go untreated." He didn't answer. Scowling, Tienna dabbed some ointment to his forehead but chided no more. When she had finished with his head and neck, she pulled back his cloak to reveal yet another ugly black bruise on his right shoulder blade. "How did you get these? This is fresh. It is not from the battle with the Daegmon."

"No. Golach's men are not overly gentle."

"They did this?" Tienna asked, shaking her head in disgust.

Thimeon nodded. Grimacing now and then when she touched a sore part of his back, he told what had happened when he came to Elynna's aid earlier in the day. Elynna listened on, along with Tienna, surprised that Thimeon could tell the story with so little bitterness or anger. And with little mention of his own willingness to take a risk on her behalf. She found herself wanting to boast on his behalf. But she remained silent.

It took several minutes for Tienna to tend to all of Thimeon's wounds, but as the various balms and lotions did their work, the color returned to his face and his voice grew steadier. A pleasant aroma filled the tent. "You are right," Tienna finally said when she was done bandaging him. "I do not sense anything broken. Still, this rib is badly bruised."

Thimeon let loose a soft but articulate yelp as she touched it. "I know," he pleaded. "You don't have to show me which one." A short time later, however, he was sitting. The three of them faced each other now. Two or more hours had passed since they had come into the tent. Outside, the sounds of revelry were fading with the light of the fires. "We need to make plans."

"Plans?" Elynna asked in surprise. Tienna's healing, and now Thimeon's words, gave her a momentary glimmer of hope. The first she had felt since their captivity. "What kind of—"

But Tienna was already nodding her head in agreement. "Yes. Let us speak while we can. What have we learned? Have you heard any talk among the soldiers—anything that might help us?"

Thimeon shook his head. "Nothing except what we heard that first morning. This is about the gifts—the 'unlawful wielding of powers' as their captain called them. We're to be imprisoned, but it's all very secretive."

Thimeon's words brought a memory back to Elynna's mind— something she should have mentioned long ago, but all that had happened and been said in the past two hours she had forgotten. She told them now. "The Daegmon is back. I sensed its presence yesterday."

Thimeon gave a quick nod. Elynna could see in his expression that her news had not caught him off guard. "We heard from

Hrevia," he said. "She and Beth spread the word this morning after you warned them. But it was no surprise. There can be no doubt it was responsible for Gale Ceathu."

"Was it following us again today?" Tienna asked.

"No. Not today," Elynna said. "But yesterday was unmistakable. I felt it just as I had when it was stalking us on the way to Gale Enebe. Not that any of this knowledge will help if we're attacked. We can do nothing."

"You're right," Tienna agreed. "Never in my life have I been so helpless."

"Then it is clear what we must do," Elynna concluded. "We must find a way to escape."

"It will be nearly impossible," Thimeon replied.

Elynna looked down at her hands, avoiding Thimeon's eyes for the moment. She knew he was right, but she did not want to admit it. Finally she looked up again. For the moment she allowed her desperation to win over her reason. "What else is there to try? What else is there to plan *other* than escape? And why not now? We're alone and untied, and from the sounds outside the tent, the soldiers have had something to drink. When will we have another chance like this?"

Tienna was nodding. "Because of my leg I had not given thought to escape. Yet now? I think Elynna is right."

Elynna felt buoyed by her friend's support. Surely Thimeon would listen to the huntress. But he was still shaking his head. "I am not sure. I think we should go to Citadel."

Elynna's jaw dropped. "What?"

"I know this sounds like utter foolishness, but something tells me we must find out what is happening there. Why has the king done nothing about the Daegmon? And why did he order our arrest? What does he know about your gifts? Even if we learn nothing of the Daegmon itself, these questions must be answered. There is something amiss in Citadel, and I fear the quest will not succeed until we discover what it is."

Elynna was in shock at his words. She glared at him. "You *want* to go to Citadel? You are right. It is insane."

Tienna's voice also betrayed her surprise. "I must agree with Elynna. I told you I felt helpless. The Plainsfolk are not bred for captivity, and a huntress even less. I would sooner be killed in battle than spend my life in prison." She paused and shook her head. "Maybe our discussion is meaningless. Maybe Fate will bring us to Citadel whether we desire it or not. Even unbound, escape is unlikely. It will take more than the skill of a Plains huntress—or of an Andani guide—to get us past so many soldiers, and we have no hope of fighting them. Yet I think we must try. If we go to Citadel—if we are left in a dungeon—then who will take up our quest against the Daegmon? What of Gondisle then?"

Thimeon was slow to answer. "I do not know. I do believe there are others who will try to fight it. If the necessity arises, there are some who will even fight against the king himself—"

"But for all we now know," Elynna interrupted, "there are no others in Gondisle who number among the gifted."

"What you say about the gifted may be true," Thimeon admitted. "But escape is not simple. Do we go alone, just the three of us? Or do we try to free the others? Even if we manage against odds to escape alone, we will be little better off than we are now. Our hope against the Daegmon lies in Cane and Cathros." He waited for a reply from Elynna or Tienna. When neither spoke, he continued. "Another thing. Suppose we manage an escape. Do you think we will be free to pursue the Daegmon again? I have already seen enough of Captain Golach to know he'd pursue us to the corners of Gondisle. Remember, Elynna, it was *you* they were after more than any of the others. How far do you think we would get?"

Elynna was silent. Thimeon's words made sense, though she did not want to admit it. Tienna still shook as if in disagreement, but she had nothing to say either.

"More importantly," Thimeon continued in an even softer voice, "there is the question of what to do if we find the Daegmon. We have not yet learned how to defeat it, even with all of us together. We thought we had destroyed it in once. We failed."

"We must at least—" Elynna started. Then she stopped as Thimeon's last word sank in. *Failed.* Yes, that much was true. They had failed. Multiple times. Why would it be any different next time?

Thimeon waited a moment, and then he completed the sentence for her. "At least *try?* Perhaps. Perhaps not. Not yet, anyway. A voice within tells me we should go to Citadel—that we will find answers there. And though I would rather go of my own will, maybe we will learn something as prisoners we would never learn if we went freely and sought an audience with the king."

He looked back and forth between the two women. Elynna tried to formulate some argument, but before any words could come to her lips, Thimeon continued. "Suppose I am wrong. Suppose there is nothing to learn. That still brings us back to the question of escape. How? How, even if we manage against all odds to slip past the guards and into the woods, would we ever be able to set the others free? Unbound though we are, what happens the moment we step out from this tent? The camp is too well guarded for us to get far, especially with all the fires."

"But in Citadel?" Elynna argued, once again unable to contain herself. "What if the king throws us in the dungeons? From what this Captain Golach has said so far, that seems the most likely result of this journey." Her voice was bitter. "We may have little hope of escape now, but there we would have *no* hope."

Thimeon look at Elynna and held her gaze for a moment. "You speak of hope, and I am glad. For hope is one thing we must not lose. And it seems to me that the one thing we would have, even in the dungeons of Citadel, is hope."

Elynna turned away from his gaze. She stared up at the top of their tent. "I don't understand," she finally said. "What hope would we have in the dungeons?"

Thimeon's answer was slow and deliberate. "As long as we are alive, we can have hope. If we are killed trying to escape, and if you are right about the gifts, then with our death is lost the current hope of Gondisle, unless the All-Maker should provide some other hope that I do not foresee."

Elynna's argument fell dead on her lips as an image of her brother sneering down at her from astride his horse popped suddenly into her mind. But now it was Tienna's turn to object. "I hear all you say. Yet the blood of the Plains is thick within me. Do you really ask that I go to prison? I agree with Elynna. If we have little hope of escape now, what hope have we in the dungeons of Citadel?"

Thimeon turned toward Tienna. "I do not know. There is yet one other thing. I wished your decision would not come down to this." His voice fell to a barely audible whisper. "It was not by accident that we were left alone and unbound. I arranged it."

Elynna remembered back two hours earlier to the guard who had led her into the tent and helped them loose their hands. She had momentarily forgotten him in the excitement of Tienna's. "*You* arranged that?" she asked.

"Yes. I spoke with one of the guards today. I asked him to bring me to you, and to unbind me so I could help you and Tienna. I knew you were sorely hurt. I promised him that if there was any trouble, I would not say how I came to be here. And I gave my word also that we would not try to escape tonight."

"You promised *what*?"

"I gave my word."

Elynna could barely contain herself. "How could you make such a promise?"

"Are we worse off than if I hadn't? Had I not given my word, I would not be here. You would not be sitting unbound with your wounds tended. And Tienna would not be healed. I have not given up any opportunity for escape that we otherwise might have had."

"But what right did you have making such a bargain for us? I did not choose to give up my chance of escape. And for that matter, why should you keep the agreement? Do you think Golach would honor his word?"

"No," Thimeon answered at once. "All the more reason that I should. If I do not, then I become what I oppose."

"But the battle against the Daegmon—"

"Thimeon is right," Tienna interrupted. Her voice was flat, as if the whole thing had suddenly become simple. "There are more battles to fight in this world than the one against the Daegmon. Some may be even more important. He has given his word. We abide by it."

Astonished, Elynna turned toward Tienna. However, the look in Plainswoman's eyes put a stop to the argument. After a moment, Tienna turned back to Thimeon. "I am curious. I understand now what you have done, and I thank you. I thank you especially for the part you played in my healing. I know well the risk you took. Little though I relish remaining a prisoner for even one more night, had you not come to join us then my leg would not now be whole. Yet I am surprised that a guard was willing to help us, and that he trusted your promise."

Thimeon allowed himself a little smile, though it was a sad one. "To our fortune it happened that I knew him. He is a cousin of a friend from Aeti, and not a bad man at heart. We were acquainted many years back. His name is Alrew."

"How did he come to be in Golach's company?" Elynna asked, with a tone of disapproval.

"His story is too familiar. He was lured to Citadel and to the service of the king by the promise of wealth and glory. Ignoring the advice of his parents, he left his home several months ago to join Golach's band. I believe he's begun to have regrets now, but isn't yet willing to admit a mistake, or to go home in failure. Still, he *was* willing to help a friend."

"Little risk for him," Elynna observed in a condescending voice.

"No," Thimeon acknowledged. "Not much. Not yet. Still, it was better for him to take a little risk on our behalf than no risk at all. Even a small step is a step. Given enough time, we might sway him. There are many, even among the soldiers, who are unhappy with the king."

The three of them fell silent then. Elynna's leaned her head back. Her eyes fell shut almost at once, and she was already drifting off to sleep a minute later when she heard Thimeon speaking softly to Tienna. "There is something we might do—something that would not break faith with Alrew. We will need to tie our hands before the soldiers come for us in the morning. I will do it in such a way that the bonds look secure but that would allow us to easily escape later on. It's a trick I learned when I was younger. The knot feels tight, but has a tag end of rope hanging at the wrist. If you pull on that with your teeth, the knot slips apart. Then, if the need arises—if the Daegmon attacks or if we are given opportunity to escape—we can free our hands.

"Won't they notice?" Tienna asked.

"Not if I do it right. I was adept at this when I was a young. And I don't think these soldiers are nearly as observant as you."

"No," Tienna agreed. "They are not. But they are brutal."

By this time, even with all the noise around her, Elynna was starting to doze. The last thing she heard was Thimeon's whisper. "We should not tell anybody about your leg. Not even our companions. Golach doesn't yet know of all the gifts. There's no reason to give him any additional knowledge. Furthermore, you will have a better opportunity of escape later if it's not known that you can use your legs."

If Tienna replied, Elynna didn't hear it. For the first night since their captivity, she slept soundly. Whatever salves and ointments Thimeon had used on her produced a wonderful effect.

15

ROAD TO CITADEL

The next morning, however, did not go as smoothly as they had planned. Elynna was awakened from deep sleep by a sharp kick in her foot. She opened her eyes with a start to see one of the guards staring in at her through the tent flap. "Get up," he growled. "Wake the others."

Elynna blinked, and out of habit reached up to push her hair back from her face. Mid-gesture, it dawned on her that her hands were supposed to be tied. The guard was staring right at her. "Get moving," he growled again, giving her another kick.

Elynna's heart pounded with a sudden rush of fear and adrenaline as she nodded her assent. She lowered her hand to her lap hoping he wouldn't notice, then turned to see that Tienna was awake and glaring at her. She turned back to the guard. He watched her a second longer. Then, more interested in inflicting pain than in doing his job well, he turned and left.

The companions flew to work. Tienna grabbed a rope and set to tying their feet while Thimeon worked on Elynna's wrists.

It was slow. His fingers were still cold and lethargic, and he fumbled with the knots and apologized for his own ineptitude.

"Hurry," Elynna whispered furiously, looking back and forth between her wrists and the tent flap. At least a minute passed before he finished with her hands and turned to Tienna. There were footsteps outside. His fingers were working now. Though it seemed as if longer, he had the second knot complete in a few more seconds.

"But what about you?" Tienna asked. "Who will tie your hands?"

Thimeon did not answer. Even if he had a plan, it did not matter for there was no more time. They heard the footsteps stop outside their tent. With the mass of rope in his hands, Thimeon dove toward the side of the tent away from the women. As the guard stepped in, he engaged in a last frantic flurry of activity pretending to be untying rather than tying his wrists, and then he tossed aside the rope as though he had just managed to undo the last bit of knot.

"Trying to escape, eh?" the guard yelled. "We won't have that." He leveled a hard kick with a booted foot and caught Thimeon in the chest. The blow sent him sprawling into the side of the tent with a grunt, almost causing the tent to collapse. The shout brought another soldier over.

"Get him," the first said. "He wants to escape." The two grabbed Thimeon roughly by the elbows and yanked him toward the tent flap. Still doubled over and trying to get his wind back, he collapsed in their grip. Twisting his arms behind him, they dragged him out.

"How did he get in here?" the second soldier asked the first as they pulled the flap aside.

"Don't know," the first answered. Then he looked at Tienna. "Can't say as I blame him though. That one at least might be worth having."

The second soldier saw the fierce glance Tienna shot him. "She'd probably knock your teeth out before you could have your way."

"Least I still have teeth, which is more than you can say. I don't notice you being too picky about where your monthly pay goes . . ." and their voices trailed away.

"Will he be okay? Can you sense whether they have hurt him?" Elynna asked. The guards' words still rang in her ears.

Tienna's closed her eyes in concentration, and she raised her right hand as though feeling the air. She opened them again a minute later. "It is hard to tell. Too many people around, and they took him away too quickly. There are no bones broken, I think, but—"

The return of two more soldiers interrupted her. One was Alrew. There was concern on his face, and he was looking back in the direction in which Thimeon had been taken.

"I'm sorry," he whispered in Elynna's ear as he stooped to give her some water. "I will see what I can do for him." Then he bent over and untied their legs. Finally he checked that their wrists were securely bound. His face registered a moment's surprise and then a smile when he saw the knot, but he said nothing. "All is well," he said to the other.

A short time later they were on the move. Cathros and Theo were carrying Tienna in her litter. Elynna had seen no sign of Thimeon after he'd been dragged from their tent. The possibility that he'd been killed did not escape her, and her heart was heavy with the thought. Golach had said on the very first day that the guards could kill any of them except her. She kept a nervous eye out for him through the morning but by midday had given up. The terrain had grown even more treacherous, and she had more than she could do just avoiding further injury to her ankle.

They had come to the end of a rocky vale between two north-jutting arms of Mount Androllin, and now faced their steepest ascent. A final narrow ridge separated them from the long descent into the wide valley where the Illengond River flowed off the great mountain, gathered waters from the central highlands, and began its long journey southward through Citadel and all the way across Gondisle to the Southern Sea. The soldiers had dismounted and were leading their sweaty horses up the slope. Still, Golach did not slacken the pace. Elynna, propelled onward by the ever-present threat of a rope across her back or a boot in her side if she fell, trudged and clawed her way onward.

Eventually they reached the top. There was collective sigh of relief among the guards as a grand vista of the fertile green Illengond Valley and the western mountains opened up in front of them. It was a clear day, and Mount Illengond was visible to the north, closer and larger than Elynna had seen it in more than a moon. Clouds clung to the sides, but the three peaks were visible around the bowl of clouds. The prisoners, however, had neither time nor energy to enjoy the panorama. They began the descent almost at once. The thought did not evade her that once they reached the road below any last chance of escape would vanish altogether.

In keeping with Elynna's sullen mood, two hours after midday the sky darkened with heavy gray clouds that moved in from the west and piled up against eastern slopes of Androllin. Then it began to rain. It was the first precipitation Elynna had felt since before Gale Enebe. She might have enjoyed it had it not been so cold and had she not been forced to march in it. But it was a different thing altogether to sit beside a fire at her home in Westwash and watch the warm summer rains that would turn the meadows around her village into a huge swath of berry blossoms than to endure a drizzling early winter rain while traveling as a prisoner.

As the rain fell harder, her cloak passed rapidly through the stages of dry to damp to utterly soaked. Her hood was all but useless. Water dripped down her forehead, and she tired of wiping it with her bound hands. As the ground beneath her feet grew laden with water, it became even more difficult to find footing. The dirt was soon slick with mud where the horses' hooves had torn it up, and the lichen-covered rocks were worse. Even the horses were having trouble. The soldiers looked as miserable as the prisoners. Still, Golach refused to halt.

Having once more reached the point of exhaustion, and not imagining she could get any more miserable, Elynna was again on the verge of giving up. About then there came one brief period when the terrain had grown especially treacherous, and the rain had turned from a steady drizzle to a driving downpour that cut visibility to just a few feet. They were in a steep gully formed by spring washouts, and muddy water three or four inches deep was rushing underfoot. Something had spooked the horses and the soldiers were occupied. Elynna had descended about a half mile or so down the gully, when she lifted her eyes from the ground, looked around in the gray rain, and realized there were no soldiers to her left. Her guards had fallen behind, or moved ahead, or stopped to calm their mounts. Her gaze fell to her wrists, and she remembered the knot Thimeon had tied.

She looked again to her left. The gully was steep, but not so steep she couldn't climb out. She glanced back over her other shoulder. The soldiers to her right were busy keeping their footing; they were paying no attention to her. All she had to do was start slowly inching away into the mist. Just a few slow feet, and then a dash. With visibility so poor, it would only take a dozen steps to disappear—as long as she did not slip and fall climbing out of the gully, and nobody came upon her from behind. She reached toward the loose end of rope, preparing to free her hands as she inched slowly to her left.

Then she hesitated. It was impossible to tell what surrounded them. Forests? Rocks? Cliffs? Wilderness? How long could she survive in the mountains without food, shelter, or weapons? Or without company? Without Thimeon. All through the quest she had relied on others, and none more so than the Andan guide whose love she despised. If she escaped now, she would be on her own.

But what if she didn't try to escape? She might not get another chance. The inner argument raged for just a minute. Then she remembered what she so furiously told Thimeon the night before. Whatever the risk, they had to try at least. She clenched her fists in determination and again continued inching her way to the left, away from the soldiers. Ten feet. Fifteen feet. The gap grew. Freedom was just feet away. She bit the knot ready to pull her hands free.

Then, without warning, they were at the bottom of the slope. The sheet of driving rain passed overhead. The sky lightened. A cluster of soldiers emerged from the gully on either side of her. Elynna was surrounded once more. Her fleeting opportunity had slipped away.

Less than an hour later, with rain still pounding down around them, they stumbled off the last hillside on Androllin's north-western slope and found themselves on the trade road. A cheer rose from the soldiers. Even Golach grinned in relief and allowed a moment's rest before ordering them southward down the road toward Citadel, still some days to the south. They continued a short distance until it was too dark to go on. They halted for the night just as the rain let up. Elynna, her legs aching, collapsed to the ground and drifted into unconsciousness. Sometime later she found herself in a tent with Hrevia and Beth, where she learned that Aram and Kayle had escaped during the descent.

"What of Thimeon?" she asked.

"No, he didn't escape," Hrevia said.

"But—" She could barely bring herself to ask. "Is he still alive?"

Hrevia raised her eyebrows. "Yes, he still lives, though he has not been treated kindly. He was with Aram and Kayle, but he did not try to escape with them. Some of the guards might wish *they* had escaped, though. Golach was furious. I heard him order short rations for his soldiers. We'll likely get nothing."

That was all Elynna heard before she fell asleep. The next morning brought clearing skies and crisper air. When she was dragged from her tent, she got a view of their surroundings. Mount Androllin still loomed behind them to the east, while in the distance to the west the Undeani mountains were now vis-ible. They had bivouacked on a plateau at the eastern edge of a river valley. It was the east branch of the Illengond River, whose headwaters were on the slopes of the Great Mountain itself. Some distance downstream it joined the Dagger River, which some called the West Branch of the Illengond. Their combined waters spilled into the Southland and flowed right to the gates of Citadel many days to the south. Elynna's gaze was then drawn in that direction. She could see where the river meandered a mile or so down toward the base of the plateau and then plunged out of view. Several rooftops of a small village were visible.

It wasn't long into the morning before they were passing through the village. Women watched with curiosity or fear as the large war band went by. A few mothers gathered young children to their sides, while older children ran up to get a closer look at the uniforms and weapons. As Elynna glanced out at the friendly hardworking faces, tears came to her eyes.

Then they were through the village and again following the cascading river as it descended toward the lowlands. No longer attempting secrecy, Golach stayed on the road, where he kept a brisk pace as they made their way out of the mountains. Traveling from dawn to dusk without rest, they passed a plethora of Andan villages, some larger and some smaller. The sky remained clear and cool, and the murky rain-swelled river slowly subsided to a sparkling emerald green. They spent another night bivouacked in an open field near the road. The prisoners were fed only enough to keep them moving. Elynna's pain slowly gave way to a dreary numbness.

Their sixth day in captivity began much like the fifth. After checking the bonds on their hands, their mounted captors led them back onto the road and started them off at a brisk pace under stern orders of their captain. The descent remained steady, following a path parallel to the river that rushed and tumbled toward the Plains. At points the river was just a stone's throw away to their right, and at other times it was out of sight. Now and then, when the road bent due south, Elynna could see straight ahead out over the distant lowlands. Then, sometime in the morning, they emerged from the mountains and into the wide green valley she had caught glimpses of. The change was dramatic. One minute the road was falling down a steep wooded hill just yards from a plunging cascade on the river, and she could see no more than half a mile in any direction. The next minute the road flattened out, and the terrain opened up, revealing views in all directions. The river ceased roaring and began a slow winding curve through a deep channel.

The dramatic change marked the northernmost tip of what the Westwashers referred to as the Great Southland. Elynna did not have maps in her head like Thimeon did, nor the same uncanny sense of direction Tienna had shown, but she had a general idea that they had now circled back almost as far south as Gale Ceathu, where they had begun their captivity, though they were many miles further west and much lower in altitude. The dull gray cliffs on the western face of Mount Androllin itself, whose shadows had engulfed them the last two mornings, were now behind them. Eastward they could still see the tall Ceadani peaks of the Androllin Range towering over them and blocking the sight of the rising sun until late in the morning, while across the valley to the west the bluffs soaring upward toward the high Plains of Tienna's folk. But ahead the land was the flattest they had seen in days. She could feel the lower altitude in the warmer, moister air. It was not yet winter here.

The Great Southland was the largest region of Gondisle, though if all the lands of the three Highland folks—the Undeani, Ceadani, and Andani—were combined, it would rival the Southland in size. The folk who dwelt here in the northern reaches of the valley were actually further north than much of both the Ceadani Highlands and the Plains, and many were of Andani descent, but they still considered themselves Southlanders. Indeed, as Elynna had learned earlier, the region was ethnically diverse with Andani, Plainsfolk, Southlanders of mixed origin, and even a few Undeani dwelling intermingled or in small enclaves. The common trade tongue of Gondisle, spoken by the Westwashers, and also by the Andani—though they spoke it with their own peculiar accent and dialect—was the language of the area. And despite its northern latitude, the region had the moderate lowland climate of the south.

They passed a few more villages during the day, but Golach kept them moving and allowed no interaction between the soldiers and the local inhabitants, who either ignored them altogether or came out to trade with the soldiers. The prisoners were given only a short rest at midday and then driven on through the afternoon. Late in the day they passed the largest settlement in the area: a trading town known as Swage spread over a large island and both shores at the confluence of the Illengond River with the Dagger that flowed down from the wild Undeani highlands in the northwest.

It was just downstream from Swage that they came to the first outpost of Citadel. With two hours of daylight still remaining in their sixth day as prisoners, Elynna saw ahead the twelve-foot-high wall of hewn timber surrounding the fort. A few minutes later they came to a halt outside the gate. The greeting from the guard in the tower made it clear that Captain Golach was known to him, and his company was expected. They passed without delay through the fortified gate and into the enclosure.

The outpost held only a dozen buildings with a small pond and a corral in which two or three dozen horses were roaming.

A few soldiers were moving about carrying out some task or another. A half dozen were at posts on a wall. Nobody else was to be seen except Golach's own men and the officer who had admitted them.

Golach ordered the prisoners led to one of the barracks. It had—and not long ago, from the look of it—been converted into a makeshift jail with bars on the windows and heavy bolts on the doors. The interior was bare and dark with not even a bed to adorn it.

Elynna stumbled through the door and collapsed in pain and exhaustion onto the wooden floor. She was sitting there holding her sore feet and bemoaning once more her isolation when, to her surprise, she heard a scuffling behind her. She turned to see the rest of her companions stumbling through the doorway behind her. One after another. The entire company that had departed from Gale Ceathu except Kayle. After a loud and clear warning that any who attempted to escape would be put to death at once, one of the guards pushed shut the door, and Elynna heard the sound of the bolt sliding across it on the outside.

Despite her fatigue, Elynna's heart pumped quickly. It was the first time since the start of captivity that they had all been together. She turned first toward Cane. He met her glance.

"Well," he said as the sound of the departing guards' footsteps faded. "This is fine."

Whether it was sarcasm that laced his voice or only his usual stoicism was not clear to Elynna. But whatever ordeals he had experienced in captivity, he appeared healthy and as strong as ever. There was no hint of any lingering injury to his arm. Not for the first time, Elynna wished she could go to him and feel his embrace. Even just in comfort, without the warmth of affection. But he had already turned his attention to his brother.

Elynna scanned the rest of the company. Some looked more gaunt than others, and several showed cuts and bruises from abuse. Siyen was as pale as seaweed left on dry sand. And Hruach was still favoring his wounded knee and leaning for support on his sister Hrevia. How had he managed to survive all the marches? But other than perhaps Hruach, none of the others were any worse off than Thimeon, and even he appeared to have improved since the morning after Tienna's healing. Whatever salves and ointments he had, they had done their job. Or else time itself had worked its healing power.

Most of them began to talk now. Several wanted to know about Aram and Kayle, but nobody could tell more than was already known. It was hoped they had escaped, but some of the guards were now saying they had been killed.

"But where are *we* now?" asked Theo. He was the youngest remaining member of the company, and while he had shown great courage and resilience in the face of the dangers and hardships they had met in the mountain, he now looked scared and very young. He was fighting to keep his voice from trembling.

"South of Swage," Thimeon answered.

"Is this Citadel?"

Thimeon shook his head. "Citadel is still many days further if we continue by foot. This is just an outpost."

"And a small one," Bandor said. "It was built to house several hundred soldiers when need demands, but there are only a hundred here at most times."

Thimeon gave Bandor a curious look. "How do you come by this knowledge? You have not traveled here before, have you?"

Bandor shook his head. "Before he was . . . before the Daegmon took him, Llian told me about his days as a soldier. He is older, but we are from the same village, and our families are acquainted. We have hunted together, and we came together to join this company. He talked with me a great deal as we traveled. Guessing from his description, this is the same outpost where he was stationed—though it was many years ago. He said it was just a short ride south of Swage, and that on his days off he would often ride north to the village to a favorite inn. Or when he was missing the Andani highlands, he would travel further north to get a taste of cooler mountain air, spending a day catching fish in the river."

"What else did he tell you?" Cane asked. "Anything useful?"

"If you mean something that would help us escape?" Bandor asked, "then no. Llian told me the names of his friends, but they were few. There were mostly only fellow soldiers. And the few who were friends are likely gone. All I can say for sure is that one hundred soldiers were normally housed there, though the place could hold several hundred when need demanded."

There was silence after that as the others pondered this information. Then they began to talk about Citadel, and about Golach and King Eughbran. A few of the Northlanders again suggested they try to escape, but a quick study of the building showed no sign of structural weakness. Even if they got outside, it would be even more difficult to get out of the fort itself. Hrevia wanted them to fight their way free in the morning when the guards came to get them, but not even Cane took that idea seriously. "We have no weapons," he said. "And you heard Bandor. There are a hundred soldiers stationed here. A hundred and fifty, counting Golach and his men. They'd cut us down."

Tienna, who remained on her litter and said nothing about her healing, suggested they at least choose a meeting place in the small chance some of them did escape later. The Plainsman Nahoon proposed the village of Hilt to the northwest, where three main branches of the Dagger River came together.

"There is a small road that leads there from Swage. We could turn back to the east toward the Andani Highlands. Or," he added hopefully, "we could escape westward through the wide pass and into the Plains."

"It's a long way from Citadel, isn't it?" Bandor wondered.

"All the better," Nahoon replied. "The further we get from that wretched city, the better."

"And yet," Bandor said, "the less time we spend traveling along the road, the better. And if we escape, we might want to meet sooner rather than later. By foot it would take us a week to reach Hilt—would it not?"

"Well, where would you want us to meet?" Nahoon asked in a slightly disgruntled voice. "Hilt is in the middle of nowhere, surrounded by wilderness. We would be safe waiting there, I think. And the people of my future wife could be found not far away from there. They would help us. I don't see why it would be a bad place."

"There is this," Thimeon said. "Hilt is an outpost town. It does not attract many traders. It was an earlier king who made that road from Swage to Hilt to help maintain a small force on the edge of the Undeani highlands to keep an eye on that folk, for they are not loyal to the throne."

"All the better for the Undeani," Hruach mumbled.

"Yes. I feel no great loyalty to Citadel right now either," Thimeon said. "Of course, the Undeani feel no great love for any folk other than themselves. But that is not my concern. I am more worried that the village is there only because there is an outpost and the money of Citadel trickles through there. There may not be many folk who dwell there, but a large portion of them are soldiers. It would be difficult to be inconspicuous in such a place."

"That is true," Nahoon said. "I had not thought of that, for in my past visits I never had any reason to be hiding. Truth be told, I was mostly hoping to see my beloved."

"I understand you, friend," Thimeon replied. "I would see my family again too, if I could."

"But where would you have us meet, then? Back in Aeti?"

Thimeon smiled. "Now you are avenged."

Nahoon blushed. "I did not mean—I'm sorry. I had forgotten your sister was there, in Aeti."

"Yes. And I would see her if I could, for we have lost our parents. But even were that a good place to meet, I would not risk bringing pursuit to my doorstop for fear of the harm that would come to her. Yet this is all a moot point. Aeti, too, I think is too far. I would suggest we meet nearby in Swage. We passed it late in the day. It is but a few miles back up the road."

"You would have us meet so close to an outpost?" Hruach wondered.

"Swage is a large town. Larger even than Aeti, though not so big as Anghata. And it is on the trade road. Strangers pass through all the time. It would not be difficult to avoid notice. There is a traders' inn there called the Lonely Rock. I got the impression when we passed through many weeks ago that some-body, or even a few people, could stay there a few days without drawing attention, especially if a few extra coins were slipped to the innkeeper."

"The beer is good there," Bandor said.

Again Thimeon looked at him in surprise. "Did you slip out and buy a mug as we passed through this afternoon?"

Bandor laughed. It was the first time any of them laughed in many days. "That's the very tavern that Llian liked to visit. He mentioned it by name and promised that if we ever made it together down this far, he would buy us each a pint there."

Thimeon nodded. "It is a good spot. So let us seek to meet there, should we be so fortunate to escape and become divided. And if you can drink it without drawing attention, you can have some of the beer that Llian spoke of in his honor. Probably more than one. I propose that whoever makes it there should wait at least a week, if possible. Of course you will have to find the coin to pay for it. But you may find help where you least expect it."

After a brief discussion, the others agreed. After that, their only success was in untying each other. As they worked on this, Tienna had all the companions come past her litter so she could check on their health. The fracture in Cane's arm had nearly healed. She thought it would be back to full strength within a few more days, else she would have volunteered to use her gift to heal it.

Elynna's ankle still throbbed with a dull ache, and as Thimeon said, it would have been better if she could have stayed off it for a few more days. But Tienna thought it had not suffered any further damage, and that it would heal on its own. She volunteered to use her gift to speed that process, but Elynna felt too stubborn to allow it. "Maybe tomorrow, if it grows worse during the day."

By the time they were done, it was too dark to see. Their discussion quieted then as the exhaustion from the day's forced march settled in. A few fell asleep almost at once, while the rest migrated naturally into smaller groups. Most of the Anghare sat together, discussing in their own tongue what they knew of Citadel and how possible it would be to escape from the dungeons. The Plainsfolk and the Andani—with the exception of Thimeon, who remained alone and silent—stayed together for a time, speaking about their treatment by their captors. But the Andani were the first to drift off to sleep and then the Plainsfolk lapsed into speaking in their own tongue. The Westwashers also conversed quietly among themselves of their homeland, wondering if the harsh winter had hit there also. Elynna, though she had little to say, was lonely for company and joined them. Tired though she was, she did not put her head down on the hard floor until all the others had fallen asleep.

The following morning the prisoners were hustled out of the barracks shortly after dawn. Guards from the outpost delivered a breakfast of bread and milk. Meager though it was, it was an improvement over the past few days, and Elynna consumed it eagerly—and quickly, for she did not know how long they would be given. Her companions must have had the same concern, for all of them ate quickly and with very little talk. She then pulled on her boots gingerly over the blisters that covered both feet, wincing in greater pain as the boot came over her sprained ankle. She wondered if maybe she should be less stubborn and accept the offer from Tienna. But it was too late now. Shortly after, their guards arrived, retied their hands, and led them all into the small clearing near the front gate.

Elynna began to prepare mentally for another day of forced march. It was already a struggle to keep track of how long they had been in captivity. It seemed like forever. At least this day's march might be on more even terrain, and perhaps the company would be held together again at night. She watched as the soldiers mounted their horses and prepared to depart. Then angry voices grabbed her attention. It took her a minute to attune her ears to the voice of Captain Golach, but eventually she got the gist of what the argument was about. To the chagrin of the outpost commander, who was still arguing with him, Golach had apparently ordered his company liberally resupplied at the expense of the outposts' own stores. Elynna realized now that several of the soldiers were riding fresh horses, and three covered wagons waited just beside the gate, each harnessed to a team of horses. One of the wagons was filled with supplies. Elynna did not guess what the other two were for until she and her fellow prisoners were loaded into the backs.

"No more walking, I guess," Cathros said aloud as he stepped up. "That, at least, is good."

"Is it?" Cane wondered. "All the more quickly we'll be in Citadel, and probably in the dungeons."

"Silence!" roared Golach, who had just ridden up to supervise the loading. He leaned over and cuffed Cane hard in the side of the head. Cane barely flinched, and just gave Golach an icy stare. "Keep them silent." Golach shouted at the guards, as he rode off wringing a sore hand. "And tie their hands and feet to the sideboards to keep them from jumping out."

As it turned out, the wagons were only a little more comfortable than walking. They were built for cargo, not passengers, and though the road beneath their wheels was in better shape than the wagon paths in the mountains, they provided a jarring ride. However, the squeaking wood and rattle of the wheels covered their voices, allowing them to converse quietly. In the long periods between conversation, Elynna watched the passing of the countryside through the opening in the back of the wagon. Sitting near the rear on the right side, she was able to see a ways off to the east as well as straight behind them. If she turned her head just a little, she could look westward as well. They were following a large river southward further from the mountains, sometimes just a few dozen yards from the nearest bank and other times a mile or more away. Downstream of the confluence of the Illengond and Dagger Rivers, the soldiers spoke of the river as the Dagger, though Thimeon said that of old the river was known at the Illengond all the way to the city of Kreavia, where it flowed into the sea. The river became less wild as they went, though from time to time they heard the roar of rapids and waterfalls.

Throughout the first morning in the wagon, Elynna still saw the mountains to the east. As they went southward, however, these curved out of view to be replaced by low rolling hills of the upper Southland. They were dotted with small farms that often came right to the road. Some had sheep, and some cattle, anywhere from fifty to perhaps two hundred head. Other farms had a patchwork of small plots growing a variety of crops: five acres of wheat, or ten acres of barley, or a small field of root vegetables, or legumes, or squash and pumpkin vines. Hedgerows and lines of trees separated the cultivated plots. There were orchards too.

Some of the harvest was now past, especially the legumes, and several grain fields were in stubble, but many crops were just now peaking in the Southland. Elynna caught glimpses of families out working together gathering large squash off of vines and putting them in wagons, or picking fall fruit off of trees. There was little real agricultural land in the Westwash, but many of the inland marshes and bogs, including those around her own village, were loaded with wild fruit: large sweet blue and yellow berries called thornberries that grew on chest-high bushes, and smaller tangy red berries known as marshfruit that grew along the ground on vines so long it was sometimes hard to find where one started.

Seeing these families out picking apples together made Elynna think of those four or five summer days each year when she and her mother, and later she and her brother, would spend all morning gathering wild berries, filling baskets of them. Many would be dried or made into jams for the winter, but quite a few would find their ways into pies, or be used as garnishes for her favorite baked fish dishes. And, of course, no small number would be consumed while they were picking.

As they continued south, however, the land gradually grew more populated. Small settlements gave way to larger villages, trading centers, and walled estates. There was also an ever-growing number of travelers on the road, and Golach kept his men busy forming an intimidating presence making sure other travelers stayed away from the wagons. Still, the wagons were left open in the back, and Elynna was able to watch the landscape as they made their way south.

After a long day in the wagons, they spent a night bivouacked half a mile off the road down near the river. She did not know how much distance they had traveled, but it seemed like two or three times what they could have done on foot. Because there was no walled fort around them, the soldiers left Elynna and her fellow prisoners tied for the night. Between the discomfort of sleeping with her hands tied and the knowledge that they were quickly approaching the dungeons of Citadel, she spent much of the night lying awake. Even through the thick fabric of the tent above her, she could see the moon pass overhead on the one night of its yellow phase. Once in the dungeon, she would not see it again. It would not shine through stone.

They started again early the next morning. By late in their second day of travel by wagon, and their eighth as prisoners, the smaller farms had disappeared altogether. They had been replaced by ever larger farms boasting fields of hundreds, to even a few thousands, of acres all devoted to the same crop.

Thimeon made this observation aloud: "It was not like this before," he said in a sad voice. "It is not good for the soil. If the new king brings this change all across Gondisle, it will destroy us as surely as the Daegmon could." He did not explain his comment, and Elynna did not ask. But she did remember how the smaller farms they had passed the day before were more like the farms of the Andani. These larger southern farms were entirely different. And once Thimeon commented on that, she noticed also that there were no longer families to be seen out harvesting together, laughing or singing. Instead, shabbily dressed and dreary-looking laborers were working the fields, sometimes behind large and unwieldy-looking pieces of equipment. She thought of Siyen's parents, and of Siyen herself, wondering if she felt like she was coming home.

What the Plainsfolk were thinking, Elynna could only guess. All along the bumpy ride, hour after hour, while others were looking north and east, scanning the hills and rivers, the eyes of the Plainsfolk were drawn unwaveringly to the west, where steep bluffs of a thousand feet and more rose up to the Plains. Had they been able to jump out of the wagon and get across the river—which by now had become much too wide and deep and swift to imagine successfully fording—and then started walking westward, they could have reached those bluffs in less than a day.

And if there were any steep hidden trails to climb, they might have been walking on the native grasses of the Plains in less than two days. That knowledge did not ease their distress.

At the end of the second day in the wagon, after the sun had already dropped beyond the bluffs into the west, the captives were led into a large fort. Unlike the wooden outpost further north where they had been kept two nights earlier, this one was made of stone and mortar and was much larger, with several cells for prisoners.

By now Elynna was feeling almost numb to the routine. The relief at being with her companions throughout the day had faded to a numb and bitter monotony. She paid only scant attention as the guards separated the companions into threes and fours and ushered them into the cells. They threw Elynna into a cell with Hrevia, Beth, and Siyen, fed them a scanty supper and breakfast, and then ushered them out to another day of travel much like the last, only with an earlier start. It was still dark when their captors loaded them into the wagons. Elynna could see the moon, in its first night in the long pale phase, low in the western horizon. They were still several miles north of Citadel, but over the next hour as the sky lightened and the sun rose Elynna discovered signs of the city all around. Even in the early hours of the day, considerable traffic moved on the roads: farmers, merchants, nobles, and various residents of the Southland traveling for whatever unknown reasons. Most were quick to get out of the way of the soldiers, and thus their travel was not delayed overmuch, but Golach kept an even closer watch on the prisoners, which brought an end to all their conversation. By then, the bluffs to the west had grown close to two thousand feet or more in height, but they had also begun to bend away westward into the distance.

16

CITADEL

L ate that morning they arrived at Citadel. The settlements had been growing steadily denser until for the final half mile it was one long row of buildings with houses so close together there was little distinction between the inside and outside of the city except for the huge wall that towered above the tallest houses. Elynna had a clear map of Citadel in her mind from her long visit many weeks earlier when she had come looking for help. The capital city had been built on a bluff above the eastern bank of the Dagger River. It was three or more miles long from north to south, and a mile and a half wide, spanning two large hills. Its outer wall, fifty feet high in most places and about twelve feet thick, ran around the entire city. Only on the west, where cliffs dropped seventy feet down to the river, was the wall lower.

East of the city outside the walls was settled land—tightly packed houses mixed with a few larger estates slowly giving way to farmland. Another small river, Rain Creek—more familiarly called The Rain—flowed through the southern third of Citadel at the foot of the smaller of the two hills. It came down through the farmland northeast of the city, paused in a small lake, and then passed beneath the eastern wall of the city through a water gate, over the broken remains of a centuries-old mill, and on past markets and inns before spilling over a high and beautiful waterfall down into the Dagger. The Rain was fed by hundreds of pure clean springs seventy miles to the northeast. Elynna had heard it told that until recently, the water in the Rain had been crystal clear and held a population of freshwater fish akin to the grelsh, even where it flowed through the city. Over the past decade, however, as the agriculture of the Southland had changed, the river had grown more polluted from farm runoff and from a handful of big mills recently built upstream. When Elynna was in the city, the river looked constantly murky as though it had just rained. She had seen some of the mills. There had been days on her earlier visit when she had not had the heart to face the crowds of Citadel and had spent the morning or afternoon wandering the surrounding lands. But the mills had depressed her almost as much as the smell of the city. Efforts to find clean water and solitude had been no more successful than her attempts to get help from the king. One farmer had told her she'd have to travel many miles into the hills to see the Rain clear or to find clean fish.

The north trade road they had followed down from the Fertile Valley ran beneath the shadow of the eastern wall and on across the Rain just below the lake. On the southeast corner of the city it hit a crossroads with the major east and west trade roads. The east-west route, as Elynna had learned many weeks earlier, ran from one coast of Gondisle all the way to the other, though she had only traveled the western road. The western road crossed the Dagger just outside the city over the only Dagger River bridge south of Swage, and wound its way through the low hills below the Plains Bluffs toward Aënport, the coastal harbor town through which much of the traffic to and from Westwash flowed. It was from there she had journeyed to Citadel. To the east, the road went almost straight across farmland to the smaller port city of Kreana, and from there on a journey that might take many weeks by foot upward along the coast into the Northland and eventually back inland to the capital city of Anghata. The south road followed the Dagger all the way to its delta and the coastal town of Kreavia.

On her last visit, Elynna had stayed at one of the few inns outside the city. She had found the atmosphere inside the walls too oppressive. The narrow streets of the city were ugly and crowded, and the people often rude. The fortified palace of the king—the *castle*, as the Anghare called it, though it did not resemble the descriptions she had heard of the castles that dotted the Northland—was inside Citadel on the larger northern hill. It was surrounded by another wall nearly as formidable as the city walls. Common folk of Citadel, she had learned, did not enter the palace except by the grace of the king.

The main entrance into Citadel with its massive gates was on the southern side of the city near to the crossroads. There was one wide road inside the city that traversed it from the front gate around the southern hill on its western side to the gate of the palace. However, there were three smaller gates into Citadel in the northern wall. They were used only by soldiers and high-ranking officials and nobles on the king's business. Elynna had forgotten about these until their cart left the main road and turned toward one of them.

At the gate, the wagon stopped for the first of two times. Elynna, fearing that once inside the walls of Citadel she would never again see freedom, bent her neck and peered through the gape between the canvas covering and the wooden wagon. The first thing she saw were the massive walls towering over her, and her heart sank. But she forced herself to remember what Thimeon had told her about hope. She looked around. The gates through which one would have to pass to enter or leave the city on this side were wide enough for two large farm wagons, or a half-dozen mounted soldiers, to enter abreast, and high enough for a soldier to carry a tall banner upright without scraping the heavy portcullis. They were a fraction of the size of the main gates of Citadel.

Golach was speaking with one of the sentries posted at the side. He then turned and began calling out orders. A half-dozen guards, who stood at the ready in an alcove just inside the gates, jumped up at once and approached the wagons. Elynna pulled her head quickly back from the gap in the canvas so they would not know she had been watching them. But they paid no attention to her. They were closing the tarp over the back of the wagons and securing it along the sides so that she could no longer see out at all.

Cathros learned over and whispered to Elynna. "More of this secrecy. They don't want anybody to recognize us, I'll wager."

Elynna did not reply. The moment the tarp was spread over, she began to feel a panicky tightness spread through her muscles and joints. It was as if they were already in prison. She could see nothing but the faces around her as the wagons jolted forward in movement.

Once in the city, travel was slower. The streets were narrow and crowded. The wagon was continually slowing and turning. Familiar odors of sweat, dust, leather, and occasionally the more pleasant aromas of baked goods, seeped through the cracks in the tarp. From the series of turns and hills, those among companions who had previously been to Citadel tried to guess where they were. Elynna had only vague guesses. Her memory of the city blurred into street after street of dirty houses, merchants' shops, and barracks. At one point she thought they were circling the northern hill to the entrance of the palace, but she was not sure. The voyage was painfully slow, and it took much longer to reach the palace gates than she would have thought. When they finally arrived at the inner gates that led into the palace proper, other guards in different uniforms looked into each wagon and then let them through.

Once through the gate, the prisoners were left waiting in the dark for several minutes. With the noise of the city gone and the wagons no longer groaning and creaking, everything was strangely quiet. It was the tensest moment of their imprisonment since the morning they had been moved to wagons, and Elynna wished one of the companions would speak. But either the others were afraid of retribution from Golach or else they were listening intently for some hint of what was happening outside the wagon, and all remained quiet.

After a time Elynna heard footsteps approaching over stone pavement. A longer conversation ensued, of which she could hear several parts. Captain Golach, whose distinctive voice she had learned to recognize, was speaking.

"Lord Prince. I have returned from the king's errand. I must speak with the king."

"I know of your errand. You may speak with me."

"If Your Highness insists, but I would rather tell you both at once, as I'm sure the king would have me do."

"You do not trust your prince?" the other replied, his voice laden with intimidating insinuations.

There was a pause. "I trust you with my life," came Golach's answer. "I also fear the king. He is . . ." Then another uncomfortable pause.

"He does not like to be crossed," the prince finished. "You may speak openly with me. I know my father."

"Then if you know of this errand, you know as well the king's wish for secrecy."

Golach's voice grew more wheedling as he spoke, and Elynna could not hear all he said. Nor did she hear the prince's response. There were more footsteps on the stone, and after that she heard only the distant drone of soft voices. She could no longer distinguish any words. She turned to Cathros, who was sitting next to her, and risked a whispered question. "Did you hear that?"

He nodded.

"What does it all mean?"

Cathrol did not reply. But Tienna, who sat on the other side of him, leaned over. "Nothing good," she said. "And yet . . ."

"Yet what?"

Tienna did not explain herself. There was a bit of hushed conversation among the companions then, but Elynna did not ask any more questions.

Several more minutes passed before the voices came back close to the wagon. "The prisoners should be brought to the dungeons," Golach said. "The fewer who know of their presence, the better—even among the palace staff. The doorkeeper and gate guards here have been sworn to secrecy. "

"I trust you have made this command known among your own company?"

"I have, Lord Prince," Golach's voice affirmed.

"Then use your own guard to lead the prisoners to the south keep."

Golach's sounded startled. "The old dungeons? But I thought . . . Wouldn't the north dungeons be more secure?"

"Why do you question me? The north dungeons are crowded with prisoners already, but the old dungeons, for all their ancient might, lie empty. You know the south keep. The ways beneath the old castle are deep and secluded. Many even among your own men don't know of them. It is our best hope of secrecy."

"But—"

"Go and see to your work," the prince ordered, his voice turning stern. "Since you are so concerned with the king's order of secrecy, I will see that your own company is assigned to guard the dungeon. Then not even the castle guards will know of the prisoners. Go. When you have seen to these duties, then report to the king. I will await you in the throne room."

"As you wish," Golach said. The voice made Elynna shiver. It seemed every bit as evil and cruel as it had on the day he had arrived in Gale Ceathu and taken them all prisoner. But now there was something else. For the first time his voice gave hint of fear. And yet it also struck Elynna as manipulative and insincere, which made her even more afraid.

A few minutes later the wagons moved forward a short distance. Then the covering was pulled off the back. They were in a dark alcove with the main courtyard and front gates visible through a low arch behind them. Two dozen soldiers remained.

The rest were gone. Lyn was nowhere to be seen either. For that, at least, Elynna was thankful. The soldiers untied the prisoners' legs, loosed their hands from the wagon but kept them bound, and ordered them down.

Thimeon helped Tienna down, feigning to support her as he had done since the night of her healing. The others dismounted on their own. Elynna remembered that they still did not know of the huntress's healing. The act, so far, seemed to be working, though what they might gain from it she did not know. The guards were keeping close watch, and soon confiscated the prisoners' packs before leading them through narrow double doors into the interior of the castle.

Elynna had been in the castle thrice before—once for her audience with the king and twice to the archives to search the Chronicles for any mention of the Daegmon. None of the trips had been fruitful, and none had brought her to the part of the castle through which their guards now led them. Golach drove them down a series of narrow corridors at the ground level. There were no windows or ornamentation, and the torchlight was sparse.

After several minutes of walking they came to one frightfully long hall, which they traversed all the way to the end. There they turned right and went down six steps into another shorter hall, turned left and descended another stairway, and so followed a series of right and left turns always going deeper. Two or three times they crossed wider corridors at right angles. Eventually they came to a long stairwell. To their left it climbed upward toward well-lit regions. To the right it went down. Golach turned right. Now they descended deeper into the bowels of the castle. They came to another long corridor with walls of hewn rock carved beneath the hill. There were no doors. At the end of the corridor they entered a large room with one wall of rock and the other three of stone and mortar.

In the room were set several strange devices the likes of which Elynna had never before seen. It took her a moment to realize they were instruments of torture. The knowledge made her flesh creep as they went down four wide steps into the room. Fortunately they did not stay there. On the far side of the dungeon's torture room were two other heavy doors, one on each side. Both had long metal rods bolting them shut. Golach looked both ways, then chose the corridor to the right. He grabbed a torch from the wall and handed it to one of his soldiers. Then he pulled a huge key ring from beside the door, slid aside the bolt rusty from lack of use, and started down the hall.

Ushered on by the guards, the prisoners followed. They found themselves in a row of cells, five on each side. Each had a heavy wooden door reinforced with metal braces. The doors had a small window with steel bars. Golach turned the key in the first lock on the right, threw open the door, and motioned to the guards. In went Cane and Cathros propelled by a rough shove. Before they could even turn around, the door was shut and locked. It was the same all the way down. Bandor and Theo went next. Then Hruach all alone. Then Hrevia and Beth. Then Marti and Nahoon. They turned to the other side. In went Pietr and Falien. Then Siyen and Tienna on her litter. Thimeon, whom the guards had labeled as a trouble-causer, was thrown in a cell alone.

Elynna was alone with her captors. "She's the one," one of the guards noted.

"Are her powers dangerous?"

Golach didn't answer. They walked past the next cell without stopping. Elynna began to tremble. It was possible they were taking her away from her companions, perhaps for immediate execution. Yet when Golach came back to the cell opposite Cathros and Cane, he stopped and unlocked it. Without another word, he pushed her inside. The lock on her cell clicked shut, and the light moved away. Finally came the slamming of the outer door, which echoed down the hallway with unnerving finality. The bolt squeaked back into place and the lock clicked.

For a few seconds a faint tap of footsteps on stone, distant and muffled, was audible through the door. Then even that faded away and all was still and dark. Elynna stood where she was staring at the locked door of her cell. The momentary relief that she was not being led to her execution gave way quickly to loneliness and despair at the hopeless of her situation as she stood where she was for long moments longing to hear the voices of her companions to reassure her she was not alone. She heard nothing. Only silence—a heavy, dead silence that suffocated even the sound of her own breathing.

Elynna stood shivering in a cell. The dim light of a torch filtered down the hall and through the grate in her door. She could see her hands and the outlines of a few rocks in the walls and floor. There might have been rats in the corners of the cell, but she would not have seen them in the shadows. The place reeked strongly of mold and old urine. Was this what death smelled like? Or despair?

Bandor spoke first. His voice sounded hollow as it reverberated between the stones. "Are all of us here?"

Elynna stepped to the doorway, glad to hear a human voice.

The small window was at eye level. She stood on her toes and grabbed the bars with her tied hands. "We are."

"Where?" came Hruach's voice.

"The dungeons beneath Citadel," answered Cane, who stood at the window across from Elynna.

"Alone?"

There was a sudden bout of coughing from a cell farther down the hall. "We are the only ones in this dungeon," Elynna answered "I was the last to be locked up. The other cells are empty." She paused, then called down the hallway. "Tienna?"

The reply was faint. "I am here."

"What do you sense?"

Tienna's voice grew louder as she walked to the door. "I sense nothing. Not even the sun in the sky. I cannot not tell if it is night or day."

"You mean—"

"I have tried. Something is blocking me. A power. Something more than the rock and dirt around us."

A long silence followed as the companions pondered Tienna's words. It was Siyen who spoke next. "Will they feed us?" She had been inconsolable with self-pity ever since they had been taken captive. "I'm so cold and hungry. They haven't left us here to die, have they?"

Nobody answered. As if triggered by Siyen's words, Elynna's stomach started to growl with hunger. She kept by the door. Cane's face disappeared, replaced a few seconds later by that of his brother. Cathros's eyes reflected the dim torchlight as he met Elynna's gaze.

His voice was quiet. "I would guess from Golach's conversation with the prince that we will face the king before many days pass."

Elynna shivered and moved away from her door. She peered more closely into the shadows of her cell. It was about six feet wide and eight feet long. Save for a low wooden bench against the far wall, it was empty. There was no blanket or bedding. The floor was cold and dirty. As wet as the Westwash could be, the dampness there never felt this stale or lifeless. She was glad for her jacket. It helped keep out the worst of the chill. But not the smell. The odor of must and mildew almost made her gag.

She walked back to the door and looked out again, trying to breathe through the grate, but the air in the hall was not much better. And her companions' faces had disappeared from their doors. Somewhere down the hall someone was still coughing, and a few of her companions murmured in low voices. She turned back to the cell, sat down, and wept.

How much time passed after that, Elynna did not know for sure. She slept off and on, but never for long and never deeply. Using her teeth, she eventually managed to free her hands from the ropes that had bound them, but it didn't help her spirits. Her few attempts at starting conversation through the grates were unsuccessful. She felt more alone than at any time since the death of her father.

Finally she heard footsteps approaching from outside. She rose, wondering whether to be eager or afraid. The footsteps belonged to two of Golach's men bringing water and bread, which they passed in through the grate in the door. When they had done their errand they disappeared again, locking the outer door behind them. The coughing grew worse. She could hear Siyen and Beth moaning.

Elynna's sense of desperation grew. They had to do *something*. "Cane," she shouted out her cell. "Cathros."

Cathros came to his door. "Yes?"

"We can't just do nothing. There has to be something we can try."

"What?" Cathros asked.

Elynna thought about Tienna's gift of healing. She had discovered a new way to use it—to heal herself. There had to be some hope in that. "What about your battle strength? Can you use it to . . . I don't know . . . to break down your door?"

Cathros shook his head. "I have told you before. As with Cane's gift, it is not something I can conjure simply because I desire strength. It comes upon me in battle against the Daegmon."

"Is there nothing you can try?"

"I can *try* anything."

"Try," Elynna said.

As Cathros took a deep breath and prepared himself, the sound of shuffling could be heard from nearby cells. Others must have been listening to the conversation. Elynna pressed her face against her own grate and glanced along the hall to see the expectant faces of several of their companions also pressed to their grates and trying to peer out. But of course she could only see those on the opposite side of the hall, and they couldn't see Cathros. She heard but did not see Thimeon speaking encouraging words in the cell two away from hers on the same side.

Elynna turned her attention back to the burly Northlander as he gripped the metal rods with his strong hands. She watched in hope as he strained against the door. Tendons on his hands bulged and his face turned red with exertion, but several minutes of valiant effort accomplished nothing. The doors were too strong to yield to mortal strength. Elynna's hope fell. One by one her jailed companions returned to their benches.

Sometime during the day more food was delivered. Elynna received a bowl of water and a small hunk of bread. The bread was fresh but bland, and the water tasted like the city. A few of her companions made attempts at conversation, but they waned as the futility of their situation settled in. How many hours passed, she did not know. It felt as if they had been there for days, though in truth it was only shortly after the setting of the sun on the day they arrived, when Elynna's nightmare returned. It was the same one she had experienced before the Daegmon's attack on Lienford. She awoke with a start, sweat dripping down her face. The presence of evil around her was palpable, and it was growing stronger. Her skin tingled with a tension she had not felt in many days: the heat of the Daegmon's presence.

17

KORANTH

ootsteps," Cane shouted down the hallway to his fellow
prisoners. "Many of them."

    Elynna sat up trembling. She could feel the heat of
her enemy's presence. She tried to warn the others, but her voice
caught in her throat. Over the pounding of her heart she could
hear something approaching. It was the Daegmon. She could feel
it. It had come to destroy them. How? The hallways were too narrow for such a great creature. She knew that. But the knowledge
did nothing to alleviate the terror.

    The light filtering through the door grew brighter as a num-
ber of torches entered the outer chamber. Many feet marched
across a stone floor. Then came the voice of Golach giving orders
to his guards. Mere human voices. Yet Elynna was drawn as taut
as bowstring from the searing heat of the Daegmon's presence.
From whence did it come?

    Moments later the door to the hallway outside the cells
opened, and she watched as the captain stepped through. He
lit the torches on the wall, then moved to his right, turned, and

bowed toward the door. Following him came another young man, of medium height and build. He had curly dark hair falling to his shoulders and a clean-shaven face with sea-green eyes. Elynna recognized him as Prince Dhan, whose voice they had heard in conversation with Golach on the day of their arrival. He was dressed in a uniform similar to Golach's but with decorations of greater rank. At his side was a richly ornamented scabbard and jeweled hilt. Though rumors told that the king had many sons by his various concubines, the crown prince Dhan was his only legitimate son born by the queen. He moved to his left, then turned toward the door and bowed.

It was the stranger following Dhan who caught Elynna's attention. He was a giant of a man, at least a head taller even than Golach, with massive hands that looked capable of crushing rock. He had to stoop just to pass through the door, and his shoulders filled the whole frame. He was dressed in a dark-green robe with a hood that covered his ears and shaded his eyes from the torchlight. In his right hand was a metal rod like a scepter, only with no jewel or decoration. Unlike the captain and the prince, he did not turn back toward the door to bow.

Elynna knew at once. She could feel it. It was from him that the sense of the Daegmon's presence had come. There could be no mistaking it. So overpowering was the heat the emanated from him that she barely noticed the entrance of King Eughbran. He was shorter than Dhan, with thinning gray hair and a paunch. Nonetheless, there was a look of power about him too. His eyes glittered dark and haughty in the torchlight. He wore the royal purple robe, and on his head was a jeweled crown. Elynna had noted all this before, but she barely noticed it now. Her attention was on the tall man. When he stepped toward her, she almost fainted.

"This is her for whom I was sent," Golach said, pointing toward Elynna. The king did not need to be told. The man who had preceded him was already looking at her. From beneath his hood she caught the glimpse of two bright-green orbs. She recoiled. For just an instant, she had caught a glimpse of his mind. It was the mind of a Daegmon.

"Open it," the king said.

"As you command," Golach answered, stepping toward the door.

Elynna fell away. A scream died on her lips as a spasm of heat shot down her back. A key rattled in the lock. There was a grinding turn and the door opened. This time it was the king himself who stepped in first, followed by the others. Elynna pressed herself against the far wall.

"I believe we have met before," the king said in a cruel voice that mocked civility. "And my loyal Captain Golach has also made your acquaintance."

"It is best to bow when the king speaks," Golach said, stepping forward with his sword as if he meant to make her follow that rule by force.

"Wait," the king said. "We must excuse her. Allow me to finish the introductions. This is my son, Prince Dhan, whose name and face you also know. Perhaps you don't yet know my most trusted advisor, the Lord Chancellor Koranth."

The tall one named Koranth stepped nearer and pulled back his hood. His face, though large and bony, was that of a human. His dark black hair was long and straight, and his eyes colorless. There was no sign of the flashing green orbs Elynna had seen a moment ago, but her sense of his evil grew stronger. He lifted his metal rod toward her chest. Her ears rattled with a resounding boom as a blast of power struck her. Searing pain scorched through her chest. She crumpled to her knees as if she had been struck by the metal rod itself.

"You see, Golach?" the king said. "Now she bows. She only needed time."

"This is the one," Koranth said. His cold hissing voice did not echo off the stone like the others' voices. "She has brought about the ill on this land. You have done well to capture her." There was only a slight pause before he continued. "Now put her to death."

"As you command, it shall be done tomorrow night at the rising of the moon," said the king.

"Sooner would be better," Koranth said, but a moment later he added, "Yet the third night of the pale moon is a fitting night for such things. It can wait one day. See that she does not escape."

The king nodded, as though accepting an order. He turned to the captain. "See to it, Golach—that she does not escape, and that the execution is carried out."

"As Your Majesty commands."

"Father, must we listen—?" Prince Dhan started.

"Does Koranth's power need to be proven to you yet again?" the king interrupted in an angry tone. He didn't wait for an answer. "It shall not be required. My chancellor's word shall not be gainsaid even by the prince himself." Then Eughbran turned and strode from the cell.

Koranth gave Elynna one last look, twisting and distorting his face so much she could not tell if it was a smile or frown or grimace. Then he turned and followed. Golach went third. The prince, departing the cell last, paused briefly at the door. He cast a last glance in Elynna's direction as she lay on the floor, breathing rapidly. Then he stepped out and bolted the door behind him.

Elynna lay where she was. Koranth's words were still in her ears. *"Put her to death."* Yet for the moment all she could feel was relief that he had departed. That she could breathe once again. Several more seconds passed before she realized there were still voices coming through the grate. It was Golach. "Do you need to see the others?"

"All of them," Koranth answered. "Those with powers must be put to death with the woman. It should be done as soon as possible. I would order it done now if tomorrow's moon were not so opportune. Do not even torture them lest their lives linger too long."

"What of the rest?"

"Do with them as you wish."

One last time the prince spoke, his voice angry and challenging. "How have you come by the magic to know which of them have these powers?"

Koranth did not answer.

The voices faded, though the sounds of footsteps moving up and down the corridor continued on for several minutes more as Elynna slowly recovered. By the time she lifted her head, the torches were gone and the cell was again lit only by torches far out in the torture chamber filtering through the grates of two doors. Her sense of the Daegmon's presence had vanished. Somewhere down the hall Siyen was wailing, repeating over and over that they were going to be killed. For once Elynna could sympathize with the half-Westwasher. She would have wailed herself, if she'd had the strength.

She was surprised when she heard Tienna's voice, calm and coherent. "There is a sickness within the king. I could feel it."

Elynna rose to her feet. Her knees felt weak, but she stumbled over to the door in time to hear Thimeon's speaking from the next grate over. "What do you mean?" His voice was also free of all the panic and despair Elynna felt as the pronouncement of their doom settled in.

"His *un*health is difficult to describe," Tienna answered. "It was not an injury but something deeper—like an animal eating him up from the inside. It frightened me. I felt the same thing in one of Golach's guards, though not as strong."

The sounds of her companions' voices, resisting panic, still seeking understanding, somehow settled Elynna just a little. "His advisor," she asked. "Koranth. Did you feel him also?"

"No," Tienna replied. "I felt nothing in him. Neither illness nor health. It was as though he were not."

"Not what?" somebody asked.

"Not *existing*," she said.

"I sensed the Daegmon," Elynna said softly.

"What do you mean?" several voices asked at once.

Elynna struggled for words to say what she had sensed. But none came. "I can't explain it. I felt his approach long before he arrived—the same way I sense the Daegmon. Sometimes I can feel its touch on my mind, as if it could read my thoughts."

"But he's a man," Hrevia said, her voice a mix of despair and confusion. "I saw him."

"What he is may not matter," Cane interrupted. "If we don't find an answer soon, we will be dead."

Elynna bit her lip and pressed the heels of her palms to her eyes. Cane had spoken exactly what she was feeling. It did not help to hear the words coming from him, from whom she always expected strength.

"Those with gifts, at least, will be killed," came an answer from another cell on the same side of the hall. The voice was quiet so it took her a moment to recognize it as Thimeon's. He continued after a pause. "I expect they will kill us all. We are witnesses and accomplices. Though, for the ungifted our deaths might be drawn out." Again she wondered why, despite the grimness of his words, his voice held no hint of despair. Did he still hold hope? She could not see his expression. He went on. "Koranth identified you at once. How was he able to recognize your power?"

He must have been looking at Cane, for the Northlander answered. "I don't know. As I said, it won't matter soon. Answers mean nothing to the dead." There was a heavy thud as he kicked hard at the door. Cathros joined him at the grate, and together they rattled the bars trying to pull them free. It was futile. Cane's face had the same look of despair as when the Daegmon had started the avalanche.

"Cane is right," Hrevia said in despair. "We're all going to be killed. What's the point of this argument?"

"There is always hope," Thimeon said in a soft voice. "Always. The Maker will not abandon us, and He will not abandon His land. Even if He allows us to be put to death in this place, He will raise up some other deliverance."

Cathros ceased shaking the door. "How can you be so sure?"

Thimeon had no answer. But after a moment, he said, "Maybe our questioning is futile, and tomorrow night we will all be put to death. But we lose nothing by trying to think. And if a way out is found, let us be sure to make the most of the knowledge we have been given."

"What we have been given," Cane said with finality, "is a death sentence. And that's something I'd rather not make anything of."

Nobody spoke after that. No longer able to bear the sight of her doomed companions, Elynna turned from the door and dropped to the floor of her cell, She buried her face in her hands, but she did not cry. Minutes passed. Then hours. Somewhere beneath the castle, far from any windows or any breath of fresh air, she could not see stars emerging by ones and twos, and then by tens and hundreds and thousands. She did not seen the moon, recently entered its long pale phase. The low smoky flickering of a torch somewhere down the hallway provided the only light.

But despite the darkness and her fatigue, Elynna did not sleep. She was aware of the passing of time by the slow inhale and exhale of breath, by the persistent coughs down the hall, and by the knowledge that each new minute drew her closer to the moment of her execution. *"Those with powers must be put to death with the woman."* Koranth, the king's counselor, had spoken the words with glee and finality. And so her brother would be proven right, finally. Everything she had done was proving futile. She could hear her heart ticking away as their end approached.

Tap-tap. Tap-tap. Tap-tap. Inhale. Exhale. How many more breaths?

Guards came at some time and dropped bread through the doors, and left without a word. Was it the middle of the night? Morning? Midday on the day of their execution? Why bother feeding them if they were to be put to death? Elynna ate it, assuming it was her last meal.

Tap-tap. Tap-tap. Tap-tap. Inhale. Exhale.

Somewhere down the hall, Tienna was in conversation with Theo, trying to solve some riddle about Koranth, the king, the prince, the Daegmon. Nobody else spoke.

Tap. Tap. Tap.

The tapping was growing louder and faster. Her heart pounded to its rhythm. All of a sudden she jumped. The sound had stopped all at once. It was not her heart. There was a pause, then a loud scraping as of stone on stone. She looked at the door fearing her executioner had come. But the sound was coming from closer—from near her head. She turned in time to see a stone move in the wall opposite the door and gave a startled yell. The huge stone moved again, sliding a few inches outward into the cell.

"Who is it?" she asked, not daring to come closer.

In answer, there was a muffled grunt. The rock moved a third time, and the grunt was repeated.

"Thimeon," Elynna cried in surprise. She rushed forward and began frantically pulling on the stone. It moved again as Thimeon pushed from the other side. A moment later, it was out. From a dark hole in the wall popped the familiar face. "Quickly. I don't know how much time remains to us."

A mingling of hope, surprise, and confusion all rushed over Elynna, but she needed no urging to obey the summons, nor was she going to wait for an explanation. She was already on her knees. In a moment, she had crawled through. "Where are we?"

"Some sort of passageway," Thimeon answered as Elynna followed him, still on her hands and knees. "I haven't explored it. It's too dark."

A passageway? Then there was hope of escape. "How do we rescue the others?" she asked.

"I don't know. Yours was the only cell I could find entrance to. We'll have to find a way into the outer room and get the keys."

Elynna guessed from the sound that Thimeon had risen to his feet. She rose cautiously and put her hands out to find him. He began moving away. She groped along the wall after him, keeping a hand on his back. He was moving slowly, feeling his way as he went. Occasionally he leaned over and felt the wall by his knees. Minutes continued to pass. He had taken about sixty steps, when after leaning over to feel the wall, he stopped. Elynna felt with her own hands. Thimeon He found a handle in the stone about two feet above the floor. In an instant he was down on his knees pushing.

At Thimeon's urging, Elynna knelt beside him. Together they put their shoulders to the stone. It slid out with a loud grind. A draft of air and a faint light came through the opening.

"Wait here," Thimeon whispered. He started to crawl through, but no sooner had his head disappeared than he backed up. "Curse this place. We've come right past the central room and to a cell on the other hallway. This won't do."

"There must be a way," Elynna cried in protest.

"Let us hope so," Thimeon replied. "We'll have to go back and try again." They turned and began inching their way back along the wall they had just traversed. This time they were more methodical, feeling up and down both walls from their feet to their shoulders. The work was painfully slow. Though she was out of her cell, the panic started to rise once again. At any moment she expected to hear the footsteps of their approaching executioners.

But it was to no avail. They found themselves back at Elynna's cell. Another fifteen minutes or more had been wasted.

"Wait a minute," Thimeon suddenly exclaimed with a hint of hope in his voice. "There was no prisoner in that other cell." Before Elynna could question him, he was already feeling his way back along the wall for the third time. He was mumbling as he went. "Of course. Of course. What a fool. Why would that door be locked?"

Elynna still didn't understand, but she struggled to keep up with him in the dark. When he stopped suddenly and dropped to his knees, she almost tripped over him. Before she recovered her balance, he was already crawling through a hole. She bent over and followed him. When she came into the empty cell, she saw his silhouette against the bars in the window. He pushed. Nothing happened. She ran to his side.

"Step back," he ordered. With a grunt, he threw his shoulder into the hard surface. This time there was a loud squeak as the rusty hinge gave way and the door opened several inches. "Stuck, but not barred," he said. "One down. One to go."

Before Elynna was even through, Thimeon was already at the next door. He pushed. Again nothing happened. He threw himself hard against the door, but it did not budge. This time Elynna had the answer.

"Try pulling."

Thimeon looked down. The door had no handle. It was meant to be opened from the other side, of course. He grabbed the iron bars and pulled. The door swung inward with his first hard tug. Together they stepped into the central room. Two torches lit the exit to the right. Elynna kept her eyes off the instruments of torture as they ran across. Again luck was with them. The key to the other corridor hung on a hook to the right of the door. Thimeon unlocked the door. The companions were at their doors when he entered.

"How on earth—?" Cane started in a loud voice when he saw Thimeon.

"Quiet." Thimeon commanded as he let the brothers out. "We must be quick." He turned, and with the key he opened the door to Elynna's cell. "Lead them into the passage," he told her. Then he spoke to the brothers. "That way. Follow Elynna."

Elynna understood the plan now. She stepped quickly into her cell with Cane and Cathros on her heels. As soon as they were in, they saw the hole in the wall where the stone had been removed. Without waiting for Elynna's instructions, they dropped to their knees and started through. Elynna watched. Before they were gone, Bandor and Theo had entered the cell. Others followed; out in the hallway Thimeon must have been going from door to door releasing his fellow captives. Soon all of them were in line crawling through the stone into the secret passageway behind the wall. All but Thimeon.

"Quiet," Elynna urged the others. She walked back to the doorway to look for Thimeon. *Tap, tap, tap.* Loud footsteps echoed through the stone hallways. She almost yelled at him to be quiet. Then she realized it was not him. Footsteps were coming from the main room. Golach was returning, she thought. And for some reason Thimeon was down the hall opening the door to his own empty cell. "Hurry," she whispered. She turned and rushed back to the hole where the last of the companions were awaiting their turns to crawl through.

A second later, however, she heard Thimeon's voice. He was at the door to her cell. "Meet me down by—"

"They're coming," she interrupted.

"I hear them. I'm going to leave Captain Golach with a false trail. Pull the rock back when you're through." To Elynna's dismay, he turned and darted out the torture chamber, directly toward the approaching soldiers.

"Wait," she cried, but he was gone. She turned. The others were all in. With a last breath, she dropped to her knees and followed. "Pull it shut," she whispered as she passed through.

Cathros obeyed. The rock went back into the hole with a loud scrape.

"Where are we?" Cane whispered.

"I don't know," Elynna answered. Her ear was pressed to the stone. She heard doors opening.

"Where does it lead?"

"We don't know yet. Be quiet."

"Are we safe?" Hrevia asked.

"Wherever we are, it's safer than where we were," Bandor replied.

"Where is Thimeon?" Cathros asked again.

"I don't know," Elynna rasped. "He's still out there."

The approaching footsteps had grown loud, and even through the stone they could hear muffled voices. Elynna rose to her feet and ordered the others to follow her. Terrified for Thimeon, she felt her way past the huddled companions and began groping along the wall as quickly as she could. When she had gone about twenty steps, she began feeling for the entrance into the empty cell. She found it a minute later. The stone was still out of place, and a faint light came through. She stopped the others, then stooped over to peer out into the cell.

There was no doubt about the voices now. They were coming from the torture room. The prisoners' escape had been discovered, and Golach was cursing furiously. Elynna was about to back up, when she noticed something moving in the shadows of the cell. Her heart stopped in sudden terror, and she tried to jump back but managed only to hit her head on the rock above her. Before she could move further, the shadow had detached itself from the wall near the door and was moving toward her.

It was Thimeon. He had his finger to his lips. Still rubbing her head, Elynna backed out of the way. Without a word, Thimeon bent over and crawled through the low entrance.

On the other side of the door the voices were getting louder and angrier. "The entrance—" Elynna started to protest.

Thimeon covered her mouth with his hand and whispered, "Not now. Too loud."

She pulled his hand away. "They'll see."

"They've no reason to look here. Did you move the stone back in your cell?"

"Yes."

"Good. Golach's men have sworn we didn't get past them, but he's yelling at them anyway."

"What were you doing?" Elynna asked in a whisper that bordered on shouting. She was surprised at her own emotions—which made her realize just how terrified she had been for Thimeon and how relieved she was to see him again. "Were you trying to get yourself caught?"

Thimeon's voice was calm. "Golach has already seen that the key is missing and that all the cell doors are open. That's what I was hoping for. And that he does not know about these passageways. If he assumes some spy let us out, and that we managed to get past his guards—or that they were disloyal—then he will not search the cells too carefully, and perhaps will miss the real clues to our escape."

Elynna shook her head in amazement that Thimeon, in the midst of everything, had managed to think about all that. All she had been able to think about was flight. She watched him now as he turned and listened at the tunnel entrance a minute longer. There were footsteps again, moving away. Golach's vehement cursing was growing distant. When the last echoes of the departing soldiers vanished, Thimeon and Cane pulled the heavy stone slab back into the hole. The scraping reverberated through the passages and sounded terribly loud but Golach did not return. Once the stone was in place, the passage was completely black.

The dark did not last long, however. Thimeon had grabbed two unused torches from the hall, and Cathros produced a small piece of flint he always kept in a pouch in his garment. It took several attempts at striking the metal tip of one of the torches against the flint to light the other torch, but they soon had two burning torches. They passed one back to Hrevia, who stood with her brother at the rear of the line. Then they looked around. It was a narrow tunnel, about an arm-span wide and just a few inches taller than Cathros. One wall was of roughhewn rock. The other—the one facing the dungeon cells—was fashioned of stone and mortar.

Cathros whistled. "I wonder. Can we get out of the castle this way? By the looks of things, we're well below ground."

"With the whole castle guard searching for us, we won't get far in the open," Elynna replied.

"And if it comes to a fight," Beth added, "We don't have much hope without weapons."

"If it comes to a fight," Thimeon replied, "we have *no* chance with or without weapons." Then he turned his attention to the tunnel. "One thing is certain. We can't stay here forever. That way leads to a dead end, so I suggest we move in this direction. Let us hope Golach does not start searching the cells carefully, because if he does, he can't miss the signs of how we left."

Without waiting for an answer, he turned and started down the narrow corridor. Elynna followed immediately behind him,

with Tienna next, and others following in single file. Being near
the front with Thimeon and his torch, she could see that the passage ran straight for about ninety feet along the back side of the
prison cells. They traversed that distance quickly, finding one
more hidden door as they went. At the end, the passage took
a sharp left. Thimeon breathed a sigh of relief when he saw it
wasn't a dead end, but he didn't pause. After the turn, the corridor ran another thirty feet, then took another left turn.

Nahoon, who was walking behind Tienna, suddenly stopped.
"Tienna!" he exclaimed. Elynna stopped and turned. Others
pulled up short, almost bumping into Nahoon. Some were looking around as though expecting some danger. But it wasn't danger that Nahoon had become aware of. "You're walking."

"Yes," Tienna replied in a quiet voice. "My leg is healed."

"How? What happened?"

Thimeon, who had also now come to a halt, interrupted
before Tienna could answer. "The story will have to wait. We
must keep moving. We do not know where we are, or who knows
about these passages, but our enemies are certain to be searching
for us soon."

The others nodded, and soon they were moving forward
again. But as they walked, Tienna gave a quick account to those
around her of what had happened, and word of her healing
spread through the company. For the first time since their capture, Elynna sensed in her companions' voices and expressions a
new hopefulness.

Thimeon, meanwhile, came now to a right turn, after which
the passage ran straight for many yards beyond the range of
torchlight. Here the floor had a slight upward slope. On their
right the wall was still solid rock and on the left was stone and

mortar. He stopped and motioned the others to silence as the muffled sound of running steps went by on the other side of the wall. Then they continued.

They had been walking about two minutes, when they came to another right turn and found themselves at a junction. Now they were faced with the first choice. To the left, stairs climbed up out of the rock. Above they could make out the back side of wooden walls. To the right, the tunnel turned downward and ran about twenty feet before ending at a rock wall. At the bottom of the wall was a low dark tunnel—a black hole about knee high.

"Here is our answer to one question," said Cane, who was looking along the upward path at the wooden walls. "There are hidden passageways at higher levels, too. So there is hope of getting through the castle without being found."

"It depends on how well those passages are known," Thimeon replied. "Unless they are forgotten altogether, they will be searched eventually. I would turn down instead. If there is a way out of the castle, it must run beneath the walls."

Cane looked as though he were about to argue, when Cathros whispered, "Listen. I heard something again. Up above us. More footsteps."

"On this side of the wall?" Tienna asked.

"I can't tell."

"We cannot take any risks," Thimeon said. "I fear our choice has been made for us."

Without waiting for an answer, he turned right and started down. In five strides he had reached the wall. He lowered his torch and looked in, then dropped to his knees and disappeared.

Cane paused a moment before following. Cathros was third, and Elynna fourth, just inches behind the big Northlander. In the narrow tunnel, the bodies in front and behind blocked the torch-light. She had to feel her way forward on hands and knees. The tunnel ran about twenty feet before opening up. In a minute they were all standing again in a taller passage that continued gradually downward, veering one way and then another, so she could never see far ahead. Afraid the footsteps they had heard might be pursuers, the companions continued on as quickly as they could while avoiding banging their booted feet on the stone. Elynna saw now that both sides of the tunnel were roughhewn rock, and the dust was thicker than in the passages they had left. Cane wondered aloud when the last time any had come that way. "Months or even years it must have been by the signs of this dust."

"That is a good thing," his brother replied.

Soon the way grew even narrower so that it was impossible to walk two abreast. In a few places where rocks stuck out from the side, Cathros had to twist sideways to slip through. Where they were in relation to the cells, nobody knew. Elynna had lost all sense of direction.

They had been walking for five minutes, when they came to a heavy wooden door with iron bands across it. Thimeon stopped before it and just stared at it without speaking. It was held shut near the top with a heavy steel pin, but there was no lock.

"Where does it lead?" whispered Elynna, who had come up beside him. The sight of a door in the middle of the tunnel surprised her.

"It would not do to wander out into a hallway," Cane warned, shaking his head. "We might open this and find ourselves in the middle of guard barracks."

"Not likely," his brother replied. "Not this far underground. In any case, we have little choice but to continue."

"I think Cathros is right," Thimeon said in a voice just above a whisper. "If such a large door were in plain sight on the other side, then these passages would not be so secret. Still we must be cautious." He motioned the others to silence, and then put his ear to the door.

Elynna copied him, and for a moment she imagined footsteps echoing down the stone behind her. An instant later a loud scraping made her jump. She looked up to see Thimeon sliding back the bolt. Tienna put her hand on his arm to caution him, but he was already pulling on the door. It opened with an eerie creak but revealed only blackness ahead. Holding his torch high over his head, Thimeon stepped forward. Elynna went forward with him, and Cane, Cathros, and Tienna crowded in behind. The torch flickered, then burned brightly.

The companions found themselves in an underground hall, ancient by the look of it. It was a high-ceilinged room, covered with cobwebs and thick dust, and large enough that the far wall was lost in shadow. Below them, where their feet had kicked up dust, Elynna saw a floor of polished stone. A pair of long tables sat in the middle of the room, but there were no chairs. The near walls were lined with old torches and lanterns, while the far walls were covered with shelves. The contents of the shelves were not yet visible in the dim light. Thimeon guessed it might once have been an archive, Cane thought a treasure chamber, and Tienna suggested a secret council room, although for that last purpose chairs would have been wanted around the table.

Elynna didn't care what it was, only that it had not been used in years, or perhaps decades. "Anyplace that's not occupied is fine with me," she said.

As the rest of the companions filed into the hall, Thimeon touched his torch to a lantern mounted on the wall beside the door. The lantern sputtered for a few seconds as webs and dust burned off, and ancient oil was wicked up from its old reservoir. Then it took flame. He lit another lantern on the other side just as Hrevia stepped in with the second torch. To prisoners recently escaped from dimly lit dungeons, the four lights made the room seem as bright as noon.

And almost at once there were several whistles and gasps of astonishment as every eye was drawn across the chamber to the dull but unmistakable shine of gold and silver, mixed with the glitter and color of countless gems. The far wall was lined with open chests, stuffed crates, and unorganized heaps of all sorts of treasures: jewels, broaches, lamps, bracelets and necklaces, small statues of precious medal, and other strange unidentified items.

Cane was the first to cross the room. He stuck his hands into one of the open chests and ran his fingers through a pile of jewels. Others of the companions were soon crowding around him doing the same. "Treasure chamber indeed," he said.

Elynna did not follow him at once, however. Though the glitter on the far wall had drawn her attention first, she now glanced about to see what else the lanterns had illuminated. Along the nearer wall, to the left of the door through which they had come, were rows of carved wooden shelves full with row after row of old books, parchments, and scrolls. Entering the room, she had not seen them in the shadows. But Thimeon had also guessed correctly, she thought. She turned to tell him so, and saw that he was already moving in the direction of the books.

Tienna, also ignoring the treasure chests, went with Thimeon. She stepped up to a shelf and ran her finger along the top of a book through a layer of dust even thicker than what was on the floors. "Who put these here?" she wondered aloud. "And why in a room with the gold and jewels and not in some archive?"

"All treasures," Thimeon replied. He blew the dust off one of the volumes and looked at it without picking it up. It was a book bound in thick black leather. It had once had a title engraved with in gold lettering, but the leather was cracked and peeling, and most of the gold was lost. "These tomes must be decades or even centuries old. And this room hasn't been visited in some time."

He turned and looked around more closely. Elynna followed his gaze. For the first time, she noticed across from where they had entered the room an arched doorway. Or, rather, it appeared at one time to have been a doorway, but the door itself had been walled over with stone and mortar. The mortar in the stone wall over the arch looked much newer than the arch itself. Though it was covered in dust like everything else, and cobwebs were draped across much of the surface, it showed no signs of chipping or age, and it was of different style and type of stone from the rest of the room. "I'll wager somebody wanted to keep this room private," Thimeon said.

Though Elynna had not yet jumped to that conclusion, upon hearing Thimeon's words she guessed he was right. Though she had no guess why it might have been kept a secret. "I wonder what it looks like on the other side," she said aloud.

"Whatever it looks like, we won't get out that way," Tienna said. "Not without a lot of work."

Thimeon did not answer. He had turned his attention back to the ancient tomes. For a short time, then, the companions were silent or spoke in low reverent voices as they wandered around. Each had soon found some pile of items that had captured their attention. Elynna looked for Cane and spotted him in a corner dusting off jewels. "These are worth a fortune," he said to his brother. "These came from Anghatte mines. No other place in Gondisle has rubies like this."

"You are right, Brother," Cathros agreed. "And of late they haven't been seen even in Anghatte mines." He held up on strikingly large and perfectly polished ruby. "I wonder if this ever made it through the markets of Anghata or Harrath. One like this would make a merchant rich for life."

So occupied were they that none of them heard the approaching footsteps until the rusted old door swung open with a loud creak. Too late Elynna remembered the footsteps she had heard earlier. She turned toward the sound in horror like a child caught stealing cherries from a private garden.

18

TREASURE

S tanding in the doorway, bedecked in his officer's uniform
with his hand resting on the hilt of his jeweled sword,
stood the prince of Gondisle. He was not tall. Most of the
Northlanders stood as tall or taller. But he was solid. Elynna
now saw that his shoulders and chest, though not overly broad,
were muscular and well-toned. His curly dark hair was bound in
a ponytail that reached the bottom of his neck. Unlike his father,
his face was friendly, but his sea-green eyes held a hint of doubt
and perhaps of pain or sorrow.

There was a long silence as his gaze swung across the room
from companion to companion, coming to rest at last upon
Elynna. Though they had never spoken, they knew each other by
sight, and after a moment his name came to her lips. Dhan. Prince
Dhan. Son of Eughbran. Months earlier he had stood silently
at his father's side when Elynna had pled the case of her people
and called upon Citadel for help. And more recently he had been
present when Koranth identified her as one of the enemies of

Gondisle, a wielder of unlawful powers. So she had taken him as one of her enemies. And now she was caught, again.

If the prince saw her as an enemy, however, his expression did not give that away. And Elynna had no sense of the presence of a Daegmon anywhere around, as she had felt with Koranth. Still, she knew their danger. She was expecting to see guards step into the room behind him, and her mind began scrambling for some plan of escape.

Still holding her gaze, Dhan took a step into the room. Finally his glance turned to the walls around him and the wealth of books and treasure hidden beneath layers of dust. Then his eyes opened in surprise, and he took another step forward

Was he alone? Elynna began to wonder when she realized that nobody had followed the prince into the room. Where were his guards? Was this a trap?

Cane, who was glancing past the prince out into the dark tunnel beyond, spoke that thought aloud. "He is alone."

The prince pulled his eyes away from the treasures and turned them on Cane. "Likely I am, Though you can never be sure. And, unlike you, I am armed."

"Sword or not, we can kill him," Cane said, and took a step forward.

No, Elynna wanted to interject. There something she couldn't figure out, like when she struggled to mend a fishing net but couldn't manage to untangle some last elusive knot. Only now things were moving quickly; it was like trying to remove a tangle with twenty big fish still flopping in the net.

"Perhaps," the prince replied, making no move to draw his blade. "If I am alone, and if you all attack me at once, the odds would be strongly in your favor—though it's beyond doubt that the first two or three of you to come within range of my sword would lose your own lives as well. And then also you would find out whether or not I am truly alone."

"I'll take the risk," Cane said, taking another step forward. Only fifteen feet separated them. Several of the other companions moved forward also. "We have nothing to lose. We know what awaits us if we're captured. I'd rather take my chances here and now."

"And risk killing one of your few allies in Citadel?"

The companions froze. Cane's mouth opened in disbelief, and for several seconds nobody moved. Prince Dhan turned slowly toward Elynna as though waiting for her to speak, but she said nothing. His words were too good to believe. Almost too good to be true. Could she dare to hope?

Thimeon spoke next, but he voiced Elynna's own thoughts. "Our ally? I would like to believe you. We have enough enemies and are in desperate need of friends. But how can it be so?" He smiled wryly. "You are, after all, the prince—the king's own son. So you must understand our distrust."

"As for your last observation, I can only answer yes, I am the prince. Yet I do not hold to all my father does or says, and of late I find myself less inclined to his policies. Indeed, I find many of his policies both evil and despicable. So I understand your distrust, or the distrust toward the throne held by any of the people of Gondisle. I suppose I could gain your trust only by proving I am not your enemy. How I might do that, I don't yet know."

"What do you know about us?" Thimeon asked. "And why would you help us?"

In answer, Dhan turned toward Elynna. "I am not yet wholly out of my father's counsels. You were in Citadel last spring looking for aid. If you remember, I was at my father's side on at least one occasion when you came before the throne."

Elynna nodded. She did remember. His had been the one sympathetic face in the throne room that day. But nothing had come of it, and eventually she had put him in the same mental net as his father—one of the rulers of Gondisle unwilling to offer aid. Was he truly offering aid now?

The prince continued. "What you might not know is that your name and your case was discussed behind closed doors. Several times while you were here in Citadel, Koranth advised the king to imprison you."

"Me?" Elynna asked. "Why? Why does he oppose us? Why won't he fight against the Daegmon?" She paused. "And if he wanted me arrested, why did he wait until I had left?"

Dhan sighed deeply. "I do not know the answers to these questions. Even as Koranth was arguing for your imprisonment, I pleaded for my father to send you aid. Alas, he would not listen to me. Long ago Koranth took away most of the influence I once had with my father. It was Koranth who told him not to aid you. Had Koranth had his way completely, you would never have left Citadel on your quest. In that small way, at least, I prevailed."

"Who is this Koranth?" Thimeon asked, taking a step closer.

"A question not easily answered. I do not know from whence he came, nor how he has gained such prominence in the Citadel court and such influence over my father. For some years he was a duke, and then a steward of the island of Entain. I was too young then to know him. Seven years ago, he returned from Entain with my father, and he has resided in Citadel ever since, always growing closer in counsel."

"How did you find us here?" Thimeon asked.

"And if you are our ally, then why were you going to let them kill us?" Cane added before the prince could respond to the first question.

"I can answer both questions. I had been on my way to prevent your execution—"

"Do you have that authority?" Cathros interrupted.

"If you mean authority in crucial matters such as the fate of important prisoners, then no. I did have such authority once. I no longer do. But not everybody knows that. If the situation had required it, I might have convinced the guards I still had the right to order your release. In that way I could have bought your freedom with my life. Make no mistake—I already tread a dangerous path. Koranth despises me. My father distrusts me. Such an open opposition to their will would have been my last act, unless I had managed to escape with you. Still, I was willing to do that. At the very least, I could have handled Golach for a time—long enough to secure your escape. There are those even among his company who still follow my command, though I would have become a fugitive with you."

"And you came to do that?" Thimeon asked suspiciously.

The prince smiled. "Koranth must have guessed my plan—to call together the soldiers loyal to me whom he had not yet ferreted out and to fight for your escape. He arranged to have me delayed. Fortunately, he guessed wrongly, for I had in mind instead the very sort of escape you discovered for yourself—these secret passageways. For though I speak truth that I was—and still am—willing to trade my life for your freedom, it is not a trade I am eager to make. I was hoping, for a time anyway, to keep secret my own part in your escape. I would preserve what little freedom and authority I have left so that I might continue to do good within the walls of Citadel and my father's palace. Just as I had already done for you. For it was I, knowing of these passageways, who ordered that you be held in that dungeon."

When the prince said this, Elynna remembered the conversation between Dhan and Golach at the gates of the palace when the companions had first been brought in as prisoners. She found herself believing him. And hoping she was not mistaken in doing so.

She turned to look at Thimeon and Tienna. To see in their eyes whether they also believed the prince. Whether Tienna sensed the same illness in him as she had sensed in the king. Their expressions gave nothing away. But in the shadows behind them, to the left of the prince, she saw Hruach inching his way along the wall. *No*, she wanted to tell him. A new fear now crept into her mind. What was Hruach going to do? What if the prince really was there to help, and Hruach ruined it?

The prince sighed. "Alas, the details of my plan didn't matter. Though Koranth was wrong about my means for helping you, he rightly guessed I was up to something. He was able to stall me. When I finally came to the dungeons, I was expecting the worst. Fortunately, I arrived to find you had escaped without my help. It did not take me long to guess how.

"After your disappearance, I diverted Golach by ordering him into the city to search for you. Then I slipped through one of the upstairs entrances and came looking for you. I went first to your cells, then retraced my steps and came this way. The passageways and tunnels are extensive. Over the past few months I've explored those above in the castle, and have made good use of them more than once. But until today, I had not followed that low tunnel and did not know where it led. I was reluctant to try just now for fear I would waste too much time, and because I do not like closed spaces. Then I heard a noise and saw your prints in the dust. And I have found not only you but also this room. What this place is I do not know, but it holds some special purpose. Somebody has gone to lengths to keep it hidden." He was looking at the wall sealing off the far door. "I can guess where that door leads, for I was on the other side not long ago."

"If you are truly here to help," Cane said, cutting to the point, "then aid our escape."

Dhan frowned. He looked down at his feet, and then back up. There was no indication that he saw Hruach. Elynna was afraid to look to see where he was. "That indeed is why I have come. But it will not be easy. I know of only one passage that leads out of the castle. It ends within the city a short distance away in the cellar of a favorite little inn. Unfortunately, that inn is still within the outer city walls, so even if I got you there, safely out of the castle, you would be hard-pressed to escape the high walls of Citadel. There are guards everywhere looking for you, and the gates of Citadel will be held against you. It is a big enough city that maybe you would be able to hide for a few days, but Koranth has many spies."

"If we make it to the city, we can arm ourselves—" Cane began.

"Yes, and you could kill a great many soldiers—good men who are your brothers and cousins and should not be your enemies. And then you would be killed yourself. But there may be—"

Before Dhan finished his sentence, there was a movement behind him. Elynna turned to see Hruach lunging forward from the shadows. She gave a cry in fear, not even sure which she feared: that Hruach would fail or that he would succeed. But either his wounded knee betrayed him, or he had under-estimated the distance, or his adversary was simply too quick. The prince's sword was out of his sheath in a flash, pointed at Hruach's throat so quickly that the Northlander had time to stop suddenly to avoid being impaled.

Still, for an instant everything hung by a thin thread. Cane and Cathros were poised to leap into the fray. Elynna found her voice.

"Wait!" she shouted. The others turned toward her in surprise. "Please," she pleaded. She finally was able to weave together the loose strands. Everything the prince had said made sense. And she remembered something else as well that the prince had not mentioned. "He speaks the truth. When we arrived at the castle, I heard him give the orders to Golach for us to be placed in that dungeon."

"I also heard that conversation," Thimeon added. "And I too believe he speaks the truth. Even if you don't trust him yet, at least give him a chance to prove himself. He may be the only friend we have in Citadel."

Dhan turned toward Elynna and Thimeon, and he bowed his head toward them. "Thank you. It is good to be trusted. There has been little trust within the palace these past few years." Then he slid his sword back into his sheath. To Elynna's surprise—and the apparent surprise of the others also—he undid his belt and took off his sword. He set it down on the floor and kicked it so that it slid over toward Cane. "I am unarmed now."

Cane stared hard at the prince but made no move to pick up the sword. "You may speak," he finally said.

Dhan nodded. "As I said, there are guards looking for you through the castle and the city. However, there may be a way. There are a few other tunnels I have not yet explored—a web of natural underground caverns beneath the palace and down deep under Citadel. I do not believe they were made by human hands. Until recently I have never had cause or time to thoroughly explore them." He smiled. "After all, as prince, I could go wherever I wanted without them. Almost anywhere, that is. Since Koranth has come, there are now places within the castle not even I am free to go. But that is a story for another day.

"Since discovering these passageways by accident, I have done some exploring, guessing rightly that the knowledge would one day be useful. One cavern leads westward toward the river and angles downward. I haven't yet followed it to the end. It may be that it comes out in the cliff side just above the river. If this is the case, you might escape by water. It will be difficult. Even there the guards will be on the lookout. Yet it may be your only chance."

"Then let us go there at once," Thimeon said.

"I would not advise it just yet. It is still early, and the moon is bright. In a few hours it will be darker. In the meantime, wait."

"Are we safe here?" Elynna asked.

"Safer than anywhere else in Citadel, I would guess. These underground passages are as old as the city itself. Rumors and hints of them surface now and then, but for most folk they are nothing more than rumor. I discovered them by accident, and only because I have permission and keys to go places where others cannot go."

"How long should we wait?" Cathros asked. "Can we get food?"

At the mention of food, several of the companions nodded. Elynna's stomach growled. They had eaten only bread and water for many days. Even Tienna and the Northlanders, who were trained for hardship, had complained of rations.

"I will do what I can," Dhan said. "But if you want food, you will have to trust me to leave you and return." He looked at Cane as he said this.

"I trust you," Thimeon said, "but I cannot speak for the others unless we have time to discuss this."

Dhan nodded. "I understand. If you want me to go, I will try to return in one hour's time with food and some word of where the search is progressing."

While the prince waited, the companions gathered at the far end of the room. The discussion was brief. Cane, Hruach and Hrevia were hesitant to trust the prince. Those from the Plains—Marti, Nahoon, Beth, and Tienna—all agreed with Thimeon and Elynna. The rest were undecided. It was Thimeon who pointed out that the risk of not trusting Dhan was greater than that of trusting him, for without him they had little hope of escape. His words and the promise of food swayed the others.

Cane, though he was opposed to the decision, picked up Dhan's sword and returned it to him. "If you betray us, I will kill you."

"I see your trust is not easily won. So be it. I do not blame you. When I return and you have escaped, you will think differently." With a final bow, he took his sword and left.

Elynna listened to his soft footsteps fading down the tunnel. When he was gone, Thimeon spoke. "We have no choice now but to wait. Let us use our time well. Sleep if you can."

The companions nodded, but few of them sought to rest. Instead they returned to the various corners of the room where they had been occupied before the prince's arrival. The temptation to slip a jewel or two into a pocket overcame more than one of them, for there were small treasures in the room that would make them rich for life if they ever managed to escape to freedom. Nonetheless, Elynna was shocked when Siyen boldly picked up three matching gold bracelets studded with costly gems and placed them around her arms.

"Siyen," she exclaimed in a loud voice.

Before the Southlander could answer, however, Hruach interrupted with a loud and enthusiastic announcement of another discovery. Half hidden beneath an old woven rug were three massive chests containing a small armory: swords, helmets, maces, shields, knives, and even bows. "This may be worth more to us right now than any treasure," he said, picking up one of the swords and removing it from its sheath. The metal glinted in the torchlight. Though obviously old, the weapon was in sound condition. He tested the edge. It was still sharp. Soon the other companions were gathering around, searching through the chests, scavenging to rearm themselves. Like the sword Hruach had first picked up, the other weapons were also of excellent make, and remained in good condition.

"One can't call this stealing," Cane said as he removed a sword and scabbard for himself. "Not after they took our weapons from us."

Thimeon, meanwhile, was in the other corner sitting on the floor with a stack of leather bound books beside him. He had one ancient tome opened and was carefully leafing through its pages. "Elynna," he suddenly called. "Come here. Look at this."

Elynna could hear the note of urgency in his voice. She walked slowly to his side, as though in no particular hurry, but something in the mysterious mood of this place had her heart beating faster, and it was with considerable curiosity that she glanced over his shoulder. "What is it?"

Thimeon held a finger inside the book to mark a page, and then closed it to show her the cover. The book, only a little wider and taller than the hand holding it, was not as ornately decorated with jewels or illustration as some of the others, but there was something curiously weighty and compelling about the faded leather binding. In the center of the cover was a simple engraved image she'd first mistaken for a three-pointed crown such as was traditionally worn by the kings of Gondisle. But when she looked closer, she recognized what any of the Highlander peoples might have seen right away. It was an engraved image of the triune peak of Mount Illengond: the three pointed spires surrounding the mysterious bowl of clouds. She had only missed it at first because the engraving did not show the entire mountain, only the top, down below the bowl to about the point where the perennial snow was able to cling to the steep rock against the constant winds. But when she saw the mountain in the image, there was no mistaking it for anything else. It was what so many referred to as the Holy Mountain. The mountain of the All-Maker. Why the image was on the cover of this volume, she did not know. Nor did she know why it would be important to Thimeon. But it obviously was.

Thimeon gave her a few moments to look at the cover, and then opened it back to the place he had marked with his finger, and again lifted it for her to see. She bent over and stared at the left page. The writing was graceful and flowing, but in a strange script she did not understand. Her eyes drifted to the other side. On the right page was a simple but mysterious drawing. It drew her eyes at once. It was a sketch of a large mountain. Not Illengond but some other nameless peak. But the artist had used only oddly shaped dots and no lines, so the drawing did not take shape at once. She dropped to one knee and continued to peer over

Thimeon's shoulder until her eyes were within a foot and a half from the page, still trying to make out the picture. He, too, was looking intently at the drawing.

"Don't look *at* it," Thimeon said in a low voice. "Look *through* it, as though you are looking at something behind the image." Elynna was not quite sure what he meant, but she tried to let her eyes glaze over out of focus. The dots blurred. The effect was slow to develop, but once it happened it was startling and unmistakable. She took a sharp breath.

There, flying at her out of the page with its evil eyes fixed right on her, was a Daegmon. It looked so real and frightening and solid that she almost jumped back. The way the image appeared in the dots was as if it had emerged from the mountain while she was watching.

"You see it?" Thimeon said.

"I do," she replied. And she did not like it. She blinked several times, then looked at Thimeon, and then back at the page. The Daegmon was gone. She could see only the mountain again.

"What do you make of it?"

"It cannot be an accident," she said in a whisper. "Just looking makes me afraid."

"Yes. Whoever drew this was not only a superb artist but had also experienced a Daegmon attack such as we did. The effect of the creature emerging from the ground as you stare at the picture is too real."

Elynna looked at Thimeon. "What is this book?"

"I don't know. Nor do I know why it was hidden." He closed it again, and looked at the cover. "The crown of Illengond. That much I recognize." Then he opened it. "I wish I could read the script. Do you recognize it?"

Elynna looked again. Though with work she could make out a few letters, the words meant nothing to her. The Highlander tongues, she knew, were related. Or at least the languages of the Andani and Ceaani. The Ceadani used the same script as the trade language, which had derived from older Andani. While in Gale Enebe she had recognized common roots to several Ceadani words. She knew nothing of the languages of the Undeani or the Plains tribes, but she had seen the script used by some of the Plainsfolk; this did not look like it. Of course the people of the Westwash for long centuries had been an isolated folk. While their tongue was closely connected to Andani, and centuries earlier had blended with the Andani tongue to form what was now the Southland language and the common trade tongue of Gondisle, at one time the folk of the Westwash had developed their own script with a separate origin from all the other writings of Gondisle. But they had long ago adapted the common script, and only a few symbols from the old Westwash script still survived as runes. There were still a few ancient stones and monuments scattered around the Westwash that had these runes. Her father had pointed them out, and told her something of their history. But he hadn't known what they meant. Only that in the far northern village around Northhaven there were many more of the monuments.

This script, however, looked nothing like the old Westwash runes she had seen.

The Anghare tongue—the language of the Northland—did have its own script. She did not know it. Even amongst themselves, the Anghare people rarely spoke their language in the company of strangers. Though it was the Anghare who had first ruled Gondisle, and who had built Citadel as the capital city at the heart of the land, they had adopted the Southland tongue as the trade language rather than share their own. Though over the course of many generations, the trade tongue had diverged somewhat with several Northland words finding their way into common speech so that the Andani dialect was subtly different.

"I don't know," Elynna finally said. "There was an ancient Westwash script, but I don't think this was it."

"It is a very old book, I think," Thimeon replied. "But no, I do not think it is the ancient Westwash script."

"Would Tienna know?" Elynna asked. "If it is a Plains tongue, I mean?"

"Perhaps," Thimeon replied. He turned and called to Tienna, who had been resting against the far wall. When Tienna joined them, they showed her the picture. Her response was the same. She looked at it for a time, moving her head first farther away and then closer, and then suddenly she clasped her hand over her mouth and looked up at the ceiling as though holding back some emotion. She brought whatever fear or dismay had seized her back in check and turned her eyes back to the book and the facing page.

"You can see now why I want to know something about this book," Thimeon said softly. She nodded, and he continued. "It might have some knowledge we have been seeking. Some clue as to what our enemy is, or how we can fight it."

"I understand," she said. "But this is not in the script of my people."

She did not recognize the writing either.

"Then we are at a loss. It is neither Andani nor Ceadani. Though I do not read Lamîn—the Anghatte tongue—I recognize it when I see it. And the Undeani language, though old, has never had a written form with these letters. If you say it is not the language of the Plains, we're stuck."

Tienna closed her eyes, and tilted her head back. "I am a huntress. There are many things I know. About tracking animals across the Plains I could tell you much. But I know less than I should about the histories of the peoples of the Plains. It may be this is writing from the Plains. I said it is not my *own* language. But there is more than one language that has been spoken across the Plains. As there is a common trade language of Gondisle, so there is a common language in the Plains, but there are other dialects spoken by the western tribes that I do not speak, and other scripts I have heard, though I do not know."

Thimeon nodded. After a moment of silence, he continued. "What we do know is that whoever wrote this book knew of the Daegmon and knew of its power to emerge from the mountainside. Might they have know also how to defeat it?"

"Could there be other books?" Elynna asked. Thimeon's words had her feeling suddenly more hopeful. "I mean, what if this or some other book could tell us more of the Daegmon? What if they told where its power came from?"

"Or how we might fight it," Thimeon added. "We know so little. Indeed, from the very start we have known almost nothing about our enemy. There were fragments of tales and legends in Gale Enebe that we might have learned from had we stayed there with Chal-char. But alas, at the time I thought we had already won the battle. I wish Chal-char were here now, or that we could speak with him again. Still, there could be a wealth of knowledge right here in this very room."

"Hidden away where it can't help anyone from Gondisle," Tienna finished.

At Tienna's words, Thimeon took a long sharp intake of breath. A thought struck Elynna at the same time, and she wondered if it was the same thought. "Do you suppose Koranth was the one who had this room walled off?" she asked.

Thimeon did not reply. But a moment later, he carefully closed the volume, returned it to the shelf, and pulled off another. The next tome looked even older. The parchment was thin and several pages were torn. With great care to protect it, he began to flip through the pages. He had not gone very far before he gave yet another a low whistle.

"What is it?" asked Elynna, who once again could not read the writing.

"This is Ceadani."

"Read it."

"I speak their language," Thimeon said, his face a little flushed, "but I have not learned to read it. Not well. The Ceadani are people of art and music. They write few books. How a book in their script came to be here, I do not know. This is very old." He fell silent as his eyes scanned over the page. He turned a few more pages. In the meantime, others had come over to look. By the time Thimeon looked up, several companions were standing around him.

"What does it say?" Tienna asked.

"Nothing about the Daegmon, as best I can tell. Here is a description of Gondisle and the island of Entain." He flipped another page and scanned the lines. "And something about a flood. I don't understand all the words—"

"Why waste your time?" Cane interrupted. "Books won't help us fight the Daegmon. We need greater weapons. Or greater gifts of power."

"Perhaps," Thimeon said, putting the book back on the shelf. Still, he picked up another volume. This one was the thinnest of the three. It looked to Elynna to consist of perhaps forty or fifty pieces of parchment bound together between old skins by a thin leather cord. Though an old and nondescript manuscript, it had a beautiful wide silver chain wrapped around it in addition to the leather binding straps. She watched with growing curiosity as Thimeon turned the book over in his hand. The chain held a curious ornament of some black metal set with a single polished blue stone just smaller than the palm of his hand. It looked more like a necklace than something that should have been around a book.

Thimeon tried to slide the chain off the binding, but it was attached to the book. He found a clasp on the back, unhooked it, and took the chain off. A look of surprise came over his face as he weighed the piece in his hand. "Feel this," he said to Elynna, handing the pendant to her.

Elynna understood what had surprised Thimeon. The stone was much heavier than she expected. She studied it more closely. Though the setting was simple and unadorned by either jewels or any filigree, it was nonetheless beautiful, and she had the strange impression it might have had as great a value as the ruby Cane had found earlier. She handed it to Tienna, who showed the same surprise in her face as she weighed it in her hand, and then returned it to Thimeon. "I've never felt a stone like this," she said. "Do you know what it is?"

Thimeon shook his head. He held the pendant a moment longer, then set it down on the floor and turned his attention to the old tome. Elynna was still staring at the black stone sitting in the dust, when Thimeon picked it up again and set it on his leg. It slid to the floor with a thunk. He picked it up and set it higher on his leg. It slid off again. He finally slipped it over his head, where the stone slid down his neck beneath his tunic.

Finally he turned his attention to the leather cord binding the pages. He tried to gently undo the knot, but the old leather simply fell apart in his hand, and the cover dropped off. He laid the cover to the side and looked at the page.

Elynna had turned her attention to other books on the shelf, when she heard Thimeon exclaim in a quiet but long and obviously excited voice, "Wow!"

Elynna turned to see at once to see what had caught his attention. In thick neat writing on the opening page was written in the common script:

OF THE END OF THE GREAT BATTLES BETWEEN THE PEOPLES OF GONDISLE AND THE DAEGMON LORD

Below the title in smaller letters was written the name:

ANATTAL I
FIRST HIGH KING OF GONDISLE
A.L. 588

Elynna's sucked in her breath and held it a moment. She read the page several times. Her eye caught the last line. The book was dated A.L. 588. Though her own people did not measure the passing of years, she knew enough to recognize this as the reckoning of the Northland—of the Anghare. Some of what she had learned in Citadel of the history of Gondisle came back. The earliest kings of Gondisle had been Anghare, and though the language of the Andani and Westwashers had been taken as the common trade language, the Northland years had once been used as a standard calendar for all of Gondisle. That reckoning had not lasted. Over the course of time other kings had arisen, some of whom had again begun to count years at zero at the starts of their reigns and insisted by law that all records did the same. Only in the Northland were the years still kept.

"Cane," Thimeon asked. "What year is this in the reckoning of your people?"

Before Cane could speak, Cathros answered from across the room. "In four weeks begins the new year. It will be the year 1109, twenty-seven years since the year of my birth."

Thimeon did some quick calculating. "That makes this book about five hundred and twenty years old."

"No wonder it's falling apart."

"That's not what I was thinking about," Thimeon said. "This battle against the Daegmon—it was being fought over five hundred years ago."

The brothers looked at Thimeon with great interest. Most of the others turned and looked at him also. He held up the volume for them to see and then read the title to them.

"Do these creatures never die?" Elynna asked, appalled.

"Perhaps they breed," Cane suggested. "Even if there was a battle five hundred years ago, we do not know that we are fighting the same creature they fought then. Only a creature of the same type."

"Maybe," Thimeon said. "Or maybe the same one. We have seen already that it is not easily killed. And yet it *was*, in some sense, defeated long ago. Gondisle has had many years of peace: such a long peace, in fact, that the creatures have been forgotten."

"And this king," Cathros noted. "He survived to write about the battles."

"Yes," Thimeon said.

"Then this book might have the secret—" Elynna started.

Thimeon was already turning the page. He began to read aloud:

> This is an account of the end of the Great War, and of the crowning of the first High King of Gondisle. A longer account has been told by the poet Aelthrith in his Canticles, with words more fitting to the greatness of the achievements. If there are names of heroes and accounts of battles not set forth herein, let not any wrath fall upon the scribe of the king. By the king's own words, this account is set forth, and though told in brief as a chronicle, the words are still true.
>
> In the ninth year of the war, when most of Gondisle had fallen under the dominion of Entain, and the Daegmon Lord's power extended almost to the slopes of Illengond, the last battles were begun.
>
> I, King Annatal, by the power of the Henetos Stone, had arisen as the general of the last army: the united host of all the people of Gondisle still free to fight against the Daegmon. Small was that army. Only two hundred free men and women came forth to fight. Twenty-five there were from each of the free peoples of Gondisle except the Anghare, who numbered fifty. Yet our hope did not lie in numbers. For among us were twenty-five of the Karsmose. Never before in any previous generation had so many of the Gifts of Power been manifested at one time.

Weapons of Power we also had in addition to the gifts. With the help of the Henetos we had reforged the great sword once called Rhomphaia so that the Ischus would have a weapon fitting his power.

But the Daegmon-Lord was mighty. Haeg-Taegs had put forth all of its power, and Gondisle itself was nigh overwhelmed. Five Daegmon were arrayed against us, and with them were all three of the Gaergaen, who led an army of human slaves. And to that final battle came the Daegmon Lord himself.

Thimeon stopped and turned over a page of the parchment. The rest of the room was silent as they listened.

To the great mountain we turned, hoping we might find help upon her slopes. For of old we were ever told that the All-Maker had hallowed her and dwelt upon her peaks. And since that time, the fiery peak of the south, Entain, had waged war against Illengond, and would continue to do so until time itself would end and start again with the All-Maker's final victory.

There also the Daegmons pursued us, for they could sense our power, and the Daegmon-Lord himself led them and was not afraid. There we made our first mistake, for we hoped to be high on the mountainside before we were attacked, but our enemy came faster than we feared, and two of the Daegmon flew ahead of us. We dreaded then that they might inhabit the mountainside as they had done before, and our dread slowed us down . . .

19

LEAP OF FAITH

It was Tienna who alerted the others to the approaching foot-steps. They all fell silent. Cane and Hruach stood next to the door with blades drawn, but Elynna knew as well as the others that there was no place to flee and no hope of fighting their way out if they were discovered, or if Dhan had betrayed them. All they could do was wait.

The approaching footsteps stopped at the door. It sounded like only one pair. There was a light tap on the door. Hruach pulled it open, and in stepped Dhan.

Cane stepped back and let him enter, but he did not sheath his blade. "What news do you bring?"

"Good news and bad," Dhan replied, meeting Cane's gaze. "But first this." He unslung a small bag from over his shoulder and removed its contents: one loaf of bread, two bottles of wine, a block of cheese, and a large package wrapped up in garden leaves. He unwrapped the leaves to reveal an assortment of sliced meats, enough so that each of the companions would get a small bite. "I am sorry I could not bring more. I grabbed all I could from my private chambers. Had I gone to the kitchens and asked for enough food to satisfy the hunger of all of you, I'm afraid it would have aroused undue suspicion."

"This is a good start," grunted Hruach, who had already torn a hunk off a corner of the loaf and stuffed it into his mouth with a piece of meat. Elynna had the same thought. At the mere sight of the bread, her mouth began to water. She felt she could have eaten the whole loaf.

"And the news?" asked Thimeon, who still held the book in his lap and was not yet reaching for any of the food.

"Captain Golach has not guessed where you are. When he found your cell doors open, and the door unlocked from the corridor into the outer chamber, he assumed somebody managed to set you free from the outside. He does not know about these passages, and with the cell doors open he did not have reason to look for any other clues."

Elynna expressed her relief with a great exhaling of the breath she had involuntarily held as Dhan was speaking. She was not the only one.

The prince went on. "Right now his men are scouring both the castle and the city. The gates to the city and the palace have been closed and guarded. Everybody in Citadel must already guess something is amiss, but my father wishes to keep your presence a secret, and so little is being said about why the guards are searching the castle. Many of the guards and soldiers don't even know what they are doing or who you are, other than very general descriptions of your appearance and the order to arrest you—and to kill you if you resist."

"Is that the good news or bad?" Thimeon asked.

Dhan smiled. "Were that the only news, I would call it good, and I would counsel you to remain here in hiding. I could arrange to bring more food, and you might be safe for several days. But my father's councilor Koranth wields some strange and powerful magic."

The very mention of Koranth sent a chill of fear down Elynna's arms. "He is not human," she said.

Dhan looked at her curiously, but he did not ask her to explain, and for that she was relieved, for she did not want to have to put into words once again how Koranth made her feel. "What power he wields, I do not know," Dhan said after a moment. "Yet it is great, and I fear him. Somehow he knows that you are still within the castle, and even now he is redirecting the search. Only by my effort were most of the soldiers sent out into the city."

"How long until he finds us?" Thimeon asked.

"My father long ago guessed the existence of these passages. There are veiled references to them in some of the archives. Fortunately, the locations of the entrances are still unknown to him. At least I believe that to be the case, for it was not the teaching of my father but accident that led to my discovery. Also, the archives that speak of these passages say that the secrets are passed from king to king, and my father—" He paused suddenly and squeezed his eyes shut. A minute later he took a deep breath and continued. "My father did not come to his throne with integrity. The throne rightly belonged to his brother, my uncle. Maybe that is why my father never learned about these passages. We are fortunate he has never taken the time to search them out. But he will certainly do so now. With Koranth to lead him, it may not take long."

"Then tell us what hope we have," Thimeon said. "For though we do not wish to fight, we know death awaits us if we are captured."

"I understand," the prince said. "All is not yet lost. I told you there is a tunnel that leads westward out of the castle. It goes downward into the rock. I have never before explored it, but have often guessed where it might lead. It may be that it leads under the river all the way to the woods on the eastern shore. But though we might hope for that, I suspect rather that there is some hidden entrance along the bluffs west of Citadel where the river flows beneath the cliffs. If you make it there, you may be able to swim to the safety of the woods on the far shore."

"How wide is the river?" Tienna asked.

"It is broad, I am afraid, and deep. Which is why I do not think there to be any tunnel beneath it. I could not imagine such a work. Yet the river is crossable for one who knows how to swim. The current is swift but not treacherous. The problem will be to reach the far shore, where it is still wooded, before the current carries you too far south. The bridge downstream is well traveled, and you are sure to be seen if you swim too slowly and drift too far down. Which leads to the second and third problems. We need to act soon, while it is dark. Even now, the search moves closer."

"He is right," Elynna said. "I can feel Koranth's mind probing for mine just as the Daegmon's did."

Again Dhan looked at Elynna with curiosity and appeared about to ask her to explain, when Cane spoke. "Then lead us onward. If we make it as far as the river, we will take our chances there. If not, we will fight. We are now well armed."

Dhan looked at the companions and appeared to notice for the first time their newly girded weapons. "Good. It is fortunate you found this place. Not even I knew of its existence. Nevertheless, by my authority as prince, I hereby grant you as free gifts from Citadel—in payment for your wrongful captivity—whatever weapons you can take from here. Judging by the wealth of what you now wear, you can consider yourselves well compensated. Now come, and I will lead you."

"You mentioned a third problem," Thimeon reminded him.

Dhan nodded soberly. "Yes. The hidden passages are not connected—at least not as far as I have discovered. To reach the tunnel leading to the river, we will have to leave these secret ways briefly and walk down a hallway in another wing of the castle. There are guests staying in that wing this night, and there is a chance you will be seen. We will have to be careful."

That was all the prince had to tell. The companions had little choice but to trust his plan. They had already shared amongst themselves all the food the prince had brought, and each of them had also had a small sip of wine. It did not satisfy their hunger, but it did take away some of its edge.

With Thimeon and Cane behind him, and Elynna next, Dhan led the way out of the treasure chamber. At the door they picked up the two torches they had brought with them from the dungeon, and they grabbed three more from the walls. The way back was shorter than they remembered. Soon they arrived at the low part of the tunnel where they had to crawl. Dhan turned and gave a final warning to be silent, then ducked and disappeared into the darkness. One by one, the other fifteen followed. When Elynna emerged from the other end and stood up, Dhan and Thimeon had already gone ahead. She jogged to catch up with them as they came to the fork in the tunnel and turned right up the stairs.

The climb was not long but it brought a dramatic change in the passage. About twenty steps up they came to a long straight hallway, narrow but high enough to walk erect. The solid rock wall was gone, replaced on both sides by brick. They had gone

just a few feet, when they heard the muffled sound of footsteps—
several pairs of booted feet approaching at a run.

"Wait," Dhan whispered, as Cane raised his sword. The footsteps grew closer until they were almost beside them. Through
the brick wall on their left, they could hear a long row of soldiers
running past. "They're on their way to the dungeon," Dhan
explained. "They will search there once again, looking for some
trace of your departure. Let us hope you hid your escape well."
He waited for the footsteps to fade, then continued on. He had
not gone more than another dozen steps, when Elynna felt it.
This time it was stronger and unmistakable: the Daegmon sense.
She almost doubled over with the sharp burning in the back of
her neck.

"What is it?" the prince asked.

"It is Koranth," she whispered as she tried to get her terror
under control. "He is coming—on the other side of this wall."

This time the prince did not restrain his curiosity. "How do
you know?"

"The same way he knew about us," she said. "I can sense
his presence." She knew it was not much of an answer, but it
appeared to satisfy the prince.

"Then what shall we do? It would be good to discover
whether he knows your exact location, or whether he has only
guessed about the hidden passageways and is leading a search in
the dungeon for the entrance."

This was the request Elynna feared—to intentionally feel for
the presence of her enemy, and the pain that presence caused. She
wished instead only to shut it out. Had one of her companions
asked—any other than maybe Cane or Tienna—she might have
refused. But there was a certain authority in the prince's request.

And she knew also that the lives of her companions might depend on her willingness.

She shut her eyes and listened for the probing thoughts of her enemy. It was like intentionally petting one of the jellied fish of the Westwash. She felt the burning sting almost at once, and several moments passed before she could speak, still squeezing shut her eyes. "He is still searching, I think. He has not found me yet."

When she opened her eyes, she was surprised to see Cane holding his sword. Flickers of blue flame ran up and down the edges as it had the two times they had been in battle against the Daegmon. The power of his gift was coming to life.

"What on earth—?" Dhan mumbled, staring wide-eyed at the sword.

"Odd." Cane said. "Almost as if—" He stopped without finishing.

"As if the Daegmon were near," Tienna finished.

"Koranth," Elynna said. "I told you. He is kindred to the Daegmon. He is one of them."

"No wonder he wants us destroyed," Cane said.

A sudden understanding lit up Thimeon's eyes. "And if he controls the king of Gondisle—"

"Of what do you speak?" Dhan interrupted sharply. He had turned red, and for the first time they saw fear in his eyes. "What do you know of Koranth? How does he control my father?"

"There is no time to explain," Elynna answered. The presence of Koranth so close was bringing her close to panic. Only the power emanating from Cane's blade was holding it off. "We must flee."

"Listen," Thimeon whispered. The footsteps had begun again, moving away toward the dungeon at a quick stride.

"Come," Dhan said. He started up the passage at a quick pace. Elynna raced to keep up, following a series of twisting corridors that squeezed behind chimneys and wound up narrow stairwells. As the steps took them further from Koranth, the panic lessened. But she knew their danger was still great, and she was just as eager to get as far from Citadel as she could.

They had walked another five minutes, when the prince motioned for a halt. There was a low wooden door near his feet. "It is here we must take our chances. This tunnel climbs another level and ends behind a banquet hall on the north wing of the castle. To get out we need to reach another series of tunnels on the west side. This door leads to a hidden panel in a guest suite. The room is empty now." He smiled for once—a sort of half-sad, half-humorous smile. "Fortunately, my father has had few guests of late. Once out of this room, we need go about thirty feet down the hall. The entrance to the other passage is through the third room on the opposite side. I don't know if that room is empty, but if not I will find a way to get rid of whoever is there. We have no other choice."

Cane raised his blade. It was cold again. So was his voice when he spoke. "If you betray us, I am close behind you."

Dhan returned the stern gaze but said nothing. Then he stooped over, took a deep breath, and pushed on the wooden panel. The door opened outward on silent hinges and the prince crawled through into a dark room. Thimeon followed him with a torch. Then came Cane, Elynna, Cathros, and the others. Siyen was last. The prince pushed the hidden panel shut behind her. They found themselves in a large guest room furnished with a huge bed and an ornately carved wardrobe. The walls were decorated with drab paintings of self-important nobility posing on horseback. The secret door had disappeared into the wooden paneling, and had they not just come through it Elynna never would have guessed it was there. The prince repeated his instructions. They were to go out in ones and twos, about a minute between each. Once out the door, they were to turn right and head down the hall to the third door on the left. He would go first and return if there was trouble. "Don't panic if you're seen," he ended. "Few of the residents know anything about you. Stay calm and keep walking as if you belong. If you draw your swords, then all is lost."

The prince turned and departed. All was silent then, except for their breathing. Thimeon and Cane stood waiting by the door. When a minute had passed, they peered out. The hallway was empty. They slipped out and shut the door behind them. Another minute passed, and out went Hruach and Hrevia. Then Tienna alone. Then Nahoon and Beth. And so on until at last only Elynna, Cathros, and Siyen were left. Elynna stood next to the door beside Cathros. Her heart pounded. She took a deep breath and tried to act calm. The hallway was still silent, and she did not sense Koranth anywhere nearby. She looked at Siyen, who stood fidgeting in the far corner of the room. Then she nodded. Cathros opened the door and they stepped out.

The corridor was empty. They turned to the right and started toward their destination. The third door was visible just a few dozen strides away. Elynna had hope they would make it.

Then, without warning, a door opened just past where they were headed. From out of the doorway emerged a uniformed soldier. He stepped into the hallway and looked directly toward Elynna and Cathros. Elynna froze as the soldier's hand came casually to rest on his sword.

"Keep walking," Cathros whispered, grabbing Elynna by the elbow and propelling her forward directly toward the soldier. A second later, out of the same door stepped a young woman in a long blue gown. The soldier held out his arm to her. With soft intimate laughs and long glances into each other's eyes, the amorous couple turned and started down the hall in the opposite direction, oblivious of their spectators.

"Is this all?" the prince asked, when Elynna and Cathros arrived a few seconds later. He didn't notice that Elynna's legs were shaking so badly she could barely stand.

"All but Siyen," Cathros answered.

The prince nodded and stood by the door, waiting to open it. Several minutes passed. Siyen did not arrive. The prince turned back to Cathros and inquired about her again. Cathros had no answer.

"Did you see anybody in the hall?"

"Yes. There was a soldier and a young woman. They went in the other direction and didn't pay any attention to us."

Dhan frowned. "Did Siyen know which door? We cannot wait much longer." When nobody answered, his frown deepened. He commanded the others to wait and slipped out the door before Cane or anybody else could stop him. He was gone for only a minute before he returned alone and with a red face. "She's gone."

"What do you mean?" asked several voices. "Was she captured?"

Dhan only shrugged. "I don't know. If she was caught, then I might as well flee with you. She will reveal all, and my life will be forfeit."

"Can you look for her?" Elynna asked. Several possibilities sprang to her mind, and none were good. Siyen must be lost. She might be captured. She might have been detoured. Was it possible she might have betrayed the company? Elynna refused to accept that possibility.

"I can, but—" He paused. "If she is already caught, the best thing for us to do is to move as quickly as we can."

"How can we hope to leave the city?" Hrevia asked. "She knows our plan."

"Maybe she doesn't," Tienna suggested. "She was not near us for the discussion, and was never one to give much concern to our plans."

"I don't know," Pietr said. "She was near me in the treasure chamber when our plans were made. I remember because she was complaining of the damp. She had also taken some jewels and had asked me what I thought they would be worth."

"So she may know—" Elynna started.

"And she may not," Thimeon finished. "She may have been caught, and she may not. She may be lost. Or she may have intentionally abandoned us."

"You mean a traitor?" Cane asked, his eyes narrowing.

"I am only saying what is possible," Thimeon answered. "We must consider all possibilities and be prepared. In any case, it would be folly to search for her, and yet we cannot remain here long."

Dhan stood still, his face showing no emotion. Cane and Cathros were also placid. Others fidgeted. Finally Elynna worked up the courage once again to take up the leadership the others were waiting for. "We will depart. If Siyen is lost, we can only hope the best for her. Perhaps she will be able to leave the castle without being recognized. She was raised a Southlander and may have friends in Citadel. And she has no gift for the creature to sense. She may fare better than any of us."

"And if she is captured and tells what I have done?" Dhan wondered aloud.

He didn't wait for a reply. He crossed the room and ran his fingers underneath a panel on the wall. There was a soft click. He placed his hand on the adjacent panel and gave a little twist to a wooden carving. There was a pop, and a piece of paneling swung open a few inches. A minute later the companions were once more in a dark tunnel. After lighting more torches, Dhan led them at a brisk pace. Their way took them on a steady descent back to the lower levels of the castle. The wooden walls gave way to brick and mortar and then to solid rock. After about five minutes, they came to a straight stair ending in a cavern roughly twenty-five feet across. Another tunnel led out of the cavern to the right. As the companions crowded in, Dhan confessed he had not yet explored beyond that point but was hopeful it would lead where they wanted. Again, there was little choice but to follow.

The prince moved more slowly now, keeping an eye out for other passages or any sign of where they were. The way was low and narrow, and much different from the passages they had been in. The rock was even rougher than it had been in the passages near the dungeon. It felt more like a mine than a castle. The taller members of the company had to stoop. Now and then they came to places where the tunnel was dug in the dirt and supported by timbers, but it kept mostly straight and level.

They came to only one branch in the tunnel. Dhan stopped for a few moments and muttered that he would like to explore the other way someday, but after a minute he made his decision and continued on. They walked in single file, and to conserve air put out all but two torches. It was a long journey, longer than the previous two portions, and the air was musty and unpleasant. When they finally came to a halt, they were again in a wide chamber of natural rock, about thirty feet in diameter and ten feet high.

It was also a dead end. The torches lit the whole cave well enough to see that the only entrance was the one through which they had come.

Elynna was among those at the front. She did not like what she saw. "There's no way forward!" she blurted out. She wished she hadn't, for the rumblings of the others behind her suggested some were once again close to panic. And for good reason, she thought. They had escaped execution by mere minutes, and had been in near constant danger and tension ever since. She felt like an overripe melon berry about to burst. She turned to Thimeon and the prince, hoping for some sign of hope.

What she saw instead was a look of concern or consternation on the prince's face. Yet all he said was, "Patience."

The companions gathered around the torches, talking in low voices tinged with fear.

"What do we do?" Elynna asked after a moment. "Must we go back?"

But the prince was now looking upward toward the rock ceiling. In the roof of the cave was a wide hole, big enough for a person. Flickering on the wall above the hole was a faint patch of reflected moonlight. "Put out the torches," the prince ordered. "Quickly!"

When the torches had been extinguished, Cane and Cathros lifted the prince up to where he could grasp a protruding rock near the roof. An instant later he was pulling himself through the hole. Elynna heard the soft echo of feet padding about above them, and less than a minute later the prince returned and stuck his head back down through the hole. "We've made it. Does anybody have a rope?"

At Dhan's words, though she could no longer clearly see the faces around her, Elynna could hear the collective exhaling of relief, echoing her own feelings.

"This will not be the last time we regret the loss of our packs," Thimeon muttered.

"No rope?" Dhan said in a quiet voice. "You'll have to get up here somehow. Start working on it while I explore. And stay quiet. This leads to an opening beneath the walls and over the river. Your voices could easily carry across the water or up the cliff." Then he disappeared again.

Cane and Cathros looked the situation over quickly, then called for Tienna. They had no trouble hoisting the light huntress on their shoulders, and with the grace and agility Elynna had so often seen in her, she pulled herself easily up through the hole. A few of the others had more difficulty. Falien and Pietr needed Thimeon's help to pull them up from above. Elynna feared she would not be able to make it at all, but by the time it was her turn, Thimeon had fashioned a makeshift rope from some belts. Soon they were all up through the hole. Cathros came last, using the belt-rope to climb since there was nobody left below to lift him. They were now in another natural cavern. On one side a tunnel disappeared into the rock. On the other was a narrow cleft through which they glimpsed a thin line of nighttime sky. Thimeon whispered that they were looking west over the Illengond River. Or the Dagger River, as the folk of Citadel called it. A pale moon hung high overhead. The third day of the pale phase, by Elynna's count, though she had not seen the moon since it had entered its last and longest phase.

It was from a curve on that side of the cave that Dhan

emerged a short time later. He was breathing hard and sweat was beaded on his forehead. "This is the way," he said.

"How far?" Thimeon asked.

"You will need to climb about twenty feet down the cliff and then a short way along the ledge. Once out there, you can jump down into the river with little fear of hitting rock. I know the river here. It is deep and the ledge drops straight down. You'll be hidden in the cleft most of the way. Only at the end, when you step onto the ledge, will you be visible from the far side. Fortunately, the other shore is thickly wooded and unoccupied. It is the King's Forest, which of old was called Ravenwood."

"What about watchers above on the city walls?"

"You won't be in their line of sight until you're at least fifteen or twenty yards out into the river. In any case, it's not a bright night and the walls are high. I don't think you'll be seen from above. The greater fear is that any shouts or loud sounds of splashes will be heard, or that you'll drift too far downstream toward the bridge. Can all of you swim?"

The Westwashers all nodded their heads at once. Elynna knew her people swam almost before they walked. Her greater fear came at the mention of a ledge and a climb. But a few of the others were hesitant about the swim.

"It will be difficult even for a good swimmer," Dhan warned. "It's a forty foot drop to the water. As soon as you hit, you'll need to start across so the current won't carry you toward the bridge. You'll have to meet up someplace in the woods. And for the sake of all Gondisle, may your quest bring you success."

"Won't you be safer if you come with us?" Thimeon asked. At his words, Elynna's thought jumped back to the disappearance of Siyen. She wondered the same thing as Thimeon.

"Perhaps, but there is more work I can do here. And I still have some friends and allies in the castle. I will spread the word among them, and we may yet bring you help."

"You have done much already," Elynna said. "For that, we give you thanks."

"May the All-Maker be kind to you," Thimeon said, and bowed.

Dhan returned the bow and stepped aside. The companions took deep breaths and girded themselves for the adventure that followed. Theo, their best climber, led the descent followed by Bandor, Thimeon, and Hruach. Elynna came fifth, just in front of Cathros. Thimeon had already passed word along to the others to be as quiet as possible, and to be careful not to lose their weapons. There was no talking as they climbed.

The great city wall lurked somewhere above them, out of sight but close enough that any guards marching a circuit might hear a stray voice. The way down was steep, but there were good handholds and footholds, and the moon shed just enough light for them to see the rocks below as well as the outline of trees across the river. Elynna made it without a problem, and she felt more at ease as they progressed. As Dhan had said, they were in a shallow cleft that protected them from a straight fall. Only at the bottom would they be exposed.

When she finished the descent, those in front were already working their way out onto the ledge. Elynna took a quick look down before venturing out. It was a mistake. The distance was greater than she imagined. Seeing the river churn past rocks against the cliff below, a wave of dizziness swept over her, and her limbs began to quiver. She leaned back against the wall and tried to hold still—and not to think about the fall. "It's okay," a voice whispered from behind. Her heart was pumping furiously. She became aware that others were waiting, but she couldn't move.

The first loud splash made her jump. She started to look down, but quickly closed her eyes. Then came a second splash. Only two more to go, then it was her turn. Her dizziness grew. There was a third splash. It sounded so loud. The fall must have been terrible. She was afraid to jump. She clung to the rocks behind her. But the rock wasn't where it was supposed to be. Something was spinning.

"No," Cathros said quietly. "Not here. Too many rocks below. Move farther down."

Why was everything spinning?

"No!" Cathros said. His voice was too loud.

Elynna opened her eyes. She was leaning too far out. She had lost her balance. Cathros reached for her. Too late. Outward she tumbled. Suddenly she was plunging toward the rocks below her.

20

UNEXPECTED
COMPANY

E lynna hit the surface hard. The shock of the concussion stunned her, and for a moment all was dark. Her body tingled with pain and pressure. Instinctively, she opened her mouth to breathe. Water came rushing in. She remembered where she was and shut her mouth. At once her lungs cried out for air, and she was momentarily disoriented, but she didn't panic. As a young woman she used to play in the surf at Lienwash with her brother and cousins and the other youths of the village, competing to do the most summersaults underwater. Fear of heights she had not conquered. But not even her brother could beat her in that game.

Sploosh! Another body hit the water nearby, and a stream of bubbles flashed through the dark water by her feet. Looking down—or the direction she thought was down—Elynna saw a faint rippling of light on the surface. She turned around and swam toward it.

A few seconds later, she broke through and took a deep gasp of breath. But it was not a gasp of panic. Just the filling of her lungs. Cathros was in the water beside her, reaching out to see if she was okay. She nodded to him, then looked back up at the distance she had fallen, amazed that she had survived. As she watched, another of the companions leaned outward and leapt. It looked like Hruach. Gripping his newly acquired sword over his head with both hands, he plunged into the water just a few yards away with another loud splash. She lowered her eyes again. The sight of that fall made her dizzy. She glanced instead at the rock wall beside her, and saw she was already drifting downstream. Turning toward the far bank, she began to swim.

After many days in the dungeon and several hours in the musty catacombs, the cool water felt good on her body. For the first time on the quest, she was in her native element. Even the stiffness and ache of her muscles from the forced march and the captivity seemed to fade as she began to swim. Her rhythmic strokes cut across the current, bringing her to a spot on the wooded bank several hundred feet upstream of the bridge. She almost regretted stepping out of the water. As she stood at the edge of the trees and looked back across the river, she saw beneath the moonlight and above the dark cliffs the walls and taller towers of the castle. Then she glanced up and down the shoreline. She was the first across, but Theo was just pulling himself onto shore a few yards downstream. Out in the water she could make out several more approaching swimmers. A few were strong. Others struggled. She arose and squeezed as much water as she could from her clothing, and then started downstream to offer what aid she could.

One by one, the others arrived. Beth, a weak swimmer, was

the last to get across. She made the shoreline several yards down-stream of the trees. Elynna was sure that if anybody had been looking down from the arch of the bridge, they would have seen her in the moonlight. To make it worse, she was so exhausted she collapsed on the shore. Thimeon and Pietr were forced to support her on both sides as she stumbled back. They could allow only a minute's rest, however, before they began to grope their way through the woods and to put some distance between themselves and the dungeons of Citadel.

Elynna walked near the front, beside Cane and Cathros. She was aware both of the loud creak of their wet shoes and of the muddy trail they were leaving behind—a trail anybody could follow. But at the moment she was more bothered by the dis-comfort of walking in wet clothes. She was thankful that here in the southern lowlands the changing of seasons was many weeks behind. The air was cool but not bitter. After the preternatural winter she had endured, it felt almost warm here.

They walked close to two hours before they finally stopped for a rest. By this time all were tired. Cathros and Pietr were prac-tically carrying Beth. Elynna leaned against a tree and breathed deeply. Others slumped to the ground. A few of the more experi-enced took the time to dry their newfound weapons on grass or leaves. Others lay where they were.

"Is it safe to build a fire?" Hrevia asked. "Sleep would come easier if we were dry. And warm."

"I would feel better if we were farther from Citadel before we stopped," answered Thimeon, who had remained standing. "I do not know how thick these woods are, but a fire would make an easy sign for anybody on the western side of the city, or for any patrols out looking for us."

"Well, I'm not one to complain," Cane replied, "but I wouldn't mind a fire. Heat and cold we Anghare have learned to tolerate, but we're not made for this wet."

"Then let us walk further and be safe," Thimeon suggested.

"We've walked for hours already," Hruach said. "We must be out of sight of the city by now."

"There aren't any settlements this side of the Dagger, are there?" Hrevia asked.

"I don't think so," Pietr answered.

"Then we ought to be safe here," Hruach grumbled. "Anyway, I'm too tired to move, and escaping won't do us any good if we freeze to death. No need to kill ourselves stumbling around in the dark, either."

Hrevia agreed. "If we had been seen crossing the river, then soldiers already would have arrived. And my brother is right. We must have walked five miles. Let's stop."

Once again Thimeon objected, but this time his concerns were disregarded. Even Elynna ignored her nagging doubts and voted with the others. "Tomorrow morning we'll begin our journey back toward the mountains," she said. "There we can look for Aram and Kayle, and perhaps find others willing to join the quest. Tonight let's be warm."

Thus it was decided. Thimeon, though still opposed to the decision, set out to gather dead wood. Bandor soon had a small blaze going in a little clearing. Their one concession to safety was an agreement to keep the fire small. However even that was soon forgotten as the companions gathered around, and in low voices discussed their imprisonment and escape. Elynna sat next to Cane. She'd had little chance to talk with him in many days. Though bruised and tired from the long ordeal, he still looked as strong and confident as ever. She wanted to tell him so. She sat next to him near the fire, hoping he'd speak with her first. He didn't. He was talking softly with his brother. She placed her hand on the ground near his and fought to stay awake until he noticed her and said something. Exhaustion overtook her, and she lost the battle, not the first of her companions to fall asleep, but not the last either.

Sometime later Elynna awoke with a start. She opened her eyes and looked around. The sky was dark gray, but a paler blue was already lighting the eastern horizon. Nearer at hand, the remains of their fire were still smoldering in the center of the circle. Her companions slept soundly. She saw that Cane had not moved but had fallen asleep within arm's reach. She inched toward him and rolled over so that her back was lightly touching his. Then, still tired from the previous day's ordeal, she closed her eyes and lay her head back down.

She was almost asleep again, when she heard the snap of a twig. Her eyes popped open. A shadow moved through the darkness at the edge of the trees. She reached behind her to wake Cane. Then she hesitated. Was it the dim light playing tricks on her imagination? Would he think her foolish? She stared for several minutes and saw nothing else. Finally convinced it was only an animal, she lay back down and closed her eyes. But her heart was still beating too fast to fall back to sleep. A few minutes passed. How many, she wasn't sure. Then she heard another snap, this time from her right. Now she was afraid. Again she reached over to wake Cane. As she did, she caught a flash of blue disappearing behind a tree—the bright blue of the Citadel uniform. Before she could warn the others, a soldier stepped out.

A trained warrior from birth, Cane was a light sleeper. Before Elynna's hand even touched his shoulder, he was sitting up. Without a noise, his hand moved toward his sword. But before he could draw the blade, several more armed figures stepped out from the trees. One of them raised his bow and nocked an arrow, aiming it at Cane's chest.

A confused rush of feelings flooded over Elynna. Anger that they had not been more careful. Fear. And over all a sense of despair that sapped her strength. Had it all been for naught?

Slowly the growing light and the soft sounds of feet on the forest floor had their effect, and the companions began to wake. One at a time each of their faces registered the shock as they looked around and discovered their new plight.

With the arrow still aimed at his chest, Cane slowly lowered his hand away from his sword. Without turning his head, he whispered to his brother. "I count only seven. They can't shoot all of us."

"I am with you, Brother," came the barely audible reply.

"Must be a Northlander," said a familiar voice. "Always looking for a fight."

Elynna started and turned. Two men stepped out of the trees and lowered their weapons. It was Aram and Kayle. Huge grins were spreading on their faces. "Are we glad to see you!" Kayle said.

Cane, Cathros, Hruach, and Hrevia were on their feet in an instant rushing over to greet their lost companions, as Aram apologized for the scare he had caused. "We didn't know who you were at first," he said. "We didn't think you were soldiers since you didn't have guards posted and weren't in tents, but neither did we expect to find *you*. We'd intended to just take a quick look at your camp and then sneak off unless we had some reason to believe you might be friendly. I guess we weren't as quiet as we'd hoped."

"Who are the others with you?" Cathros asked. Aram turned and motioned with his hand. The five strangers with him and Kayle now also lowered their weapons and stepped forward from the trees. Two wore Citadel uniforms. Elynna recognized the young Andan soldier who had helped them during their captivity. She did not know the other. Aram introduced them as Alrew and Lluach, recent defectors from Citadel. Then he gestured toward the other three, who were not wearing uniforms. It took Elynna a few seconds to recognize them. When she did, she was startled and disturbed. It was three of the villagers from Gale Ceathu: Noab, Noaem, and a dark-haired Ceadani woman with sharp eyes and a soft chin. Kayle introduced her as Anchara, but Elynna barely heard. She was still thinking about her unpleasant departure from Gale Ceathu and the betrayal of those same villagers after all the help the companions had given to them.

When the greetings were over, Aram looked around again. After a second count, he furrowed his brows. "Where is Thimeon? It is a grave loss if he was left behind in Citadel."

For the first time, Elynna noticed Thimeon's absence. Nobody recalled seeing him since the previous evening. "He must have slipped off and abandoned us during the night," Cane said. "He was angry we did not heed his warnings. First Siyen, then Thimeon."

"No," Tienna replied sharply and with complete certainty. "If you think for a moment Thimeon would betray or abandon us, then you have not begun to know him. He will be back."

Meanwhile, several of the companions were eyeing the Ceadani suspiciously. "You are bold to come into our midst after betraying us at our capture," Cane said.

Elynna had similar feelings, though something about their honest and pained expressions suggested Cane might have been too quick to judge.

"I wish to explain," Noab replied. "We had no intention of denying you. We knew you were not responsible for the destruction of our village, and we will never forget the aid and comfort you gave us on that day. If we could have helped you, we would have."

"Then why didn't you speak the truth about us?" Beth asked.

Noab frowned. "The truth? That is a good question to ask. It was truth I was seeking, and truth I was speaking." Several companions started to object, but Noab raised his hand and his voice and forestalled them. "Think back on my words. I did not speak any falsehood. But neither did I speak all the truth I knew, for speaking those truths would not have helped. The captain already knew the truth about you. He *knew* you were not responsible."

"Why do you say that?" Elynna asked, though she had no doubt Noab was right.

"I could sense it in his speech. His words were twisted; he did not speak truth, and he did not care about truth. If I had chosen to speak on your behalf, it would have availed you nothing, but perhaps it would have cost my people their freedom. And so, though I did not lie, I chose to remain silent." He paused and looked around from face to face. After a moment, he continued. "In any case, do not think we abandoned you. As soon as my people were on their way to safety, I turned with Noaem and Anchara and we began to follow you. Though we had little hope of rescuing you by force, we thought in some other way to give you aid. We followed you for several days, at first keeping to secret trails known only to the Ceadani, and later through caution and knowledge of highland forests we were able to keep pace and avoid being discovered."

Elynna found that she believed Noab's story. Indeed, she was impressed at both the risk they took and also the effort they made. But now another question popped to her mind. How, with all the miles of territory around Citadel, were Aram and Kayle able to find the Company again? How did they even know about the escape? But she didn't have a chance to ask. Noab was still speaking. "Whatever skill these Citadel warriors have in battle, they have little woodcraft. For that, at least, we can be thankful."

"He speaks the truth about helping us," Aram interrupted. "When Kayle and I escaped, we were not a hundred yards away from our guards before Noab emerged from the shadows. We were startled at first and almost fought them, but they convinced us of their intentions and led us to safety."

"If it had it not been for their help, we would never have succeeded," Kayle added. "The soldiers were quick on our trail, and we didn't know where to go to escape. But Noab led us to a hiding spot and covered our tracks."

"We are not used to these mountains," Aram added in his own defense.

"They also arranged for some of the food we ate on our journey when the soldiers were not feeding us well," came another voice. Elynna turned and saw Thimeon. While the others had been talking, he had somehow returned undetected and stepped back into their midst. Before anybody could question or even welcome him back, he continued. "They called to us several times from the hills as we traveled." He raised a hand to forestall the obvious questions. "Not so that our captors could hear them. They spoke in the calls of birds and beasts. But I heard and understood, and from time to time was able to reply. They went ahead of us several times and left packages hidden on the trail for me to find—roots and berries and herbs for our strengthening. Several of you benefited from these, and our captors were none the wiser. I would have told you all about them in order to bring some hope, but for the time, the fewer of us who knew about our secret benefactors, the safer we all would be."

"But where have you been this morning?" Falien asked Thimeon.

"Scouting," he replied. "I will give you details later. First we should move. The search for us has extended past the city. If Elynna is right about Koranth, he will sense that she left Citadel. It cannot take them long to guess how we escaped, and we can be assured they will soon be looking for us here. We have not been so careful hiding our trail as we might have been, nor have we traveled as far as it might have seemed in the dark of last night."

Several questions broke out. Cane's was the loudest. "Have you seen a search party?"

"Yes," Thimeon answered. "Or so I guess." Then he gave a brief account of his disappearance that morning. "I was nervous about our fire, so I went on a scouting trip back toward the river. That was about an hour before first light. I saw them coming," he said, pointing at the newcomers, "and I watched them until I knew who they were and that you would be in no danger, but I avoided them for the time so that I could continue my errand. I went as far as the western edge of the wood and a hill overlooking the southern road. There I saw a large detachment riding westward at good speed. Then I veered back toward the river and did what I could to hide our trail, which we left as plain as day. Fortunately, the smoke from our fire had died out by morning. If you were to climb one of the taller of these trees, you would still see the northern walls of Citadel high on the hill."

At this, several of the companions' eyes opened in dismay. Thimeon shrugged and continued. "It may have come to worse, but it didn't. My guess is that the first party—the one I saw a short time ago—will ride hard toward Aënport and make sure to cut us off from reaching there. They know Elynna is from the Westwash, and they may expect her to try to escape back there by boat. Others, however, will soon follow and search for us through the wood."

Then Thimeon turned toward the three Ceadani. "I add my voice to that of my companions and give you my welcome. I was glad to hear your story and to see that the friendship between the Andani and Ceadani still runs strong." He added something else in the Ceadani tongue, to which Noaem replied. Then Thimeon turned to the soldiers. "And you also, Alrew. I feared that you were more a prisoner than we were. I am glad you have cast off your chains. But we will speak later. For now, I suggest you rid yourselves of those uniforms. If we are caught, you will be better treated if it is not known you deserted the army."

"Your warning is well taken," Alrew agreed. "Unfortunately we left Citadel in rather a hurry. All we have are the clothes and weapons you see. I wish we could have brought food, for I see you are not well supplied."

"It is true," Thimeon acknowledged. "We took nothing from Citadel except a few weapons." He turned to Aram and Kayle. "What of you? Did they leave you anything of use in your packs?"

"A few items of warm clothing, nothing else. No food. And we don't even have our weapons."

"We have some food remaining," Noab said. "But for this many, it would not be more than one meager meal. We also have our bows and knives. And a rope, should we need it."

"But how did you find us?" Elynna asked, finally getting out the question that had been in the back of her mind. She directed the question at Aram and Kayle, who had been part of the company, but a moment later she added, "And how did you find each other?"

Aram answered. "We told you already how we found the Ceadani. Or, rather, how they found us. After that, we followed you as closely as we could. But it became hard to do so in secrecy once you left the forests and hit the trade road. Finally we just took a risk, since Noab, Noaem, and Anchara were unknown, and the five of us could travel together without arousing suspicions. We trusted the soldiers would be looking for two people, and would have expected us to flee in the other direction and not follow you. Still, we had to keep our distance, following the rumor of your journey—which was not difficult until you apparently took to wagons. Then we fell ever further behind."

Kayle took over the story then. "We kept following your trail as it grew colder hoping perhaps another of you might find a way to escape, and that we'd be there to help. We didn't arrive at Citadel until late in the day yesterday. Had we not found a merchant with an empty wagon willing to carry us the last day, we might only be arriving at the city now. Anyway, at that point we assumed you were prisoners in a dungeon somewhere, and we weren't sure what if anything we could do. But clinging to a shred of hope, we decided to investigate the city. Aram and I were afraid to go into Citadel for fear we would be recognized. Noab also had conversed with Golach, so he didn't think it was safe. So after some delay and discussion, Noaem and Anchara agreed to go in."

"But less than two hours later," Aram said, picking up the story again, "the gates were closed for the night—which I had forgotten was the custom here. They only just got out in time, or we would have been separated for the night."

"Longer," Alrew said. "The gates were guarded today. Nobody was to be let out of the city."

"Then we were more fortunate than I knew," Aram went on. "Anyway, we were eager and hopeful that they might have learned something, but they had nothing to report."

"My brother's understanding of your speech is not so good," Noab admitted.

"I don't know what any of us could have learned," Aram admitted. "And we had no idea what to do next. The five of us found a place in the shadows where some beggars slept and we joined them, hoping to remain inconspicuous. Even there, we were too nervous to sleep more than a few winks, as we took turns keeping a lookout. Suddenly, in the middle of the night, Lluach and Alrew appeared right in the midst of us. As I think I said, we were terrified at first at the sight of them in uniforms. But of course it proved to be very good fortune. A wonderfully lucky accident. They will have to tell you what happened."

Elynna turned to the two recently defecting soldiers, eager to hear how the rest of the story unfolded.

"We had been looking for a chance to escape for several days," Alrew said. "The two of us. Though we patrol in different companies, we have been in barracks together for the past year.

There may be others too, but of course it was not something we could freely talk about. Golach's men live in fear. He has spies among us to watch out for traitors. It was enough of a risk for us to make plans together, me trusting Lluach not to betray me, and him trusting me.

"Anyway, the castle went into turmoil last night, but as soon as we were called and told to begin searching, we guessed what had happened. That is, we guessed there had been an escape, though we didn't know how. We also saw our chance to escape. Feigning to take part in a search of the city, we made our way to the main gate crossing, and shortly before the big public gate opened, we were able to leave through one of the soldier's gates behind a detachment on horseback. The commander of the detachment was sent off down the east trade road in search of you.

"In the all the confusion, and in the predawn darkness, nobody was paying attention to us. We didn't even have horses. So when the horses galloped off, we just ducked into the shadows. And we ran right into these five as they stood with the beggars around a small fire. I recognized Aram and Kayle as the prisoners who had escaped, and when they realized we weren't there to arrest them, we agreed to work together. After that, we just took a wild guess which way to go."

"We really had no expectation of finding you," Kayle added. "Alrew was quite sure you had escaped—that your escape was the cause of the turmoil in the castle—so we had *some* hope. But with a big search going on, we were afraid to stay near the city for fear we would be recognized and caught. Not just us, but these two also, since they were now deserters. The three Ceadani were the only ones who could have stayed there safely, and we talked about that option but decided to stay together instead. So we were fleeing as much as we were seeking you. Since we knew from Alrew that all the roads would be guarded, we thought we could hide by crossing the bridge and entering the nearby woods. We'd been walking for several hours when we stumbled onto you."

"Without any supplies," Aram added. "But that is the story."

Thimeon nodded and turned back to the two soldiers. "We will make do with what we have. And you are welcome among us. Whatever brings you to us and whatever hardship we find together, I trust you will not regret your decision. Be welcome. I am Thimeon."

"I am Lluach," the soldier replied in the strong coastal accent of Aënport. "Though I can offer no supplies, I might be of help. If we can get to the coast, I have family and friends who will give us aid. My father is a merchant and has ships and horses both."

Elynna's heart quickened just a bit at this news. Trading vessels from Aënport routinely sailed up the coast to the Westwash. To Elynna's home. Or what had once been her home.

"My family has no love for our current king," Lluach continued. "They were not proud when I went to Citadel—though I tell the truth when I say I was conscripted into the army by a compulsion of which I will not speak."

Thimeon nodded. "We are grateful for your offer. We will need the help of many before we are finished. But as to whether our path now leads westward, that is something we must decide together. And something we must decide soon, though some thought must be given to the decision. It is both important and urgent."

"How do we stand now?" Tienna asked.

Thimeon rubbed his chin. "Except for Aram and Kayle, we all have weapons again. Yet we cannot go far without food and more gear. In addition to food, we will also need warmer clothing if we are to head back into the mountains. And tents too. Yet these will wait until we are farther from Citadel. Our enemy will give pursuit. We will have to travel by hidden ways and not trust any folk we do not know. The King's Forest where we now are is a narrow strip of land between the Dagger River and the high bluffs that guard the Plains. We are only a few miles north of the Aënport road. To the south is cultivated land. Lluach may know more of this region than do I and can add to this knowledge, but from maps I have studied, I have learned that if we could travel west and then south, we might make it to Omuon Hills. Though not as rugged as the mountains we have left, they are wild and would offer hiding *for a time*."

Thimeon looked at Lluach, who nodded his agreement and added, "I've passed through them on the road. It's an uninhabited region, with some heavily wooded areas. We could hide, especially in smaller numbers, though what we would eat I do not know, unless we took to raiding local farms."

"Yes," Thimeon said, "food will be an issue we must take into account. In any case, from there we might even eventually reach the coast if we can skirt a few settlements. The more heavily settled farmlands are further south and west. Still it would be risky, as the road will be patrolled. Just to reach Omuon we would have to cross the highway and several miles of open ground, and it will be well-guarded and heavily patrolled especially this near to Citadel. I fear that going south would be like walking back into a trap. And even if we reached Aënport, I'm sure every boat departing there will be watched and guarded against us. Northward stands our best hope, I believe. Even beyond the King's Forest, the land remains uninhabited and wooded on the west side of the river."

As Thimeon spoke, Elynna tried to picture a map in her mind. She had traveled the Aënport road once, though in the opposite direction traveling eastern toward Citadel. But she knew nothing of the extent of the King's Forest. Only what she had heard from Prince Dhan: that it lay across the river west of Citadel and was also called Ravenwood. Again she was glad that Thimeon was there to lead, and that the burden of the decision did not fall on her.

"Will we return to Aeti?" Bandor asked hopefully.

Thimeon shook his head. "I cannot look that far ahead. North of the Fertile Valley, both notches that lead into the highlands are narrow and sure to be guarded against us. We may have to find a way across the great river and into the hills. From there we could swing around back to the southeast, through mountain passes into Ceadani land from the south, perhaps even up the Ana River. I do not think they will expect us to go east. But no way will be altogether safe, or unguarded. In any case, that decision is still at least one day off. In my estimate, our first steps should be north."

There was no debate. Though Lluach looked disappointed, nobody gainsaid Thimeon's words, and all agreed they needed to move soon. Since learning the walls atop the high bluff of Citadel were still visible, a few expressed regret at their decision to halt the previous night. But Elynna wondered if they would have been able to continue any further even if they'd had to. She didn't think Beth would have been able to walk another step. And Hruach's limp had grown worse again. Within minutes of the discussion, they struck off northward. Lluach and Alrew had traveled the region often and took the lead. They were in a forest dominated by giant hardwoods. Nearer to the river, it was mostly a tangle of great sycamores and swamp maples, but where the companions now traveled they found flowering oaks, red birch, and blue beech, which combined to form a thick canopy high overhead. Even had the sky not been as cloudy as it was, there would have been little blue to be seen through the leaves. Yet beneath the canopy, the forest floor was clear and travel was fast.

Heeding Thimeon's warning, they moved quietly, talking only when necessary. When the sun was directly overhead, they paused for a rest in a clearing. Lluach found a patch of wild fall berries near a spring on the edge of the trees, and each got a handful to lessen their hunger pains. After a drink, they continued on their way. As the afternoon wore on, the sun disappeared behind a growing bank of clouds. Late in the day they were forced to detour around the edge of a dense thicket. Passing through a stand of young evergreens, they unexpectedly struck the western edge of the forest. There they stopped and lifted their heads in awe. Cliffs of some twenty-five hundred feet towered above them and dominated the view as far north and southwest as they could see.

"We've veered too far west," Alrew said. "I have not led us well." A short distance away, a small herd of deer was grazing in a patch of clover near the edge of the wood. Two does had lifted their noses to scent the air. However, Tienna's eyes remained upturned, unaware of the deer. Beside her stood Marti, Nahoon, and Beth gazing upward with her. Above them, tantalizingly close, was the edge of their homeland. The Plains. Only a mile-wide strip of grasslands separated them from the base of the bluffs. Of course, once at the base, it would be no easy task to reach the top and step onto the Plains. Elynna did not even know if it was possible. But she remembered then that Nahoon was betrothed to be married. Though he spoke no word, surely he must have been looking up those bluffs and thinking of his beloved.

"Is it possible?" Thimeon asked.

It took Elynna only a moment to guess what Thimeon was thinking—or what he was guessing about Tienna's thoughts. The cliffs were sheer in most places. Only the most skilled and hardy of the companions would be able to scale them. Yet that had not prevented Tienna from gazing longingly toward her home.

"For one who knows the secret ways, it is possible," Tienna answered. At her words, the eyes of her fellow Plainsfolk lit up, but they said nothing.

"Do you mean we should go to the Plains?" Elynna asked in surprise. "We agreed that our place of meeting would be an inn in the town of Swage."

"Only if we were separated," Thimeon replied. "But we are now together again."

"Why the Plains?" Cane queried. "What can we find there? We should return to Ceadani land and continue our pursuit of the Daegmon."

Noab and Noaem nodded their agreement.

"You speak of one Daegmon," Thimeon said. "We now have reason to believe there are more than one. Indeed, we now *know* that at one time there *were* more than one, and we know also that they have been attacking all over Gondisle. In any case, even if there is only one, we have been gone for several days. It seems unlikely that the Daegmon that destroyed Gale Ceathu, or that Elynna sensed following us, remains there. The place he captured us before, however, is the most likely place for Golach to search for us again."

There was a long pause before anybody answered. Then, one by one, the voices began to interject opinions. Earlier, in the urgency of escape while still under the shadow of Citadel in the King's Forest, all had been content to listen to Thimeon. Now there was real disagreement among them. The Plainsfolk were in favor of returning to their own land and argued it was the closest and safest course. A few of the Westwashers agreed, as did Thimeon. But the rest of the Highlanders and Northlanders were inclined to return east to where the Daegmon had last been seen. And some of the companions for the first time questioned the entire quest, saying that it was hopeless to fight both the king and the Daegmon. They'd be hard pressed to just stay alive.

At those words the debate grew heated. "Nobody is forcing anybody to continue," Cane shot back. "You can leave whenever you want. You can go to Entain for all I care."

"I'm not saying I'm leaving," Falien answered. "Not with the debt I owe to Tienna. I'm just saying—"

"We heard what you said."

All the while their voices were growing louder. In the passion of the moment Elynna forgot their need for secrecy until Thimeon reminded them. By then the cloudy sky had grown dark. "Let us wait until morning and take a vote," Thimeon suggested.

"Since when do we decide by vote?" Cane asked. "Elynna has led us and is leader still. The gifted will stay with her. As for the rest of you, decide what you want."

At this, everybody turned toward Elynna. Her shoulders drooped at the sudden burden. The responsibility Cane put on her shoulders was one she did not want. At the same time, she knew he was right. Without her gift, there was little hope of finding their enemy or knowing its plans. If there were others like

Koranth, she would be needed to recognize them as well. She was a leader by necessity. And even if she wanted to flee from that responsibility, where was there for her to go? To her brother to admit her failure? No. She would not give up until she had avenged her father.

Yet that conviction did not make clear the path they were to take next. "I fear the morning won't bring anything new," she grumbled. "But neither do I know what to do now. We will wait until morning."

"So be it," Cane said. "Then we will need to organize watches through the night."

"And we should sleep ready to depart at a moment's notice," Thimeon added. The two of them then organized shifts through the night, with Cane assigning half of them to watch the open grasslands to the west from the edge of the trees, and Thimeon organizing the others in shifts to watch for movement in the forest to the south and east.

Dispersing in three and fours, the companions found places to rest on the soft grass near the edge of the forest. Tienna, pacing a few yards away from the tree line and taking the first shift on guard, saw the approaching soldiers first. "Riders," she whispered, running back toward the circle. "Coming over the ridge. They will be upon us soon."

Thimeon reacted at once. "Into the woods. Quick," he called. "Grab your weapons."

Those who were awake jumped up at once, but it took several seconds to rouse the others. Then they were rushing headlong into the darkness of the trees retracing their earlier steps.

Elynna found herself a few steps behind Thimeon. Around her was a loud din of pounding footsteps and clattering weapons.

If they had been spotted, they would have to fight. She wondered if Golach was there. Where were they running to? In the growing darkness, it was hard to see where she was going. She started to slow down to avoid stumbling. Then she heard—or imagined she heard—hoofbeats coming from behind. She ran blindly ahead until, without warning, someone caught hold of her and pulled her to the ground. She struggled to rise. A hand across her mouth stifled her cries.

"Quiet," came a soft voice. "We're over here."

Recognizing Noab, she stopped struggling. She crawled along the ground behind him into a hollow in a small stand of cedars where three other shadowed figures waited in the darkness. She pressed herself to the ground and squeezed in.

"Did they see us?" she whispered.

"I do not know," came Thimeon's voice.

Only then did Elynna realize it was his body she was pressed up against. She could feel the warmth in his side and the quick beating of his heart. For once she didn't try to move away. When Noab slipped in beside her, she found herself pressing closer to Thimeon to make room. "We were close to the trees," Thimeon whispered. "In the failing light they might have missed us."

An answer came from the other side. It was Noaem speaking in the Ceadani tongue. For a few minutes he and Noab conversed. "What is it?" Elynna finally asked, unable to control her impatience.

"Elynna?" Thimeon asked in surprise. "I did not know it was you. I thought I was with the Ceadani." There was an awkward moment's silence as he inched away a little. "I'm sorry. I know you don't want . . . I wasn't trying—"

"It doesn't matter. Just tell me what happened."

"The riders went past us," Noab said. "Noaem said the horses did not communicate any urgency."

Elynna was confused. "The horses?"

"Yes," Noab answered. "Noaem understands the thoughts of animals—especially horses and domestic animals, but he also can understand some of the thoughts of birds and wild beasts, simple as those thoughts may be."

"Of course," Thimeon said, as he made the connection. "On the day we were captured near Gale Ceathu, Noaem knew the soldiers were coming before any of us heard them."

"Yes," Noab replied. "He is rarely wrong about such things. He has an ability—"

"One of the gifts!" Thimeon interrupted. "Could it be?"

21

VERTIGO

I t was a long time before Thimeon and Elynna had succeeded in gathering the company together again. Though the area of forest across which they had scattered was not overly large, they didn't know how far away the soldiers were, so they couldn't risk calling aloud. Instead, they moved painstakingly from tree to tree and hollow to hollow whispering as loudly as they dared until finally all were together again in a circle of trees a stone's throw from the edge of the forest where they had been earlier. The woods were black by then.

"Who were they?" Beth asked.

"Soldiers," Tienna replied. "From Citadel."

"These regions are not often patrolled," Lluach said. "I'll wager my last five months of service they were looking for us. This is exactly what I expected."

"Are they gone?" asked Hrevia in her distinct northern accent.

"They are gone," Noab replied. "My brother listened to the horses. They have ridden about a mile past us and stopped. The horses are now tethered while their masters sleep."

"Perhaps you should explain," came Thimeon's voice.

Noab cleared his throat, and then explained his brother's ability to understand the speech of animals—or rather the *thoughts* of animals, especially horses. He repeated what he had explained earlier to Elynna and Thimeon. At this there were several murmurs, either of astonishment or disbelief. Noab went on to tell that his brother spoke only a little of the trade language.

"What Noab is saying," Elynna explained, "is that Noaem is one of the gifted. The strength of our company may have grown in more ways than we knew."

At this comment, several voices broke out at once. Alrew and Lluach had to warn them to stay quiet. Then talk resumed in lowered voices. Noab once more repeated what he had said, and this time Noaem himself described in broken phrases his comprehension of the horses' thoughts, switching every now and then into Ceadani, which Noab or Thimeon translated. He explained how even a few minutes ago the horses had been complaining of ill treatment and were glad of the soft ground. Then the whole explanation of the gifts had to be given to Alrew, Lluach, Noab, Noaem, and the silent Anchara. Alrew knew something of it from fleeting comments he had heard during his service under Golach, but the other four had heard nothing, not even in rumors or old stories. They were amazed at the descriptions of the flames that encircled Cane's sword, and of the strength that came upon Cathros in battle. Elynna said little of her own gift but described Tienna's sense of health and her power to heal.

"You call these powers 'gifts'," Noab said, when Elynna was done. "I think I now understand the word. They are not skills one develops. We have women and men in our village we say are *gifted* in healing, but we mean something different; they have worked

hard and learned old wisdom passed from generation to generation about the healing properties of herbs. They study where these
herbs are found, and how they can be made into medicines, and
how best the medicines are applied. We might better say that they
were *skilled* in healing, or *knowledgeable* in healing. But Tienna,
you say, is able to heal somebody without this special knowledge?
That is, indeed, a gift. A great gift. And, like the skill and knowledge of our healers, perhaps a great burden as well. But that is not
the point. A gift comes *from* somebody, does it not?"

Several of the companions stared a little blankly, but Thimeon and Tienna and couple of others smiled at this question. "It
does," Thimeon said. "I believe the gifts are from the All-Maker."

"Then I think I understand the same way you do," Noab said.
"And understanding this, I will tell you that I, also, have what
you might call a *gift*."

His announcement was followed by a stunned silence. Some
companions stared in disbelief. Others in hope. Everybody in
anticipation. "Tell me it is something that will help us in battle,"
Cane mumbled.

Noab tilted his head. "Battle? I do not know. I had not
thought of it in terms of battle. I am able to tell when somebody
is speaking the truth."

"You call this a gift?" Cane asked, incredulously. "Many of
us can tell when somebody is lying."

"There is, I acknowledge, a skill in discerning truth—one
that can be developed, much like a skill in healing. Some people
reason about words, to discern truth. Others look at the eyes of
those who speak and can see truth there, having learned to see
through the masks we so often wear. But I do not claim either
of those skills. I simply know when somebody is truthful. It is

not just their words. It is the person. Truth and falsehood taste as differently to me as honey and bitterroot. When that captain came to our village, he and his words tasted more thoroughly of falsehood than any person I had ever met."

There was another long silence, and all Elynna could think about was the feeling she got in the presence of Koranth or the Daegmon. Does falsehood burn and smell? She could not bring herself to ask.

"That," Thimeon said quietly, "may be the greatest of all our gifts, for truth is one of the most important things in this world."

Cane, however, merely shrugged. He asked again how Noaem's or Noab's gifts could possibly be useful in their battle against the Daegmon.

Tienna reminded him that her own gift seemed to have little or nothing to do with the enemy either. "Healing wounds received in battle is of great use, at least for the warrior," Cane said.

"Yes," Tienna agreed. "So there are gifts that are not weapons and yet which may still help in times of war."

Cane did not respond. After that, the discussion came back to what their course was now. The same arguments that had been raised before were raised again, by the same voices but more heatedly than before, until Tienna, in a contrastingly calm voice, reminded them all that the route north had just been cut off. "I don't see that we have any choice at all, now," she said.

"Why?" Cane asked. "We could make our way through the forest as we originally planned. They will not see us."

"I fear the Plainswoman is right in this," Lluach said. "The forest does not go on forever. I know this region. I have been here often. It becomes narrower as we go northward, and finally comes to an end long before the mountains begin. If we reach that northern edge, we will still have several miles to travel in the open before we reach the wooded slopes. Besides, the woods themselves will be guarded, and we may not even see the sentries. Can we trust to luck?"

"You two know how the Citadel army thinks better than any of us," Thimeon said. "What do you advise?"

"I know little about the Daegmon," Lluach answered. "It has not yet come to Aënport. What I have learned of it I have heard only from the refugees coming south from the Westwash."

"When the time comes to pursue the Daegmon, we will learn where we must go," Thimeon said, and Elynna cringed for she knew he was speaking of her. "First we must escape Citadel."

"Well," Lluach answered. "Alrew may think differently, but I will tell you what I think. They have already guessed where we are and have sent a force to waylay us and cut us off. I don't know this Captain Golach, the one of whom you have spoken, but I know other captains in the army. Dunat, at least, is not dumb. It cannot take him long to guess the direction we have gone. El-Phern is another. He used to hunt these woods—against the law, of course, but it was before he was a captain—and he is probably already calculating roughly where we are and how far we could have traveled. And if his guess is right, we're in trouble. They will surround the forest and slowly close a net searching it from one end to another."

"That is how Golach would work too," Alrew agreed. "And even if they don't know for sure that we've come this way, once they start searching the woods, they're sure to find our tracks, and then it won't be long before they find us. They won't even need horses except to patrol the boundaries. The Citadel army is big enough that they can simply surround us and close us in.

It would only take a rider stationed every half mile or so along the perimeter to keep us from escaping. He'll do it slowly and make sure we have time to be afraid before we're caught."

"What then is our hope?" Thimeon asked.

"I spoke of trying to slip past them," Cane said. "But if their company is small enough, we could simply overwhelm them and destroy them all so that word never reaches Citadel. If we act now, we can catch them unaware before any other forces arrive."

"No," Thimeon said emphatically. "For one, it is too great a risk. They are on horseback. If even one of them escapes, they could be back with reinforcements before we had traveled a mile. More importantly, these men are not our enemies. We must remember that, or we will end up doing the Daegmon's work for it, destroying Gondisle ourselves. There must be another way."

There was a pause. Then Lluach spoke. "Well, I must have thought I had some hope or I wouldn't have risked joining Alrew when he talked me into leaving. So maybe the band camped over the hill is just a scouting party looking for tracks, or hoping to catch us in the open. Maybe they don't know where we are. I don't know. We can only guess. Either way, though, it is unlikely that we will reach the end of the forest before the riders do. Unless perhaps we travel all night through the woods. But then in the morning they will pass us again. We can't outrun mounted soldiers—"

Tienna spoke again. "But we needn't. The horses can't climb cliffs. If we can cross a short space of ground, we can reach the bluffs. A half-day's climb will bring us to the top, and to the Plains."

"Climb up those bluffs?" Elynna asked incredulously. "They must be a thousand feet high." Just thinking about climbing the cliffs she had seen in the daylight brought almost as much fear as the thought of capture.

"More," Tienna replied with a smile. "Indeed, more than double that height. We are at the bottom of the highest ledges on the eastern side of the Plains. Only in the extreme northwest where the land drops away to the sea are they higher. If we climb here it will be twenty-five hundred feet to the top, much of it cliff. Then we will be in the hills east of the Plains, from which it is a five-hundred-foot descent—though a much more gradual one—to the grasslands. "

"You can't be serious about climbing," said Elynna. She thought again of her near catastrophe on the ledges above the river.

"Why not? Their height is our advantage. The soldiers won't expect us to take that route. Even if they do, they will be hard pressed to follow. They will lose any advantage. Their horses will not be able to climb. And they will have to climb with far more gear than we have—the one advantage of the fact that we are carrying almost nothing."

"Of course they won't expect us to go that way." Elynna raised her voice. "Because we'd be insane even to try."

"Perhaps. If you did not know the secret ways."

Four hours later Cathros and Thimeon were waking the companions. Tienna, in her training as a huntress, had learned of the ancient descents: the hidden and half-forgotten trails down the cliffs from the Plains to the lowlands of the south. When she told that they were near such a place now, the companions had agreed it was their best hope of escape. Only Elynna had raised a weak dissenting voice. But Cane, despite his earlier comments, had not left the decision to her. So he and Thimeon roused the others in the dark, and they made themselves ready. Tienna had already gone on a quick scouting trip, and she returned about the time the other companions were ready to go. In a low whisper, she announced that the way ahead appeared clear. Then she reviewed their plan one last time. They would cross the open space in the predawn hours hoping to sneak past enemy eyes. Once across they would decide whether to begin the climb at once or wait in hiding at the bottom of the cliffs until morning. Both plans had their dangers, but all choices now held risks.

As she spoke, Noab and his brother doled out the last of their food supplies. Each of the companions received one small piece of dried meat and a bit of hard gyurt cheese. When they had finished their meager portions, they left the protection of the woods and began jogging across the mile-wide strip of grassland. The clouds had thinned, and the light of the pale moon glowed through just enough to give the tall grass a dim gray glow, but it still would have taken an owl to see them from more than a dozen feet away.

The cliffs were visible only as a towering void where no stars could be seen, but Tienna knew where she was going. The others followed her lead, angling just north of the descending moon. With their swords wrapped in cloth to keep them from jangling, they made little more sound than the sough of the breeze through the leaves. They had not gone a third of the distance before they had run into the moon shadow cast by the cliffs. In less than an hour they were safely across.

At the base of the cliffs, Elynna looked upward and tried to swallow her fear. The rest of the companions looked to Tienna. The tireless Plains huntress gave them only a moment of rest before she began traveling northward along the cliff face.

Now and again she paused to look upward, but she said nothing. Once, coming over a slight rise, Cathros caught a glimpse of the smoldering remains of a campfire a mile off to the right near the edge of the woods, but there was no other sign of the soldiers. Lluach had guessed that any sentries would be posted in the woods and not against the ledges. So far, his guess was proving well founded. After another thirty minutes, they came to a long vertical crack in the rock. Tienna stopped. For a rare instant, she appeared unsure of herself.

Elynna risked another look upward. Above them was a sheer vertical face, several hundred feet high. "This can't be it," she mumbled.

"There are false paths and misleading signs," Tienna admitted. She turned to her fellow Plainsfolk who stood beside her. "Beth?"

"I have never heard of these secret ways," Beth admitted. "But I come from the Lake. Perhaps Marti—?" But Marti shook his head also.

Tienna turned to Nahoon, the last of the four Plainsfolk in the company. "I'm thinking," Nahoon said abruptly. "On a hunting trip many years ago I was shown some of the trails, and also some of the false trails that would start you down the cliffs and then disappear, leaving you with no place to go. I don't remember which was which, and even if I could remember, it was always from the top, never from the bottom."

"Are we lost?" Beth asked.

"No," Tienna replied, her voice sure once again. "This is where we need to be. About sixty feet above us there should be a ledge that leads to a deep crevice through which one can climb in concealment for a hundred feet or more. Then the way opens up for a short distance. That will be the dangerous part—not because of the climb but because we may be spotted."

"Then let us wait," Thimeon said. "It would be dangerous to attempt the climb in the dark. Even if we were to succeed in the climb, the sun will soon rise. In such a short time we could not climb far enough to avoid being seen. We should wait until the sun climbs past midday when this face is in shadow."

"But is it any safer waiting here?" Aram wondered aloud. "At least if we're spotted up there, we've got a good head start."

"Do you want to climb an unknown cliff in the dark?" Thimeon asked. "This hollow is surrounded by tall grasses and brush. Unless a rider passes within twenty yards, we will not be seen here even in broad daylight. Let us take some rest. The climb will be difficult."

Aram acquiesced. Following Thimeon's suggestion, the companions lay down and rested again—all except for Tienna. Elynna watched her walk to the edge of the hollow, where she stood still and silent staring eastward toward the northern edges of Ravenwood or perhaps over them toward the horizon, where the sun would soon be rising. The ground was soft and dry, and the dread of climbing hung over her such that her fatigue and the softness of the ground caused her to fall asleep along with most of the companions. So sound was her sleep, in fact, that when she awoke, the sun was more than halfway up the sky in the east.

She sat up. The air felt warm next to the dark rocks, and her sleep still clung to her, so that for a moment her thoughts wandered aimlessly in a fog and did not dwell on the climb. She took a drink of water and looked around. Her fellow companions were sitting. Some were sorting through their gear and preparing for the climb. Tienna was still at her post, staring eastward as if burdened by the responsibility she had taken upon herself. Elynna knew what that responsibility felt like. She had borne it for many weeks. She was glad not to be bearing it now. She was glad also when Thimeon finally went to Tienna and spoke a few words, which none but the two of them heard. Tienna nodded. She looked once more at the cliffs, then rejoined the others. After a quick drink, she lay down, closed her eyes, and fell asleep at once.

At midday all were awake. For a few minutes there were no shadows and the sun was directly overhead. Then all at once the shadow of the cliff engulfed the whole company and began to move outward into the grass at a visible rate. "It is time," Tienna said, and then the reality of the trial ahead rolled back over Elynna.

Cane and Theo had scouted out the crevice and found a series of handholds and footholds that led at least thirty feet upward.

"I will lead," Theo volunteered. "These are tame compared to the mountains north of Aeti. When my father takes me to hunt the big wild sheep of the high mountains, or the shaggy crag-goats, we spend days on the cliff sides." He took a coil of rope from Noab and began his way up. Elynna could not watch. The best she could do was stare at the stone faces of her companions as their eyes followed Theo's slow movement. Only once did they all gasp in unison as a handful of sand and small rocks rained down on them. But Theo was still hanging by his hands. A moment later his feet had found a hold and he was moving again. Soon after that, the rope came down. It did not reach the ground but dangled just above the reach of the tallest of them.

"That rope is fifty feet long," Noab commented.

"If any of you cannot make the climb, tell us and we will pull you up," Thimeon said. "I will go first and help Theo."

"No," Tienna objected. "I have led us here. I will go next." Without waiting for an answer, she turned and began her climb. Using the same holds as Theo, she pulled herself up the first ten feet, and as Elynna watched trembling Tienna reached over for the rope and was soon out of sight. Bandor was next. Then Thimeon. Noab and Noaem followed, then Alrew and Lluach. But after Noab went, Elynna had to turn away. They more she watched, the more she grew afraid. When Nahoon was halfway up, Cathros motioned for Elynna to begin.

"I cannot do it," she said in a low voice.

Cathros eyed her more closely. "Are you too tired?"

Elynna looked away in shame. "I am afraid."

There was a pause, then Cathros nodded. "We will do what we can."

"Pulling her up will not be easy despite what Thimeon said," interjected Cane, who had been listening. "And it will be painful for her." He turned to Elynna. "If you are not careful, you will bounce off the rocks."

"I cannot climb," Elynna repeated. "If I look down, I will fall."

"Then do not look down," said Cane in his flat Northern tone.

Elynna winced. Cane's accusing tone felt like a physical blow. But for all her shame at her own terror, and her desire to be able to make the climb, she knew that her body would simply not work. She hadn't even begun to climb and already she was reeling with dizzying. She was grateful when Cathros came to her rescue.

"I will help. We will need another rope."

Elynna did not know what Cathros's plan was, but it could not be worse than her attempting the climb alone. She held her tongue as Anchara stepped forward and produced from her pack a shorter rope. Cathros tied it around Elynna below her arms. Then he climbed up the rock and secured the two ropes together to form a single longer piece. Turning back down toward his brother, he said, "I will precede her to the top and help those above. If the ledge is wide enough, I can help lift. Can you climb beside her?"

Cane shrugged. "It will be dangerous to be climbing. If she swings into me, it could knock me off."

"You are right, Brother," Cathros said, climbing back down. "You climb up and help from above. I will aid Elynna."

"I am not afraid," Cane replied coolly. "If it must be done, I will do it. And you have greater strength for lifting her."

"No, Brother. It was my idea. You precede us up. Your strength will suffice."

Cane shook his head. "You are stronger than I. You go to the top. Secure the rope as we go so that if Elynna is dropped she will not fall far."

There was long silence as the brothers measured each other. Then Cathros nodded. He turned back to the rock and began up. Elynna closed her eyes as he climbed, trying to will away the dizziness. If she felt this now, while still on the ground, what would she feel like above?

All too soon, Cathros had reached the top. She felt him tug on the rope. That was the sign for her to be ready. She risked a look up. All that was visible was the long snakelike rope crawling upward toward eternity. She squeezed her eyes shut. Only as the rope pulled snug about her arms and her feet lifted from the ground did she realize that Cane had been talking to her.

". . . feet on the rocks," he was saying. "Or you will swing all over the place." The pressure on her chest kept her from answering. The rope was biting into her armpits, and her side was scraping painfully against the rock face. "Hold the ropes," voices were calling softly from below. "Keep your feet on the rocks."

Elynna reached up with her right hand and tried to grab the rope and take some of the weight off her chest. Just as she caught it, her elbow swung into the rocks with a hard jolt sending a shot of pain up her arm. "I'm going to fall," she groaned, barely aware that she was speaking aloud.

"You are secure," came a reply from nearby. She looked through squinting eyes to realize that Cane was climbing beside her, keeping pace with the speed at which she was being lifted. His presence gave her courage. She reached again for the rope, while he leaned over to steady her. "Keep your feet on the rocks," he said. "Brace yourself to keep from swaying."

Elynna finally got hold of the rope and relieved some pressure under her arms. But then she spun a little, and a protruding rock gouged her right side. She heard her tunic tear. "Use your feet," Cane barked softly.

"I'm trying." Another sharp rock caught her as she was hauled past it. Then, by good luck, both her feet hit the rocks at the same time and she was able to plant them firmly. Holding the rope in her right hand, she reached out with her left and braced against the wall. Upward she went, slowly but continuously, bouncing and jarring along the way. All the time, Cane was still climbing a few feet away.

Then, without warning, she stopped moving. What was wrong? She glanced down. It was a mistake. The same mistake she'd made on the bluffs below Citadel. The mistake Cane had told her not to make. That she'd told herself not to make at the start of the climb. The ground was already far below. Her head began to spin. She felt herself lurching sideways. She reached out toward Cane to steady herself. Her body bumped into his feet. She felt the contact, felt him slowly giving way as the rope brushed him off his precarious grip. "Go back," he said, almost calmly. "You're too—"

He never finished. With a shower of small rocks, his feet popped loose of their hold and he started to fall.

"No!" Elynna yelled.

Cane was quick. Already his hands were reaching toward her rope. There was a moment of hope as his hands found a grip. Then Elynna's yell changed to a scream. Those above were not ready for the sudden increase in weight. The rope pulled free. Suddenly both of them were plummeting outward. Elynna's scream ended abruptly by a jolt in her arms. Her hands were ripped from their grip. A split second later she felt a hard blow to her ribs and grunted in pain. Then came another jolt as something landed on her and crushed her against the rock wall. Then all went black.

When Elynna awoke, she was lying on her back on something hard. Her whole body ached, especially her rib cage. Then she remembered Cane and tried to rise. A hand held her down. "Just rest a moment," came Tienna's voice. "You'll be okay after a moment. You are fortunate there was no serious injury."

"Did I fall?"

"Only a few feet. The rope caught you."

"Where am I now? Back at the bottom?"

"No. We're on a ledge."

Elynna opened her eyes. "At the top?"

"No, my friend," Tienna replied. "We have a long climb ahead, and soon I must leave you to lead the way. But the worst is past. There are no more cliffs."

Elynna swallowed, then voiced the question she was afraid to ask. "Where is Cane?"

"He is unhurt," Tienna answered. Then she smiled. "For that, he can thank you. It would appear you managed to get between him and the rock wall and cushioned his fall. You'd feel a lot better now if it had been the other way around."

Despite the pounding in her head, Elynna felt a rush of relief that Cane had not been hurt. Still, she did not think he'd be inclined toward much gratitude. "You'd better tell him that," she said.

A short time later, Tienna rose. "I must go now. The way is narrow, so we ascend one at a time. Rest a few more minutes and then follow. Thimeon will stay with you."

"No—" Elynna started, but it was too late; her friend was gone.

Several minutes passed before Elynna sat up. Her ribs and shoulders ached fiercely, but her head had cleared somewhat. She looked around. She was sitting on a flat rock floor deep in some sort of crevice. Forty feet ahead she could see a thin line of blue sky. Between her and the opening, Thimeon and Anchara sat waiting for her to recover. Anchara was staring out over the landscape. For only the second time since joining the company, she had her hood back revealing long dark Ceadani hair streaked with gray. Despite signs of age, her face was beautiful in a way that was deepened by the sadness in her eyes.

When Elynna announced she was ready, the three of them rose to their feet. Anchara led the way. Thimeon let Elynna pass, then followed. The path wound up a steep crevice, but there were natural stairs and footholds. They climbed for several minutes. From somewhere above, the faint sounds of other climbers were audible. Or perhaps it was the wind whistling past the face of the rock. After a time, the crevice widened and grew less deep. Elynna caught a glimpse of open sky around a corner. Another minute of climbing brought her to a wide ledge that wound to the left along the cliff face. Tienna had warned them it would be the part of the climb where they would be most vulnerable to being seen from below. Elynna, however, was more afraid of traversing the open ledge than of being seen. She inched her way forward, but stopped before she was close enough to look down. The sun had already passed far to the west, and there was a cool breeze coming from the east. Several of the companions were gazing over the edge, intent on something below.

"What is it?" Elynna asked.

"Soldiers at the bottom of the cliff," came Nahoon's reply. "We've been discovered."

22

THE PLAINS

Thimeon, Anchara, and Elynna joined the others on the small jutting shelf. "How many?" Thimeon asked.

"Thirty," Cane answered.

"Have they spotted us?"

Cane shrugged. "They may not have spotted us yet, but they know where we are. We left signs at the bottom that a blind man could follow."

"Where did they come from?" Theo asked. "How did they find us?"

"Elynna's scream could have been heard for miles," Cane answered in a dry voice.

Elynna looked down at her feet and bit her lip as a wave of guilt swept over her. "Have they started after us yet?" she asked without looking up.

"No." Alrew replied from a few feet farther down. "It's just a scouting party. Not enough to pursue us. But I saw two messengers galloping off. Only a matter of time until a larger company arrives. Probably with one of the captains."

"They can't attack us up these cliffs," Lluach replied with confidence. "Not if they had five hundred men and only five of us to defend." He looked at Alrew. "I say we climb back down and make sure they don't follow."

Thimeon's eyes narrowed. "What will you do to stop them?"

Lluach looked back as though the answer were obvious.

Thimeon shook his head. "No."

"The soldier is right," Cane argued. "We could defend this way with just a few, even against a much larger army. It would be easy enough to stay hidden from archers—"

"I do not doubt the effectiveness of Lluach's plan," Thimeon interrupted. "But what is the price? Too many lives. Ours and theirs. The soldiers of Gondisle are not our enemies."

"Well, we can't let them follow unhindered," Alrew said, "but I agree with Thimeon. Those soldiers are our cousins and friends. They do not know what they do. They follow orders. I don't want to kill them."

"What do you suggest?" Cane asked. "We cannot fight the Daegmon if we are running from them. There's no way around it. Sooner or later we will have to fight."

"Then let it be later," Thimeon argued. "If the folk of Gondisle fight one another, the Daegmon has already won."

"What other way is there?" Lluach asked. "I don't know what awaits you if you're caught, but I'll be marked a deserter. My death won't be pleasant."

"Then stop wasting time," Tienna interrupted. "It will take them many hours to reach where we are. By then we can be long gone. We will be at the top before sunset."

"And then what?" Cane asked.

"We will disappear." The mysterious tone in Tienna's voice

prompted Elynna to look up. The huntress had a mischievous expression on her face—one Elynna had not seen before. "You forget where we will be and with whom you travel. If we reach the top first, they will never find us. Not with fifty thousand men. The Plains will swallow us without a trace. I could guide an army across the Plains under their noses and they would never see us. And I tell you this also. My people will give us whatever aid we ask for. We will be rearmed, resupplied, rested, strengthened, and a thousand miles away before Golach even knows we've left."

There was a long pause as the companions searched Tienna's face. Whatever they saw must have reassured them because nobody gainsaid her. As for Elynna, she was eager for any hope that something would lessen the guilt of her most recent failure, and the burden of leading this company.

"Then lead on," Thimeon said. "We will follow you into the bowels of your land and see if these Plains really can swallow us—or perhaps swallow our enemies."

Cane, however, was not yet to abandon his alternate plan. "Go ahead. I will stay behind and leave something that will, at the least, give them cause for fear and perhaps slow their ascent."

"And I will stay with Cane," Lluach added.

Thimeon sighed. "Do what you must. But remember this: the ground of Gondisle will not easily forgive us if we spill blood needlessly." Then he added to Cane, "Remember also that there are Anghare amongst our pursuers. Your people's blood flows thick in the veins of the kings."

"All the more reason to take these soldiers seriously," Cane replied. "We will make sure we are not followed anytime soon. We will put into their hearts the fear of Entain." He turned with Lluach and disappeared back into the crevice.

When Cane was gone, Tienna took her place at the head of the company. She started forward without a word. Silently and in single file, the rest of the companions followed. Elynna came near the back with Thimeon and Cathros. Her legs shook when her turn came to step out onto the open ledge. It was no more than four feet wide with sheer cliffs falling away several hundred feet. She froze just an instant. Then Cathros stepped up beside her and placed his broad hand on her shoulder between her and the ledge, and she was able to continue. In this way they traveled for some time, winding their way along the face of the cliff in a northward direction. All the while a broad panorama of the Fertile Valley was open to their right with Mt. Androllin visible in the northeast.

Eventually they came to a break in the cliffs, and the trail turned inward into another narrow cleft. There they found a rude staircase cut into the rock. As they paused to share drink, Tienna explained that origins of the trails.

"Legend tells that several such ascents were carved in secret many centuries ago by enemies of the Plainsfolk. They were planning an attack on the Plains, hoping to bring an army up this unguarded way in secret. The attack was discovered and it failed. Our enemy was destroyed and his armies lost, as the legend tells, for they were caught in the ascent and thrown back to the ground by the hundreds and thousands. The paths, however, my forbearers did not destroy, for once they knew about them they knew also that they would be easily defended, just as Cane and Lluach are now doing. Yet over time the gradual shifting of the earth has erased all but a few of them. None now reach all the way from bottom to top. The few remnants have, like the people who made them, been lost and forgotten, and now lay in disrepair."

She paused and smiled. "Little did our enemies know that the stairs would one day provide an escape back to the Plains. The All-Maker works that way at times."

"Too bad we can't thank them," Theo said.

"No, but we can thank Him," Thimeon said softly.

When all had taken a drink, they continued. They were now headed straight up the mountain. The way was steep, and the steps were uneven and worn with age. Pietr and Falien as well as a few of the Northlanders grumbled at the climb and the lack of food, wishing they had kept some remnant of what the Ceadani had brought. But Tienna encouraged them. "Once we reach the Plains, we will have food in plenty."

It was while they were eating that Cane and Lluach rejoined the company. Thimeon and Alrew questioned them, but Cane answered only that he had arranged a few surprises that would make pursuers fearful to follow quickly. But Elynna gathered from his answer that they had not actually engaged in battle, nor had they even seen any enemy approaching yet. With this reassurance, they continued. Before sundown Tienna announced that they were near the top. The crevice had opened up and was no longer as steep. Soon they were climbing a gentle rocky slope, and at last they crested the final ridge and emerged atop a high hill looking across the Plains. The view was breathtaking. Far to the west the sun was just setting across a terrain as endless and flat as the sea. The red light reflected off vast golden swells of autumn grasses and grains that rippled like waves in the gentle breeze. To the north the distant peaks of the Undeani, edged in snow, glimmered like distant islands with reflected light. The company stood still for a while, mesmerized by the sight.

Tienna's face was wet with tears and as radiant as the sun it reflected. "I have forgotten how greatly I missed my home," she said. "The land of the evening fire."

"It is beautiful," Thimeon said, coming to stand beside her. "I am so enamored by the mountains of my own home, I forget how much beauty the All-Maker has caused to be all across Gondisle. So much splendor in all its diversity and vastness."

Without looking at him, Tienna leaned against him and clasped his hand in hers. All fell silent again. For the moment they seemed to have forgotten the urgency of their situation and the possibility of pursuit coming behind them. They breathed in the fresh autumn air tinged with the scent of spruce and gazed across the Plains, still and wordless as many folk are when moved by the beauty—as Elynna's own mother and father had been at times when watching a particular magnificent sunset from the beaches of Lienwash. Of all of this Elynna was aware, and she was glad for the momentary respite. But she was also aware of the sudden closeness between Thimeon and Tienna, and the inexplicable skip in her own heart at the sight.

"Come," Tienna said a minute later, releasing Thimeon's hand and stepping away from him, as though only just realizing herself what she had done. "We will be safer at the bottom. There is a deep warm river that winds southward along the base of these hills. If we follow it upstream, in less than a mile we will come to a cave where we may spend the night. We will be well hidden. Then, if we do not tarry in the morning, by midday we will find welcome from the folk of this land."

So down the hill they went, with Tienna leading at a fast gait. The sun was gone before they were halfway down. The moon had not yet appeared over the high hill behind them, and the sky was dark blue. At the bottom they found the stream. It ran quiet and deep through the soft soil, with only the reflection of stars on its smooth surface to reveal its presence.

The companions stopped at the edge for a drink. The water had a faint mineral taste and was surprisingly warm for so late in the autumn. Tienna's assurance that it was good to drink was enough for the travelers who plunged their faces into the surface, wiping off two days of dust and grime while they quenched their accumulated thirsts.

As Elynna knelt drinking, she heard a loud splash. She turned to see the Plainsman Nahoon surfacing several feet out in the river. After the long climb, the lure of the river's placid surface had proved irresistible. Marti, though not an especially good swimmer, was next. She heard Thimeon's voice a few feet away.

He was speaking softly. "Is this wise?" He was standing next to Tienna watching Nahoon and Marti splash out in the water.

"I think it is good for them," the huntress answered. "This is their home, and the water here is good. They have missed it. And tonight we will have a fire and a warm place to rest. It will not hurt them."

"Let us at least post guards," Thimeon replied. The edge to his voice reflected his concern. He turned and found the North-landers Aram and Kayle and sent them back up the hill to keep watch on the trail. Then he turned back to watch Marti and Nahoon refresh themselves in the water. By then three others had joined them. Elynna could not see who they were yet, for only the tops of their heads bobbed in the water.

Tienna was speaking again. Her voice sounded light—not plagued by the worries or pain that had been burdening her at the bottom of the cliff. "You are prudent," she told Thimeon. "I should have done the same. There is much at stake, and I know we cannot risk foolishness."

Yet despite the gravity of her words, her voice sounded light. Was it just being home again, or had something else lifted Tienna's mood? Elynna looked again at Thimeon standing close to the huntress, and one possibility arose to her mind unbidden. Elynna was not sure what she thought of that guess.

"Citadel will surely pursue us," Tienna was saying. "There is evil there that won't rest. But it is my belief that Golach will not attempt to follow us up the bluff. Not right away. If he were the one fleeing, he would not hesitate to kill anybody who tried to follow. He will not guess that you would be more merciful."

"We are still vulnerable," Thimeon said.

"We are," Tienna replied. "So I don't know how to say what it is I now feel. I simply feel right now that we are free for a moment from danger."

"Let us hope so," Thimeon replied. All the others were joining Nahoon and Marti in the water—all except for Aram and Kayle, who were keeping watch somewhere up the hill, and Tienna and Thimeon, who stood with Elynna watching the scene. The ground was covered with a pile of cloaks and boots. There were loud laughs and no small amount of splashing as some suddenly sensed relief and joy washing over them. Even Beth—though she did not wade out past her waist—ventured into the water. Thimeon made several futile attempts to quiet the others, warning them that their voices would carry and that they weren't safe here. He finally gave up.

Shaking his head in disbelief, he looked over at Tienna and shrugged. "If Golach catches us, at least we'll die happy." Then he pulled off his boots and his own outer garments and jumped in. Tienna smiled. Then, concealed by the darkness so that only Elynna saw her, she dropped *all* her clothing in a small pile by the water's edge and dove beneath the surface. Elynna went last. Not sharing Tienna's abandon, she pulled off only her boots and left her clothes on. The current was stronger than she expected, but the water felt good.

The revelry lasted only a few minutes. One by one the companions began emerging, most often several dozen yards downstream, where the current had pulled them. Thimeon was the first out. Elynna saw him disappear back up the trail, and a few minutes later as she stood on the shore dripping, Aram and Kayle came down and dove into the water.

Unfortunately, only Noab, Noaem, and Anchara had extra dry clothes to wear—and Tienna, who had slipped out of the water and redressed without anyone's knowledge. Standing in wet clothing, a few of them expressed regrets at their rash decision, but none of the complaints were serious. Nahoon assured them that in the dry autumn air, their clothes would dry quickly enough.

True to Tienna's word, they had a short distance to go before they turned aside toward the hills. After retrieving Thimeon from his post, they started after her toward the secret hideout of which she had spoken. They were in her habitat now, and she had traveled the Plains since she was a small girl. Though the entrance to the cave was hidden in a small hollow beneath the shrubs, she led them straight to a large dry area. Then she disappeared outside again bringing Thimeon back outside with her. They were gone only a short while before they both returned bearing a bundle of sticks and chunks of wood. They soon had a steady fire going near the back of the cave, where a natural vent sucked most of the smoke up and away. The wet companions gathered around the fire to dry off.

However, just as Elynna was feeling warm and sleepy, to her surprise she saw Tienna standing by the entrance preparing to depart though she had not said where she was going. "Be careful," she warned the others. "Even this far south, tigers are known to hunt the hills. Especially in the autumn, when wild sheep descend from the highlands. Do not go out alone. I will return before morning."

"Where are you going?" Elynna asked. "And should *you* be going alone?"

"I will be safe in these hills. I feel safer than I have for many days. I am used to traveling here alone."

"But *where* are you going? And why?"

"To scout behind us. I don't think we will be pursued up the cliffs, but I wish to make sure. If we are pursued, I want to know how far back our pursuers are."

"I will come with you," Thimeon said.

Tienna did not answer. She simply turned and ducked out through the cave entrance. Thimeon watched her go, and seemed to ponder whether or not to follow. He made up his mind and ducked out after her.

Elynna watched them go. Wet clothing, the thought of roaming tigers, and a jumble of emotions she could not put a finger on kept her awake a short time. Then fatigue took over. With her back pressed up against Beth for extra warmth and her feet toward the fire, she fell asleep dreaming of tigers, the Daegmon, and falling.

It was not the hardness of the ground that woke Elynna in the morning but hunger and the sounds of voices. Sitting up, she looked through the cave entrance and saw it was already light. The voices came from outside. She arose and stretched. Had she been in Lienford, her heavy clothes would have been wet for days. In the air of the Plains, though, and with the help of the fire, they were already dry. She brushed the dirt off her legs, made one failed attempt to get the tangle of sticks out of her hair, and walked outside.

Tienna had obviously just finished explaining something. Others were gathered around her in a half circle questioning her. "What does it mean?" Noab was asking.

"I do not know," Tienna said. "Only that my guess was correct. There is no sign that anybody has followed us up the bluff."

"I don't believe it," Lluach argued. "I served Citadel for too long. They would not give up."

"No," Alrew agreed. "Not Golach. Are you sure they aren't following?"

"I am sure," Tienna repeated. "Late last night and again early this morning I ventured far down the trail. There is no sign of them."

"You may not have seen them—" Lluach began, but a fierce look from Tienna cut him short.

"Forgive him," Thimeon said to Tienna. "He does not know you as well as we." Then he turned back to Lluach. "I was with her on the first trip. And in any case, if Tienna reports that there is no pursuit, then we can be sure there is not. But you are right that Golach will not give up. Perhaps he is leading an army up the Dagger and down into the Plains from the village of Hilt in the northeast hoping to cut us off."

"That would take several days," Lluach said. He thought for a moment. "Unless there is a garrisoned army already waiting at one of the northern outposts. But even so, just getting a message to them would take time."

"Yes," Thimeon agreed, "but Golach could still reach Hilt before us, and we'd be cut off from going that route." Then he explained to Lluach what Tienna had suggested the evening before. The bluffs were easily defendable, and Golach, being ruthless himself, would expect the company to act with the same brutality.

"Perhaps," Lluach consented. "And last night Cane and I did give them reason to think that was the case. But I still expect direct pursuit. Do not underestimate him. There are even Plainsfolk—trained hunters such as yourself—in the service of Citadel as scouts."

At this, Tienna's turned her head. "I have never heard of any Plainsfolk serving as a scout for another army."

"Nevertheless, it is true."

Tienna shook her head either in dismay or disbelief or just in sadness. There was a long silence before they resumed their discussion of what course to take next. After Tienna's news, none of them were any longer in favor of going northward through Hilt and trying to make their way to Swage or Aeti. If their pursuers had taken that route, there was little chance of slipping past them. Westward was the remaining option, at least for a time.

According to Nahoon, ten days of walking would suffice to bring a tall man from the northeast corner of the Plains to the far southwest, or from the eastern boundary where they now were to the western corner by the sea. Seven days, if one were hardy and took little rest. Then he told that Tienna had once crossed in six days, running day and night with only a few rests, hunting her own food on the way. The others looked at Tienna in awe, but she blushed and quickly continued where Nahoon had left off.

The Plains were bounded to the north by a range of peaks that started near Hilt and ran westward to the sea, veering just slightly south as they went. These guarded the way to the mountainous land of the Undeani. To the east, south, and southwest of the Plains, the land dropped away in cliffs. To the south and east the drop ended in the lowland regions surrounding Citadel. In the west and far southwest, the cliffs fell straight into the sea. One or two of the Westwashers suggested they go that way. There was a range of large uninhabited islands not far off the coast where they could hide for a time. But Tienna shook her head. The descent to the sea would be almost impossible. Even if they survived, they had no boat and no place to land a boat. "And," she concluded, "those islands are uninhabited for a reason."

That left two possibilities: either remaining in hiding on the Plains or crossing the mountains to the north. Most of the Plainsfolk were wandering herdsmen and hunters, or nomadic gatherers of wild wheat. There were three large villages. Two were by the shores of the great lake Umgog. The large fishing settlement of Tanengog was nestled on a bay on the south shore, while the smaller village of Arnog straddled one of the major tributaries coming into the north side of the lake. A third village was situated in a river valley far to the northwest, but the dwellers of that region were of mixed blood descended in part from the Undeani. They were less friendly to other Plainsfolk, and many did not even consider it a Plains settlement. Tienna's idea was to cut due west into the heart of the Plains as far as Tanengog. Then, crossing Umgog by boat, they could continue northward through the passes into Undeani land, then back eastward toward Illengond—or wherever their pursuit of the Daegmon took them.

"Will the pass still be open this late?" Theo asked. "As we well know, it has been an early winter."

"There are no signs of early winter on the Plains," Tienna replied. "The winter we felt in the Ceadani highlands was the unnatural work of the Daegmon. Yet if you fear that route, let us winter in the Plains. The whole army of Citadel could not find us."

"No," Thimeon said. "I do not doubt that you could keep us hidden from Golach, but I fear he would blame your people and exact from them a price for what he would see as treachery."

"They would not fear," Tienna said proudly.

"And there is this, also," Thimeon went on, ignoring her comment. "Even if we evade our human foes, the Daegmon may be able to find us and lead the army to us. It may be that even the Plains will not be enough to hide us from this enemy. We have seen already that it senses the presence of the gifts even as Elynna can sense its presence—"

"Who says we *want* to escape it?" Cane asked.

Thimeon turned toward Cane. "The time will come when we will have to face it. Whether sooner or later, I do not know. But I want to face it when we choose—when we are ready. In particular, I don't want to find ourselves fighting the armies of Citadel at the same time we battle the Daegmon. One enemy alone is enough."

"What other choices do we have?" Cane asked.

"Follow Tienna's plan. Head into the Undeani wilderness. Fleeing, if you want to call it that. Staying away from Golach until we can find a way to defeat the Daegmon."

The debate lasted only a few more minutes. But even Cane agreed that Tienna's plan made sense. When the last of the company had emerged from the cave and washed their faces in the river, they began their trek. They followed the line of hills northward for about an hour, staying on the rocky soil beside the river. At a shallow gravelly stretch of river, they forded and turned westward toward the heart of Plains.

Once away from the hills, travel became slower. The land was crisscrossed with deep gullies, and in other places the grass was waist deep or deeper and almost as difficult to wade through as snow. More than once the leaders were startled as an antlered deer leapt out of the grass a few feet away, or some large bird half the height of a man took wing almost beneath their feet. Fortunately they had Tienna for their guide and she led them on a good path, all the while keeping her eyes open for some sign of the inhabitants of the land. Shortly after midday she returned from a brief foray ahead with news that a small clan from the Uëtha tribe were heading westward to winter near the lake.

"Can we catch up with them?" Thimeon asked.

"Not if they don't want us to. They will already know of our presence."

"How many are they?" Cane asked.

"It is a very large clan. Four hundred, counting children."

"Surely they can't all hide," Cane protested. "Not that many. Not out here in the open."

"The Plains are not as open as they look," Tienna replied.

Cane looked at the flat land around him, with not a hill in sight and no more than ten trees visible within a mile. Then he looked back at the trail they had left behind them. Finally he looked back at Tienna as if she were crazy. The other Anghare were also incredulous.

"Did you see the pair of tigers following us for the past two miles?" Tienna asked.

Elynna's eyes opened wide. She turned and looked back along their path as did several of the other companions—all except Thimeon who was smiling. Even Cane's face registered momentary fear or surprise. "Then what shall we do? Anghare

are hardy enough folk, but I would not complain if we were offered food."

"I will go ahead. If I am alone, they have no reason to hide. The rest of you wait several minutes, then continue on westward." She looked around and called Nahoon. "I know some of the Uët dialect, and my face and name will be known to their leaders and hunters, but it may do us well if they know there are other Plainsfolk among our company."

"I speak the Uëtha tongue," Nahoon said.

For once Tienna appeared surprised. "How do you know it?"

"My mother was an Uët. She taught me her language when I was young, and I have spent some winters among them. If my grandfather is traveling with them, he will recognize me." He paused, and then added sheepishly, "And my beloved is Uët. We would have been married this month had it not been for the Daegmon on this quest."

"Why did you not say so earlier?" Tienna asked. "About your knowledge of the language, I mean."

Nahoon shrugged. "I had no reason to believe you would need any help. And also, my heart longs too much to see my beloved. I did not trust my motives."

They looked at each other for a moment, then Tienna bowed. "Come," she said. "Your knowledge of the language will be most useful. And perhaps you too will benefit from the trip."

The companions watched as the two of them loped off at an easy gait. Tienna had gone only about twenty-five yards, when she disappeared into the tall grass. Nahoon disappeared half a minute later. The companions waited several minutes, then followed their course westward, marching silently across the Plains.

It was late in the afternoon when Tienna returned alone. Nobody saw her coming until she was standing in their midst. Several of the Northlanders jumped in surprise, and everybody asked her questions at once. The first thing Elynna noticed was that she had replaced the ragged clothing she'd been wearing since their capture many days ago and was redressed in a knee-length sleeveless shift. It was loose-fitting, though she had it belted around the waist, and was of a fabric woven of soft fibers of a mix of colors: dark brown, light sandy flax, and other shades of tan and ochre. It blurred and blended with the grasses surrounding her as she moved. She also had several fur bands adorning her arms and legs, and her hair was now braided and bound in a dark-green ribbon, the only bright color she wore. Across her shoulder was a wooden bow of the style born by Plainsfolk: shorter and thicker than the longbows favored by the soldiers of Citadel but with a strange backward bend developed over many years by Uët and Arnei hunters, giving arrows a speed of flight rivaling those of long bows. She also bore a new long dagger, hanging sheathed at her belt, along with several fine coils of tightly woven leather strips. The companions also saw, strapped to her back, two large brown satchels of a fabric similar to her dress though less soft. They looked bulky enough to weigh down even Cathros, though she carried them with ease.

Thimeon commented aloud that Tienna looked like herself again, and the others also voiced their admiration. For a rare moment, Tienna appeared pleased with herself, particularly at the comments paid to her appearance by Thimeon. Most of the companions, however, expressed more interest in discovering what she carried in the satchels, and also where Nahoon was. She revealed that one satchel was full of food and the other of clothing, and that Nahoon had remained for the night with his Uët kin and would meet them sometime tomorrow with an even larger stash of provisions.

After several days with scanty or no fare, the companions needed no urging to eat. Tienna doled out several round loaves of flat bread, made for easy carrying, along with wild nuts and a few strips of dried meat. While the hungry companions attacked the food, she distributed the extra clothing to those most in need. "We were very fortunate," she said as they all ate. "They were away from their village at the very start of the Festival of Rest. Because it was the last moon of the harvest, it was a three-day-long festival, and they had abundant fare."

"I'm glad they saved some for us," Theo said as he tore off another hunk of bread from a loaf being passed around.

"That was not by accident," Tienna replied, her voice suddenly soft and reflective. "We were blessed on many counts."

Thimeon stopped chewing. "What do you mean?"

"Do you know what the Festival of Rest is?" Tienna asked. "Do other peoples still celebrate it?"

"I didn't even know any of the Plainsfolk still celebrated it," Beth said, sheepishly. "Between gathering harvest and hunting and fishing and making clothing, who has time to rest?"

Tienna nodded sympathetically. "I admit that my own people are less good about following the tradition. But some of the Uët still keep the festival, and they don't appear to be lacking in food or clothing because of their choice to put aside work."

"What is this festival?" several voices asked at once. But in the middle of those voices Elynna caught Thimeon asking, "Is it the mid-moon festival?"

Tienna took a quick breath and explained. "It is said, in

our tradition, that when the All-Maker brought the first people to these Plains, refuges from some great war, he promised that there would always be food for all: wild grains that would grow on this soil, always in a different place, and always in abundance, as well as wild game, both prairie birds and fish with white flesh as well as meat that is red. But we must put our trust in him. We could plant berries and grow roots, but must not till the soil to plant grains of our own. We could raise animals for milk or wool but not for meat." She paused a moment, while Beth and Marti nodded their agreement. Then she continued. "Because the All-Maker brought us to this land as a place of rest, we were to remember that rest by having a Festival of Rest on the twentieth day of each month—one week after the moon enters its pale phase, and eight days after the yellow moon. On that day, we were to do no work, and to celebrate in abundance with feasting and song. And on the eighth month, the last moon before winter, we were to have a special Festival of Rest lasting three full days, starting the eighteenth day of the month and ending on the day of mid-moon. No matter how much or little food was stored for the winter, we were to eat and celebrate abundantly."

"And you still follow this?" Thimeon asked. "The mid-moon festival? For my people also have the same tradition."

Tienna shook her head, a bit sadly. "We haven't forsaken it completely, but neither do we fully obey. Our people still do not break the Plains with metal plows to plant grains, as they do in the Southland. But while the tradition persists that we only raise animals for milk and wool, I think many people now gladly slaughter these 'milk animals' for food whenever the desire is upon them. As for refraining from work one day each month, to celebrate the

Festival of Rest, I fear only a handful of the Uët people still obey that command. There is always work to be done, it seems."

"I wish more of us did rest," Beth said. "We might be happier. And I don't think anybody would starve."

"No," Tienna said. "We would not. In any case, we can be glad that Nahoon's mother's people were celebrating. And we can be glad of one other thing, and this I do not fully understand. One of their seers told the people to bring extra food this year to the festival and not eat it—that it would be needed for hospitality. This food was *ready* for us when we came."

"So they did not know who we were?" Hruach asked. "They just gave us this food?"

Tienna tilted her head, as if pondering how she might explain. "Those are two different questions. They were prepared to give the food to whomever needed it. One thing about practicing rest and peace, no matter how busy we feel, is it teaches us to acknowledge our dependence on others—on the soil and rain and sun to provide our food, and on the All-Maker himself to sustain us." She paused, then added, as though speaking to herself, "That, I suppose, is reason the practice is so important, and why I hope my own people will renew this practice. And when we remember who and what sustains us, the practice of hospitality also becomes easier. The Uët people do not live an easy life, but they have learned these lessons.

"And yet," she continued a moment later, "they rejoiced all the more, I think, when they learned to whom they were to give the food and clothing. For they did know something about our company. They knew the purpose of our mission, and the names of the Plainsfolk members of the company. We have been in their prayers to the All-Maker for many weeks, for they believed the fate of Gondisle rests with our quest."

"I'm grateful for what they've provided us," Aram said, "but I'm not sure if I'd call it hospitality. In the Northland, it is custom to welcome strangers into our *homes* and not just leave food for them."

"Maybe that's because you *have* homes," Beth replied, a little defensively. "The Uët have no permanent homes. Only a few seasonal settlements."

"It *is* a good custom you have," Tienna added, speaking to Aram, "though I have heard it is not always followed. But these are uncertain times. There are rumors of war and violence, and of unrest in the Southland, that go beyond just the attacks of the Daegmon. Since we left our home many weeks ago, bands of raiders have appeared in the east and south of our land. The Uët were aware that a band of strangers crossed into the Plains. They did now know it was we who had returned. They feared we might be some of these raiders."

"I thought they were told to feed us," Hruach interrupted.

Tienna smiled. "They were. They were prepared to feed us even if we were enemies—if indeed we turned out to be the ones whom the seer had told them to prepare for. All they knew is that somebody in need would ask them for food and clothing, and they should have extra ready to meet that need. But they were *not* told to allow us to attack them, or rob them, or harm the women, as some of the raiders have been rumored to do as of late. Some young women have disappeared. Taken into slavery, they fear."

"We Anghare," Cane interrupted in a flat tone, "would *not* have hidden if an armed band came down out of the mountains into our land. Especially if we outnumbered them four hundred to twenty as they did us. We would have captured raiders, or killed them, to defend our land. We would not have hidden in fear."

Tienna looked at him, and Elynna saw the pride of the Plains-folk flash across her face. In a tone matching his, she replied, "Do you speak of cowardice? The Uët have already given their word that they will give no aid to the Citadel soldiers, and though they are not yet ready to declare open war against the king, they will do what they can to waylay or confuse any pursuit. Be sure that this will cost them. But there are reasons for their caution. They had heard I was dead, our company was destroyed, and our quest had failed."

At this news, several of the companions started asking questions at once.

"Where had such news come from?"

"Why did they think the company had failed, or been destroyed?"

"Had this news spread to all the corners of Gondisle?"

"Has *everybody* heard this?"

Elynna understood the concern. If such news had indeed spread, then the families of her companions would have presumed them dead. It would be heartbreaking for the families. And hard for her companions to know that their families believed this. This knowledge, however, only made her remember that she had no family left. Only her brother Lyn.

"News came from the Southland that we were enemies of Citadel and had been captured," Tienna said. "Then other rumors spread as well—that we had been killed by soldiers in battle, or executed in Citadel, or perished in a storm in the mountains. The last rumor, and the one most believed, was that we had been killed by the Daegmon. And there is another reason they believed the stories," Tienna went on. "The Daegmon, which they had not seen on the Plains since my departure, has returned. The Uët scouts have seen it."

418

23

THE VOICE OF THE ENEMY

E verybody who was still eating now stopped, and several jaws dropped. "When?" a half dozen voices cried at the same time.

"It has attacked twice over the past ten days. One of the northern tribes has suffered great loss. More often it has been witnessed flying high overhead. It was last seen three nights ago, coming out of the east and flying low over the ridges."

"The day we escaped from Citadel," Hruach commented, after a quick calculation in his head.

"This cannot be coincidence," said Cathros.

"Perhaps not," Cane agreed. "But remember that three days ago when it appeared here, we did not know ourselves that we would be coming to the Plains. We only left the forest early yesterday morning, and did not arrive at the top until last night. So it could not have known we would be here, and so perhaps it does now know where we are now."

"Unless it is in communication with Citadel," Cathros said. "Or with Golach. He knows now where we have come."

"But he didn't three days ago," Cane argued again.

Elynna had kept silent to that point, trying to enjoy the taste of food on her tongue and the absence of growling in her stomach. But Tienna's latest announcement had brought back the memory of her cell in the dungeons of Citadel and of her encounter with Koranth, and she had followed closely the discussion between the two brothers.

"I think Cane is right about one thing," she said to Cathros. "The Daegmon could not have known on the day of our escape where we would go. We didn't know ourselves. Still there can be no doubt that the Daegmon came—or was sent—to find us. Or to wait for us. And so it knew of our escape. I am sure that the Daegmon is in communication with Citadel. Koranth is one of them—one of the Daegmons. I could sense it in him. He has tremendous power. And he is evil."

Cane looked at her with skepticism. "I have no doubt that he is evil. Nor even that he is powerful in some way. But how can you say he is one of the Daegmons? We have all seen his human form."

"Elynna is right," Tienna interjected. "I too sensed something wrong—an emptiness, as if his body were an illusion."

"Then supposing he is a creature akin to the Daegmon," Cathros said. "What do we do?"

"If Citadel is in league with the Daegmon—" Aram began.

"Not *all* of Citadel," Thimeon interrupted. "We have met some there who are not."

Aram shrugged and went on. "For our purposes, Citadel is against us. If the prince is correct, Koranth now governs the king of Gondisle. We already know he ordered our capture."

"Koranth," Lluach spit. "The soldiers hate him. The captains do too, except Golach and Dunat, and maybe El-Phern. They're the ones who pursue us, I'll wager."

"Yes," Elynna said, rising to her feet. For all of this discussion brought back upon her the sense of urgency from which her night's rest had given her momentary respite. She knew what this meant. Whether the Daegmon knew three days ago where they were going to go didn't matter. What mattered was that wherever they went, it would eventually be able to find them. She said aloud, "And with the Daegmon searching for us and able to sense my presence, the captains will soon enough also know where we are."

"Then let us be ready," Cane replied. "Maybe we will be saved the trouble of pursuing the creature."

Nobody then spoke any more on the matter. The company traveled only a little further that evening. They held to their trail for another three miles, then Tienna turned northward and led them a final mile to a shallow gully cutting southwest. Water flowed along the bottom, and a few large trees along the sides. They made camp in a circle of sturdy oaks about fifty feet across. "We will have to go back southward tomorrow if we are to find Nahoon and the rest of our supplies," she explained. "But I thought this a better place to be in case we are attacked by the Daegmon. The trees, which are few in the Plains, will provide some shelter and slow its flight. If it attacks us, it will have to attack from the ground. Among the trees, as in the ravine back at Gale Enebe, perhaps it will be less maneuverable."

Thimeon and a few others nodded their agreement. They had seemed in good spirits since arriving in the Plains and for a time had spoken little—and perhaps as Elynna had thought little—of their pursuers. But Tienna's news had cast a shadow on them again. At dusk, Cane gathered them together to plan a defense in case of attack.

"Our enemy is not invincible," he began. "We have seen that. Its talons and jaws are deadly, as is its tail, but its eyes and neck are vulnerable if one can reach them with spears. For that reason my brother and I will attack it from the front. Those with spears may join us if they are willing."

Lluach and Alrew, who had fled Citadel fully armed, stepped forward. They had given their swords to Aram and Kayle but still bore their spears and daggers. Bandor, having attained a spear from the ancient armory, also stepped forward. Cane nodded his approval. He then divided the rest of the companions into three groups to attack from the rear and flanks as chance allowed. Thimeon would lead the Highlanders, Hruach took charge of the Anghare, and Tienna commanded the Plainsfolk and Westwashers.

"Sleep with your weapons near at hand," he concluded. "We do not know if it will attack us, but if it does, Elynna will warn us and we will be ready. If we do not flee, we will gain a victory."

The companions dispersed to various places around the small stand. They had gained from the Plainsfolk a few more blankets, but had still only one tent among them, so once more they were forced to sleep in the open. They lit no fire, but many gathered in groups of three or four to talk. Elynna sat near Cane and some Northlanders, when she felt a hand on her shoulder. It was Thimeon.

"You have misgivings," he said, lowering his hand.

Elynna looked over at Cane, who was watching and listening, then turned back to Thimeon. "No." She turned away from him before he could reply. He stood a moment longer, as if wanting to say something else. Ignoring him, Elynna lay down, pressing her back up against Tienna's sleeping form, and kept silent until he walked away. However, the huntress was the wrong person to use for warmth; back in her own land, she had resumed her long-trained habits. She allowed herself half an hour rest, then snapped wide awake and rose to her feet.

"Where are you going?" Elynna asked.

"Our sentries are posted nearby. I will go further afield and scout the land about us."

"For what?" Elynna asked, feeling perturbed that her friend was abandoning her. "Whatever weakness I may have, one thing I can offer. I will know if the Daegmon comes."

The bitterness in her voice at those last words must have been apparent, for Tienna reached over and placed a hand on her shoulder. "I am sorry for the burden you bear. But as for our safety, there are other dangers on the Plains" Then she was gone.

Elynna rolled over and tried to sleep. She heard the soft conversations of a few of her companions who were still awake mingled with the snoring of those who slept. A few yards away, Marti and Beth were talking in the common tongue about how much they had missed the tall grasses and wide, flat space—how the mountains had made them feel claustrophobic and how good it was to be back home. With Bandor listening, Aram and Kayle were telling Cathros about their escape from Golach and how they had been hoping to rescue the others somehow. Thimeon was speaking with Noaem, Noab, and Anchara in the Ceadani tongue. Slowly, however, even these voices faded as Elynna grew more tired. Eventually only one voice remained. It was a familiar one, though Elynna did not at once recognize it.

"*We are in trouble,*" the voice said. It dawned on Elynna that she must be dreaming. She was sure her eyes were closed, but she was seeing things. Familiar visions swirled round her head. A fire. A house. People running. It was her nightmare of the Daegmon attack on Lienford returning to haunt her, she thought. Only, now the images were strangely detached. Then she realized it wasn't Lienford at all. This village was set in the cliffs beneath the mountains, not on the wetlands of the Westwash. And all along the voice was speaking. "*You must return. We need your help. The creature has come back.*"

Unfamiliar faces flashed across Elynna's mind. Then came the face she knew. Cathwain. It was as if the young Ceadani woman from Gale Enebe were looking right at Elynna, talking with her. "*Help us. Help us.*"

"Help!" This time the voice was audible. Woken from her vision, Elynna sat up. It was dark. Someone was calling from the edge of the trees. She looked around. Others were on their feet. The sudden flare of a torch revealed Thimeon's face. An instant later he was racing toward the cries. Elynna rose to her feet and followed, though more slowly. An answering torch lit up some distance away. Then came the low ferocious growl of a large beast—a sound that sent chills of terror up Elynna's spine.

"Stay back," came Tienna's voice out of the shadows. Many yards ahead of Elynna, Thimeon had already halted. Ahead of him, at the edge of the trees, were the glittering eyes of two giant tigers—beasts twice as large as even the largest of the other wild cats of Gondisle, like the rare lions of Anghatte or the darker tigers that lived in the interior marshlands of the Westwash. The larger of the two was almost as tall at the head as Thimeon. Though there was no breeze, their orange and white fur shimmered like wheat in the wind as they took a step forward on their massive padded paws.

They had come upon the company at night, perhaps looking for an easy meal. And they had almost gotten one, Elynna thought. Pressed against a tree just a few feet away from them was the slim form of Anchara, her face wild with fear as she stood shoulder to shoulder and eye to eye with the great feline.

"Nobody move," Tienna repeated.

Ignoring her, Cane took another step forward with a torch in one hand and a sword in another. Another low growl stopped him. The slightly smaller tiger opened its mouth in a wide yawn to reveal a row of teeth as long and sharp as daggers. It was letting him know it saw him. Though several of the companions stood between her and the cats, Elynna took a step backward. Then she saw then that Anchara was not alone.

Noaem stood just a few steps in front of her, between her and the tigers. With his dark cloak, she had not seen him at first—not until the torch had flared brighter. He was unarmed, yet he did not look frightened. There was a strange, almost eager, expression on his face. To Elynna's surprise, he took a step toward the tigers. One of them padded back a step, but the other turned to face him. Its bright striped side now glowed orange, black, and white in the torchlight. It was easily seven feet long without the tail. Noaem took another step forward. Only twelve feet separated them now. One quick leap and he would be dead before anybody could help.

Thimeon, Cane, and Tienna all started to inch forward, each looking for some way they might come to Noaem's rescue. Tienna held a knife in her left hand and a long loop of rope in her right. Cane had a spear. Thimeon held a bow, but he had not yet nocked an arrow. The great cats saw them all. One growled a third time, baring its teeth at Cane in an unmistakable warning. The other turned toward Tienna and took three steps in her direction, still showing its grin. The companions froze again.

Noaem spoke. "Wait," he said in the common tongue. Then, more slowly, he said something else in his own language and took another step toward the larger tiger.

"Noaem, what are you doing?" Tienna asked, holding still. "It can take off your head with one swipe of its paw."

Noaem did not answer. Perhaps he did not know the words in the common tongue for what he wanted to say. Or perhaps his concentration was too intense to be distracted. He took the final step forward. His eyes were just a few inches above the tiger's. He reached out and placed his right hand upon its forehead. The tiger gave a soft growl, but it did not back away.

"Beware the paws," Tienna warned. Even as she spoke, the tiger raised its own right forepaw. The animal was magnificent. Even in that simple gesture, its strength was unmistakable. The companions were speechless. The tiger now raised both paws off the ground and placed them on Noaem's shoulder. His knees buckled under the weight, but he stood firm. The tiger opens its mouth wide and gave a low roar just inches from his face. Noaem was pale, yet he did not flinch as it licked him once in the forehead. Then, quite suddenly, it dropped to its forepaws, gave one last look at the others, then disappeared into the darkness with its mate.

Several seconds passed before any of them were able to move. Tienna appeared the most astonished of them all. She walked over and touched Noaem as if to make sure he was truly alive and human and not some dark ghost. Then she moved to Anchara's side. Anchara was trembling and could barely keep on her feet.

Tienna walked her back to the small circle where they had been sleeping.

"Brother," Noab said, when all were gathered together. "Tell us what happened."

"It spoke to me," Noaem replied. "That is why they came to us this night."

There was a long pause as Noaem's words sank in. Then the questions began. It took some time for him to give the full explanation, in part because so many questions came at him at once, and also because much of what Noaem had to say he could say only in his own tongue, which Noab and Thimeon had to translate. He was also so stunned that he was having difficulty speaking. He seemed as surprised as the rest of them at his own behavior. He had gone for a walk with Anchara when the tiger had appeared. He had wanted to run, but some strange compulsion had urged him instead to move toward the beast. He realized it was speaking to him. As he had earlier understood the thoughts of the horses, so now he understood the thoughts of the great cat. The difference was that the tigers were intentionally communicating to him, as though they *knew* he could understand them and had chosen him to hear their message.

If there was any doubt about the extraordinariness of what had happened, Tienna assured them that what they had seen was not normal behavior for the tigers. Moreover, this was one of the giant snow tigers, the largest and fiercest of their kind. They hunted people as well as four-footed beasts. Though, unlike their smaller cousins, which also roamed the Plains to hunt deer, antelope, and elk, the snow tigers rarely left the hills.

"But what was it saying?" several voices asked, impatient with Tienna's interruption.

"It warned us," Noaem answered. "The Daegmon will come again. And it is evil. They want our help."

He said something else in the Ceadani tongue, and Noab explained. "The tigers have told us that the Daegmon is not a beast like them. It is not natural to the land. It is evil. They fear it will destroy them or enslave them just as it will do to the man beasts. They tell us we must fight it and not let it rule."

"Did your brother give them an answer?" Tienna asked Noab.

"He did," Noab replied. "He told them we will fight it."

Elynna was the first to wake the next morning. The Daegmon was coming. She felt it. She woke Cane, who roused the others. They soon formed a circle facing outward. Cane, willing to take the brunt of an assault upon himself, was on the east, where the trees offered the least protection. With him were Aram and Kayle, the fiercest of the Northlanders, along with Lluach. In a change from the original plan, Cathros stood on the west side of the circle guarding a thirty-foot gap between two large trees. Hruach and Hrevia, the other two Anghare, were with him, along with Alrew. Noab, Noaem, and Anchara, who had no experience with warfare and had not yet faced the Daegmon in open battle, stood to the north, along the edge of the gully where the thick trees offered the best protection. With them went Falien also. Tienna guarded the southern end, where there was more open ground around the trees. With her were Marti and Beth, along with Theo, Pietr, Thimeon, and Bandor.

The Daegmon was not long in coming. They heard its cry high in the dark-gray sky. Elynna ducked cowering, but she did not run. Something was different. In the past she had felt an overwhelming fear. Something that went beyond the rational knowledge of the power of her enemy. She still had that same knowledge, and the fear that went with it. She did not know if they had much hope of victory, and she feared who among her companions might die in this battle. But some other thought or strength kept that fear from paralyzing her. It was more than the knowledge that they had defeated the creature at Gale Enebe, though she clung to that also. More even than the way Cane's power fought off the terror. It was as though that power had grown.

Down it came. Even from afar Elynna heard the wind whistling over its huge wings. It passed over them only once, slamming its tail so hard into the earth outside the trees that the ground shook. Yet whatever power it wielded, terror did not possess Elynna as in past encounters. Before its presence could have its paralyzing effect, Cane's blade burst to life. It burned hotter than ever before—an inferno of pure blue. Even Cane looked in amazement as flames shot into the sky.

But that was not the greatest surprise to Elynna, nor even the brightest light in the grotto. There was yet another light, simultaneously both deep and very bright, even bluer than the flame of Cane—as blue as the winter sky on a cloudless day, or as the deep crystal clear spring-fed lakes in the highest peaks of the Andani highlands.

It was a light the companions had not seen before. And what surprised Elynna the most is that it came from Thimeon. It burned upon his chest, too bright to look directly upon. In the mingled glow of the two flames, the little grotto was lit more brightly than if the dawn had come.

Elynna turned in surprise. How could it be? Thimeon was not among the gifted.

But the Daegmon gave them no time to wonder. No sooner had it passed overhead than it spun on its huge wings and dropped to the ground with a terrifying crash. Its mighty talons smashed the earth, ripping loose a tree the size of Cane's leg. With two long strides, it was at the southern edge of the circle. Its eyes blazed red, alive with fire. Beneath its feet, the grass withered.

While Tienna and those with her gave ground, Cane and Cathros rushed in to the attack from opposite sides. Others followed. Cane's flame was intense. It had engulfed the whole side of his body and burned five feet in the air past the end of his sword. Either he had grown in power or something else was at work. Still the Daegmon advanced. And more clearly than ever before, Elynna could feel its thoughts. Its intentions. Its evil. It sensed the presence of the gifts, just as she could sense it. It was there to destroy them. And it chose Tienna as its first target.

It lunged toward her with gaping jaws and thoughts of destruction. Elynna screamed in horror, partly at the intensity of the creature's will and partly at the suddenness of its actions. There was no place for her friend to hide. No place to run. No escape. Yet somehow it missed Tienna by five feet. Standing on the grasses of her homeland, Tienna's grace and agility seemed even keener. She dodged to her right, rolled to her feet, and came up poised and ready.

The Daegmon did not slow. With its tail still slashing about near Tienna, it turned suddenly toward Thimeon.

It stopped. Its wings were spread wide, arching to their full forty feet, as it stared at him. In his right hand Thimeon held his sword. His left hand hung loose at his side. He had turned his back toward Elynna so she did not see his face, but she saw the bright halo of light around him. She looked at the Daegmon and saw the wicked intelligence in its eyes. She read its thoughts. It was not pleased.

"*You have returned.*" The thoughts sprang from the Daegmon's mind as clearly as words. Elynna stepped back, surprised at how plainly she had understood. Her own power had also grown.

"Returned?" Thimeon said aloud. He, too, had heard the Daegmon. Or had the creature spoken aloud? So many thoughts crowded her mind—the Daegmon's as well as her own—that she could not tell.

"*Do not think that I cannot recognize you. I can taste your power as clearly as you taste mine.*"

Elynna saw in Thimeon's expression that he was confused. He did not know what the Daegmon meant. He did not understand what was going on. "What power?" he asked, his voice trembling. The Daegmon was just a few feet from him—close enough to strike. Cane and Cathros had come close to his side, but they made no move. "You mistake me for one of the gifted."

The Daegmon studied him a moment, then laughed. "*For a moment I was afraid, but I see already that your power has diminished greatly while ours has grown. You do not even understand what you wield.*"

Thimeon did not answer at once. He was struggling against his fear. "You are mistaken," he finally said. "Your power has not grown. You sense my own power, and you are afraid."

What was he talking about? Elynna wondered. Thimeon didn't know anything about their power. Or about his own. But a moment later a flicker of insight passed across her mind, as though she could see his thought as well as the Daegmon's. She could see what he was doing. He was bluffing. Feigning knowledge. Trying to get information from his enemy.

It was a dangerous game. The Daegmon bent its powerful neck forward, bringing its eyes several feet closer to Thimeon, who lifted his left arm and gripped his sword in both hands.

"The gifts of your people have waned or been lost," the Daegmon said in its thoughts. *"We destroyed them while you slept. There are too few now to defeat us. You are too late in coming back."*

"Who are you? Of whom do you speak?" Thimeon asked.

How long, Elynna wondered, would he continue to play the dangerous game? And what would they learn?

"Do you jest with me?" the Daegmon asked. It paused, and again for an instant Elynna thought she sensed fear in it. But only for an instant. Then the fear was gone. The creature almost laughed. Perhaps it too could sense Thimeon's thoughts. *"No. I see you do not. You ask questions because you do not know the answers. Yes, I see now that you are ignorant. You are even weaker than I thought. My brothers and I shall destroy you easily. Perhaps I will destroy you without their help. How my own power shall grow when I consume you!"*

Suddenly it struck. With one great flap of its outstretched wings, it sent a huge torrent of air swirling around the feet of its intended victims. While the companions tumbled backward in the near gale, it lunged with its teeth toward the blue light. There was an explosion of flames and sound. Red and blue flames and bolts of light shot high into the sky. For an instant all was chaos. Shouts of terror filled the air from several points of their circle as Thimeon was momentarily engulfed.

But his light did not disappear. It grew, mingled with another blue light—for Cane had come to Thimeon's side and countered with his own attack. Whether his blade itself struck the

Daegmon, or whether it was the flames alone that held it off, the creature backed away. Thimeon and Cane were still standing there, unscathed and bathed in blue.

"*It is nothing,*" the Daegmon roared. "*You are nothing. Send your minions away and face me alone.*"

If Cane heard the creature's cry, he did not heed it. He rushed suddenly forward. The Daegmon slashed at him furiously with its talons. He was knocked aside by some invisible force, but the talons did not touch him. Others rushed in. Lluach lunged with his spear. It snapped uselessly on the creature's hide. Noaem and Noab both released arrows, which burst into flames and disappeared as ash before they even reached their target. Hruach, seeking to dart in and strike with his sword, was hurled aside by the mighty tail.

Then from the tall grass came a flash of orange and white. In three powerful bounds, the mighty tiger had crossed the open space. Its fourth leap carried it high into the air, where it landed several feet up the Daegmon's back, just below the wings. Strength for strength, size for size, the tiger was no match for such a foe. For all its fierceness—for all the mighty strength it had in comparison with a man—it was but a small thing to this enemy. And yet such was its ferocity that even the Daegmon was stunned. It tossed its head from side to side trying to shake the tiger loose. The mighty feline dug with its powerful claws, trying penetrate the scaly hide.

Noaem and Noab came rushing in, seizing the opportunity to inflict a wound. Or perhaps merely coming to the aid of the cat. Their spears were leveled at the Daegmon's side but to no avail. With a final toss of its wings, the Daegmon shrugged the tiger off. Eight hundred pounds of muscle crashed to the ground and bounded to safety.

Noaem was swept aside with the back of the Daegmon's claw. He too rolled to safety. Noab was not as lucky. His spear snapped and he fell. One swipe of the Daegmon's talon and he lay helpless on the ground.

The Daegmon stood towering over Thimeon as if to crush him, yet something held it back. As it hesitated, Thimeon stepped forward with the blade he had taken from the ancient chamber. He swung it toward the creature's belly. The blade glanced aside without leaving a nick, and yet the Daegmon was stunned. Elynna could feel it. There was a power at work on their behalf—a new power the company had not before known.

In rushed Cane, slashing once more at the enemy's side. His blade flared brightly. The blue flames engulfed his whole body. The other companions fell away from him. Even his brother could not go near his side. Thrice Cane slashed. The third blow found a mark. The Daegmon stepped backward, roaring in anger. It towered high on its rear talons, poised to strike, but the blow never fell. While the companions stood watching, it raised its giant wings and with a single powerful downstroke rose into the air.

"You will all find an eternal home in my master's dungeons," it cried, laughing as it disappeared northward.

A great cheer rose—a cry of victory led by Cane's loud voice.

Elynna barely heard it. Even as she was released from the pain of the Daegmon's presence, another presence struck her. *"Help us,"* it cried. This time, Elynna knew who it was for sure—Cathwain, the young Ceadani woman, the granddaughter of the Elder of Gale Enebe.

"Help us," she cried again. There could be no mistake. She was speaking to Elynna. And somehow, from far across Gondisle, her call had found its way. *"You must come back to us. The*

Daegmon is here. It has taken our sanctuary and killed our gyurts. My people are dying. Please. Help us."

Elynna fell to her knees overcome by the terrifying passion of Cathwain's plea that cut away at the jubilance of their small victory. She heard the others still cheering and congratulating one another. She saw Noab lifted to his feet and was aware of him being helped back toward one of the trees where his brother tended to the huge gash in his left side. But Elynna did not move.

"*The Daegmon is here.*" She had heard Cathwain's words as clear as day. Her voice was still echoing through her mind. But how could they be true? "*Help us. My people are dying. Please. Help us.*"

ACKNOWLEDGMENTS

Thanks to Deborah, my wife of twenty-six years (and counting), for continued support and encouragement in my writing; for partnering with me in raising three great sons; and also for good cooking, bike rides, a welcoming home, weekly dates, great family vacations, and all the other countless ways you show your love to me daily. May the next twenty-six be just as good.

Thanks to Mark for persistence with the map. To Thomas and Mark and Peter (in advance) for reading the book and telling all your friends about it. To my parents for starting me early on reading and helping to shape my imagination.

Thanks to the Chrysostom Society for providing a model of good writing, and especially for the encouragement. And thanks to all the staff at AMG, and to Susanne Lakin for comments on the first draft.

A NOTE ON THE
PRONUNCIATION OF
VARIOUS PROPER NOUNS

In the Anghare tongue of the Northland, the TH is pronounced hard, as in the English words *the* or *then* (and not as in *with*.) Both the Ceadani and the Andani pronounce TH as *T* followed by a very slight breath. Thus Cathwain is pronounced Cat – *HWAY* – in.

With the exception of Ceadani names and a few older Andani words, G is pronounced hard, as in the English words *give* or *great* (and never as a *j*, like the G in *giant*.) However, in the Ceadani tongue (in place name words such as *gale, gali, galena*) or in a few older Andani words, such as *daegmon* or various traditional names, the G is pronounced as *y*, or like the G in *filet mignon*.

Among the Plains and the three Highlander tribes, it is common to accent the second syllable of names, and double consonants are pronounced twice. Thus *Thimeon* is pronounced Ti-*ME*-on (with a slight breath after the *T* and long "e" in the second syllable). *Tienna* is pronounced Ti-*EN*-na. Westwashers, by contrast, accent the first syllable of names (despite their common linguistic roots and their eventual sharing of a language with the Andani). Thus *Elynna* is pronounced *EL*-lin-na.

A NOTE ON THE HISTORY OF
THE LANGUAGES AND PEOPLES
OF GONDISLE

After the All-Maker cast the Daegmon Lord out of the southern half of Gondisle, the Fisherfolk of Westwash were the first people to settle the Southland, coming down the coast by boat and arriving on the western shores, where they settled the harbor of Aënport. A generation later the Andani also began a migration south from Aeti and their settled highlands northeast of Mount Androllin. They came south through the center of the land, following the Illengond River, settling first in the upper valley near Suage beneath the western slope of Androllin, and soon after continuing south from there when they realized the land was fertile and welcoming.

As the Andani moved further south, they found established settlements of emigrants from the Westwash. The two peoples, both peaceful, began to mingle and intermarry. It is written in the official history books of Gondisle that the first settlement where the two peoples dwelt together was at the present location of Citadel, but some traditions claim that the location was on the west side of the river and further north. What all accounts agree upon is that the languages of the two peoples bore a recent common ancestry and were still very similar. That, in addition to their peaceful nature, explains why they so readily began to interact so easily and freely. And as the Andani and the Westwashers mingled, so too did their already closely related languages, soon forming into a single new language that would become the common trade language of Gondisle.

After many years, the more warlike Anghare came into the Southland from the east. They were at first peaceful—though distrustful—and content to settle unoccupied land, which there was much of, especially east and south of the Rain River. But as they settled and began to cultivate the land, they built first walled towns, and then small forts and outposts, and then larger forts they called "castles." Within two generations they had begun to carry out raids and to lay claim to lands that had already been settled and to demand tribute. There is little recorded history of those times, but it is known that the first kings of Gondisle were Anghare. However, though the Anghare ruled Gondisle, they did not teach their own tongue but rather took the common tongue already established in the south as the trade language of the land.

Most of the names of the peoples of Gondisle were given by the Andani in their own tongue. The oldest names, given before the Andani and Westwasher languages merged, were for the other highland tribes. In Andani the suffix *ani* means "people" or "people of." *Andani* is the name by which they refer to themselves, and it means "people of peace," in contrast to the highland tribe dwelling to the west, whom the Andani refer to as the *Undeani*: the "people of war." *Ceadani* is the name given by the Andani to the tribe dwelling in the highlands to the south of them, and it means simply "people of the south." The *Ceadani* are linguistically the most closely connected to the Andani, and there is no history of the two folk every being at war with each other.

The geographic names Westwash, Southland, Plains, and Northland are all later names that emerge in the trade tongue. The Fisherfolk do not refer to their own land with the generic and non-descriptive "Westwash" but rather speak of various parts of their land more specifically as *Riverland*, *Island*, *Coastland*, or *Barrens*—the latter referring to those places where nobody can live, though in fact the *Barrens* of the Westwash are teeming with life. Neither do the Anghare folk refer to their own land as the Northland but rather as Anghata. It is from the name of their land that the Andani began to call them the Anghare. The tribes of the Plains have their own set of distinct tribal languages, distinct from all the other languages of Gondisle.

When you buy a book from **AMG Publishers**, **Living Ink Books**, or **God and Country Press**, you are helping to make disciples of Jesus Christ around the world.

How? AMG Publishers and its imprints are ministries of **AMG** (*Advancing the Ministries of the Gospel*) **International**, a non-denominational evangelical Christian mission organization ministering in over 30 countries around the world. Profits from the sale of AMG Publishers books are poured into the outreaches of AMG International.

AMG International Mission Statement

AMG exists to advance with compassion the command of Christ to evangelize and make disciples around the world through national workers and in partnership with like-minded Christians.

AMG International Vision Statement

We envision a day when everyone on earth will have at least one opportunity to hear and respond to a clear presentation of the Gospel of Jesus Christ and have the opportunity to grow as a disciple of Christ.

To learn more about AMG International and how you can pray for or financially support this ministry, please visit

www.amgmissions.org